THE QUANTUM GENE

BrianMcKinstry

Copyright © 2025 Brian McKinstry

All rights reserved

The characters and events portrayed in this book are fictitious. Any similarity to real persons, living or dead, is coincidental and not intended by the author.

No part of this book may be reproduced, or stored in a retrieval system, or transmitted in any form or by any means, electronic, mechanical, photocopying, recording, or otherwise, without express written permission of the publisher.

ISBN-13: 9781919188812

PROLOGUE

From under the couch, behind the cloth flap, Kerry could hear the creaking floorboards and just glimpse the shoes of the men who had broken into the apartment a few minutes earlier. Donald's cat had dived in with her. He trembled and she stroked him, as much to sooth herself as him. His fur tickled her nose, and she desperately tried to suppress a sneeze. Doors and drawers were loudly opening and closing.

"I was fucking sure she was going to be here! I didn't believe that Stirling guy for a moment," said the first, a deep voiced London accent.

"Were the plods who checked the CCTV sure it was her?" This voice posher, harder to place.

The first sighed. "Yep, it was a 98% match, captured two hundred meters from here. Where the bloody hell else could she have been heading?"

"Who knows, she might have friends this side of town, I suppose."

"What about Stirling. Where's he now?"

"Well, who'd have thought it," his voice dripping with sarcasm. "Look at this. His phone just happens to be on its way here now."

"Clocked off a little early, hasn't he?"

"Well, isn't he in for a surprise. Might as well make ourselves at home while we wait."

One sat heavily on the couch, shifting to get comfortable. Kerry winced but didn't move the buttock he was crushing. *Please don't find me.*

"You have checked all the cupboards and under the beds Phil?"

"It's hardly Buckingham Palace John. Yes of course I have."

"What about that couch?"

"What about this couch?"

"Under it?"

"Why is she a contortionist?"

"Just look."

CHAPTER 1

....

Seven hours earlier.

"And now some good news. St Julian's secondary school in Edinburgh is celebrating getting eight students into Oxbridge! The first of their students to have ever achieved this," announced the beaming, perma-tanned breakfast television host.

Kerry Pearson choked on her muesli. That was her old school! One of the most deprived in Edinburgh, and until now she had been its only student to have ever got to university. Just surviving the day in that place without having your lunch stolen or your head put down the toilet was counted as a success. What the hell had happened? On the screen, her old headmaster, Mr Bhopal was wittering on about hard work, dedicated teaching staff and novel teaching methods devised by an organisation called the Odyssey Initiative.

What bloody dedicated teaching staff? Had he sacked all the old ones and got new ones? What sort of teaching methods could turn that hellhole around? She shook her head. *Well, good luck to them, if anyone deserves a break, those kids do.*

Intrigued, but also a little bit deflated that she was perhaps no longer the school's greatest success story, Kerry searched for the Odyssey Initiative on her iPad. The website was super slick, the home page background, which looked vaguely familiar, was of a black square with a sun rising above it and a crescent moon above the sun.

The strapline "Raising horizons Inspiring ideas" appeared at the bottom of the screen with slowly changing glowing images of handsome young people living the dream as successful professionals. There was very little detail on what it actually did, but it mentioned they were working in partnership with schools and businesses internationally.

She linked to the St Julian's website where the partnership with Odyssey was right on the home page. The same black logo was there, alongside the more familiar rainbow double Helix of Chi-Gen, a big research company based in Oxford with whom her department had some collaborations; presumably the industry partner the headmaster had mentioned. The text below the logo extolled the opportunities that Odyssey was providing as paid internships for the top five students to be undertaken, if they wished, in a gap year between school and university.

Seems too good to be true. What's the catch?

A raised voice caught her attention once more. The, now serious, presenter listened to a scowling narrow-eyed man expound loudly on the dangers of immunization, listing the 'totally proven' calamities which were about to befall mankind as a result of mass vaccination. The presenter nodded, turned to the camera, gave a considered look and said "Food for thought there" before briskly moving on to the next item.

"What?" shouted Kerry. "No challenge? No balancing argument? For God's sake they give as much time to any crackpot who rolls up having 'thoroughly researched the topic' by surfing the web as they do to Nobel prize winners!"

Kerry thought of her twitter feed, full of this sort of nonsense; conspiracists with thousands of moronic followers who got all their news from the internet. Not that the broadcast news was much better. No news item seemed to last more than 30 seconds these days, the apparent attention span of 'homo social-mediaensis'.

She picked up her phone. There was a pop-up warning her that there had been access to her university account from a new server. *Odd when did I do that?*

Shit is that the time!

She tossed the bowl and mug in the sink, already overflowing from yesterday's lunch and last night's take-away. Then grabbing her bag she ran out and slammed the door behind her, leaving the beaming presenter to talk to some C-list YouTube star about his upcoming reality show.

It was a typical bright, cloudless, freezing Edinburgh autumn morning and she was regretting leaving her puffer jacket behind. She shivered as she zipped up her hoody and began weaving through the exhaust clouds of the stalled traffic. As she reached the pavement, she caught sight of a huge electronic billboard, recently installed and running down the side of one of the university buildings, displaying an animated Odyssey logo. The logo gave way to slowly changing images of visionary young people gazing at distant galaxies, then in lab coats with safety goggles holding up test tubes, then in front of computers displaying complex 3D graphs finishing with the exhortation to 'Be your best self" alongside the website and QR code.

She frowned. *Who* are *they?*

CHAPTER 2

Hurtling up the white-walled stairway of the new genetics building, Kerry pushed by several colleagues tossing them hasty salutations and explanations that she was running late. At exactly at 8.59 she arrived sweaty and breathless at the lab, collapsed into her desk and booted up her laptop to await her video connection with her supervisor Peter Munro.

Seconds later he appeared on screen, clean shaven, jacket and tie (*Who still wears ties?*) his left upper lip curled, seemingly ready for battle.

She started to say hello and ask him how he was, but he talked right over her.

"Kerry, I'm literally tearing my hair out! You have just three months funding left on your grant. Normally, at this stage students are sending me the second or third draft of their finished thesis not still collecting data! Will you get a grip! I must warn you that I don't think I can justify an extension to your grant. If you don't submit on time, then you'll have to find your own means of support."

Kerry, wisely, decided to forgo the opportunity to explain that he was metaphorically rather than literally tearing his hair out.

"I'm sorry Peter. I've already written most of it up. Just the last chapter to do, but I've found something new, and I think really exciting."

He rolled his eyes and shook his head.

"Come on Kerry! Not another one of your wild theories! How many times have we been here before only to end in a blind alley?!"

He leaned forward to the camera and emphasising every syllable shouted. "Concentrate on your original research question! Get the thesis finished!"

With that, he hung up.

"Rude bastard," she mumbled… suddenly panicking then sighing with relief, that he had indeed signed off.

Kerry was truly sick of her 'original research question' because it was actually Peter's, and he was using his PhD student to do the sort of grunt work he couldn't be bothered to do himself. He had paid scant attention to her for the last three years and ignored most emails requesting help. He usually surfaced only a few days before any annual departmental review to play the interested supervisor for the review committee and criticize what she had been doing. No doubt, however, he'd be all over it when it came to writing for publication, making sure of course that he was named as senior author.

Anyway, this time she was sure she had found something. Her research focussed on what was considered to be apparently redundant DNA in the human genome. Over millennia humans and the animals from which they had evolved had been infected by thousands of viruses some of which had left part of their DNA in reproductive cells. This had gone on to become fully integrated with the genome, replicating as the cell replicated. These additional genetic sequences, sometimes referred to as junk DNA, seemed to serve no useful purpose. However, in recent years it was becoming clear that at least some may have important functions, and several scientists had posited that in the past such inclusions may have been responsible for some leaps in evolution.

By chance Kerry had noticed a particular sequence in some new tissue donations that she hadn't seen before. It was odd because the genetic code was identical in all the samples in which it was present. Older redundant sequences generally varied due to random mutations over time. She wasn't sure if this was just due to chance or if it suggested some new process was at play, for example a novel retrovirus like HIV. The sequence did not appear to have been described before, but that wouldn't be surprising since a large proportion of the human genome was composed of this non-coding junk DNA and it might easily have been overlooked.

Her interest piqued, she approached a friend who worked for a Scottish Biobank, ScotGene, that had been collecting blood samples for genetic sequencing from volunteers over the last ten years. With what remained of her equipment grant (and without her tutor's permission) she had paid for the genetic sequences of 2000 donations, 200 from each year for the last 10 years. The email with the results had pinged into her inbox during Peter's rant.

With some trepidation she opened the file and started to analyse it.

Well bugger me!

The genetic code was absent in all donations up until 3 years ago when it started to appear with increasing frequency. In those collected in the last year the frequency was 8%.

She frowned and shook her head. *Surely if this had been the result of a viral infection then it would have had some symptoms, and someone would have noticed it.*

She worked through other possible

explanations. New viruses, with this sort of infectivity were usually devastating. The ScotGene database was largely collected from patients who were having a blood test for health reasons but had given permission for the sample to be also used for research. Had the people who donated these samples been ill? Were these people still alive and well? What if anything did the new code do?

Her next thought was whether she should contact her supervisor or wait until she knew more. She knew Peter would be furious that she had 'wasted time and money' on this and he seldom let her finish a sentence in explanation. However, there was another geneticist, Donald Stirling, with whom she got on well.

She had first met Donald when she was attending a conference in Stockholm. She knew no-one there but spotted him sitting alone and, screwing up her courage, asked if she could join him. He was very friendly, not to mention *so fit*! She smiled as she remembered how her hopes of a conference romance were dashed when an equally lithe and handsome young man joined them and patted Donald's knee proprietarily.

Nonetheless she was delighted to discover when she took the PhD position in Edinburgh that he was working in the same laboratory, and they hit it off from the start. As she got to know him, she discovered that he had something of a maverick career having worked in laboratories all around the world including a stint at Porton Down, the government's biological military research facility. She knew he had been conducting research on the potential of using retroviruses like HIV to repair faulty DNA. She knew also that he had been very vocal about the dangers of unregulated gene editing and its potential for creating dangerous mutations in infectious viruses. Could she trust him with what she had found? This discovery could be huge, a paper in *Nature* maybe. She wouldn't be the first PhD student whose work had been appropriated by a professor and passed off as his own. However, over the last two years Donald had helped her far more than Peter and had never suggested she name him on a paper.

Her stomach turning, she lifted the phone with a sigh and dialled his office.

"Donald here."

He sounded irritated and Kerry almost lost her nerve.

"Hi Donald, it's Kerry here. How are you?

His voice softened.

"Oh. Hi Kerry. How's it going, any closer to finishing your thesis?"

"No, not exactly, but I have got something new,

something I think is important, something I think you might be interested in. Have you got five minutes?

"It's never five though, is it?" he quipped amiably. "Let me finish what I'm doing, and I'll join you in about 30 minutes."

"Thanks, I'd really appreciate it."

As Kerry ended the call, she started to worry about the departmental politics of it all. Peter and Donald didn't really get on, and she worried that Peter would be upset if he were to find out she had gone to Donald first. Maybe, she thought, she should call it off, but, just as she reached for her phone again, the door opened, and Donald strode in smiling and breezy. She sighed. *He always looks so cool. Close cropped hair, well cut blue shirt and grey chinos. Why are all the best-looking ones always gay?*

"Well, what have you got for me?" he said grabbing a swivel chair from the desk behind

Kerry was about to say that maybe she had gone off half-cock and perhaps she should wait a little longer, but then she remembered that Peter had never taken her seriously, seldom offered constructive assistance and that Donald had been much more help to her even though he had no obligation to do so.

She took a deep breath, passed over the results and explained how she had noted an identical long stretch of unusual code in two samples and then a third and that by the time she had found a fourth she knew that something was up.

"It does seem a bit unlikely," mused Donald while clearly looking intrigued. "The code really looks very similar in these samples though."

"It's identical, Donald."

She proceeded to explain how she had asked her friend at ScotGene to help and that the results seemed to suggest this was a new finding and something which was becoming more common.

"OK, I think you definitely have something here, Kerry. Who else knows about this? Have you told Peter?"

Kerry was immediately wary. She wanted to be sure that her discovery wasn't about to be purloined. She decided to invent a colleague who could corroborate that she had made the discovery first.

"I emailed a friend in Oz, but she didn't seem that interested, more concerned with the negative findings in her own research."

"Well, I'd keep this under wraps for a bit. This could be a huge step in your career. The question is, do you want me to collaborate with you on it and what do you want to do about

Peter? I think you'll have to involve him, or he'll make a stink about this."

"To be honest, I'd rather not, but I realise it may be the politic thing to do. I'd be really sick if he grabbed the credit for this given that he's tried to stymie me in every way".

Donald's look showed that he thought this was a real possibility. Kerry could see there was clearly no love lost between the two men.

"OK, I have some funding for a year. If you complete the PhD, you can come and work with me on it. Don't get me wrong. This is your discovery, I'll not be seeking credit, but you may have to prepare yourself for an onslaught from Peter when he finds out. Where are you with the PhD?"

"Despite what he thinks it's actually more or less done. I'm working on the final chapter and sorting the references. The only reason I haven't sent it to him so far is that he never responds to anything I send him."

"Send it to me and I'll look it over. We need you to pass first time. Meanwhile, also send the first six chapters to Peter. That will keep him quiet for a while. Focus on getting that done for the next few weeks, but in the meantime get back in touch with your friend in ScotGene to see if there's any way he can give you more information on the samples. Did you tell him what you were looking for?"

"I said I was looking for particular viral sequences but didn't tell him why."

"That's good. For the time being the fewer people who know about this the better."

Kerry frowned and blew slowly through pursed lips.

"Well... I guess I was stupid I posted a question on the GenCom website to see if anyone else had seen the code"

Donald's expression showed that he thought that had been a mistake.

"When did you do that? Did you get a reply?"

"Yesterday morning. No reply, I'll take down the question right now, probably hasn't been noticed."

She logged on to the site.

"That's odd it's not there, it says it was removed by me just a couple of hours after I posted it, but I didn't remove it" she said turning with a questioning frown to Donald.

The phone rang.

It was Cheryl her old lab-mate.

"Kerry, there were a couple of weird looking guys in here looking for you a while ago. They thought you still worked in this building. I didn't like the look of them so said I didn't know where you worked now. I don't think they believed me. Do you know who they could be?"

"No, but I think someone has been in my university account."

"I'd be careful Kerry. They did not look like nice people."

Kerry started to tell Donald, but the phone rang again. It was Peter.,

She sighed "I could do without this." She rolled her eyes at Donald and then put it on speaker.

"Kerry, what the hell have you been up to!" he said speaking quickly in a whisper. "I've just had a phone call from someone who says he's from the Security Services. Wanting to know where your lab is. He says they have been tipped off that you're a green activist extremist and that you have been involved in developing potentially lethal viral mutations. They thought I was in on it! I told them I knew nothing about this research, but that I know you'd been going off piste a lot lately with your own wild ideas. They asked me if I had read your Instagram pages. I couldn't believe the stuff on that! I told them that I'd be astonished if this were true. Kerry, I know we haven't always seen eye to eye, but you seem to be in serious trouble. Got to go there's someone outside my door".

Peter hung up.

Kerry looked stunned and turned to Donald.

"I hardly ever go on Instagram; I haven't posted anything in months and that was just a holiday snap. This is nonsense!"

Donald frowned and shook his head.

"Get out of here now Kerry! Go out the back, put on your hoody. Leave your phone. Here's my keys and the address of my apartment."

"Go there and don't leave, don't go online and don't answer the phone. We need time to think about this. You've clearly inadvertently poked a hornet's nest."

"But it must be some mistake I've never been in trouble before. I just need to explain it."

"Please don't argue Kerry, I've seen these guys in action. They have no problems finding the evidence they need, whether or not it exists. I'll try to find out what's going on. Back up what you have on this stick for me, leave the laptop and then go."

Donald popped his head out the door to check the corridor and told her to go. Her heart pounding, Kerry pulled on her hoody and, head down, exited the rear of building into the cold autumnal air. Fortunately, the security on that exit was always lax as the door was almost continuously propped open for cigarette breaks. Trying to remember every spy movie she had ever seen; she kept her head down to avoid security cameras and slowly threaded her way down the gently curving Mound to Princes Street which was teeming with football fans heading for a derby in Easter Road. She stopped at a kiosk selling match gear and bought a Hearts bobble hat and shirt. She ditched the hoodie, and headed down Leith Walk towards Donald's flat, situated not far from Hearts' rivals Hibernian's football ground, the site of the derby, the crowd thickening as she went.

Shit, if they do manage to track me, they really will think I've something to hide.

Meanwhile back at the lab, Peter, frowning and jittery, arrived with two very large solid looking men with dark suits and closely cropped hair.

"Hi Donald, you haven't seen Kerry, have you?" he asked, his voice quavering.

Donald thought he had never seen Peter look quite so flustered before.

"Yes, I saw her about an hour ago. She said something about going across to the Royal for some samples. She'll be back soon. Is there a problem?"

"There may be. These gentlemen are…"

The larger of the two grasped Peter's elbow and smiling, and in an educated English accent said

"From the Chief Scientist's Office… we have

been doing spot checks on our grantees. Some overseas students don't appear to have been working here despite it being a requirement of their visa.

"Kerry's not an overseas student"

"Political correctness gone mad. We have to check everyone equally," added his colleague with a smile.

"Would you like to wait? I'm expecting her back in the next 15-20 minutes." Which, thought Donald, should give her the chance to get clear of the place.

"Have you been working with Kerry too?" asked the taller of the two.

"No, she works most closely with Peter. Peter is the international expert in her field". Thinking that on this occasion flattery would throw poor Peter under the bus.

"Not this work, I know nothing about this work!" exclaimed Peter anxiously.

"Redundant DNA, Peter? Surely, it's your field? If not that, what *has* she been working on" he frowned and raised an eyebrow.

"We don't want to take up more of your time Dr…?" Said the taller of the two.

"Stirling, no problem. Always happy to help. Have you tried phoning her?"

"Yes, but it is switched off, last seen here."

"How would you know where it was last seen?"

"As I say, we've taken up enough of your time, Dr Stirling, if you see Kerry, please let us know. Here's my number." The card had only the name John Speirs and a telephone number. Turning to Peter he smiled and said, "Professor Munro call us as soon as you know anything. Is this Kerry's computer? Does she have any back-ups of her work here?"

"Everything is automatically backed up on the University server."

We need to take the laptop with us. We also need to speak to your IT lead."

"Can you just do that? All her work is on that," said Donald.

"This computer was provided by a grant from the Chief Scientist's Office, so it belongs to us as does the work she was undertaking. We'll return it once we have established that her work is bona fide."

"Of course, it's bona fide. Peter, tell them."

However, they were already going through the doorway, leaving Peter visibly trembling and pale.

"Peter what the hell is going on? If they're from the Chief Scientist Office, then I'm a banana. They look more like the SAS".

"They told me not to tell anyone, but since

you have seen them, I'll tell you. Kerry has got herself in serious trouble. They say she may have been developing biological warfare agents, that her Instagram pages are full of animal rights crap, about humans having destroyed the earth and how 'the meek' should inherit it."

"That doesn't sound like Kerry, and she's not done any DNA synthesis work of any kind, so I think that is very unlikely to be true. She eats steak tartare for God's sake. She's about as green as the Chinese flag!"

"Well, she's done something to annoy some powerful people. I for one do not want to get caught up in it."

"You're already caught up in it. If there's anything in what she's done, and it certainly isn't making germ warfare agents, then as her supervisor you're bound to be in the crosshairs."

"Oh God! I haven't a clue what she's been doing recently. I guess I haven't really been paying much attention to her. She always seemed capable if a bit lax about deadlines. If you see her, will you tell her to phone me right away? I'd better have a word with the head of department. Damn, I was up for promotion, this is all I need."

It was now approaching 2.00PM. Donald felt

for the data stick in his pocket and headed home. Aware that he too may be under surveillance, he stopped off for groceries along the way and tried to make his journey home look as normal as possible.

CHAPTER 3

As he wandered around the aisles of the Tesco Metro, dodging trolleys and baby buggies, Donald wondered what Kerry had uncovered. *It's clearly something to do with that genetic sequence but what does it do? Whatever it is, there's a bunch of people wanting to shut down her investigation, but how far would they go?*

Donald fingered the data stick. He had a friend he could trust whom he worked with at the defence facility at Porton Down. This was his field. He might be able to cast some light on what the mystery gene sequence did, if anything. He worked in Oxford now, but how could he go there without raising suspicion? He scrolled through the multiple email invitations he received every week to attend symposia and conferences and found one taking place in Oxford the following day. He emailed the organiser asking if it was too late to register. They'd be delighted to have him. He turned into Waverley station and used his credit card to buy a ticket.

Just as he started walking down Leith Walk his phone rang.

"John Speirs here. We met earlier today. I'm just phoning to see if you have heard anything more from young Kerry."

"No nothing more… Sorry but this is extremely odd, what has Kerry done and please don't give me any guff about the Chief Scientist Office and overseas students!"

"I'm not at liberty to say what that is but be assured that her recent activities are considered a potential threat to the security of this country".

"As far as I know, the work she's been involved with has been about ancient viral DNA remnants. I can see no potential for that being a threat to national security. She's never been trained in any processes which could alter an existing virus or make a bioweapon."

"It's amazing what you can get hold of if you know the right sources. Kerry seems to be a determined young lady with very strong views about many things from big pharma to the destruction that humanity has wreaked on the planet. Sorry, but the carefree girl you think you know is a carefully constructed persona. She is dangerous and you should let us know as soon as you see her so we can prevent her from doing serious harm."

"My God, who'd have thought it… Kerry of all people. I'll let you know if I see her. Did she not return to the lab?"

"No, we suspect she was tipped off."

"Not by anyone in our department I should think. Does Professor Munro know about this?"

"We'll be speaking further to him later this evening. Goodbye, sir we'll be in touch."

Poor Peter, mumbled Donald with a satisfied grin.

Donald proceeded down Leith Walk towards his flat. He stopped at an ATM and took out £200. Heading off to a side street and out of the view of traffic cameras, he dropped into a "Cash Generator", picked up a second-hand laptop for £60 and took it to a local café. From there, using an email address he had used last on a secondment in India eight years ago, he logged on to a VPN in the Philippines and from there to two different secure servers.

He smiled. *I'm on fire! I can't believe I can still do this stuff!*

He uploaded Kerry's files from the datastick then deleted all the files, over-writing the stick with several episodes of a mildly pornographic TV series. He slipped the laptop down a gap behind the cistern in the toilet of the café. From there he made his way home.

He climbed the stairs to his first floor flat and picked up the spare key from above the lintel. As he opened the door he shouted "Hello".

John Speirs answered. "Who did you think would be here Dr Stirling? I thought you lived alone?"

Speirs was standing next to the window smiling cynically. His mate was seated on the couch. The window had not been open earlier which suggested that one of them had used it to enter the apartment.

"How the hell did you get in here?"

"Let's not mess about Dr Stirling. Where is Kerry?"

"I've no idea" he said in a tired tone. *Which is true. Where on earth is she*?

"We have CCTV footage of her coming down Leith Walk, where else would she be going?"

"Anywhere, she could live this direction for God's sake!"

"She doesn't"

"We checked her laptop. A copy was made of her files just prior to our arrival at the lab. Do you have that copy?"

"No! Why would I?"

"Why did you say hello as you came through the door?" asked Speirs' companion.

"I have a very anxious cat which dives for cover

when strangers come in. Where is he, have you done something with him?"

"You bought a train ticket to Oxford today."

"Yes. How do you know that?! I'm going to a conference there tomorrow, staying overnight and coming back the following day."

"Do you mind if we check your bag?"

"Would it make any difference if I did?"

Speirs' tall colleague forced a smile, rose from the couch and took the bag.

"Nothing here"

"Oh well, Sir we need to search you."

"This is ridiculous don't you have to read me my rights?"

"Could do, but we aren't going to bother. Phil, search him."

The firmness of the agent's grip (he was surely military) told him resistance would clearly be futile. The agent produced the data stick.

"What's on this then."

"It's personal. Nothing to do with Kerry."

"Then you won't mind us checking it". He moved towards Donald's desktop computer.

"You can't look at that on a university computer." said Donald.

"Really? Why?"

Donald looked down, sighed and frowned.

"It's nothing illegal, but the University has programs which look for skin tones and people have been in trouble in the past. I've another laptop here."

Donald moved to the cupboard and pulled out a battered laptop. The man called Phil switched it on, asked for the password and plugged in the data stick.

He looked at Speirs. "They all look like video files"

"Open them."

One by one the six files were opened to Speirs' evident disappointment.

"Hmm… Didn't have you down as a bender, but I guess you can never tell. Still, I can see why you wouldn't want the university to catch you watching those."

"Bender? Really? Were you off sick on the day they did the diversity training, or do you just not give a crap?"

"Where did you download them? The files all have this afternoon's time on them. "What was on this stick before then," asked Phil.

"More of the same"

"So, we won't find Kerry's prints or DNA on this will we?"

"Can't think why they would be." *Shit why didn't I think of that?*

"Sir, if we find you have been less than truthful with us, it won't go well for you. If you see Kerry, you call us right away. OK"

"Of course."

With a passing scowl, Speirs and his sidekick left the apartment, fortunately leaving the data stick behind. Donald closed the door and locked it.

"Kerry where are you?" Donald said to himself in a loud whisper.

"Here!"

Donald started as Kerry drew herself from under the couch.

"I heard voices outside the window and then heard it slide open. I did what you said and hid under here. For once, I was glad I'm skinny! I then heard the window opening. Your cat came under with me. I heard them walking about and opening drawers then one of them lifted the flap at the edge of the couch. I almost shit myself, but your cat jumped out at him, and he didn't look any further. Who are they?"

"Not sure. They look like MI5 or special branch but who knows? This must be about what you found and posted online. Kerry, I was going to ask you to come with me to Oxford to see an expert friend of mine, but it's too dangerous. They are clearly watching me and almost certainly keeping an eye on this building."

"Donald, I promise you I'm completely innocent. What should I do? Maybe just go and see them and explain?"

"You need to stay here a while; they think you aren't here so it's probably the safest place now. I'm not sure what they want from you. They clearly think you know more than you do. We need to find out why these genetic changes are so important. I'll head to Oxford tomorrow and see if my friend can help. Meanwhile, keep out of sight of windows and after I leave don't turn on any lights. Is there anyone that is going to miss you that you need to reassure? I could try to get a message out."

"No-one will notice for a few days except at work. Sunil and Sean in the lab are on holiday just now and won't be back until next week. I don't really do social media, so my pals won't miss me. Not for a few days at least. Do you think they'll phone my parents? I'd hate them to be worried. My mum gets really anxious."

"They'll have contacted them, and almost certainly have spun them a story. Don't think about contacting them just yet. I know that'll be difficult for you. You haven't emailed or phoned anyone else? "

"The last thing I sent was my thesis when you asked me to earlier today. There's nothing in that about the new genetic code, but they may think I've sent it to you."

"You can be sure they have already read that email and, that if you'd included anything about it, it would have 'mysteriously' disappeared too. Let's get some food and watch the telly…. By the way, I'm not into porn usually, not that I've any objection to those who are, but it seemed the best thing to overwrite the code with. The code is safe, by the way. "

"What could it be that has these people so twitchy?" said Kerry.

"I don't know. I hope it's not true, but the only thing I think that could cause this would be some sort of virus which could have inserted the code. The people behind it clearly don't want that to come out and want you scared enough to stop what you're doing."

"So, what are you saying? Some sort of government or big pharma experiment that has gone wrong? Maybe a manmade retrovirus which has got out of control and infected a load of people?"

"I know it sounds wild. Whatever it is it couldn't be causing any sort of immediate medical problems or surely it would have come to light before now. Shit! You can imagine the scandal if people find out about this. The armchair conspiracists would have a field day. People would be ascribing all sorts of illnesses to it. There'd be lawsuits and, if it has spread outside the UK, an international incident. China would certainly feed fat on it after the flak they took on COVID in Wuhan."

"We really need to know what the genetic sequence is encoding, if anything, and what it might do. Although it doesn't seem to be causing problems now, who knows what it might do in the future.

"Your friend in Australia that you sent the file to. She may be in trouble too."

Kerry pursed her lips and blew through them.

"I lied to you about that. It's pathetic I realise, but I've just heard so much about people's ideas being stolen. I'm sorry."

"Don't be! That was smart."

"What does the friend at ScotGene know?"

"Not much. I said I had found something interesting and wanted to see how common it was. He didn't seem overly interested."

"If you've found this, it will only be a matter of time before others do too. I don't think they'll be able to keep a lid on this forever. I suspect they are playing for time to control the narrative of how it unfolds. In the meantime, you have to lie low, and I have to look as though I've no idea what's been happening. Let's get something to eat. You have a seat and watch some telly; I'll get on with some work".

Donald took out his laptop and started work on Kerry's thesis, determined that he was seen to behave 'normally'. He suggested potential improvements, but found it well written for someone at this stage of their career.

Cognizant that everything he wrote was being intercepted, he attached the annotated chapters to an email saying that he hoped she was OK as he had heard there had been some trouble and to get in touch if he could help. He looked at the time and was surprised at how speedily he had done it.

Tesco lamb curries on their laps they, sat down to watch television. There were a couple of quiz programs, the first, 'Only Connect' was an IQ based program which involved different types of reasoning, the second, University Challenge, a straightforward, knowledge quiz. To his delight he hammered Kerry at both.

"Try not to look quite so smug, Donald. Some of us didn't get a posh education."

As he was due to catch the train to Oxford at 07:00 the next day Donald suggested they get some sleep. He suggested it would be foolish for her to take the spare room in case people were watching the flat but noted a sudden flash of discomfort on her face.

"No! No! Sorry! I wasn't going to suggest we share a bed!" he smiled. "What do you take me for? I was very nobly going to suggest you take the couch in the living room instead! I'm a bit too tall for it".

Kerry laughed and countered unconvincingly that she had thought no such thing.

With instructions to her to lay low all day, he left the flat at 6.30 AM. As he walked the dark, deserted, streets towards the station he tried very hard not to look like he was checking every doorway and alleyway.

He saw no signs of anyone tailing or watching him either on the train or as he changed stations in London but then realised that they didn't need to as they were probably tracking his mobile phone. The Oxford meeting, held in one of the ancient colleges was surprisingly productive and was worth the visit even if he hadn't had an ulterior motive. Following the meeting he found a working payphone from where he called his friend Alan to arrange to see him that evening. He dropped back to the hotel and put on his running shoes and tracksuit. He left his mobile in his room, set out on a run, but after a couple of kilometres he stopped for a bite at a Burger King and headed off to Alan's house.

Alan and he had once been close. They had shared a room while undergraduates and had had a brief affair which ended amicably. Alan had since got a girlfriend, but they kept in touch and had met up a few times at conferences but never more than on a friendly basis. Later, they had worked together at Porton Down. Their work was meant to be about countering foreign and terrorist biological threats, but it became clear that it was being subverted to actually create such agents. Their protests about this only led to intense scrutiny of their lives, sinister reminders about the consequences of breaching the Official Secrets Act, and thinly veiled threats about their continuing ability to work in any biology field in the UK if they revealed anything of what they had uncovered. They had both been forced to resign and had had to go abroad for a few years where they advanced their careers before anyone in the UK would employ them again. Donald was sure he could trust him.

Alan's house was in a broad, tree-lined avenue, set back from the road in a well-cared for garden. *How on earth has he afforded this on a research scientist's salary? He must have inherited some dosh or kept a lottery win under wraps!* In the driveway sat a large newish BMW SUV. *Definitely things are looking up for Alan!* He rang the bell.

The door opened. Alan smiled and pulled him in for a hug. "How very London!" said Donald. "No kiss though?"

"We've given that up remember," laughed Alan.

"Well, you're doing well for yourself Alan. The Medical Research Council are clearly paying better than they used to!"

"Not working for them anymore. The MRC didn't extend my grant, so I've gone over to the dark side and am working for Chi-Gen now. A guy's gotta live!"

"And live well by the looks of things!" Donald's eyes flicked from the large screen television to the Bang and Olafson sound system and stylish leather suite.

"I know. It's a crazy salary, but what are you doing in Oxford?"

"I came for a conference and thought it would be good to see my old pal again, but if I'm honest I also came to ask your opinion on a problem. I'm not sure if I'm onto something or not."

Donald decided to omit mentioning the MI5/special branch or whoever they were. He didn't want to embroil his friend in any trouble. However, as he told the story of how his PhD student had stumbled on this recurring genetic code, he noticed Alan look more serious.

"This could be massive, Donald. What do you think it is, some new virus?"

"That's why I've come to you, to find out what this encodes. It seems like a longish sequence and not typical viral DNA. Could you look at it? Maybe use another laptop rather than the company one? It would be a shame to have this scoop pinched by big Pharma!"

"I'll get another laptop. It's at times like this that I'm glad the old lady next door hasn't a clue about computer security. Her wi-fi is wide open" he smiled.

He turned it on and passed it to Donald.

"It's on a secure server, "said Donald

Donald typed a few keys and passed it back.

Alan spent about ten minutes moving his mouse back and forward over the genetic sequence all the while clearly getting more and more interested.

"This is quite a coincidence. Chi-Gen has been working on a drug for attention deficit disorder. A year ago, we found a gene which seemed to occur more frequently in people who have the disorder."

"It can't be that, surely people would have noticed if they had started getting symptoms of ADHD!"

"No, it's not that. This new genetic sequence

that Kerry found isn't that gene. It's just that I recognise where it's situated. The coincidence is that it is *right next* to the part of the genome on which we were working and which in some people is faulty. It may of course have no function at all, and this is just a coincidence, but it conceivably may have an impact on attention and concentration, some sort of regulatory function. But how did it get into so many people's DNA? This really could be huge Donald. Who else knows about it? "

Donald decided to come clean with his old friend and told him how events had unfolded over the last 48 hours and the involvement of Speirs and his sidekick.

"Who are they?"

"I'm not 100% sure but I think they may be secret service." He handed over Speirs' card.

"For fuck's sake, Donald. Are you off your fucking head! Remember what happened to us before! This could be career ending for you, if not jail-time! And now you've brought it to me! Does anyone know you're here?"

"No, I've been very careful. My phone is in my hotel room. I left by the back door; I called you from a booth and walked here. I could see no-one following. I was careful to check for cameras and there were none."

"Thank God for that. Where is the server you

stored it on, can they not find it?"

"It's in the Philippines. No-one but me knows about that. I uploaded it on a burner laptop".

"Where's the girl? Not in your flat I hope?"

"No, she's staying with a friend I think," he lied.

"Is this the only copy you have of the data?"

Alan's tone seemed oddly breezy, and Donald became a little suspicious.

"No,"

"OK. Well Donald, I want this off my computer and all traces of links to this server. I'm deleting this."

"What the fuck! Why did you do that?!" exclaimed Donald.

"Saving our careers and our asses. Get rid of any other copies you have. Whatever you've got into is way bigger than anything you can cope with alone. From what you've said they've nothing on you. Keep it that way. I don't know how much you care about the girl, but one way or another she's being thrown to the wolves. The only question is whether you want to go with her."

"You really did cross to the dark side, didn't you? This isn't the Alan I know. Don't you care what this is about?"

"I care, that for the first time in my life I have a nice house and a nice car and a salary on which

Emma and I can finally get married and have a family. I'm sorry Donald, you know I've always really liked you, but I'm not going to jeopardise all that. I want you to sneak back to your hotel the same way as you came and forget you saw me."

Donald thought that at least Alan had the decency to look ashamed. While fleetingly angry with him, he realised that he really didn't have the right to entangle him in this.

He stood up held out his hand and said, "I'm sorry Alan you're right. I shouldn't have brought this to your door. No hard feelings?" Alan shook it and looked at him as if for the last time and just said "Sorry." No hug.

As the door was closing Alan added.

"If there was any way to find some of the people who had this new code to see if they have noticed anything different it could be useful. The whole ADD connection could be a red herring but checking their cognitive abilities is where I'd start. You also need to discover how this got into their genes. It must have been an engineered virus. I can't think of any other way. This doesn't look like a natural phenomenon. It would take a very sophisticated outfit to come up with it; no-one I know could do it. Goodbye Donald. Don't contact me again."

Donald took a different route back to the hotel.

To his relief, the side door was still open. He made his way up to his room and opened the door. His things had been moved.

He walked cautiously into the room, looked in the bathroom, then spotted a note on the pillow, and alongside his phone.

the same business card he had been given the day before. It just said to call.

Donald moaned. He knew these guys could trace him if they wanted to, but hoped they hadn't followed him to Alan's house. Alan had been right; he had had no right to drag him into this. He sat on his bed and wondered what to do next.

Donald picked up his phone and dialled the number. If the news was bad, then he might as well know.

"Hello?"

"Ah, Dr Stirling. Thank you for calling back. We were wondering if you'd heard from Kerry."

"Something tells me that if she'd tried to communicate with me, you'd know it" replied Donald.

"Well, there are many ways of communicating Dr Stirling. May I ask where you were this evening after your meeting with your colleagues?"

"To be honest, I don't know what business

it is of yours. I'm getting just a bit sick of you following me everywhere. I'm sure if you follow my journey on the local webcams, you'll see that I went for a run and grabbed something to eat. Perhaps you should focus on finding Kerry if she is so important to you. Although not that for one moment do I believe that eco-terrorist crap. Perhaps you should be up front and tell me exactly what you and your bosses are worried about and maybe I could be of more assistance. She is a gifted PhD student, but her skill base is limited, and her work focus extremely low risk. What has got you all so uptight?"

There was silence.

"OK Dr Stirling. May we make it clear that it is your duty to contact us if you hear from her, otherwise you'll be seen as an accessory." The line went dead.

Donald was relieved that they still hadn't managed to find Kerry, but realised it was only a matter of time. Perhaps the best thing to do was for them both to go to the lab tomorrow and try to find out what was going on, maybe with some legal representation… although these guys had not demonstrated much respect for the rule of law so far. The only ace still in Kerry's deck was the data held on the server in the Philippines. Someone clearly wanted that kept under wraps. Perhaps some sort of trade could be made.

*

Back in Edinburgh, Kerry was bored. She examined and sneered at what passed for Donald's 'library', an assortment of genetics books he had reviewed and several crime novels.

Not exactly highbrow are we Donald?

Nonetheless she was deeply into a novel about a cop fighting corruption and organised crime in Georgia when she heard a clatter at the door and dived for her hiding place under the couch but, after five minutes palpitating and sweating, decided it was probably the postman. At least this time she didn't need to pee. Yesterday she had been bursting, waiting for Donald to come home with those two spies in the room. She crossed her legs just thinking about it.

She had lost the urge to find out what happened next to the luckless hero of her crime novel. Would it really hurt to go online? Looking through Donald's drawers she found the laptop he had let the 'thugs' use, but after a few attempts and a final warning she gave up guessing the password. However, there was an old mobile phone and charger. She plugged it in, switched it on, typed in the password 1234 and it opened. *Bloody hell! What an idiot*!

She immediately instructed it to forget the flat wi-fi. She discovered a moderate signal from a coffee-shop across the road. It wanted a password. It was called the Happy Bean, so she tried happybean 2020, followed by 2021 and 2022 which worked! Grateful for everyone's lax computer security, she was online.

She looked for conspiracy theories about DNA insertion. Most of it was around HIV and its origin. Retroviruses such as HIV could be used to alter DNA, but she found only completely bizarre claims of alien or rogue billionaire insertion of DNA using this method. Theories about COVID vaccination as a means of societal control also arose. She knew that couldn't explain her findings as several of her positive samples had been added to the database before the vaccine was available.

Bored, she flitted through websites eventually landing on the BBC where she caught sight of the article about her old school. There wasn't a great deal more there, but now that she had time, she tried to find out more about the Odyssey initiative. According to Companies House, Odyssey was part of another organisation, Future Now, which was incorporated only five years previously. She clicked on the executive director, Marion Spitz. Her Wikipedia page said she had been born in Argentina but educated privately in England at Cheltenham Ladies college and then Oxford. She held directorships of several companies and one of these was the main British subsidiary of CreativeCom the giant tech conglomerate run by Abe Markov.

Intrigued, she remembered that Abe Markov had co-authored a controversial book called 'Falling Man', in which he and his business partner James Barton agonised about the failure of the brightest and most accomplished people in the world to procreate and the consequent gradual erosion of IQ and human achievement. They argued for a voluntary eugenic approach to maintaining the quality of the human gene pool by offering incentives to the brightest to reproduce and, more contentiously, payments to those that were termed 'less able" not to. The book caused an uproar with its authors effectively 'cancelled', a call for a boycott of CreativeCom and a subsequent crash in its share price. They had disappeared for a while from public view following this, although CreativeCom recovered and continued to do well.

So, is his company now interested in an alternative educational approach to improve humanity? If it works as well as it has in St Julian's, then they are certainly on to something.

A rattling at the door pulled her out of her reverie about CreativeCom and had her diving under the sofa once again, the cat springing away from her with a loud yowl. She waited a few moments, but nothing happened. She slowly crept towards the door to see a leaflet from a local pizzeria on the hall floor.

"Oh God I can't live like this" she mumbled to the cat.

Why are these guys so worried? If this gene transformation is spreading as rapidly as it seems it is, they're not going to be able to keep it hidden for very long. What is their plan? What do they want with me?

Kerry felt her eyes fill with tears as she thought about how worried her parents might be and how much they really didn't deserve this after what had happened to her younger brother. He had died by suicide a year ago, his depression a side effect of a novel pain killer, one that it turned out had been known about but concealed. She shook her head angrily wondering if some out of control big pharma experiment was behind the gene transformation too. With a sigh, she closed her eyes and for the first time in a very long time she whispered a desperate prayer to please get her out of this mess.

She hoped that Donald would be able to get somewhere with his friend in Oxford. But what could he do? Perhaps she had made a huge mistake running away, although Donald seemed very certain that they needed time to think and plan. But what if they catch Donald? She thought of Johnny, an old boyfriend with whom she had amicably broken up about a year ago but with whom she kept in touch. He was a smart guy, a computer whiz, green enthusiast, but always hopelessly fixated on the latest conspiracy theories... one of the reasons they had split. She knew he still carried a torch for her and would almost certainly help.

But how to contact him without alerting these creeps?

Smiling she remembered a thriller in which the terrorist cell communicated using online gaming. She logged on to a role play fantasy game which she knew was her friend's obsession. The game displayed the "avatar handle" of everyone on-line and sure enough there he was, *@extinction2012* (chosen as it was the end date of the Mayan calendar). This game allowed player-to-player coms. She seldom played and had never used the coms but thought it should be safe to do so. Using her avatar *@princessandthepea* (based on her reluctance to sleep in his grotty apartment) she sent a message.

- *Are you alone?*
- *Yep. What's up?*
- *In trouble. Need help.*

A few seconds went by before words started to

appear across the screen once more.

- *Where did we first meet?*
- *Youth club Leith.*
- *Sorry, had to be sure it was you. What do you need?*
- *Can you come to Flat 2, 21, Larmar St. Come in your Deliveroo outfit. Will explain when you arrive. Delete this thread.*
- *Sounds serious. On my way.*

CHAPTER 4

....

In Oxford, after a sleepless night, Donald rose to take the 0520 train back home to Edinburgh. As the East Coast scenery passed by, he wondered how he might be able to hold on to their one bargaining card, the evidence of the increasing frequency of the new genetic sequencing. One way was to set up an email containing a link to the data targeted at a large number of colleagues with a time delay, which would be sent automatically if he didn't cancel it before a set deadline.

Next to him a woman was playing Sudoku. He used to find it a frustrating game but looking over her shoulder he found could see the solutions easily even the supposedly hard ones.

You really are on fire. Stress is good for you Donald!

Slowly a suspicion arose in his mind, as he linked his performance on the TV quizzes the night before last, the speed at which he had read and annotated Kerry's thesis and his newfound ability to concentrate on Sudoku. As a child he had been diagnosed with mild ADD but his parents had taken him to a psychologist who taught him strategies for dealing with it. Could it be? Surely not. Then he remembered an annoying viral infection he had had a couple of months ago which lasted about a fortnight or so with a dull headache and slight fever. He had been doing outreach at an Edinburgh school. Some set-up where young scientists were paid pretty generously to visit schools to talk about their careers to encourage kids from less advantaged backgrounds to do science. He had blamed his illness on the biology teacher there who had had a streaming cold. He remembered thinking at the time that, given the lessons of COVID, the guy should have worn a mask.

Shit! I need to get my blood tested.

The train pulled into Waverley station a full five minutes ahead of schedule. Donald thought he'd have to buy another 'burner' laptop, but on the off chance he dropped into the same run-down café where he had left the last one only to find it still neatly ensconced behind the stinking toilet cistern where he had left it. He retrieved it, raising an eyebrow at the notice on the door proudly indicating that the toilet had been inspected every three hours. *Yeah. From a distance with a gas mask.*

He wiped the urine-stained seat and sat down, logged into the Philippines server, and sent duplicates of the remaining copy of the data to several other locations. He then set up a group email to a list of geneticists with a link. The message was timed to dispatch in one week if he didn't log on to change it

There was a loud banging on the door.

"What are you doing in there, mate? Some of us are desperate out here!"

Donald deleted his history, closed the laptop and put it back where he had found it and apologising as he opened the door, to meet the chef who was wearing a truly disgusting 'white' uniform. Smiling he said

"Sorry pal, I think you must have had the same burger here as I did".

"Ye cheeky git! There's damn all wrong with ma burgers!"

He reflected with a smile that he perhaps shouldn't have made his visit to the café so memorable.

As his apartment door opened his cat ran towards him and started to rub against his leg. Where was Kerry? Had they found her? He reached down to stroke his cat behind the ears when he felt a sudden touch of cold metal on the back of his head and a deep voice saying. "Don't move!"

"Don't hurt him! He's on our side!" yelled Kerry

"Looks like the filth to me."

"Who the hell is this?" shouted Donald.

"Donald, meet my friend Johnny. Johnny is the smartest person I know. There's nothing he doesn't know about computers. Johnny, meet Donald".

The cold metal was a piece of metal piping. The man who held it was of mixed race, small, thin, unshaven, his curly hair badly cut and dishevelled. He wore a black tight-fitting hoody adorned with a large screen print of the smiling Guy Fawkes image from "V is for Vendetta" on the front. There was no corresponding smile on his face.

"Kerry, I told you to call no-one" murmured Donald.

"The way I called him is untraceable".

"Let's hope so. Have those men been back?".

"No, but when I didn't hear from you, I started to worry that they had maybe got you. I got frightened and called Johnny".

"I don't think we'll be able to keep ahead of them for long. We should maybe think about going in."

"What are you crazy!" shouted Johnny. "These guys have tried to frame her. What's to stop them putting her away?"

"Please be quiet we don't know who may be listening. What will stop them is the fact that she still has the data and I have set it up so that if anything happens to her or me it will be sent to geneticists all around the world".

"And you're sure that'd stop them?" said Kerry, looking sceptical.

"No, but I'm pretty sure they are going to eventually catch up with you and it would be better to do it on your terms".

"I don't like it. I wouldn't trust those bastards" sneered Johnny.

"I don't trust them at all, that's why we have that bargaining chip" replied Donald.

"Why are they so interested? What are they scared of?"

"I think I may have a bit of an idea as to what the genetic sequence does. Where it came from is another matter"

"Really, was this from your friend? What did he say? Can you trust him?

"Yes and yes. He says that the sequence sits next to a part of the gene that his company had been interested in. They were planning to develop new drug treatments for attention deficit disorder, ADD. They had found that variations in that gene were associated with ADD. So it could be that your new sequence might have an effect on concentration or cognitive ability."

"Well, that'd explain why the world is going to hell in a handcart!" said Kerry.

"I'm not so sure the effect is necessarily negative. Ideally, we need to find out more about the people who were affected by this and to check their cognitive abilities. That'd be a big project, not the sort of thing we could do in secret. We would have to identify these people and then approach them. We would have to get funding, go to an ethics committee. These people aren't going to let this happen."

"Not necessarily," said Johnny. "There are other ways to find out. Most people have some sort of social media presence…. At least the younger ones. If we identified them, we could just look up what's been happening to them".

"How do we identify them though? All we have is anonymous data" replied Kerry.

"Where is the ScotGene biobank?" said Johnny.

"It is behind a National Health Service firewall it is unbelievably well protected. Attempting to breach it would be career ending for Kerry and me."

"I'm pretty sure my career has already ended Donald. You're still in the clear and you have to stay clean. These guys are fighting dirty. Well, I can fight dirty too. I'm leaving. As far as they know you never saw me after the lab on

Monday. We have to hope your pal in Oxford will keep schtum. Give me the location of the data and how you have protected it. If you need to contact me, use this number. Don't use a traceable phone, don't assume it's necessarily me on the other end. Remember where I first met you? That's the code. If we need you, you'll get a message from a gay website offering specialist services", said Kerry smiling mischievously.

Kerry handed over a piece of paper with the number of the burner phone Johnny had given her which Donald memorised and in return he gave her the location and password for the data. She picked up Johnny's hoody, donned his Deliveroo bag, pulled up a face mask and left. She picked up his bike downstairs and headed off on a tour of Edinburgh to make sure she wasn't followed. Johnny, having got Donald to check the landing was clear, set off 15 minutes afterwards on foot.

Later that evening Donald's phone rang. Unknown number. He was going to ignore it as he really didn't feel up to talking to Speirs or his sidekick but then thought it might be Kerry or her anarchist pal and decided to answer.

"Dr Stirling"

Shit. "Yes, hello Mr Speirs or do you have some other title I should know like commander, inspector or some such?"

"Mister is fine."

"We'd like to see you again, Dr Stirling. Could we meet in your lab tomorrow morning?"

"Well, I can tell you now, I don't know any more about Kerry's whereabouts than the last time we spoke."

"I discussed our last conversation with my superiors, and they have decided that it's time to let you know more about what's been happening. We think you may be able to help us. May we see you in your lab tomorrow at 10.00 AM"

CHAPTER 5

Johnny and Kerry met up again at a flat in a council housing estate in the West of the city. Johnny assured Kerry that no-one, but he knew about this flat. As far as the council were concerned it looked like it was rented by a Ukrainian couple, and the rent was apparently paid every month. There of course was no couple and no money was ever transferred. "Their computer security is mince" he told her by way of explanation.

The surrounding neighbours were from a variety of countries and not concerned with making friends. The doorbell was linked to one of Johnny's burner phones so that he could reply to casual enquiries to keep up the semblance of occupancy.

"I set it up as a bolthole should I ever need it. The electricity is on a pre-paid card, but there should be plenty of credit".

"It's a hell of a lot tidier than your own gaff!"

observed Kerry.

"I could do with a little less attitude and a bit more gratitude" he laughed.

"Thanks Johnny. You're a good mate. I just wish I knew what to do next. One thing Donald said was that he thought the gene sequence might have a positive effect. It got me thinking while I was cycling here. On the news there was an article about St Julian's getting a load of students into Oxbridge!

"St Julian's! Seriously! Oxbridge prison maybe! Sorry I know you went there, but my mum changed address to make sure I didn't have to. It was a mad house. Our school wouldn't even compete in games with them as so many of the kids ended up with injuries!"

"Yes, I thought it seemed crazy too. The website says it's in tow with a company called Odyssey and another genetics company called Chi-Gen is mentioned on its list of corporate sponsors. It would appear that Odyssey has strong links with CreativeCom".

"You're bloody joking me! You think that Nazi Abe Markov has something to do with this?"

"I know this sounds like one of your wild conspiracy theories, but there just *may* be something in it."

Johnny affected mock umbrage at this characterisation but whispered

"Well now that is really interesting. I'd *love* to take that bastard down."

"Hmmm. Improving the lives of young people and helping them to get to university may not be everybody's idea of a bad guy. However unsanctioned unconsented, genetic manipulation may be just the sort of meddling our eugenics-loving billionaire would get up to."

"We need to get into St Julian's. Shall I start with a nice hack of their computer and find out what I can about when and how this started?"

"That'd be great. Leave ScotGene for now, it will be a much bigger nut to crack, and we don't want to reveal our hand too early. Let me try the traditional route with St Julian's. When I left, I was something of a star. I think I could blag my way back in. According to the website the school secretary is still Mrs Ahmed. I'll try her first thing tomorrow. What phone should I use?"

Johnny pulled open a drawer which contained several phones.

"Take your pick!" he grinned. "Just use it once though."

He showed her the bedroom. Clean sheets! Kerry could hardly believe it.

I'll pop by tomorrow with some breakfast. There's some tea and coffee there if you want it. He reached out to her and pulled her in for a brief kiss on the cheek.

"Don't worry we'll beat them!" He smiled, hugged her again and left.

Kerry suddenly felt exhausted. She had slept very poorly on Donald's couch. She was desperate for a good sleep but was sure it was going to evade her. She stripped off, pulled the covers over her and decided to count sheep. Five minutes later she was snoring.

She woke to Johnny shaking her. It was 8.00 AM. He stood clutching a tray with two large, generously filled bacon rolls and two large cups of coffee.

"Did you sleep?"

"Like a log!"

Johnny smiled.

"Cool hand Kerry!"

At 08:30 Kerry, picked up the phone took a deep breath and dialled the school number while Johnny looked on.

"Hello, Mrs Ahmed. Hi, you probably don't remember me I'm Kerry Pear....Oh. Well thank you. I haven't forgotten you either... I'm fine... how about you? Glad to hear it. The reason I'm calling is to ask if it might be possible to speak to Mr. Bhopal. I realise he's probably busy and may not have ti… you think so… well that'd be great… Well today if that's possible… Yes 11.00 AM would be great… It's about the research I'm conducting… Oh I hadn't realised that the school was so involved in that type of thing… Yes it certainly does look as though a lot has changed. See you tomorrow."

Kerry looked reflective.

"She sounded so happy and upbeat. Last time I saw her she was ready to resign. Some of the parents there gave her a very hard time. She used to dread phoning them when their kids were skiving off. I used to spend time in the office on the pretext that I wanted to learn a bit about administration. The real reason was that it was one of the safest places in the school. It will be interesting to see what's changed".

Johnny, pulled out his laptop and started typing, calling up the St Julian's website to start cracking it.

"This should be a doddle."

Sixty minutes later Johnny was still tapping the keyboard with increasing frustration.

"I don't believe this. You'd think it was bloody MI5! What does a school need this level of security for? They must be hiding something!"

"I guess having one of the world's biggest tech firms as a collaborator comes with certain advantages. One of the boasts on the school website is a first-rate informatics department. When I was there, there was hardly a computer in the school which wasn't crippled with viruses from porn sites. Let's see what I find when I go along there. See what more you can dig up on Odyssey and also check about any links Odyssey or CreativeCom may have with Chi-Gen."

An hour or so later Johnny called Kerry to look at something.

"I can't find any direct connection between Chi-Gen and Creative Com although you're right about the connection with Odyssey. It may not look it, but it is a wholly owned subsidiary albeit via a couple of offshore shell companies. However, there is a connection with ScotGene."

"What with CreativeCom? That'd be astounding!"

"No with the school. The lead for ScotGene is Sunita Bhopal, who just happens to be the daughter of … drum roll… St. Julian's headmaster. The photo here shows the ScotGene stall at the parents evening. It appears that they have a drive every parents' evening to sign people up asking their families to do so too. Along with signing up they give a saliva sample. Amazing what people will do for a free pen! Although I'd imagine that in a school like St Julian's a free anything is very welcome, no offence!

"None taken. I'm just looking up the ScotGene website. It appears that Sunita Bhopal has been the lead for five years, so I suspect the recruitment has been going on for a while."

"Ok so that takes it out of the realm of just a coincidence. We really need to speak to the headmaster."

"When do we go public with this?

"Let's hold off until I've spoken to the school. You keep trying to get into their systems. I need to let my parents know I'm alright. I don't think we can risk phoning them."

"Do they have email? I can get a message to them. It will be untraceable. What do you want to say?"

Kerry's eyes filled with tears.

"Just say, that I'm sorry I can't get in touch directly, that I'm OK. That no matter what they may hear that I haven't done anything wrong. I just hope that doesn't spook them… what if they haven't contacted my parents?"

"They will have and upsetting them won't be something they'll be concerned about." Noticing her distress, he took hold of both her shoulders. "They'll pay for this Kerry. I promise."

Kerry smiled, remembering why despite his crackpot ideas she liked him so much. She pulled him towards her and kissed him hard on the mouth hugging him tightly.

CHAPTER 6

After a night of broken sleep, Donald walked up Leith Walk, yesterday's blue skies had given way to a fine drizzle and a light breeze. He pulled his raincoat collar up and wished he'd brought his cap. He dodged the confused tourists trying to find a way around the never-ending roadworks and shook his head as he went over the events of the last few days, wishing to God that he had never been involved.

Kerry's discovery was undoubtedly real. He wanted to believe her when she said she didn't know what the significance was of the DNA sequence she had found. However, what were the odds of her having 'just noticed' such a needle in a haystack? Moreover, Kerry had suddenly seemed remarkably at ease with subterfuge and rule breaking. Her close connection with Johnny who seemed an absolute stalwart of the counterculture was a little worrying. Was she really the innocent he thought she was? Could there be something he was missing? She had always seemed a regular sort of person, but how many times had he heard that expression used by people when they were asked about neighbours and friends who turned out to be terrorists? Was he being used? With a sigh, he realised that he had made his choices now and tried to dismiss his misgivings. However, he knew he had lost control of the situation and dreaded that he might well be held accountable for what Kerry and Johnny did next. He had so much more to lose than they did.

As he approached the laboratory, he spotted Speirs and his sidekick through a doorway. They were sitting at one of the benches alongside a tall well-dressed darker skinned man. He was about to enter when Peter Munro shot out of another room and pulled him into one of the side offices. He had dark circles under bloodshot eyes, his normally immaculate shirt and tie askew. Donald thought he could smell whisky. Munro's eyes darted towards the lab, and he whispered, hardly pausing for breath.

"Have you heard anything Donald? Has Kerry been in touch? Those two have been phoning me constantly asking if I've heard anything and if I was sure that I didn't know what she was doing. It's just so unbelievable. I'd never have thought it of the girl, but surely she must be guilty or she'd have turned up by now. I think they think I'm in on it! Should I be thinking of getting a lawyer? When they turned up today... I'm not joking, I thought, this is it, they're going to arrest me!" He sobbed and shook his head quickly, composing himself.

"Peter. Don't you think that even if Kerry *is* innocent, but she thought people had framed her as a terrorist, she might not feel that inclined to turn herself in. She's probably laying low while she tries to work out what's happening. Quite frankly, I'd be amazed if they thought you were in on it. However, seriously, if you carry on being as jumpy as you are right now, they may start to!"

Seeing the alarm in his face he added in a firm voice emphasising each word.

"You have done nothing wrong Peter. You don't need to worry." He squeezed his shoulder. Peter collapsed against him. With another sob he said

"Thank you, Donald. You've been so good about this. I know we haven't always got on in the past, but you have been so kind, and I won't forget it."

Donald managed a guilty smile. "Don't mention it Peter."

A voice came from the laboratory.

"Dr Stirling. Thanks for coming. We don't need you anymore Professor Munro, you can go."

Peter looked pathetically grateful, forced a smile, and scurried off.

"Why don't we go into my office?" said Donald.

He led them into his office, a mess of piled-high paper stacks with seemingly randomly extruded post it notes, interspersed with half-finished coffee cups. It was a long-running joke in the department and, much to Donald's delight, the cleaning staff had long refused to enter it. No-one could ever understand how he could find anything, yet he could. If ever you needed a paper or a book, he always seemed to know exactly where to find it. Donald smiled as he wondered if the two spooks had tried looking there. *They'd have had a nervous breakdown!*

Donald lifted three piles of papers from chairs and with some rearranging made room for them on his desk.

"Well, please make yourself comfortable. What can I do for you?"

Speirs sneered and gave a short humph.

"You can start by telling us why we shouldn't just arrest you for aiding and abetting a suspected terrorist."

Donald raised an eyebrow and pulled his head back.

"What on earth are you talking about?"

"We know you know about Ms Pearson's gene sequence, Dr Stirling. Your friend McPherson in Oxford wisely decided to talk it over with his boss in Chi-Gen, who contacted us right away. Professor Singh here has since been working with us on this problem."

Prof Singh smiled.

"Good afternoon, Dr Stirling" said Singh in a 'posh boy' accent that annoyed Stirling. "We have actually met before, albeit briefly. I spoke to you after your fascinating lecture on the potential bioterrorist threat of CRISPR technology."

Singh turned to the other two men.

"This is a technology which facilitates the grafting of DNA into genes in a very precise way."

"We know what CRISPR is, Professor." Speirs sighed with a tired look.

Turning back to Donald, Professor Singh continued.

"Your friend Dr McPherson copied your file before he deleted it and passed it to me. I'm his boss.

Donald struggled not to show the profound

sense of shock and betrayal he felt.

How could Alan have done that?

"He and I have spent quite a bit of the last 24 hours looking into it. What Dr McPherson, hypothesised about the potential nature of the genetic code is correct. The genetic sequence is closely positioned to the gene which we thought was damaged in people with ADD. Looking at the distribution in the ScotGene data you provided it looks reasonably common. The most likely cause of this is, as he suggested, some form of gene insertion using a virus as a vector."

"As far as we're aware this has only been detected in Scotland or in people with a connection to Scotland. It seems likely the source is here. We need to know a bit more about how it is spreading before we go public and cause a panic," added Speirs.

Donald narrowed his eyes and tight lipped replied tersely,

"Did you guys learn nothing from COVID? You have to act quickly, you can't just hope it is all going to be OK? What is Chi-Gen's role in this? Did you create this?"

"No, nor would we. As I said, given the position on the gene, this new mutation, if it does anything, may have an impact on people's concentration for good or ill. We were interested in this area of the genome because we were trying to find a drug which might help people with ADD focus better, but we have no idea what the mutation which Ms Pearson discovered will do. I should add, Dr Stirling, despite your righteous indignation at our seeming immediate inaction, neither you nor Kerry got in touch with Public Health when you wondered if it might have a viral cause. You may wish to question your own motives for keeping it secret," he ended tetchily with a sneer.

"OK let's just calm down. As you can imagine, this could cause serious upset in the general population if news of this finding gets out" interjected Speirs.

"When, not if, it gets out!" murmured Donald. Turning to Speirs he said.

"So why all that guff about Kerry being an eco-terrorist? Why not just come clean and explain things as you are doing now?"

"We first found out about Kerry's supposed activities on the morning we visited you in the laboratory. We received a tip-off from a group with which we work periodically, and which usually provides reliable information. They said that they had been informed of a very credible threat to create and deploy a novel infectious agent, based on an archaic virus and that Kerry was actively involved in this. We then checked her social media and found it to be full of the most appalling stuff about the destruction of the planet wreaked by humans and the need to stop it."

"She said she never posted any of that."

"We now know she didn't. We were able to trace the source of the Instagram entries to an unknown agent working through the dark web".

"We believed it at first Dr Stirling, because Kerry isn't like you. She may not be an eco-terrorist as you put it, but she's expressed some very strong views about Big Pharma in the past and is very bitter about the death of her brother which she lays at their door. We also discovered that she keeps pretty close company with some very dodgy green anarchist hackers, but then you probably already know that don't you?

 "I've been in touch with my boss. We need this to be kept quiet… at least for a while until we can discover more about this code's origin and what it can do and just how far it has spread. We need a plan before this information is unleashed on the world."

Donald was silent as he thought this through. There was little point in dissembling further. It would not help, and his career would certainly be in ruins if he did. He sighed.

"OK, this all needs to be checked out, but I

think it may be transmitted by a respiratory virus. The reason I believe this is that I suspect I could have been infected. I think I may have contracted it on an out-reach visit to a school. For a couple of weeks after that visit I had a cold and a really bad headache."

Speirs started to interrupt.

"Let me finish. As a child I had many of the features of ADD, but I was lucky to have parents who understood it and to have a high enough IQ to compensate for it. Nonetheless it has been a problem for me to focus on one issue for long throughout my career. I always have to have two or three projects on the go simultaneously. These last few weeks I've noticed that I've been much more productive, my recall and problem solving has improved hugely. "

"Interesting, which school?"

"St. Julian's."

Speirs bent over his tablet and started to google it.

"There are several relevant hits. The most recent and possibly relevant is that they have just got a load of kids into Oxbridge. There's also a piece in a local newspaper from a few years ago about sick building syndrome in the school and how several children had complained of headaches one being admitted with suspected meningitis. However, it looks like all the children recovered after a day or two with no apparent after-effects. Interestingly, there seems to be a connection with your company professor, and with an organisation called Odyssey."

He continued to scroll.

"There's another article here about a presumed viral meningitis cluster in West Edinburgh where the school is situated, with a few adult cases too. Public Health were involved but they never got to the bottom of it. I can't see anything recently about it. "

"So, what's Chi-Gen doing there, Prof Singh? When I was there your logo was all over the place along with Odyssey?" said Donald

"That's true. We were invited by the headmaster at the suggestion of Odyssey. Our understanding was that they were an educational institute that were fostering a novel approach to teaching and learning and that they felt a company like ours which was considering opening a branch in Edinburgh might provide a good role model for children interested in science. For our part, we had been looking for something that showed we had a community conscience… cynical I know… and this seemed to fit the bill, so we joined in. I was only peripherally involved; I wasn't aware it was St. Julian's. I can assure you we have had nothing to do with this. I'm beginning to wonder now if we have been fitted up to take the fall when this all comes out."

"By whom? What is Odyssey anyway?"

"Well, that's interesting. Odyssey seems to have some sort of connection by shared directors with CreativeCom," said Speirs

"But that's a computer company. It doesn't have a biotech division, does it?" asked Donald

"Not that we know of. However, Mr Abe Markov could really buy just about anything he wanted, and as I recall, improving the human race is something about which he has controversially expressed an interest," replied Speirs.

"It would require people with very high skills to produce something like this," said Donald. "People at the very top of their fields. I can't think of anyone in the world never mind Scotland who would do this."

"Would or could? It could have been developed anywhere, a rogue lab either in China or the US. There are a few European centres possibly capable of this too," answered Singh.

"Assuming this is a man-made virus and not some chance mutation. Is it being unleashed all around the world or just here? It seems a very unlikely sort of place to start!" said Donald with a quizzical look.

"We only know about Scotland," said Speirs.

"OK so far this doesn't appear to be doing any harm, in fact it may actually be producing some benefit. However, we have no idea if there may be longer-term ill effects. It is scandalous that, without consent, this has been unleashed on the public. We need to ask Odyssey, don't we?" asked Donald

Speirs raised a hand.

"Hang on. We have to be careful about what we say to Odyssey. If they aren't involved, then we risk revealing this before we know enough about it to inform the public in a way which won't cause panic.

We think you can help us Dr Stirling. As can Miss Pearson. Whoever has unleashed this knows about her. The attempt to incriminate her, we assume, a chance to buy time to grab the narrative. There's a chance they'll speak to her if she approaches them. Can you get in touch?"

"I'll see what I can do as long as you leave it to me. No following me, no tracking. If she gets a whiff of that it will all be over. She is a very bright woman with very suspicious friends. I'll get back to you once I've spoken to her."

CHAPTER 7

....

Donald left the lab and walked directly to the Cash Generator store. To his surprise, the assistant recognised and greeted him.

Never thought I'd be a regular here! he smiled.

He asked for a cheap mobile phone and bought a £10 SIM. He walked to a nearby green space and called the number Kerry had given him. There was no reply, and it rang out. There was no invitation to leave a message. He was about to try again when he received a text. "Where did we meet?" He replied, "At the conference in Stockholm". The phone rang.

"Hi Kerry?"

"Donald. Are you OK?"

"Yes, we need to talk. I just bought this phone and SIM, and I'm in the middle of a park."

"OK, but best to keep it brief."

"I met with Speirs. My pal in Oxford sold me out... told his boss the bastard! Speirs says that his crew were not behind the Instagram posts.

He claims that they had been alerted to them by another group they work with from time to time. When they checked up on you, they found connections with some anti-big-pharma groups, and they knew about your relationship with Johnny and his friends which made them think the source's allegations might be true. However, they now know that the posts are false."

"I'll await their apology."

"A Chi-Gen boss was there. They deny all knowledge of it, but then they would, wouldn't they. He said he thinks Alan was right about the possible impact on ADD or cognitive processes of the gene and the possible viral vector to disseminate it. I didn't tell you yesterday, but I'm beginning to suspect I may have been infected. I think it may have happened when I was visiting a school."

"St Julian's by any chance?"

"Yes! How did you know?"

"I'm on my way there now. Am I going to bump into Speirs or his mob?"

"Not that I know of. That's the part I'm coming to. They want us to work with them. They think there may be a link through a company called Odyssey to …

"CreativeCom," interjected Kerry.

"Yes! how do you know all this?"

"St Julian's is my old school. They seem to have had a rather sudden and dramatic transformation in their academic fortunes. What does Speirs want?"

"He thinks that CreativeCom, if it *is* them that's behind it, will want to get a hold of you."

"I bet they do!"

"Apparently, Speirs and his bosses think, as we do, that they can't keep this under wraps, but just want to have time to control the narrative, to have something to offer when it all comes out. They think that the best approach might be for you to get in touch with Odyssey. I could do so with you."

"So, we risk getting kidnapped or worse while they sit and watch?"

"It would be easier to find out more about Odyssey if you seemed to co-operate, possibly saying you're excited and delighted by the impact of what the gene alteration has done for the kids. I suspect if you followed that line they just might fall for it."

"Do you really trust Speirs and his gang. They seem pretty ruthless."

"What they said seems to make sense. They also hadn't made the CreativeCom connection until I told them about thinking I had been affected."

"And in what way have you been affected?"

"I'm able to focus on things much more than I could previously and…."

"That explains your performance on 'Only Connect' the other evening. I felt a real dunce next to you!"

"That and a few other things I've noticed."

"So, this gene insert may not be all bad"

"Well, if we're right then it wasn't… well not for me, but we don't know if it works well all the time or if it can hurt some people. Could it make some people over focussed on stuff for example? We just don't know."

"These guys are crazy. Why release it like this? Why not do a trial?"

"Can you imagine how controversial it would be to do a trial like this? You can just hear the conspiracists, the state manipulating people's minds, the devaluing of some people because they are a little different. There may be some truth in these things. Abe Markov isn't the kind of guy to sit around and wait for all the argument to settle."

"What's to stop them just kidnapping or killing us? "

"We still have the ability to blow this up early if they do."

"They don't know about you. Unless Chi-Gen is in on it or there's a leak in Speirs' department.

You should stay out of it. I can go to the school and if they haven't already, I can make sure the school lets Odyssey know I'm there."

"If you do meet them, how do you get in touch with us."

"I'll call you on this phone. If I don't call by this afternoon, Johnny has fixed me up with a tracker. Its tiny and well concealed and can send a panic signal if I need to. I'm texting you another emergency number."

She hung up. Donald rang Speirs on his own phone.

"She's willing to help. You haven't got anyone going to the school have you. She is on her way there now."

"We do, but they aren't there yet, and we can call them off."

"Do that. She's pretty cynical about your trustworthiness. I am myself. However, if she sees any of your guys around, she'll be off. She says she's going to phone me again this afternoon after she's seen them."

"Phone me again after you have spoken to her."

CHAPTER 8

The first thing Kerry noticed about her old school were the new gates. They were an elaborate organic design in stainless steel.

These must have cost a packet! When I left, they could hardly afford to repair the gym roof.

The walls on either side of the path up to the school were strangely free of the 'cock and balls' and gang related graffiti which had previously decorated them. Passing through the door in the entrance hall she saw two students, in full uniform behind a desk, tapping away at keyboards. They looked up.

"Hello, Kerry, isn't it? I'm Hana and this is Josh. We're expecting you." The speaker was a young woman wearing a hijab in the school colours.

"Hi! Great to meet a St Julian's legend!" said her companion a tall, somewhat gawky young black man, standing and reaching out his hand beaming a winning smile.

"Hi. I don't know about that…"

Kerry looked bemused and gestured around her.

"We never used to have anything like this when I was a student here."

"What, you mean the student reception? The student council thought it would be a good way both to greet visitors and students as well as to help students build up their own social skills. It also gives them a bit of a handle on who's coming and going."

Student council! Just getting kids to come to school at all was an achievement before. What the hell has happened here?

"Let me take you to the headmaster's office," said Josh indicating a room at the end of the corridor.

Mrs Ahmed beamed as Kerry entered her office. The downtrodden, jumpy person she remembered had gone. Instead, here was a confident well-dressed, subtly made-up woman who stood up and gave her a hug. The office too had undergone a transformation. A beautiful modern wooden desk, free of clutter just one large computer screen, keyboard and mouse.

"Kerry! Lovely to see you again. Come in! It's been far too long!"

"Would you like a tour? You'll find things have changed a lot, I think. Michael Flannigan our head prefect has offered to take you round. He has a free period at the moment."

"Not *Mad Mick* Flanigan?!" exclaimed Kerry, "The same Mick who painted the headmaster's car yellow, the year I left? I'd have thought he'd be long gone!"

"Well, that's not a very PC way of putting it!" said a voice behind her.

Kerry turned and there was a tall, good-looking, smiling young man in a school uniform with a prefect badge who was clearly a grown up 'Mad Mick'.

Kerry flushed bright pink.

"Oh God Michael! That was so rude of me. I'm sorry."

The young man laughed.

"Believe me I've been called much worse. Kerry, you were one of the very few people in this school back then who was actually nice to me. Do you remember when the police were chasing me, and you hid me in the mail room?"

Mrs Ahmed frowned. "I didn't know about that!"

Kerry laughed. "Yes, I do. Served them right the creeps. Four of them chasing one wee kid."

"Would you like a tour, Kerry? I think you'll see a few changes."

Michael indicated the corridor with an

outstretched hand. Kerry meekly stepped forward and they both ambled down the corridor. Kerry was speechless as Michael showed her computer suites brimming with PCs, laboratories with serious looking students in clean white coats working on experiments, an amazing fitness centre with multipurpose exercise rooms, and a completely revamped assembly hall with state-of-the-art audiovisual equipment. Kerry couldn't contain her amazement.

"Michael, where did the money come to pay for all this? When I was here, it was a struggle just to keep the lights on."

"We have a very generous sponsor. We're so lucky Odyssey have chosen St Julian's as their flagship to test their educational theories. We think they thought if they could make them work here, they'd work anywhere!" he laughed. "And it looks like their bet has paid off. Did you see the article on the BBC? We have had amazing exam results this year."

"But just buying stuff wouldn't do that though?"

"I think if you start to treat people as special, they start to act special, don't you think?"

"Maybe, what are these new educational theories you're talking about?"

"Psychological techniques for improving focus

such as mindfulness, or meditation as we prefer to call it, and reward-based systems are the basis of it, but it's a little more sophisticated than that. The logical thinking courses are really popular. We have a resident psychology team and a research group."

"Could I meet them?"

"Of course! They were very keen to meet you as it happens, however they are away on a course today."

Oh! Look at the time. I told Mrs Ahmed I'd get you back to see Mr Bhopal 11.00."

"Do you mind if I use the loo first?"

The toilet was another revelation. Previously a smoke-filled, foul-smelling site for casual violence, there were now new sinks, new loos, electric dryers. *Hand cream too for God's sake!* She slipped into a stall and pulled out her phone. She quickly texted Johnny to tell him what was happening. She wondered how much to tell Donald knowing it was it going back to Speirs but thought that shady government was probably better than shady big business… just. She then deleted the record of the texts, flushed the toilet, used the sink and dryer for appearance's sake and rejoined Michael.

"Well, I'll leave you now Kerry I have advanced maths at 11.00. It was so nice to see you again."

"It was lovely to see you too Michael. I'm so

pleased that things have started to work out for you."

"This is a brilliant school now Kerry. The funny thing is the knock-on effect it seems to have had. You know my dad and my younger sister Kathy were a bit of a mess. We're all so much better. I guess the stress of my antics was pulling them all down. Dad has a job now and Kathy is doing brilliantly here."

"I don't think that could have been all your fault Michael. Anyway, let's catch up again and let me know what happens with your exams."

Kerry entered the office. Mr. Bhopal stood up and embraced her.

"So *wonderful* to see you, Kerry! Did you get the tour? What do you think?" he asked in that posh Oxford English accent the kids used to torment him about.

"I don't know what to think. This is a completely different school from the one I attended!"

"I know! I can hardly believe the transformation myself. We have been *so lucky*! This all happened because of a letter I wrote five years ago. The school was in such dire financial straits I sent begging letters to hundreds of companies asking them if they'd consider supporting us. I realised it was a long shot, but I was desperate. Out of the blue a letter came from Odyssey. The strange thing was, I hadn't heard of them and hadn't approached them! However, they said they could offer considerable support as part of a development project in education they wanted to try out and asked to meet me.

They came... I saw them with a few of the senior teachers and the chairman of the board of governors. When they told us of their plans we were blown away! They were offering equipment, refurbished accommodation, paid staff training courses on their new techniques, an educational psychology team and a full-time nurse! A couple of teachers were wary, with the old adage 'if it seems too good to be true it probably is', but we all knew the school was on the edge of an abyss and just about anything had to be better."

"What did they want in return?"

"They just wanted to see if their techniques worked and, if they did, they'd market them around the world. Honestly, Kerry, it has been nothing short of *miraculous*! The morale among the staff is terrific, truancy and episodes of violence have almost disappeared. Even sickness absence is down among the students and staff. The school nurse has made sure everyone is immunised against everything."

"How are they testing the outcomes of their

approach?"

"They have a clinical research team who ran some physical and cognitive tests on the children when they first started and now do it twice a year. Don't ask me what they do, I don't know the details of those, perhaps our clinical psychologist Dr Huber will be able to fill you in on that.

"But the exciting news is that I just this minute got a call from the actual head of Odyssey who is coming here tomorrow! I've only ever had meetings with her by video before. It's the first time she'll have visited the school. I had just mentioned you were coming today, and she said that was a great because she really wanted to meet you and would visit in person. I thought, what an incredible coincidence! Can you come? I more or less promised you would Kerry even if it's only for half-an-hour? As a bonus, you could also have a word with Dr Huber about your research. She'll be back from her conference then. I can promise first class coffee and biscuits, made here by the students of course.

Kerry remembered the 'brownies' that were prepared in home-economics when she was a student here.

"Yes, a coincidence indeed. I'd be delighted to meet her." *But maybe just coffee!* she smiled.

Kerry was ushered out by another smiling student. She stood at the main entrance, apparently checking her phone, but simultaneously looking for observers. She took a bus into town where she visited the National Gallery leaving by a different doorway from the one she entered. She then took a complex route through several stores, pushing her way through the throngs of tourists.

Convinced she had left any possible tail behind she started to walk home. However, noticing a public telephone call box, she was overwhelmed by the desire to contact her parents, whom she knew would be frantic with worry. She realised that their phone would almost certainly be monitored, but thought, that if she kept the call brief, she could be gone before they could tag her again. To her relief the payphone was working and her bank card still worked. Her mother answered the call after just a couple of rings.

"Mum, it's me. I can't stay on the line long. I just want you to know that I'm fine, and you're not to worry."

"Oh! Thank God! I thought we'd lost you too!" sobbed her mother.

Kerry's eyes filled with tears. It felt so unfair that her parents who had been nothing but good to her were suffering because of something she had done however innocently.

Her mother continued, her voice high pitched and quivering.

"What have you been doing?! The man who came to the house said they were concerned you'd got in tow with some very nasty people and that maybe they were using you. They told us to contact them if we heard anything from you."

"It's OK, Mum it's been a big mix up. I haven't done anything wrong nor have my friends. I think if you phone the number you have after this call, I hope they'll confirm that, or that they will soon. I can't see you right now, but I promise you I'll keep in touch. I must go. Phone the number you were given and tell them I called and what I said. I love you. Tell dad I love him," she said, her voice breaking. She thought as she hung up that those last few words were what people said when they believed they were leaving for good or about to die.

Pulling herself together she once more dived in and out of several shops before heading along backstreets to Johnny's safe house. If what Donald said was true, they no longer suspected her of bioterrorism, but she was pretty sure they still wanted to talk to her. Nonetheless, she was determined, if she was going to talk, it was going to be on her terms. She wasn't as trusting as Donald when it came to the police.

CHAPTER 9

Donald ended his call with Speirs and noticed on his own phone that he had a missed call, Alan McPherson. He grimaced and felt his stomach turn. He still couldn't believe the guy had sold him out. He couldn't imagine a situation where he'd have done that to Alan. He wasn't sure if now was the time to phone back when he felt so furious, but he pressed the ring button.

"Hi Donald, thanks for calling back. I know you must be feeling angry with me right now."

"I'm fucking furious, but actually… if you want to know, more sad and disappointed."

Alan sighed.

"Well, I'm sure it's no consolation, but my guilt gauge is off the scale. I was so bloody anxious after you left. I was sure those guys had followed you. You know what they're like. We've seen them in action before when they thought we might leak what we knew about Porton Down. Then I thought our careers were over and we'd done nothing! I just couldn't take it again. I thought if I said nothing about what you'd told me they'd assume I was in on it, I'd lose everything, and they'd get you anyway."

Donald could hear Alan's voice breaking as he spoke. There was no doubting the genuine contrition there. What was the point of making him feel worse when it had been he, after all, who'd brought the trouble to his door?

"OK Alan, I know I'm not blameless here. I don't want to fall out. Let's put it behind us. What's happened since?"

"I've been working on this non-stop since we met and I spoke to my boss. I think he told you that."

"Yes, he did, does he know you're talking to me now?"

"Yes, he thinks we should work together if you're willing to do so? He's a bit pissed that Chi-Gen appears mixed up in it. He is adamant we have nothing to do with it."

"He would say that though, wouldn't he?"

"He said that you thought you'd been affected. Could we start looking at you, that wouldn't risk breaking cover."

"OK, but you know this won't stay under wraps for long. Are you going to come here or do you expect me to come to Oxford."

"Chi-Gen has a lab with a small team here in Edinburgh. It's run by Emilio Sanchez."

"Emilio Sanchez is working in Edinburgh? Yes, I know him a bit. I didn't know he was here though. Didn't he work for NeoPharmatics? I met him at a conference a few years ago and he was really pissed about the company. Talented guy though. His research was on using viral vehicles to insert DNA into cells, wasn't it?"

"Yes, so that may be of some help to us. I plan to come up this afternoon, do you think that'd be OK?"

"Do you want to stay at my place?"

"Are you sure that'd be OK? I wouldn't blame you if you didn't want me there."

Donald sighed. "I could do with the company actually."

"See you around 3.30 then." Alan's voice sounded a good bit lighter than when he first called.

As Donald hung up, he once again started to doubt the integrity of yet another friend. Could Alan really be trusted, he hadn't been great so far? Was Chi-Gen as innocent as Alan's boss made out? He resolved to watch his step with both Alan and Kerry. He had to look out for himself too. Later, in his flat as he sat stroking his cat, he thought that he had never felt quite so isolated. He needed to know what was going on and working with Chi-Gen was one way of doing so. He also really wanted to know what was going on in his own body.

His cat was purring loudly his eyes half closed

At least I have you Schrodinger, you won't let me down… well as long as I'm providing the cat food.

At around 3.30PM, Alan phoned Donald to say he had just got off the airport tram close to his apartment and a few minutes later the doorbell rang. Donald wasn't sure how to play it. He was still sore about the betrayal, but was there any point in going on about it? When he opened the door Alan stood there with a worried apologetic look.

Donald found himself smiling.

"Come on in! Fresh start? eh?"

"I was expecting you to punch me, and I wouldn't blame you. I feel a total shit."

"Let's put it behind us and get to work. Can we go to Emilio's lab this afternoon? Does he know we're coming?"

"My boss phoned him this morning and told him I was coming up. He didn't say what it was about. He thinks we need to keep it under wraps just now."

"How well do you know Emilio, Alan?"

"Only by reputation. People don't like working with him. He has a ruthless streak. I've heard that he drops collaborators as soon as he feels they are no longer of use, usually after appropriating their work. Their names don't appear on papers even though they have clearly contributed. I was warned off working with him. However, there's no doubt that he is a leader in his field. He had been working with NeoPharmatics but moved to Chi-Gen. Rumour has it the departure from NeoPharmatics wasn't his idea. Shall we go there now? I think he's expecting us."

They arrived around dusk at the Chi-Gen research laboratory on the southern outskirts of Edinburgh, a large cube made entirely of greenish glass, but which glowed a brilliant orange in the setting sun, casting a glow on the road and buildings nearby.

"I've always wanted to see inside this place but never managed to persuade anyone to give me the tour, despite some heavy sucking up to the guys who worked there when I met them at conferences." said Donald.

"I've not been here either. Looks plusher than the lab in Oxford. Certainly newer."

Alan pressed on the entry phone and stated his name. There was a buzzing, and the door opened. The security guard at the station asked for his ID and an iris scan and he was asked to sign in Donald. Donald too was asked for ID and to look at a camera.

"I'm afraid you have to leave phones and all recording materials here Sir," said the guard.

They passed him their phones and he put them in zip-lock containers.

Donald noticed Alan's quizzical look as he put two phones in the tray.

"Work and personal," he said in response, hoping that Johnny's security was better than his own.

They crossed the large empty atrium to a bank of elevators. Alan used his ID and an iris scan to call one. Donald felt like he was back in Porton Down. Alan, however, did not seem put out by it. Perhaps, he thought this was the new normal for biotech companies. What was clear was that, without Alan, he'd not be able to move about this building.

They stopped at the 10th floor and stepped out into a wide corridor. There were glass walls on either side, with rooms filled with equipment and people in bright white coverall suits moving around and seated at various types of apparatus. At the third door on the left Alan used his badge and scan again to gain entry to a small brightly lit room where they donned coveralls and boots.

They pushed through a door and heard a hiss of air blowing towards them as it opened. Closing it behind them a tall figure in similar coveralls approached.

"Doctors McPherson and Stirling I presume," he said with a Spanish accent.

"Alan and Donald," replied Donald smiling. "Actually Emilio, we have met briefly before in Milan."

"Of course, I knew I recognised you. I got a message from Professor Singh to offer you all necessary assistance. He didn't say what it was about."

"It is a bit hush-hush Emilio I'm afraid. We have been told not to discuss it. Sorry. We need to do some DNA sequencing," said Alan.

Emilio looked a little crestfallen then puffing himself up and with more than a hint of disdain in his voice said.

"OK. Do you know how to work this Forrest 3000 sequencer."

"You have a Forrest 3000!?" exclaimed Alan. "It's not due to be released until later this year!"

"We helped develop it" replied Emilio with a slight smile.

Donald felt there was more than a hint of contempt in the reply. He realised they had not made a friend of Emilio. He wondered briefly if it was just down to Latin machismo (immediately rebuking himself for indulging in stereotyping) or if there was more to it.

"I'll leave you to it."

"Thanks Emilio, hopefully it's as intuitive as the earlier versions. I'll give you a shout if we need help," said Alan.

Sanchez gave a forced smile and moved to a bench nearby even though the lab was half occupied.

Alan looked at Donald, raised his eyebrows and flicked his eyes towards Sanchez.

Donald loudly told Alan he needed to pee, but his intention was to extract a small blood sample without Emilio knowing. On his return he made a show of apparently removing a sample from his satchel and they started work on processing it.

The process took a few hours. To build bridges and pass time, Donald started to engage Emilio.

"What are you focussing on these days Emilio? You were exploring viral delivery systems a couple of years ago. Are you still doing that?"

"Yes. That's correct."

"Professor Singh said that your work was cutting edge and a potential game changer," Donald lied. "Sounds terrific. Nobel prize in the offing?"

Emilio visibly puffed up a little and smiled.

"Professor Singh said that? Sorry, I can't say too much about it. Like yours, my work is very confidential. I can't take all the credit" he said with a look that implied self-modesty. "We have a partner that contributed to it too."

"Ah!" smiled Donald, "So it's true! Who's the collaborator, let me guess, Wang Li?"

"No way!" he said with evident disdain. "He couldn't come up with this. I can't say but it's no-one you've heard of."

Alan looked up quizzically. It was extremely unusual in their field for them not to know leading players. Donald, however, thought that for the time being they had probed enough. He was beginning to get a little suspicious. It seemed a bit of a coincidence that Chi-Gen were working locally on precisely the type of technology which would have been needed to make the sort of genetic changes they had encountered in the ScotGene samples.

Alan called him back to view the results which were appearing. As suspected, Donald carried the genetic mutation.

"How dare they!" he whispered to Alan, glancing quickly at Emilio to check he hadn't overheard.

"Look how long this sequence is that Kerry discovered! And there may not be just one alteration. This type of gene insertion is way beyond what I understand to be current state of the art."

"It would be useful if we could run the ScotGene samples through an AI program to look for other possible anomalies. The problem is that it's likely to find a lot of matches. However, if we compare the older samples with the newer ones and restrict it to looking for sequences which are the same in all the newer samples but which don't appear in the older ones that should cut it down a lot. Do we know anyone who could do the programming?"

"I think I may know someone," said Donald. I'll have a word with him.

"Did I hear you say you wanted an AI programmer," said Emilio who unbeknown to them had been standing behind them.

Donald jumped. "Eh, Yes.. Do you know someone?" then wondered to himself how long Emilio had been there. He really didn't trust him at all.

"Yes, let me know what you're looking for and I'll ask her."

"Once we're clear about what we want, we'll take you up on that" replied Donald jauntily, while thinking *No bloody way!*

"I think we have done all we can for this evening. Let's head off," said Alan

"I've a few more things to do" said Emilio, "I can tidy up for you".

"Thanks Emilio, but almost done," replied Alan

with a smile while encrypting and saving his files.

They warmly wished Emilio farewell saying they'd see him the following day. Emilio's eyes darted worriedly from one to the other. Dissembling was clearly not one of his strengths. All he could manage was a grunted goodbye as he turned towards his own workstation.

"That guy is hiding something" said Donald through gritted teeth as they passed down the corridor.

"Agreed, I wish I could be sure that he won't be able to access the work we carried out this afternoon despite my best efforts to conceal it. I think we should assume that he'll soon know what we have been doing."

CHAPTER 10

....

As Kerry entered the safe house, she heard a rustling then the back door slammed. Had Speirs found them? She turned to leave, and her heart leapt as the kitchen door pushed open. It was Johnny holding a laptop.

"Bloody Hell, Johnny. You scared the shit out of me!"

"You scared the shit out of *me*! I didn't know who was coming in. How did you get on with the school?"

"Incredible, but I also heard from Donald. He's seen Speirs, who now says he knows we're not bioterrorists, that they discovered that, although it appeared to come to them through a reliable source, the disinformation about me on Instagram was placed by 'agents unknown' through the dark web. Maybe you could check that and see if you can find who was behind it? They want us to cooperate with them."

"You must be joking! Would you really trust those bastards!?"

"No, but Donald thinks that while we have a copy of the data, we have some leverage. At least it would get them off our backs for a bit."

"What did you learn at the school, Kerry?"

"The school was a revelation, incredible. I'll tell you about it, but we need to set up a meeting with Donald. Do we need to meet in person?" asked Kerry.

"Always riskier. While it's definitely more reassuring to eyeball someone, we only have Speirs' word that they are still not after us."

"I'll call him and see if he's free to talk then," she said, pressing his most recent number.

"No reply, that's strange."

Donald heard the phone ring, but unsure as to whether the one he had checked in at the Chi-Gen lab might have been compromised, he let it ring. Because of this he had dropped into a Tesco and bought another phone He sent a message to Johnny explaining the change in phone. After a delay of around 10 minutes his new phone rang... a different unknown number. He and Alan were almost back at the apartment.

"Hi, said Donald, "What's the question?"

"Where did you first meet her?" asked Johnny

"Stockholm"

"Where are you?"

"Walking home to my apartment, I don't think we can be overheard."

"Have you heard from Kerry?"

"She's here."

"Look I'm with Alan. We've just been at the lab. We have some news. We'll soon be back at the apartment. We'll call from there."

"No, do it from outside. You don't know who could be listening at your apartment. Can you trust Alan?"

"Yes, I think so.... As much as anyone, I guess. I'll call back in a few minutes."

Donald and Alan found a park bench away from traffic and re-dialled Johnny. He told him he had it on speaker and that Alan was with him. Alan looked a little downcast. Donald suspected that he still felt guilty and had to reassure them of his trustworthiness.

"Alan and I have something important to report, but tell us how you got on today, Kerry."

"God, you wouldn't believe that school! Honestly if it weren't for the kids' accents, you'd think you were at Eton. It's a complete transformation. Polite, well-behaved kids, working with state-of-the-art equipment. It's hard to believe it could all be down to educational techniques and improved resources. However, I guess it's just possible."

"Seriously, you think?" said Donald.

"One of the students, who was a total psycho back in the day suggested that previously they were all expected to be losers and so they acted like losers. If you treat people with respect, he said, you get it back in return. The headmaster said that the offer from Odyssey apparently came out of the blue. They offered educational psychologists, masses of new equipment, training support on their educational methods, all just in return for seeing the impact of their intervention."

"And who's doing the testing?"

"The in-house psychology team. They test the children twice a year. He was vague about what they were measuring. However... this is perhaps the most interesting thing... I've an appointment tomorrow to speak to the head of Odyssey and the chief educational psychologist. The Odyssey head specifically asked to speak to me. It's the first visit she's ever made to the school, so I think we have made an impression!"

"Well, if we weren't sure about a link, I think we are now. Are you happy enough to go tomorrow? Do you think it will be safe?"

"I think I must. I doubt they'd try anything too dodgy. They must know there's more than just me involved... at least I hope so."

"What about you Johnny? How have you been getting on with getting into their computer systems?"

"Well, it wasn't easy to get in! The security was mental! I've been digging around. There are a few things that are interesting, mainly in the medical files."

Donald sighed. He immediately felt uneasy at the casual breach of medical confidentiality that Johnny was describing and worried what else he had been up to. However, he also wanted to know what he had discovered, however unethically.

Johnny hesitated for a moment. He slowly blew out through pursed lips.

"Most of what you see in the files seems positive. Prior to four years ago, the records report quite a lot of injuries from fights in the school and an incredible number of positive pregnancy tests. What psychology reports there were, dealt with dyslexia, behavioural disorder, ADHD and Autistic spectrum disorders. However, about three years ago the picture starts to change. In the last year, there are far fewer injuries, usually due to football, none as a result of fights, no new referrals for ADHD or generalised behaviour problems. Even dyslexia seems to be less of a problem... which I guess doesn't fit in with your ADHD gene theory. Oh, and there were only two positive pregnancy tests compared with a previous average of about 10-12 per year."

"Well at least that sounds OK. Anything negative?"

"If anything, there's a slight rise in autistic spectrum disorders, but even that seems to reflect the same number of children being seen but more often. On the educational side, the exam results are the big change though. It wasn't just those kids getting into Oxbridge; right across the board the results have been higher. Extraordinary, and a lot higher than my old school anyway."

"Any cognitive testing results?"

I couldn't find any evidence of cognitive testing. The psychology research records aren't on the school server. I guess I'd have to hack into Odyssey to get those. That could be risky. I'd imagine their security is considerable stronger than St Julian's."

"Hard to believe that all this happened as a result of better educational techniques", interjected Alan.

"We have some news too," said Donald "Alan and I spent the afternoon in the Chi-Gen lab in Edinburgh. We both think there's something going on there despite the denials of the Chi-Gen boss. However, the big news is that I have the same genetic sequence that you uncovered

Kerry. I'm pretty sure I got it as a result of a respiratory virus when I visited St Julian's. Whatever this is can spread from person to person."

"Oh my God! This is massive!" replied Johnny. "We have to tell the world"

"Let's learn a bit more first. Johnny, we'd like some help from you if you can do it. We think there may be other genetic changes apart from the one that Kerry discovered by accident. Would you be able to compare the genetic sequences in people who have the changes and those who don't to see if you can uncover any other transformed genetic sequences in common. It'll not be easy. Clearly there will be a huge amount of overlap, but, if we're right, there will be similarities present between those affected that aren't present in those that aren't."

Johnny frowned. "Hmmm... that will require some major computing power.... but I know some people that can maybe get me time on a super-computer here in Edinburgh. I'll get back to you."

"What time is your appointment with the Odyssey head Kerry? Is that the Marion Spitz person we found online?" asked Donald.

Yes, and it's at 10.30. I also have some time set aside to meet the main educational psychologist."

OK so let's reconvene after your meeting tomorrow Kerry. Can we change code words. When we contact each other the first sentence should contain the word 'great'."

After ending the call Donald turned to Alan.

"This is crazy. You can't help but think there has to be a downside. From what Johnny says our suspicion that more than one gene is involved is likely to be true."

"What do you think about Johnny?" said Alan screwing up his face. "He seems a bit fast and loose with data protection, don't you think?"

"He's certainly not the sort of ally I'd normally choose, but I guess needs must. Kerry seems to think he is something of a genius when it comes to computers. I just hope he doesn't get caught doing something stupid and drag us all down with him. Anyway, not sure what more we can do this evening. Let's go and get some dinner. There's a great Italian near here."

Back in the safe house. Johnny seemed energised and set to on the task he had been given by Donald. Kerry heard him on the phone to a colleague asking about computer access and being suitably cagey about what he was going to use it for. It was all very pally. Kerry wondered just how many of what we would consider to be 'regular guys' working in informatics subscribed to Johnny's big conspiracy theories. *God knows. Perhaps he's been right all along,* she smiled. Feeling a little redundant she asked Johnny if there was an untraceable way to download her corrected thesis from her email. She might as well get on with it.

CHAPTER 11

It was a sparkling sunny day, making up for the drizzle of the day before. Kerry walked through Princes St Gardens towards the railway station. She glanced up at the familiar ancient fortress, perched on an extinct volcano, sweeping down to the beautifully manicured gardens below and began to feel more relaxed than she had felt for a couple of days. She tried to reassure herself that despite there being an apparently appalling ethical breach, what was happening in St Julian's appeared to be positive. However, they certainly needed to know more, particularly about any possible long-term consequences. She doubted she'd get anything from Marion Spitz but thought the psychologist might be able to give her more information. She knew there was some risk attached to walking into the 'lion's den', but she had the tracker Johnny had given her which he had assured her was 'virtually' undetectable. She reassured herself that surely too many people would know about her attendance this morning for them to try anything.

Leaving the gardens, she hopped on a bus which took her to the gates of St Julian's. Hana and Josh were on reception duty once more and after a cheery welcome, Hana took her along to the headmaster's office. He was sitting with Mrs Ahmed when she arrived and jumped up immediately.

"So glad you could come again Kerry! Dame Marion is so keen to see you. She is particularly interested in your research project! Anyway, let's not keep her waiting". To Kerry's surprise, and mild discomfiture, he took her arm and steered her to an office a few doors down from his own.

Marion Spitz was petite, grey haired and bony thin. Kerry noticed her well-cut floral dress and that she was holding a beautifully crafted Mulberry handbag. It looked just like one her dad had bought her mum as a 25th wedding anniversary present. Her mother loved it although feigned annoyance at the extravagance. The handbag was just about the only thing this woman had in common with her mother. She felt she was being greeted with the practised smile of a head waiter who had already weighed her up and found her wanting.

She really thinks she already owns me!

"And you must be Kerry," enunciated Spitz, in a voice that reeked of confidence and expensive education. "Thank you, headmaster. I'll speak to you later once this young lady and I have got acquainted." She gave a brief smile and raised her eyebrows.

Mr Bhopal pulled back, his face betraying a degree of dismay at the casual dismissal, but he attempted to make light of it.

"Well, ... I... I'll leave you two scientists together then," he said, emphasising the word scientists while glancing at the tray that clearly had three cups alongside the coffee and brownies.

"He's such a poppet, isn't he?" said Spitz with another forced smile as he closed the door behind him.

"He really cares about the children in his care. He always has," said Kerry evenly.

"Yes, very commendable," she replied dismissively.

"Mr Bhopal said you were keen to see me." Kerry tried to take the hostility she felt out of her voice.

"Well, yes. Always keen to meet a St Julian's star!"

"There seems to be something of a constellation of them now."

"Indeed. Kerry, what do you know of our work here?"

"Really just what I've heard yesterday from Mr Bhopal and a couple of the students. "

Spitz continued to smile, a few seconds passing as she weighed her up.

"All good, I hope? We're very pleased with the difference we've made here. The headmaster said you wanted to speak to him about a research project. I checked you out on the university website. Your work is on redundant DNA, isn't it?" she said with knitted eyebrows. "How does that fit in with St Julian's?"

Kerry knew she was up against a slick operator. She wondered just how much this woman already knew. She wouldn't be surprised if she knew all about her discovery but couldn't be sure. She smiled and tried to look enthusiastic.

"This really isn't anything to do with my PhD project. I'm dying of boredom with that and can't wait for it to finish. One of the things I discovered in the course of my work is the concerns people have about genetics, possibly out of proportion to any real danger. I was planning to apply for a grant to explore these issues. I saw the news about St Julian's on the BBC, and I got the idea that it might help my application if I could demonstrate that I already had a cohort of young people lined up to interview."

"Fascinating. Odyssey, as you may know, has many interests of which education is only one. Research such as that you propose would be of great interest to our main funder and believe me Kerry, he has very deep pockets. Would you be interested in meeting him?"

Is she's trying to bribe me? thought Kerry, while still smiling and trying to look excited by the offer.

"Of course!" exclaimed Kerry. That'd be great. All the while an alarm was going off in her head, worrying that maybe that things were moving a little fast, but more convinced than ever that Odyssey was thigh deep in all of this.

"As it happens, I've a phone call with him scheduled for this morning. I'll have a word with him. Why don't you speak to Brigitte our lead psychologist to get more of an idea of how we have wrought the changes you see, and I'll see you again around lunchtime once I've spoken with Mr Bhopal. Would that be convenient?"

"That sounds great".

Spitz looked towards a smartly dressed young man in the corner of the room and raised her eyebrows. He stood up and opened the door for Kerry and followed her out. With a confident smile, he introduced himself as Larry, Ms

Spitz's PA, and expressed his hope that she enjoyed her visit. Kerry wondered if the slick social skills on display in the school were part of some sort of package. Chatting amiably about what a great organisation Odyssey was to work for, he led her to another office and introduced her to Brigitte Huber.

Brigitte had clearly missed the session on social skills. She didn't look up as Kerry entered but typed with one hand on a keyboard while with the other indicated a chair on the other side of her desk. Larry gave a look of apology and resignation which seemed to suggest this wasn't the sort of behaviour one would expect from Odyssey. He gave a brief wave and left.

After another twenty seconds of typing Brigitte looked up and pushed her spectacles onto her upper brow.

"What do you want?"

"Ms Spitz, thought it would be a good idea to talk to you about the methods you employ which have had such a dramatic effect on the children here."

"Oh God, I hope you didn't call her Ms Spitz. It's Dame Marion since the last birthday honours list," replied Brigitte in an exaggerated posh voice which made it clear she didn't have much respect for the concept of ennobling or indeed for the Dame."

Kerry couldn't help smiling. Despite her reservations she felt herself warming to this person who seemed at least to be straight talking.

"Not a fan then?"

"Whatever gave you that idea?" replied Brigitte in a fairly broad Glaswegian accent."

"You're not what I expected. With a name like Brigitte Huber I thought you'd be a severe European intellectual type like Simone de Beauvoir or something."

"Hmm, not sure that's much of a compliment! My dad was a German truck driver, who disappeared shortly after knocking my mother up, and she was a fan of Brigitte Bardot. It's not a very typical high-brow bio!" she said with a wry grin.

"So, what's the story with these kids and this school? I can't believe the difference. What are you doing to them?"

"To be honest, it's a bit of a surprise to all of us. The methods we have been using aren't new although, because of the resources we have here, we can apply them much more intensively than is usual in a school setting. The techniques are around positive reinforcement, sticking to routines, reducing distractions, encouraging physical activity, meditation, self-confidence building and the use of logic to solve problems. We worked with the teachers too, who, believe me, needed almost as much work on their self-confidence."

"So, what's the surprise?"

"Well, we would normally expect to see *some* improvement with this, but what we have found is off the scale and we're not quite sure why. Maybe it is some sort of group effect that when you put enough resource into a big enough proportion of students and combine it with a big investment in equipment, which clearly shows that someone values them, it just takes off. We need to repeat it somewhere else to see. "

"How long did it take?"

"Well, that's the odd thing. When we first came in the first term it was very hard to engage the students. We really thought it was going to be a struggle, however after a few months it all started going really well. The students were much more attentive and able to benefit from the techniques we were teaching them. I'll be honest I've never seen anything like it. What's your interest here, Kerry? What do you do?"

Kerry explained that she was a geneticist and her current PhD work and that she was interested in people's views on gene editing and thought that her old school would be a good place to hear young people's views on this.

Brigitte looked thoughtful.

"There's something you're not telling me. I'm good at this game Kerry, I know when someone's holding something back. Why are you really here? People who do lab-based genetics don't suddenly discover a yen for social science."

Kerry was taken aback. Was she really so easy to read? She had a good feeling about Brigitte, who appeared to have been straight with her so far, but was worried about revealing her full hand.

Brigitte could see her internal debate.

"Just tell me. I know there's something very odd happening here and then you come here talking about gene editing. I like this school, and I like these students, and if they've been the subject of some crazy experiment I want to know, especially if I've been an unwitting part of it."

It was clear that although Brigitte did not talk like the European intellectual Kerry had initially expected that she was no slouch. If Brigitte had sussed this then Spitz, with her remarkable offer of funding, probably had too. Brigitte might be an ally, and she certainly needed one. With a deep sigh, Kerry told her the whole story and her suspicions.

"Those bastards! How dare they!"

"We don't know anything for certain yet. It could all be coincidental. Look you can't say anything yet. Anyway, from where I'm sitting it all actually looks incredibly good. I can imagine after the news report the other day, schools all over the country are looking at this."

Brigitte looked away thoughtfully into the distance.

"It's not all good. Not everyone may have benefitted from this."

"What's the problem then."

"A small number of kids, you know the quiet ones, nerdy a little obsessive. Some of them have got quite a bit more withdrawn. In fact, most of our work now is with them and not the kids with ADD. We thought at first they were just a bit taken aback at how some of their classmates whom they had written off as 'nut-jobs' were suddenly getting much better marks, but it may be more than that. For kids like them a variant on that ADD gene may actually have been a little helpful and fixing it may have made their condition worse."

"We don't know any of this for certain Brigitte. We have no idea for example how they'd get the gene inserted. We had wondered about an infectious agent."

"There was a spell a while back when there was a mystery ailment. Just about all of us got it, bad cold, headache feeling shivery. One or two of the kids wound up in hospital, but nothing was ever found. We were all a bit cheesed off as we had all been given the flu immunisation… Shit! That was it wasn't it? The school nurse was obsessed by it. Odyssey said that for their programme to work they needed the kids not to miss any teaching. They bribed them to take it with a whole range of goodies as a reward. Because it didn't involve injections, everyone had it, even the teachers, just a squirt up the nose. We get it every year, but there have been no bad effects the last few years".

"They might have to give it only once. The following years might be just the standard flu immunisation or possibly you have become immune to it. Brigitte, do you know if any other schools are involved?"

"There's a whole troupe of schools lined up in Scotland wanting the Odyssey solution as it's called, especially after the BBC news programme. We've had a ton of middle-class parents, who previously wouldn't have touched us with a barge pole, wanting to enrol their kids here. Mr Bhopal got his knuckles rapped by Odyssey for giving that interview, but to be fair, it is hard to keep exam success like that secret. As far as outside Scotland's concerned, I overheard Larry this morning talking to 'her ladyship' about flights booked to the USA and Naples, but it may have nothing to do with this."

"If what we think has happened then we need hard evidence, a real smoking gun like a sample of the virus in the flu vaccine. What's the school nurse like? Does she know what's going on?"

"Paterson? I'd be very careful with her. When she first came here she was very contemptuous of the kids and their parents, a bit of a racist too. She's not the sharpest tool in the box, but she's sly. You can be sure that anything you say will be reported up the line."

"Don't do anything just now Brigitte and say nothing to anyone else. We don't want to spook them and risk losing the chance of getting some hard evidence. There are other people working in different ways on this. We're not alone. I need to get in touch with them though and tell them what I've found here".

The door opened. Spitz came in. She looked at them both curiously. Brigitte however, turned on her brightest smile while standing up.

"Dame Marion! How nice to see you. I've just been telling Kerry here about the fabulous results our psychology techniques have had here. I've told her that if her research goes ahead that I'm sure we'll be able to find children who are willing to help."

Brigitte's interjection seemed to assuage any lingering concerned curiosity in Spitz. She smiled back.

"Great. And more great news Kerry. Our funder is very interested in your plans and wants to meet you to discuss them. He's in London at the moment but returns to Santa Clara tomorrow. Would you be able to go and see him? We'll arrange to fly you down. You can't miss this opportunity, Kerry!" she said in slightly high-pitched voice that she clearly thought passed as companionable but sounded as sincere as Donald Trump pedalling bibles.

"Wow, that's wonderful! Does he want me there today!?" replied Kerry trying her best not to overdo the enthusiasm. "I mean, I'll have to go home and get my ID for the plane! Would that be OK?"

"Yes of course. I'll get Larry to take you there. There's a flight in 2 hours, so you need to get moving. Larry! We're leaving now!" she yelled.

As the door closed after her Kerry quickly scribbled Donald's telephone number on a pad and gave it to Brigitte along with the burner phone. She had a bad feeling about this trip to London and didn't want to explain at the airport why she had two phones.

"Use this phone to phone my friend Donald. Tell him what's happening and tell him to contact Johnny."

"Who's Johnny?"

"Another friend who's helping."

Larry pushed open the door. Brigitte smoothly slipped the phone in her pocket and Kerry gave Larry an excited smile raising her shoulders and her thumbs up.

"Ready to go. This is so exciting!!!!" she squeaked in her best 'girlie' impression.

CHAPTER 12

Larry smiled back and ushered her towards the main entrance. Josh and Hana had been replaced at the welcome desk by two equally smart looking young people who smiled and bade them good day. A polished black Mercedes was waiting in the carpark, the chauffeur smartly dressed in a suit, overcoat, and peaked cap. The engine purred into life.

"Do you need my postcode? "Kerry asked the driver.

"I have your address Ms Pearson" he replied. "Marchmont isn't it?"

Kerry gave a small gasp. She hadn't given the school her new address but replied.

"Yes, that's right, thank you."

The driver carefully threaded his way through the traffic and roadworks, diverting frequently. He was clearly knowledgeable about Edinburgh's confusing and ever-changing one-way systems.

When they arrived at her apartment. Larry jumped out of the car with her.

"I won't be a minute, you can wait here," Kerry exclaimed brightly.

"Dame Marion said I was to make sure you weren't delayed and not to take my eyes off you until you were on the plane. Sorry I know she's a bit of a control freak, but I don't want to lose this job."

Kerry was now convinced that Spitz and Odyssey were onto her. She took a deep breath. There was an opportunity here to find out what was going on, but how dangerous was it likely to be? She remembered her fearless brother and those kids that may have been damaged by the Odyssey programme.

"Sure, but no comments about the state of the flat!" she said, wagging a finger.

Kerry bounded up the stairs to the fourth floor and opened her door. Larry, somewhat breathlessly, arrived a few seconds behind her.

"I see what you mean" laughed Larry surveying Kerry's living room chaos. "Pretty obvious you haven't been through the Odyssey program!"

"I said *no* comments about the flat" she smiled back.

Larry followed her around the apartment as she rooted through drawers looking for her passport.

"Your driving license would do, Kerry" he said.

"I don't drive."

Throwing aside a couple of pairs of pants she triumphantly produced the passport.

"Now if you don't mind, I need to pee."

In the bathroom, she pulled out her phone. She quickly sent a message to Donald, cognisant that at some point someone else might read it.

"Won't be in today. Going to London to meet potential funder from Odyssey, will let you know how it goes. A new friend may phone you."

When she returned from the bathroom, Larry was on his phone. He turned to her making a forced apologetic face.

"They say you should pack an overnight bag as they don't think they'll get you back on time this evening. Is that OK? The company will pay for your accommodation. I'd take it Kerry; they really don't stint; it'll be somewhere nice."

Kerry wasn't surprised by this but that didn't stop her stomach churning. However, the need to know more steeled her resolve to press on.

"Yes, I thought it would be tight to go there and back in a day. OK, I'll get some things."

"Quickly though Kerry, the plane leaves in 90 minutes."

Forty minutes later they entered the airport. A smartly dressed young woman approached them.

"Ah! At last, you're here. Hi Kerry, I'm Eleanor, I'll be travelling with you to the meeting. "

Larry wished them both a pleasant journey in a sing song voice waved and left.

"Quick we need to get through security and it's a nightmare today. The flight boards in 20 minutes"

They skipped to the express queue but even it was backed up with aircrew. Kerry set off the security alarm and had to be hand searched. She was shaking with anxiety believing they had found Johnny's tracker, which was lodged in her bra strap, but was waved through. She then waited for her bag to come through the x-ray machine. Five minutes went past with no sign of the bag. Eleanor kept looking at her watch anxiously.

"I'll see what the hold-up is."

"It needs to be checked. You didn't put liquids in it did you?"

"No."

After a further five minutes the bag was checked and handed over.

"OK, Kerry, let's run. The gate is miles away.

They approached the gate and joined a thinning group of last-minute passengers and boarded the plane. It was Kerry's first experience of front row travel. She reached into her bag to switch her phone off but couldn't find it.

"My phone! It must have fallen out when my bag was being searched. I really need it!"

"I'll phone security," said Eleanor with a slight tone of exasperation.

Kerry felt like a country bumpkin next to her. *She probably thinks I've never been on a plane before!*

Eleanor was speaking then arguing with someone about the phone. The aircraft doors were closing. Kerry started to feel very anxious and alone. She unbuckled her seatbelt.

"I really need my phone I have to get off!"

Eleanor leaned over and pushed her back in her seat.

"Kerry, we can get you a replacement phone in London, the plane's about to go."

The flight attendant unbuckled her seat belt, came towards her and asked her to sit down.

"I need my phone. I left it at security!"

"Sorry the plane is taking off, it's too late to leave now. You can speak to lost property when we land. Someone will have handed it in."

"Kerry turned around. Eleanor was initially, stony faced but immediately gave a concerned look."

"Oh Kerry, what a bummer. I'm so sorry about this. If we hadn't rushed you, this wouldn't have happened."

Kerry thought that this was all too much of a coincidence. She prayed that Donald had got her message, and that Brigitte would come through for her. She hoped she hadn't been wrong about Brigitte who certainly looked like she was genuinely angry about what might be happening in the school but then remembered that Eleanor had given the impression of being genuinely distraught when she had lost her phone and she didn't believe that for a moment. Hopefully the tracker was working and, if need be, Johnny would be able to find her. Kerry wondered just what sort of offer this 'funder' was going to make her. One she couldn't refuse she suspected.

CHAPTER 13

Donald and Alan had returned to the Chi-Gen building, and they were just about to pass through security when Donald's phone chirruped.

"Bloody hell! That girl!" he spat.

"Kerry? What's she done?"

"She's gone to London. She says to speak to a funder. She must know she's possibly walking into a trap. I need to let Speirs and Johnny know what's happening."

Donald started to phone Speirs when his burner phone rang, Kerry's own burner number. Thinking it was Kerry, he hung up on Speirs before he got a reply and answered right away.

He was immediately wary when he heard an unfamiliar voice on the line. Brigitte explained who she was and told him that Kerry had asked her to call him. Donald asked her to hold on while he moved away from the security desk and away from Alan to an open area in the atrium. He asked if she was speaking securely or better if they could meet, but Brigitte said it would definitely raise suspicions if she was absent from the school so soon after meeting Kerry and that it was essential that she give him some information now.

She spoke quietly and quickly outlining her meeting with Kerry, their suspicions about Odyssey and their belief in a definite link between the novel genetic code and the extraordinary achievements at St Julian's. She then spoke of her concern about Kerry's pressured decision to go to London.

"I'm worried about her; I don't believe a word about this supposed funding. They never pay for outside researchers. Should we be calling the police?"

"The authorities are already involved Brigitte. I can let them know that she is going to London. Don't do anything else just now. I'll text you on the burner phone you have just used to let you know what is happening. If you haven't heard anything in forty-eight hours, phone me. I know this sounds very James Bondish, but to be sure we know that we're talking unobserved, the first sentence either of us utter on that call or in a text, should contain the word 'great'."

As he hung up, Donald wondered again whom

he could trust? Surely Brigitte wouldn't have revealed what she had if she were not sincere. She could be extremely useful, but could he really trust Alan and Speirs? Odyssey seemed an amazingly powerful organisation and the police were notoriously leaky. He decided to stay quiet about Brigitte to Alan and Speirs for the time being.

"Who was that?" asked Alan, a worried frown appearing.

"Just Peter Munro, Kerry's supervisor. Still crapping himself that he might be caught up in this. Told him not to worry but to call me if he had any news."

"Right, it's just that the call came in on the burner number, I hadn't realised Peter knew that."

Donald thought Alan was going to say something more but had changed his mind. He hated that he was holding back in his friend. He then phoned Speirs. He related Kerry's suspicions about the school including the concern about potential harmful effects on some children. He left out Brigitte's contribution. Speirs became quite excited when he heard that Kerry had gone to London. He saw it as a clever move on her part and didn't appear at all worried that she may be at any risk.

"Let us know as soon as you hear from her."

The staff at the security desk appeared to be looking towards them somewhat suspiciously. Donald thought it couldn't be that uncommon that people finished off calls before handing over their phones, but perhaps he was being a little paranoid. He needed to phone Johnny but that would have to wait.

After they passed through security Alan looked dejected, like someone who had just failed an exam. His voice had a slightly hysterical tone.

"Who were you really phoning? You don't trust me, do you? I don't blame you. Believe me, I panicked the other night when I phoned Singh. I promise I'll be straight with you from now on. I really will!"

Donald sighed. He thought that perhaps he was being gullible, but Alan did sound sincere.

"OK, Alan, I believe you, I just don't know how much I can trust your bosses."

"Me neither."

"Let's head off to the lab and see what we more can find."

Emilio Sanchez was sitting at a bench when they entered the lab and gave them a desultory acknowledgement. As Alan and he were getting seated at the bench, Donald wondered how he might get more information from Emilio about what exactly he was doing and if it could possibly be related to what was happening St Julian's.

"Emilio, would you settle an argument. What would you say was the longest genetic sequence that could be transferred to animal cells using viral vectors? I was pretty sure that only pretty small segments could be transferred that way. I'm right, aren't I?"

"Why are you asking?"

"Well, it came up in an argument a couple of weeks ago. I hadn't realised then that I'd be sitting next to one of the world's experts on the subject!"

Emilio visibly puffed up.

"There have been significant developments in that field, several of which I've been responsible for. As I mentioned yesterday, my work is a little hush hush just now, but I think it would be safe to say that there's now really no limit on what can be transferred and integrated into mammalian cells."

"And that can be done without destroying the host cell? That's incredible."

"I'm working on a paper at the moment which describes the process."

"When can we expect to read it?"

"It may be a little while. My collaborators wish to be sure the process is patented properly. I've possibly told you more than I should," he said with a slow wink and tapping his nose.

What a prick! thought Donald.

"Don't worry we'll keep schtum! No plans to buy large shareholdings in Chi-Gen just yet!" said Alan with a smile.

Donald thought they should leave off interrogating him as they didn't want to raise his suspicions. He thought the guy was so vain that he wouldn't be able to resist telling them more anyway. He turned to Alan and asked what they could be doing while they were waiting for Johnny to analyse the results.

"It would be good if we could get some samples direct from St Julian's. Maybe Kerry could help there when she gets back."

Alan noticed that Emilio turned towards them at the mention of St Julian's. He looked confused and unhappy. Alan gave Donald a quick kick under the bench. He looked Emilio in the eye making it clear that he had spotted his interest.

"Do *you* know *Julian* St John Edwards Emilio? He's a drug rep for one of the big pharma companies. Donald was just saying he had doubts about his mental stability. Apparently been offering ridiculous bribes, fine dining, golf anything to get people to use their reagents."

Emilio looked relieved. "No, if he does send him my way… I could do with a night out."

They laughed together.

Realising that they had almost given the game away, and that what they could do usefully in the lab was limited until they heard back from Johnny, Donald decided it was time to leave. He turned to Emilio.

"We have to go to a meeting now Emilio. See you later this afternoon?"

Emilio looked a little suspicious but murmured that he'd see them later.

Alan encrypted his work, and they left together. As the door opened for them to leave Emilio picked up his phone.

"I wonder who he's phoning. Who's his boss in your outfit? Is it Singh?" said Donald.

"I don't know but we need to find out. Did you see his ears prick up at the mention of St Julian's"

"Yes, nice dummy you sold him there by the way. Quick thinking!"

When they got their phones back Donald suggested Alan find out what he could about Emilio while he brought Johnny up to speed.

Johnny replied on the first ring.

"Great to hear from you?"

"Great to hear from you too."

"OK, what have you got for me? "

Donald brought him up to speed, this time, out of Alan's earshot, including Brigitte's contribution. He outlined his concern about the risk Kerry was taking.

"Yeah, it's a bit of a worry, but she's a big girl. Knows how to handle herself. Let me check where she is."

There was some tapping in the background

"That's odd. Her phone is in Edinburgh and the tracker has gone offline."

"Oh God, that doesn't sound good!"

"The phone is at the airport, and she may still be in the air. The tracker won't work there. Hang on…. it's just appeared she's in the City Airport in London. I'll keep an eye on where she's going."

Donald sighed. Why was he the only one that seemed worried about her? There's no knowing what these people were capable of.

Alan was unusually quiet as they walked the few hundred meters between the Chi-Gen building and his office in the university. His lips were moving, deep in thought.

"Penny for them?" said Donald.

"I'm just trying to get my head around this business, why would Markov get involved with this. It's bizarre. If you read what he wrote in his book, the St Julian's underclass is precisely the sort of people he wanted to stop breeding. I can't help thinking there must be some sort of drawback."

Alan came to a sudden halt, his face a mask of horror.

"What if the drawback is reduced fertility?"

"Fuck's sake! Surely, he wouldn't do that!"

"Plausible though don't you think? Jesus, Donald. It just gets worse. We have to go public."

"Let's wait and see what Johnny comes up with first. We don't want to go off half-cock."

Donald could see his friend's angst. "OK?"

"Its's just that Emma and I really want a child. How easy is it to get this? I mean could *you* be infectious? It seems like this mutation can spread like a flu or cold virus."

"I have no symptoms. When I got it, it was from someone with a streaming cold weeks ago. I think it's unlikely I'm infectious"

"I think we need a drink, don't you?"

CHAPTER 14

Kerry and Eleanor disembarked the plane and made the short walk across the tarmac to the City Airport arrivals hall. Eleanor was speaking on her phone.

"That was Larry. They've found your phone. Apparently, it was left in security. He's arranged to get it back to you"

No doubt after they have given it a good going over. Well, they're in for a disappointing time! Kerry smiled brightly and gave a sigh of relief.

"Oh, thank goodness they found it. It's not that old and I hadn't insured it."

There was a man in a dark suit holding up a card with the name Eleanor James on it in large type.

"There's our lift".

After a cursory greeting they headed to the carpark and set off for central London.

How the other half live Kerry mused.

"Where is the meeting?" asked Kerry trying to keep her voice even and light.

"At one of our offices in Canary Wharf. You must be starving, I know I am. We can pick up a sandwich and a coffee on the way. "

Eleanor told the driver to pull in at a sandwich shop and asked Kerry what she'd like. A few minutes later she returned with a couple of wraps and coffees. Kerry started to eat the wrap but was halfway through the coffee when she started to get worried.

Surely they wouldn't try to drug me? But then surely, they wouldn't infect a bunch of kids with a gene altering virus.

Realising that these people might well do anything, she ate the wrap and made a show of drinking the coffee but left most of it. She decided to try to strike up a relationship with Eleanor.

"What's your role in the organisation Eleanor?"

"A sort of general factotum, girl Friday. I do what I'm told but get well paid for it."

"Were you in the services Eleanor? My aunt was and she had the same sort of bearing and mannerisms that you have."

"I hadn't noticed I had any particular mannerisms! What do you mean?"

"The way you hold yourself, quiet efficiency,

forces accent".

"Well, I am impressed. I was in fact in the Navy for ten years. What did your aunt do?"

"RAF, she was a navigator, there weren't many women doing that job. Not so easy for a woman in the Navy either I'd have thought."

Eleanor shrugged and smiled.

"I think the guys under me thought it wasn't easy for them!"

Kerry laughed. "I could believe that!"

The car turned into an underground carpark where they grabbed their bags. Eleanor used a security pass to take a lift to the 37th floor. They emerged into a bright reception area, deep-pile, cream carpet, a large faux fireplace and a mahogany reception desk which seemed as big as Kerry's apartment. The views across London were spectacular. The receptionist looked like she modelled for Vogue in her spare time.

I'm not in Kansas anymore.

"Hi, you must be Kerry", said the vogue model with a surprisingly strong Cockney accent. Kerry had felt sure she'd have been the daughter of baroness on an internship.

"I'm Natasha, pleased to meet you. Mr. Markov is expecting you."

Kerry thought it was wise to feign ignorance of any connection with CreativeCom, pretending to notice the company logo behind the desk for the first time.

"Markov…. Not Abe Markov?" she laughed.

"The very same"

"Seriously? You're having me on!"

"No. You're seeing the main man."

"But what has CreativeCom to do with St Julian's?"

Before she got an answer, the door opened, and Abe Markov was there. He looked smaller than Kerry expected with a well-groomed, three-day stubble beard. He wore ecru chinos, a light blue polo shirt and blue leather mules.

God! He only looks a few years older than me. Expensive facial products or good plastic surgery? she wondered.

He was smiling.

"Hello Kerry come in. Thank you…eh?" he said with a gentle West-Coast drawl.

"Eleanor Sir"

"Yes of course Eleanor. Thank you, I'll take it from here."

Eleanor gave Kerry a smile and raised her eyebrows to signify how exciting this all was and left.

They entered an office which was almost as big as the reception area. Kerry took in a large desk, a small meeting area with a large video screen and some soft furnishing beside full-length windows. A man sat on the sofa beside the window. In contrast to Markov, he was dressed in a dark Savile Row ensemble with some sort of club tie.

"This is my lawyer, Ralph Hinton-Bruce. Ralph, this is Kerry Pearson, who has some exciting ideas I want to discuss."

Kerry greeted Hinton-Bruce and continued to smile as naturally as she could.

"Good afternoon." Kerry said a little emphatically, smiling quizzically. "This is a bit of a surprise. I thought I was coming to speak to someone about a small grant to interview some young people about genetics, not the world's biggest tech entrepreneur!"

Markov returned the smile with a measured one of his own and after a few seconds deliberation.

"Did you really?"

Kerry felt her smile faltering. She knew she was in trouble.

"I'm going to speak frankly Kerry. As you may have guessed we have been having quite a close look at your research. It's impressive. Indeed, making a link between St Julian's and a relatively minor DNA trait was close to inspired. I'd really like to know how you did that. "

"I don't suppose I'd have done, if you hadn't set your heavies on me," she replied

"Now that's the interesting thing. I know you're going to have a bit of a problem believing this but please listen to what I have to say. We weren't responsible for that. Without giving too much away we do have some 'friends' in the British Secret Service who alert us to potential cyber threats and other issues of interest. Until we were contacted about your work and the proposed link with the St Julian's situation, I knew absolutely nothing about it. For the last thirty-six hours we have furiously been playing catch up trying to find out what the heck is going on."

Kerry raised an eyebrow. Markov clearly registered the cynicism but continued.

"Have you heard of James Barton? … No? He was a partner of mine in the early days of CreativeCom. His interests were in artificial intelligence and quantum computing, but he increasingly started to become obsessed with the future of humanity, with what he saw was a deterioration in the species and the mindless destruction of the environment. He even dragged me into it for a bit… to my detriment. However, he was spending less and less time on his day job, so we parted ways, reasonably amicably, around 8 years ago. He took most of his close team with him and we shut down almost all his projects. However, one of the ventures he ran was Odyssey. When we looked at it, it seemed a like good fit for CreativeCom in terms of public relations, working with challenged and disadvantaged people in several countries in a variety of fields. It was relatively inexpensive. It seemed to be running well with an efficient team and James offered to stay on the supervisory board. We put Marion Spitz nominally in charge, but it was always intended to be light touch."

Kerry noted the lack of the 'Dame' honorific.

"So here we are now with something of a troubling situation on our hands. One which I certainly didn't plan. James has disappeared of course, and we're left with the problem of trying to sort it all out. We have called in his team to try to find out what's been going on. Unfortunately, Ms Spitz over the last few years seems to have taken the suggestion of a 'light touch' approach as more of a 'no touch' approach and claims to be completely in the dark about what they have been doing. I was astonished when I saw the scale of it. Most of it has been funded directly by James or it would have raised alarm bells sooner."

Kerry had to subdue her schadenfreude. It did not sound like Ms Spitz would last the week.

"However, I have to say that the more I saw,

the less sure I was that what James had done was completely bad. What did you think of St Julian's, Kerry? Is what's happening there so evil?"

"If what's happened there is what I think has happened, then it is at least unethical."

"Unethical to give some of the poorest, most deprived children in the country the chance to achieve something with their lives? If you told them that you'd a magic wand that could reverse what has been done, do you think they'd want you to use it? "

Kerry exhaled loudly.

"We have no idea what the long-term consequences are of this kind of genetic meddling. How do you know it's safe. Will everyone benefit? Are *all* the kids in St Julian's doing better? This may be wonderful, but he should have gone through the usual processes of getting research approval, got consent from the kids and their parents."

Kerry immediately regretted raising the potential side-effects, worried she may have implicated Brigitte.

Hinton-Bruce raised his head. "Well apparently, they did get consent. "

"What?!"

"All the children signed consent forms as did their parents. No-one was treated without consent."

"Did they have any idea what they were signing? You know a lot of those parents are poorly educated themselves. What did he bribe them with?"

Hinton-Bruce smiled and continued.

"I'm pretty sure many of your colleagues get research subjects to sign consent forms they don't understand, often for experimental treatments much more dangerous than this and with little benefit to them."

"Yes, but they have gone through ethics committees to assess the risk. Do you honestly think an ethics committee would have let them do what they have done?"

Markov smiled.

"Well of course not! As I recall it was James' favourite tenet that it is always much easier to get forgiveness than permission."

"And what about the spread outside of the school?"

Hinton-Bruce looked at Markov. Markov had stopped smiling.

"What do you mean?"

"I mean the people who have been subsequently infected with this virus that did not agree to anything. At least some people were infected through contagion with immunised children and teachers."

"I think that is highly unlikely. From what we were led to believe by the people we have consulted, the types of viruses used to transfer DNA are normally incapable of sustained replication. What makes you think this has happened?"

Kerry hesitated, shaking her head briskly from side to side.

"Theoretical at the moment, based on history only."

"What history?"

"The fact that there appear to be behaviour changes not just in the children of the school but their families too."

Kerry decided not to mention Donald's concern that he may have been infected. She wasn't sure how much they knew of Donald's involvement or that he and Alan were planning to test him.

"That could be just coincidence. It would certainly be troubling though if it is true. We'll look into it." He said glancing at the lawyer who nodded and tapped his tablet.

"You may have wondered why I arranged to see you here. I dare say you had concerns about what might happen to you. You don't need to worry. Nothing bad will happen to you. I'd like to try to convince you that we're on the same side here. We want this to stop here and to minimise any potential harm."

"OK, but tell me why did he choose St Julian's?"

"Not sure, but it looks like it was complete chance. Apparently, James was visiting me here in our London office and while waiting outside he overheard may PA talking to her assistant about what turned out to be a slightly pathetic begging letter from the headmaster. She remembers him asking if he could deal with it. At the risk of sounding callous, he probably saw a desperately low performing school with one of the most deprived catchment areas in the country, a readymade community of people with nothing to lose who would risk anything for a bit of cash and if it all went belly up wouldn't know how to go about complaining. What's not to like?" he said smiling.

Kerry started to flush with anger but controlled her urge to scream at him. She took a deep breath.

"You'll have to understand that I find this a little hard to believe. Your views on the 'descent of man' as you put it are well known. Then we find you have been meddling with people's genes. The very sort of people you and James Barton were trying eradicate. What else have you done to them."

"I haven't, as you say, 'done' anything to them.

This is all James Barton. I agree that improving the quality of humankind and preserving the environment from overpopulation is something in which I've always been interested. However, it was an obsession for James Barton who as you may remember co-authored that book, indeed he was the principal author, even though I took most of the flak for it. Let's face it, our suggestions in the book on how this might be achieved have…. well let's say they've not always met with universal acclaim.

"To say the least!"

"I realise the voluntary sterilisation was a bit naive; although frankly it would have been a win-win for some of those people and the state that has to support them. This solution to upgrade the current stock rather than stop them breeding certainly seems more acceptable.

However, before you make your mind up about this, perhaps I should tell you about some more of James' projects. The whole thing is much bigger than St Julian's. James believed, as do the small number of his acolytes who had some knowledge of the project, that this may be the greatest leap forward for humanity in the last 300,000 years. However, I'm not so sure that's true. That's why you're here Kerry. I'd like you to come and work for us."

Kerry opened her mouth to speak

"And no, before you say anything it's not a bribe… you are *clearly* a very talented young person with the right skill set and, as you and your colleagues already know about the problem, you're probably the best group to take over investigating this and shutting it down. You can decide after you have heard what I have to say. If you decide you don't, you'll be free to go if you wish."

"But, please. Sit down. Take some coffee, this is going to be quite a ride."

CHAPTER 15

Markov pressed a button on his desk, the windows dimmed and the wall opposite them came to life.

"We brought in James's team leads.... at least the ones we know about. They are managing the Odyssey projects on the ground, but we have no reason to believe that most of them know anything about any sort of genetic manipulation. They are all surprised and delighted by the apparent success of the interventions that they introduced which have gone far beyond what they had expected. They reason that this is because of the unprecedented intensity of the teaching and behavioural approaches as well as the massive infrastructure investment. We haven't been able to find any of the team responsible for the genetic research and the creation of whatever agent was used to bring about the genetic changes. James has kept that group separate."

Kerry wondered if they had approached

Brigitte. She assumed so. She thought it was unlikely Brigitte would reveal their suspicions to Markov's team. She just hoped that she could keep a lid on her rage... at least for a while. Markov seemed to be one step ahead of them.

He started to show a series of photographs of schools with children of different ethnicities.

"You're already aware of the work that's going on at St Julian's. This is mirrored in similarly challenged schools in Naples, Birmingham Alabama, Rio de Janeiro, Jakarta, Lagos Nigeria, Chengdu and Mumbai. What they all have in common apart from the poverty of the children who attend them is enthusiastic staff and headteachers desperate and willing to try something new. St Julian's was the first, but the early results from the other trial sites are showing the same sort of improvements as you've seen there."

The slide changed. This time to what looked like a prison.

"James' team haven't restricted themselves to schools and children. This is work from a secure youth treatment centre in the USA where the toughest long-term young offenders are sent."

The slide showed a series of graphs.

"Since the programme started, violence rates have fallen dramatically, the number of prisoners involving themselves in educational activities, provided by Odyssey, has soared. Some are doing university degrees. Staff absence has fallen. The number of positive drug tests is a tiny fraction of what it was previously. It has revolutionised the lives of the prisoners and could potentially save the state a fortune.

We also heard about a small project in sheltered accommodation for elders in North London. The team involved there have seen a surprising improvement in cognition... which they put down to Odyssey's enhanced structured activities."

The slide show ended with the Odyssey Logo. Markov turned to Kerry.

"These are the projects we know about, those that we're involved in paying for either directly or indirectly. There may be more. We know this intervention appears to be associated with increased intelligence and better attention span, there's a suggestion from the prison work that it may have an effect on violent behaviour and addiction. I'm not a geneticist but I'd guess this could not all be as a result of one mutation."

"I suppose it's just possible that improved cognitive abilities combined with the psychological methods that Odyssey are employing may have improved these attributes."

"Maybe, but there are plenty of brilliant people who are addicts and I personally know plenty psychopaths who are super-smart. I wish it were as simple as that."

"What do you see my role in this as being?" said Kerry musing that, to her mind, one of those super-smart psychopaths was sitting opposite her.

Markov smiled.

"As I said, you are clearly a talented researcher and have shown remarkable skill in discovering all of this. Without wanting to cause offence Kerry, you're also close to the kind of people that seem to have been targeted for this treatment. We know that you and your, sadly deceased brother have often stood up to defend them."

Kerry visibly flinched at him mentioning her brother. How dare he! However, she stayed calm as he continued.

"We need to know what else is going on here. Are there other mutations we don't know of yet and what do they do? Revealing the limited knowledge we have right now could be catastrophic which is why we want to keep this to the people who already know about it, at least until we have as much information as possible before we go public. We want you and your colleagues to explore this. You'll have complete independence, however with the proviso that you do not make public either your research or what you already know until we have a better idea of what is actually going on. We can put all the resources you need in your hands. You'll be handsomely paid for your work."

Kerry was taken aback. This wasn't what she had expected. This was an incredible offer, although it would mean becoming part of it. It felt wrong and dangerous. However, if what Donald suspected was true, the genie might already be out of the bottle and these genetic mutations were spreading like influenza all over the world. She didn't ask what would happen if she refused the offer. From what she had seen and heard she didn't doubt they could cover it all up, discredit her, and make any attempts to reveal what they knew look like the work of just a few more conspiracy theorists. She admitted to herself that if Johnny had come up with this story a few weeks ago she'd have laughed and dismissed it herself. She decided that, at least for the time being, she'd have to play along.

"Would I be able to work with my own team. I certainly don't have all the expertise I need for this?"

"Yes of course, although they'd have to

be vetted. If you're thinking about Donald Stirling, Alan McPherson and Johnny McCabe, then assuming they can be convinced to play ball, we would have no objection."

Kerry flushed. *So, they know about everyone.*

"Don't be so surprised. We know about Dr Stirling's involvement from our contacts in Chi-Gen and Mr McCabe's from his strenuous attempts to hack into St Julian's then our own servers. By the way, he also unsuccessfully tried to hack into the ScotGene biobank to obtain more information, leaving just enough of a trail to identify *him* as the person who introduced a virus which has *destroyed* all the records. We know he didn't of course… James did. I hope the back-ups are safe, but James is known for being thorough"

Kerry could not hide her shock. The biobank had been 10 years in the creation, and now It was destroyed. *That idiot Johnny*! she thought. *Donald had warned him, and he'd played right into their hands! God, I hope he hasn't dragged down Donald too*!

Markov smiled, raising one eyebrow, apparently imagining her internal dialogue.

"It seems that James Barton has been one step ahead of both you and us."

"I think you need a little time to ponder this, Kerry. I'll ask Eleanor to take you to your hotel.

She'll contact anyone you wish to reassure them that you are well. I'd like to hear your decision, or at least what you think, after you have spoken with your collaborators. When I said earlier that your theory that improved intelligence might reduce psychopathy was wrong, I very much had James Barton in mind. He is ruthless and you can be assured that any attempt to reveal what you have found to the wider world will no doubt be vigorously quashed and you and your friends with it. He has huge resources to call on. However, hopefully it won't come to that and that we can get in control of this by working together."

Kerry had never felt quite so helpless. It was clear that if what Markov said was true (and she only had his word for that) James Barton and the people he worked with held all the cards. She needed time to think. She needed allies, but was Markov to be trusted?

"Thank you, you're right. There's a lot to think through. When do you need to know?"

"I'm heading to Santa Clara tomorrow morning I'll see you first thing to hear your decision. "

Markov pressed the intercom, called for Eleanor to come in and asked her to take Kerry to her hotel.

However, just ahead of her a jolly looking elderly lady pushing a trolley came in and spoke in a broad cockney accent.

"OK to pick up the coffee things?"

Then as she looked at the Odyssey logo on the screen

"Ooh, 2001! Den Den Den De-Den! Bom Bom Bom Bom" to a tune vaguely familiar to Kerry.

Markov looked at her as if she'd gone mad.

She smiled and gave a quizzical look.

"2001 A Space Odyssey? Before your time love maybe. A 60s movie about aliens making apes intelligent and them evolving into humans, a rogue computer going mad and killing everyone. You'd probably call it an AI now I suppose. Anyway, sorry to interrupt."

She picked up the cups and left, leaving the three open mouthed.

"The conceit of the guy! He hasn't even tried to hide it!" exclaimed Hinton Bruce.

"Well, that's sorted out my transatlantic flight recreation anyway. Do you know that movie Kerry?"

"I knew I had seen the logo before but hadn't twigged. Yes, I saw it a long time ago. It's a classic.

Eleanor appeared and they left.

After she left. Hinton-Bruce said

"Do you really think you should've revealed so

much of our hand? You think you can trust her?"

"No, not at all, but it's worth a try. She is obviously a very bright scientist, and she uncovered Barton's damn shit show way before he expected anyone to."

"Why did he not just neutralise her right away? Why involve biosecurity and MI5. Surely that just made matters worse?"

"I suppose he didn't know how many other people were involved. Better to discredit her than to make her disappear. However, he, or the people who were working for him, overplayed their hand. The destruction of the ScotGene data, putting the blame on her and her team is a much better ploy. One he should have thought of first. It gets rid of the immediate evidence and destroys them in the eyes of the scientific community."

"So how does CreativeCom get out of this? Should I be selling my shares?"

"At the moment, as far as we're aware, the only people that know about this, apart from Barton and his people, are Kerry and her immediate colleagues, two agents from the biosecurity section of MI5 and their boss. Their boss and I have a longstanding arrangement which has been pretty lucrative for him, at least compared with his salary. We still don't know the extent of the implementation of this, but it seems containable. If we can stop Barton or persuade him to go legit with this. Let's face it, it looks fantastic. Why did he just not bottle it and sell it? That's the niggle. What is it we don't know about it that stops him doing that?"

"What about the Chi-Gen boss"

"He's shit-scared that Chi-Gen is going to get the blame for this. That's why he's got one of his men working on it. We'll have to keep an eye on him though. Frightened people often don't act rationally."

"What about Pearson's theory that it is spreading from person to person? We can't contain it if that's true."

"If it's true then we're definitely fucked and, depending on what that asshole Barton has up his sleeve, the whole human race may be too."

"If you seriously think that, should we not blow the whistle now?"

"Let's find out a bit more first."

"Are you really that relaxed that Kerry and her pals won't try to go public with this?"

"If they try then I'm sure they'll be pretty easy to discredit and the whole story… well, let's face it, it all sounds unbelievable."

"Let's see what she says tomorrow."

CHAPTER 16

It was 9.30 PM by the time they arrived at the hotel. Eleanor had suggested they take the car although the hotel was only a short walk from the office.

Obviously worried I'll make a dash for it! thought Kerry.

"How did the meeting go? Did you get the grant?" said Eleanor bright eyed with what appeared to be genuine excitement and goodwill. Kerry realised that Eleanor almost certainly had no idea about her bosses' plans.

"Yes, they offered it to me. I'm definitely thinking about it. Just not sure I'm the right person or good enough for what they want."

"Don't say that! They clearly think you are. I've *never* been asked to give anyone the sort of treatment they gave you today. They seem to value you *very* highly!"

They reached the check-in desk. Eleanor gave the booking under the name Markov. The receptionist visibly jumped to attention. "Oh yes for Ms Pearson! Welcome to the Marriot Ms Pearson we hope you'll enjoy your stay. We have you in one of our superior suites on the executive floor. Breakfast is served in the executive lounge from 6.30 AM. Do you need help with luggage?"

Kerry declined holding up her small backpack. Eleanor blew through pursed lips and said "I don't know about you Kerry but I'm starving, would you like some dinner? The food here is fantastic. They have a Michelin star. Normally it takes months to get a reservation, but the Markov name does miracles."

Kerry didn't feel like eating anything but realised she ought to.

"You know, I don't think I want anything fancy Eleanor. Could we just have a pizza?"

Eleanor couldn't hide her disappointment but tried to put a brave face on it.

"Yes, eh, there's a pizzeria just round the corner."

Eleanor decided that if she wasn't having a decent meal, she was having a decent drink and ordered the most expensive wine on the menu. Kerry never felt more like getting blasted than she did at that moment but knew it would be a bad idea. She let Eleanor consume most of the bottle and demurred when asked if she wanted to order another one.

"But we're celebrating! Aren't we?" slurred Eleanor.

"You can take the girl out of the Navy, but you can't take the Navy out of the girl!" said Kerry smiling. She decided she liked Eleanor but, pleading exhaustion, asked to go back to the hotel. To her amazement the car had been sitting there the whole time.

Back in the hotel room, she tried to get her head around all the ramifications of the day's revelations. She needed to speak to Johnny and Donald, but she was dog-tired and thought there was nothing to lose by waiting until tomorrow. She brushed her teeth and removed the complimentary chocolate from the beautifully turned down bed saving it for her morning coffee. With a sigh she slipped between the cool smooth sheets and tried to get to sleep.

CHAPTER 17

....

Donald's phone was ringing. He glanced at the wall clock. 11.30 PM. Shaking his head to clear his sleepiness, he sat up in bed and reached over Alan to take the call.

"Damnation! How did I let that happen. The guy has a partner for god's sake!"

They had gone for a meal, but one drink had led to another and another and then a brief goodnight kiss had wound up being something more.

"Hello" he croaked. He heard Johnny say that he had a pizza delivery and it would be *great* if he could buzz him in.

"Hi that's *great*. I'll just come to the door."

Alan was coming round. He nudged him and told him to get up, that Johnny was coming.

"Jesus! Don't let him know about this," he whispered, grabbing clothes and running to the spare bedroom.

"I don't suppose he'd care." Donald shouted

after him.

Donald grabbed some underpants and a T-shirt and pressed a buzzer to open the main door. A few minutes later the apartment doorbell rang. Johnny stood there in his Deliveroo outfit.

"Come in."

Johnny sniffed as he entered the room and eyed the two scientists.

"Well, I won't ask how you two have been passing the time while I've been slaving over a hot server!" he smiled

Shit! thought Donald. Alan just looked crushed.

"What have you got for us Johnny?" said Donald in a resigned tone.

"It's early days and, as you said, a huge amount of overlap, but there are a few additional shared gene changes which appear in the people who have the mutation that Kerry discovered. I've no clue what they mean though."

"What do you mean by a few?"

"There are at least five other distinct sequences apart from the one we know about that are appearing in the those who have Kerry's mutation that aren't in the others."

"OK, let's have a look at these."

"Maybe put a pair of trousers on first Donald, you're not doing anything for me," he smiled.

"Ha Ha," he said with a scowl. "Anything from Kerry. Do you know where she is now?"

"I've been checking every hour or so. She is in the Marriot near the CreativeCom building. Very posh! I hope she's working her way through the minibar and ordering steak frites on room service. Her phone, interestingly, also moved from Edinburgh and was taken to the CreativeCom office where it stopped working."

"Ran out of battery?"

"Nope, switched off, no doubt prior to being taken apart and interrogated. It's encrypted and, even if they crack it, all they'll get is a record of the calls she made to you. If they give it back to her, she'll know that it won't be safe to use."

"I just hope she's OK" Donald replied pulling up his jeans.

"She knows how to handle herself."

"Ok let's look at the results. Is it safe to use your computer Alan?"

"I don't know, better not to."

"Just as well I brought one" said Johnny with a smile removing a laptop from his backpack.

They sat down together around the laptop. Donald plugged it into a big screen.

Alan scrolled through the data.

"OK, let's look at this sequence first, it's the

shortest and it's on the X chromosome. Any ideas Alan?"

"No, not really, without a bit more work and we would need to map it to known sequences to try to decide what their function is."

Johnny rolled his eyes and blew out, making it clear he didn't know what they were talking about.

"Sorry Johnny. The X chromosome is involved in sexual differentiation and fertility but also mutations in it are associated with all sorts of other things like muscular dystrophy, depression, even aggression," said Alan.

Alan was continuing to scroll through the data.

"There's another area on the Y chromosome," added Alan. "So that's both female and male chromosomes targeted. Fuck! Johnny, you mentioned that pregnancy rates at the school had fallen, didn't you?"

"Surely he wouldn't do that!" exclaimed Donald. "Well, we were looking for the sting in the tail and this could be it."

"What do you mean?" asked Johnny

"Well, we need to do a lot more work on this, but it could be the changes in the sex chromosomes could render people infertile. Clever, you give a generation the chance of a smarter more productive life but only if they don't have kids," explained Alan.

"Let's not get ahead of ourselves we don't know if it'll do anything like that or not. We need to do more research on this."

"It's enough for me! I'm going live with this." said a clearly delighted Johnny started pulling his phone from his pocket.

Donald's phone rang. Unknown number.

"Hello, it's your Swedish nemesis again. Sorry to phone at this time. I just couldn't sleep with all this stuff going around in my head. I'm phoning from a payphone from the Marriot in Canary Wharf, but who knows if it's secure."

"Thank God Kerry. Are you alright? Good. Anyway, hi, it's fine. We were all up anyway. I've Johnny and Alan with me. You're on speaker but we think this phone could well be compromised, so you should assume they are hearing everything."

There was some hesitation at the other end of the line then a long sigh.

"They know everything anyway about you and Johnny. Anyway, Markov denies he is behind this. A former partner James Barton…"

"Another fascist bastard." Johnny interrupted loudly looking from Donald to Alan with a smirk.

"…appears to have set this up without the main company's knowledge."

"He's a clever bastard no doubt about that," Johnny interrupted. "He was definitely the brains in CreativeCom. Headed up their AI division and then moved on to quantum computing. There were rumours of a big breakthrough in the new company he set up. Apparently, he had found a way around the big error problem in quantum computing. When he left CreativeCom the share price took a tumble."

"If I could finish Johnny," replied Kerry with a sigh. "Markov seems as keen as we are to find out more and to shut it down. Needless to say, not for any humanitarian reasons, but to save his company from taking responsibility. However, Barton is one step ahead of us and is clearly determined to keep control of both the roll out and the narrative around it."

She stopped for a second and took a breath.

"There was a major data breach at ScotGene, a virus was introduced, and the files have all been wiped. Markov said that you Johnny had tried to hack it and left some sort of signature; enough for it to be used to have you carry the can for it and probably all of us by association."

"Fuck you, Johnny! I told you not to touch ScotGene. How are we going to prove what we have found without evidence!" shouted Donald.

"We still have evidence; we have it right here." said Johnny, indicating the screen but looking considerably less cocky than a few minutes previously.

"All we have now is an anonymous data set. They could say that it was all just constructed, just another looney conspiracy theory about genetic manipulation by tech billionaires.... They're ten a penny on the internet."

"Not if it comes from you Donald. People respect you."

"Really? So, I send the information and 10 minutes later they send an email, apparently from me, saying my account has been hacked and denying any involvement in what is a ridiculous proposition. What would my colleagues do then? They're busy people, they'll drop it straight in the bin. Ask Alan!"

"You could reveal it at a meeting."

"Well, that might work, but then they start discrediting us for real, for stealing confidential material, trashing ten years of work in ScotGene, invent some grudge against CreativeCom that'd explain my need to produce such fanciful nonsense, dig up and enhance any past scandals. We could be jailed, certainly academically ruined."

Alan blew out through pursed lips and despondently nodded his head in agreement.

"We are fucked," he said, looking worried.

Donald caught sight of the look and felt a wave of guilt for having dragged his friend into this; not to mention so casually trifling with his emotions.

"You're still clean Alan. You've done nothing wrong."

"What have any of us done wrong?! …. Well apart from Johnny of course" Alan said giving Johnny a scowl.

Johnny shook his head from side to side nonchalantly and shrugged his shoulders.

"But" continued Alan, "do you really think that the people behind this are going to trust anyone who knows what we know? We're all in deep shit."

"I've been in worse." said Johnny with another shrug and a nonchalant grin.

"What else did you find out Kerry?" asked Donald, ignoring Johnny with a roll of his eyes.

Kerry sighed again. Donald frowned. She sounded so depressed.

"It's all so much bigger than we could have imagined. Much more than just boosting the IQ of a few school kids. The genetic transformation affects much more than that".

"Yes," replied Donald, "we've just started working on that. Johnny used an algorithm to analyse the genetic code for new mutations and we found multiple localised mutations affecting a small number of genes, and one or two more extensive ones."

"I only know what they told me yesterday. There may be more. Markov pulled in all of Barton's team to find out what they had been doing. They didn't seem to realise there had been any sort of genetic manipulation and, like the people at St Julian's, thought results were down to the methods they employed."

There was a thoughtful silence in Edinburgh as she continued.

"They have tested it in a juvenile prison, and it has resulted in a sudden decline in violent behaviour and reduction in drug use. I suspect that one of the genetic variants you have uncovered will map to several of the known associations with aggressiveness or for addiction.

 "Markov wants a team to start working on this right away but wants to keep it secret for a while until we know exactly what we're dealing with, while no doubt doing what he can to shore up CreativeCom. He's offered us all jobs, which he says will be very well paid."

"They can stuff their jobs!" spat Johnny. "I don't care what happens to me. I'm going to get this out."

"I'd think hard about it." said Alan sternly. "The people we're up against are clearly very powerful and tap into the smartest programmers in the world. You're already in serious trouble because of ScotGene. They almost certainly have a backdoor into one of your computers. What if they filled it with paedophile porn. We've seen what they did with Kerry's Instagram. Who'd listen to you then."

Johnny blinked slowly, taking it in, realising that Alan was right.

"We've been outmanoeuvred at every turn. What about Chi-Gen? Have they been lying too?" asked Donald.

"Chi-Gen wasn't mentioned as culpable. I'm pretty sure they'd have said if they thought they had been involved."

"There's Emilio Sanchez. He seemed very excited about that breakthrough in delivery systems," mused Alan.

"Yes but remember he mentioned a collaborator" replied Donald. "That collaborator would have to have contributed a lot for someone like Sanchez to be willing to give them credit. He has a reputation for pilfering ideas; maybe one of the reasons he had to leave NeoPharmatics. Your boss said he was worried that Chi-Gen was being set up to take the fall should this come out. He may be right."

Alan was shaking his head

"If you'd asked me who in the world had the expertise to do what they appear to have achieved in the way they have carried it out, I'd have said absolutely no-one. We are right at the beginning of this type of technology and what this represents is way beyond the state of the art. Who could it be?"

"Sorry, Kerry. We keep interrupting you. Anything more before we drop our bomb?" Asked Donald.

"Unfortunately, the worst is still to come. It's not just Scotland. They are conducting 'trials' as they call them all over the world on just about every continent…. who knows how many people have been affected already. "

"What!" said Alan and Donald simultaneously.

"One thing though. From what they had heard from Barton's team there was nothing to suggest wild, person-to-person spread. We need to know for certain if that really is happening. "

Donald shook his head taking in what Kerry had just said and answered in a despondent tone.

"We do, and it has. I have the mutation, so no playing daddy for me." He whispered with an ironic smile.

"What? exclaimed Kerry.

"That's our bomb. The mutation is associated with changes on the X and Y chromosomes. We think it might affect fertility. It's early days but we could see this might be sold to people as a package. You get to be smarter, more focused …. You just can't have kids. Now it sounds from what you say that it may be a cure for addiction and violent behaviour too."

"This is monstrous! what will people do when they find out? I can't begin to work out the consequences of this" said Kerry with a sigh. "What do I tell Markov in the morning?"

There was a long pause.

"Are you still there?"

"Yes," said Donald. I think the best thing to say right now is that we're interested and need to hear his terms. Arrange a meeting with him by video link. It doesn't look like he knows what we know. Leave it that way just for now."

"No bloody way!" shouted Johnny. "I'm not working for that bastard!"

Kerry spoke up.

"Think about it Johnny. It makes sense to at least appear to be working with him for the time being."

"I agree, let's not do anything hasty," said Alan.

"There's an opportunity here to find out exactly what's been happening and check how bad… or to be fair, how good it is. You know, I think if they offered this package…. as an option to people, there might well be a big uptake."

"That's true," replied Donald. "Think about the choice *we're* being offered here. We have the chance to investigate possibly one of the biggest events to hit humanity in thousands of years, with the potential to head it off, if it looks like being a disaster. The alternative, at least in the short term, is to end up broke, discredited maybe even in jail with no influence at all. I know these guys are smug, manipulative, patronising bastards, but they do hold all the cards!"

Kerry cleared her throat and added

"We have only Markov's word that he wasn't responsible for this, but it sort of made sense and I was inclined to believe him. If so, the real criminal is James Barton and we need resources to find out exactly what he's done, how this is likely to develop and to plan how to deal with it. So far, as I said he's been several steps ahead of us. Markov is prepared to put necessary resources at our disposal. It sticks in my craw too, but I think we have to go with this for now."

"But it does mean we become a part of it" replied Donald gloomily.

"Yes, that's the price I guess, "replied Alan. "However, we're only co-operating until the time is right to reveal all. Should we not be letting the secret service guys know?"

"It is strange that after phoning me every 3 or 4 hours for updates that Speirs and his mate have suddenly stopped communicating" replied Donald.

Johnny was looking into the distance, seemingly lost in thought. "One of the things I discovered when I was checking out Odyssey was that there are several ex-government ministers listed as advisors and two members of the House of Lords on the board. It could be this thing goes very high."

"We have to realise that not everyone will think this is bad. Maybe bad the way they went about it, but the end results could look attractive. Markov reckons there are plenty of politicians who would love this. Reduced crime and drug addiction and improved educational attainment. If we also chuck in reduced cognitive loss in old age it will look brilliant to a lot of people. One for which they'd probably take a drop in the fertility rate. Once they get over the initial shock, it may be that people will be happy with their brighter, more ordered lives," said Kerry

"There may not be a choice with direct case to case spread happening" said Donald gloomily.

Alan was nodding his head.

"We don't know if Barton is just using these case studies you described as test beds and will then go public with the benefits giving people a choice. We don't know if the changes will fade with time or if the effects can be reversed or ameliorated, or if there will be unexpected consequences. They have altered huge swathes of DNA by the look of things. The school psychologist was already worried about some students. What else could happen? There's just so much more we need to know."

Kerry loudly exhaled. "My head is aching with the consequences of it all. Can we try to sleep on this and meet again tomorrow morning. I'm seeing Markov at 0800. I'll tell him that we're interested and already working on the problem, but we want a meeting. Until that meeting I won't reveal the additional information we have. What about Speirs? "

"I'll phone him and tell him we have a meeting with Markov tomorrow after which we'll be able to give him more information. It'll be interesting to see what his attitude is. I can't help thinking that they have been hobbled in some way. Alan and I will continue working on the data that Johnny gave us, and we'll see what we have by tomorrow evening when Markov should have arrived in the States and can take a call. Any other loose ends?

Alan raised his eyebrows. "Emilio Sanchez?"

"Yes, we need to see what more we can get from him. There's something fishy about that guy and he is over-interested in our work.

"What about Singh? He knows about this too. You said you didn't think he was part of this to begin with Alan? Who else has he likely told. I presume he'll have let his board know?" Asked Donald

"I don't think he did. He said we should keep it to ourselves until we were sure it was important. I guess that could be little suspicious in itself, but he was only just recently appointed chairman of the board and maybe was worried about sounding off and subsequently looking foolish."

"You need to feed something back to him, but not everything, not yet."

Johnny was tapping on this phone.

"Well, well, well." he said with a sneer and passed the phone to Alan. "I don't think he's your boss anymore. At least not your top boss. According to Bloomberg, Chi-Gen has been bought out for just over a billion dollars, five percent above previous valuation. It seems to have created speculation about some sort of breakthrough. "

"Well, someone has had their mouth stuffed with gold! I wonder what Singh's cut was of that?" said Alan. "Who bought it?"

"Some big private equity company… I don't think we'd have to dig too deep to know who owns it."

"Well, it must be Markov or Barton. Either way Kerry, you certainly seem to have cost someone a lot of money!" said Donald with a crooked smile.

"They sure are tying up loose ends," replied Johnny. "Let's hope we aren't next."

"OK let's call it a night. Can we reconvene tomorrow about midday? Alan and I should have more results by then. "

Kerry hung up. Donald turned towards Johnny.

"Johnny, we don't know if Barton has implicated you yet, but if he has you'll be a wanted man. I'd lay low for a while. Please stick with our plan. Do not reveal this to the world until we have had a chance to get more information."

"OK… for now… but not for too long. I'll leave you the laptop. Text me the details for the call tomorrow."

Johnny pulled up his hoody, grabbed his backpack and, after a brief check of the landing through the spyhole, left.

Donald turned to Alan.

"I think we should call it a night too. We're

both still feeling the effects of all that wine and unlikely to do our best work. Well at least I am."

He hesitated then continued

"About what happened… I'm sorry. We shouldn't have let it happen. Can we forget it?"

"Yes, you're right on both counts. I'm sorry too."

As Donald, climbed into bed he remembered Brigitte and resolved to check with her the following day as promised.

CHAPTER 18

Alone in the hotel room Kerry really needed to sleep so helped herself to a scotch from the minibar, smiling that at least for once she didn't have to worry about the price.

"Nope. One won't hack it," she mumbled as she twisted the top of a second Glenmorangie and ripped open a packet of the most expensive nuts she had ever seen. She couldn't stop thinking about it all.

The consequences for humanity were immense. She could well imagine millions of young people grabbing the chance to be smarter and be more focussed and to hell with fertility. However, she could see whole countries and religions banning the mutation, while no doubt a chosen few of their plutocrats, politicians and priests unbothered by the consequences for underlings secretly made use of it. The conspiracists would go crazy, except this time with justification.

Whole races could be rendered sterile, having to go cap in hand to technologically advanced nations for a cure (if there was a cure). What impact might it have on women? She could envisage some societies where boys could store semen samples and benefit from the mutation while it was denied to girls pushing them even further down the hierarchy.

Shaking her head, she remembered that these possible 'choices', no matter how illusory, might vanish if Donald was correct and the mutation was already spreading from person to person like influenza.

"What has Barton unleashed on the world?" She whispered.

She glanced at the clock. It was getting late. She was exhausted and, having brushed her teeth again, slipped once more between the covers determined to get to sleep, trying to banish rumination with happier thoughts.

But where are those happy thoughts when you need them? Just four days ago she was a happy postgrad whose only concern was a pig of a supervisor and a looming but manageable deadline. Now she felt the fate of the world was in her hands.

She scoffed and chided herself for being overdramatic, but then thought… *It really is!*

An hour later she was still tossing and turning

glancing at the glowing blue numerals on the bedside clock counting off the minutes. Her mind lurched from one depressing possible permutation of the future to another. Finally with a screech of frustration, she launched herself forward and punched the bed with balled up fists. Kicking away the thick cotton sheets, she sprang from the crazy-big bed. Wearing a long 'Munch: The Scream' T-shirt, a gift from her brother, and hugging herself against the overchilled air she started to pace, striding furiously back and forth from door to window.

"Markov, Barton, the Secret Service all of them have us every which way! Free to fuck us over how they like" she whispered.

Sighing, her thoughts turned to Donald, a decent guy, whose only crime had been to try to help her and whose career was almost certainly in ruins now, then slowly shook her head as she thought of Johnny, whose reckless attempts to hack ScotGene, despite Donald's warnings, had given Barton the means to totally lay waste to it while leaving them the blame. *Idiot!*

She stopped at the floor to ceiling window where a crack of amber light, from a gap in the black-out curtain cut across the floor. In exasperation she dragged and pushed at the rows of drapes.

How many damn curtains do you need!

Pressing her head against the cold glass, her breath billowing and condensing in irregular opaque circles she looked out over the Thames. 3 AM, but a steady river of headlights still inched towards the Rotherhithe tunnel. She could just make out the odd shout reaching the 14th floor from revellers on party boats.

"If they only knew what was about to hit them" she whispered. "Those bastards are so casually ripping up their lives, leaving what sort of world behind. And who's going to come out on top in this brave new world?

She sighed. "The same people that always win I guess… or will we all be losers?"

CHAPTER 19

The following morning Brigitte, quietly seethed in her office. Donald had said do nothing, but how could she sit there doing nothing?! She had barely slept the previous night, furious about what had been done to the kids but also fuming that she had been taken for a fool. She had known there had been something fishy about the kids' performance and was annoyed with herself that she had been blinded by pride and the adulation that had come with the success.

She remembered her last encounter with Spitz. Leaving the school for home she had passed her as the chauffeur was holding the car door, simpering Larry not far behind. Spitz had leaned forward from inside the car, her neck stretched out like a snake with a supercilious smile and a "Lahvley to meet you again, we must catch up prop'ly some time."

How I'd love to punch that smug, upper-class

bitch's lights out; hers and Larry the lapdog's! Damn it! Kerry said she needed a smoking gun. Let's find her one!

She calmed herself, practised a cheery smile in the mirror then, realising everyone would find that suspicious, reverted to her usual scowl and marched along the corridor to Mrs Ahmed's office. Mrs. Ahmed looked uneasy as Brigitte entered. She had always found her direct manner disconcerting. She was somewhat taken aback when she sat down opposite her and asked her how she was. Small talk had never been Brigitte's forte.

"Fine, thank you Brigitte and you?" she answered somewhat hesitantly.

"Great, I was wondering if you could tell me if Nurse Paterson has any free time today. I'd like to discuss one of the children with her."

"Oh, I'm sorry, she went off sick yesterday because of a dental extraction and called in today because she's still in some pain. I don't expect her back until tomorrow."

Brigitte could hardly hide her delight. However, she adopted a concerned demeanour. "Oh, that *is* a shame. I'll catch up with her next week."

"I'll let her know you asked for her," replied Mrs Ahmed with a puzzled look, bemused by Brigitte's uncharacteristic caring streak.

"No need Mrs Ahmed. I'll leave a note on her desk."

Brigitte crossed the quad to the block which housed the medical room. The door was locked but was no match for a girl brought up in Glasgow's East end, whose twin brother, once a gang member but now a financial sector whizkid, had provided her with a somewhat eclectic extracurricular education and a healthy contempt for authority.

The door clicked open, and she slipped in, closing the door behind her. The windowless room was in darkness. She switched on her phone torch and could make out an untidy desk, a couple of chairs and an examination couch. There was a poster about influenza immunisation and an eye test chart on the wall just above a set of weighing scales. She then caught sight of the object of her search. The fridge, in which she hoped she'd find Kerry's smoking gun stood in the corner.

It was locked, but after a brief search she found the key under a batch of puzzle and celebrity gossip magazines in a wire tray on the desk. *Well, someone has plenty of time on her hands!*

She noted that the fridge had a round thermometer on the front which clearly marked the safe temperature storage levels. This was linked to an audio alarm and a printer on the filing cabinet beside it which slowly spooled out temperature data every 15 minutes printed on what looked like a long till receipt. She realised that she'd have limited time to explore without triggering an alert or a temperature fluctuation which would show the fridge had been tampered with.

She opened the door, the harsh internal light casting shadows on her white coat. There were several boxes of different vaccines, but right at the back she found a box of intranasal influenza vaccines, similar to the ones she knew all the children and staff had been given. She removed one. Given the general disorder of the office, she thought it unlikely that Paterson had recorded the numbers very assiduously. However, as she was about to close the door, she saw a box labelled with a child's name, Patrick O'Donoghue. Brigitte knew that Patrick had recently joined the school. She remembered that Kerry had said that the virus might only have to be given once and that subsequent vaccines could just be normal ones.

Well, if anyone is going to have the rogue vaccine it'll be you, Patrick. When she opened the box, she saw an intranasal flu vaccine which looked identical to the other flu vaccines. However, it had a different batch number.

She emptied the contents of one of the routine vaccines into the sink and rinsed it away. She squeezed half of the vaccine scheduled for

Patrick into the empty syringe. She then took another vaccine and topped up the one for Patrick.

Satisfied that it did not look like it had been tampered with, she slipped it into its box once more and the one containing a sample of Patrick's into her pocket. The others she discarded in the 'sharps' box. The fridge thermometer was about to move into the red so she quickly closed it the door and prayed that an alert wouldn't sound or be recorded, but just as she was closing the fridge she heard the door creak.

She turned quickly to see a tall shape silhouetted in the doorway. Her heart started to pound.

"Dr Huber? What are you doing here in the dark?" a male voice asked. "Shall I put on the light?"

Brigitte did not immediately recognise him, but as the light went on, with some relief, she realised it was Michael Flannigan.

"Oh! Hello Michael. You startled me. I couldn't find the light when I came in. I was just about to leave a note for Nurse Paterson. I was looking for a pencil or pen."

"You should try your top pocket then," he said with a brief laugh.

"How are you these days? I haven't seen you in a

while," said Brigitte with a smile, trying to keep her anxiety out of her voice.

"I'm fine. Better than I've ever been... Like most of the kids here I guess."

There was something about his even tone which alerted Brigitte. He continued to look carefully at her. She felt that his gaze was slowly peeling back the layers of her deceit. She needed to leave. Brigitte looked at her watch.

"Wow! Is that the time. I really should be going. I've a few reports to write."

"I shouldn't keep you back."

He looked like he was about to turn away but added, in a steady even voice, holding her gaze.

"Dr Huber, things are great here, in no small part thanks to you and your team. It would be a shame if it didn't stay that way. The kids here… their lives have been transformed. Please don't let anyone take that away."

Brigitte was almost overwhelmed with compassion for him. This boy was so sincere. She wanted to hug him and say everything was going to be alright. He clearly knew that something was wrong.

"Oh Michael! What brought this on? Why are you thinking this way?" she said as breezily as she could muster.

"First Kerry appears out of the blue, with some

cock and bull story about researching gene editing, then Dame Marion turns up for the first time ever, then I see you rifling through the fridge and lying to me. What am I supposed to think?"

"I wasn't…"

She sighed. The game was up. She decided that dissembling would get her nowhere.

"Michael, Kerry isn't sure that all the improvements that have happened here are due to my team and a bit more equipment. I've had my suspicions too but was too caught up in the success of the whole thing to really question it. The very last thing I want is for you and the other students to be hurt in any way. She's worried that the kids here may have been experimented on. That's why I'm helping her investigate."

"All I can see is good so far. And, if it's not broke…"

"All we can see so far… but what are we not seeing? Are there consequences we don't know about? Not everyone has benefitted believe me. You have to ask why big corporations are interested in this and possibly… and we don't know this for certain… using you as unwitting guinea pigs."

"Well, as 'an unwitting guinea pig' I want to know what's going on. I want to make sure that anything you or Kerry or anyone else decides doesn't take away this fantastic gift we have been given, even if it has been by altering our genes."

He glanced at the fridge.

"I won't grass on you Dr Huber, but I'm to be kept in the loop from now on. OK?"

"You're right Michael, you and the kids here have the biggest stake in all of this. Kerry and her friends are doing their best to find out what they can, but I suspect it won't be easy. I promise you I'll share everything they tell me with you. However, I don't think it'd help to tell the other kids here anything until we have hard facts and hopefully some choices about how to go forward."

"Perhaps. What about Mr Bhopal and the teachers. Are they in on it?"

"I'm pretty sure they aren't. Some of the more astute ones may suspect something a bit odd is going on, as I did. I had briefly wondered about a new drug being secretly administered given the programme's emphasis on healthy eating and the sudden improvement in school catering but had dismissed it. However, I'm absolutely sure none of the teachers would have suspected gene tampering in a million years. Until Kerry showed up it had never occurred to me. I suspect nurse Paterson knows something. I'm pretty sure we can't trust her."

"None of the students trust her. She's always been a cow. OK, for now I'll keep this quiet… although I know how I'd feel if I thought one of my pals was keeping this from me. I want updates every time you get an update. Be sure, I'll be revealing this to the others at some point, the only question is when."

"I promise you I'll tell you everything I know." She said with as much sincerity as she could muster. "Is it OK to tell Kerry you know about our suspicions?"

"Yes, I trust Kerry. I'm sure she'll be on our side."

"As will I Michael," she affirmed. Brigitte nodded to him and started to leave the room, followed by Michael. He glanced behind them.

"Was that paper on the floor when you came in?" he said.

"No, it must have fallen."

"Anything else changed?"

"I don't think so.

She retrieved it and put it back where she thought it had been. Looking at the disorder on the desk she thought it would be unlikely that Paterson would notice anything was amiss.

"Arrange for some daily sessions with me Dr Huber. Tell Mrs Ahmed I'm struggling with some problems at home. She'll believe that. I'll see you tomorrow. Now let's get out of here before anyone sees us."

Brigitte, realising she needed to keep her 'smoking gun' refrigerated went straight to Mrs Ahmed and told her she had developed a migraine and had to go home.

"Oh, you poor thing! Are you able to drive?"

"I'll be fine on the bus. I've had them before. They usually only last a couple of hours."

On the bus she sent Donald a message.

"Great if we could meet up! Call me!"

CHAPTER 20

....

The sound of the telephone jarred Kerry from sleep. She sat up, confused at the unfamiliar surroundings. She glanced at the clock. "6:50AM! Shit, I didn't think I'd sleep at all!"

"Hello"

"Hi Kerry, Eleanor here. Hope you had a good night and sorry to wake you so early. I certainly regret all last night's wine! Mr Markov is expecting you at 0800. Could I meet you in the foyer about 07:40? We got your phone, by the way. We had it couriered as you were so upset at losing it."

"Wow! Thank you! I'll just get washed and a bit of breakfast and see you at 7:40"

"You're booked into the exec lounge so be sure to use it. The Eggs Benedict are to die for!"

After a brief shower Kerry presented herself at the executive lounge. The smiling hostess checked her room number. Kerry noticed that her name had an asterisk next to it.

"Ah, Ms Pearson. Is this your first time here? We have a special table for you."

Kerry was ushered to a table by the window. She felt a little out of place among the expensive suits and occasional tourist dressed in clothes that looked as though they had been bought that morning. However, her discomfort was worth it as the view was spectacular almost vertiginous. She ordered coffee and orange juice and decided to see if the Eggs Benedict really were worth sacrificing her life for.

They *were* good! She packed up her paltry belongings and took the lift to the ground floor where Eleanor was waiting with a big smile.

"Well Kerry? Have you decided?"

"Yes, I'm going to take up the offer."

"Oh fantastic! I'm really pleased for you. Most of the people I meet in this job don't even give me the time of day and a few of the bastards think their invitation includes the right to shag me. I was really, really hoping that a genuinely nice person would get something for a change."

Kerry smiled. She liked Eleanor. Markov was lucky to have her, and she told her so.

They arrived at the CreativeCom office just before 08:00.

"Good morning, Natasha. Goodness, what time do you start in the morning?"

Natasha smiled, clearly impressed that Kerry had remembered her name.

"When the boss is here, I'm here," she replied with a laugh. "He's expecting you. I'll take you in."

Markov was sitting by the window looking out. Hinton-Bruce and another distinguished looking dark-skinned man with a grey beard sat opposite. They stood up as Natasha introduced her and ushered her into the room. Markov looked up. He seemed tired and, Kerry thought, a little dejected.

"Good morning, Kerry. I hope you had a comfortable night?"

"About as comfortable as you, I think by the look of you."

Hinton-Bruce frowned but Markov smiled. He hated sycophants and Kerry clearly wasn't one.

"Let me introduce Professor Singh who heads up our latest acquisition, Chi-Gen. No doubt your friends have mentioned him."

Kerry feigned surprise.

"Really CreativeCom owns Chi-Gen now?... Yes, good morning, Professor Singh."

"Have you an answer for us Kerry?"

"Yes, I'll work with you, as will my colleagues. They've already started work. They understand the need to know more about it before it goes public. However, please be assured that we won't sit on this to save CreativeCom's blushes. I know you're flying out this morning. Will you be able to speak with us when you arrive in California?"

"Agreed, and Mr Hinton-Bruce here will draw up the necessary contracts. Kerry, if there's one thing you need to know about me is that I'm a realist. From what I've heard, I think the odds are that CreativeCom won't survive this. However, I'd very much like to not be in jail at the end of it, although I suspect that regardless of my innocence, the lynch mobs will come after me. Believe it or not, I really do care about the future of humanity and that should take precedence over everything else. I'm leaving now but you should start work with Professor Singh right away. Natasha will provide you with office space and communications. Goodbye Kerry. I look forward to an update this evening."

Kerry was struck by his change in mood since last night and wondered if he had discovered more about the mutations since they last spoke. Could Alan have passed information to Singh? It was a possibility. However, Singh had access to the same data that Alan and Donald had been working on and could call on an army of geneticists to replicate their work, possibly parcelling it out so that none saw the whole picture. Whether he knew or not was a moot point anyway. They clearly had to work with him as they needed the resources of a big biotech company.

"Yes, we'll see you then. There will be a lot to speak about by the time you arrive in California."

She turned to Singh.

"Shall we go Professor? "

"Call me Raj, Kerry. We're on the same team now."

Natasha found them an office, a small meeting room with eight expensive looking chairs around a pine table, on which sat some sophisticated video conferencing equipment. There was a large screen on one wall.

She pointedly looked at the camera and said, "I think we should assume that everything we say in here is overheard and possibly recorded Prof… Raj."

"Well, there was a time when I'd have thought that was a little paranoid but not now. Let's make a start. Where are you and your colleagues up to. The brief update email Alan sent this morning didn't tell me anything I didn't already know, but then I suspect he was holding off until you and Markov made a deal."

"Do you trust Markov?"

Singh looked at the camera, hesitated but then decided there was little to be gained by pretending. Markov would see through it anyway.

"No, but what can we do? I have to ensure that Chi-Gen isn't left with the blame for all of this. Markov has a hold on you. Although we know it was Barton who deleted the ScotGene data and laid the trail it could suit Markov to hang both you and the previous Chi-Gen management out to dry."

"Do you believe he had nothing to do with it and that Barton did it all, hidden in plain sight?"

"It's a hard one to swallow, but if he is lying, he's a good liar. If he were behind this, he could have had you all arrested and behind bars by now and maybe me too. I think we have to work on the assumption that his intentions are all bona fide for now."

"I feel the same way. He seems sincere, but being able to fake sincerity goes a long way in business… and he is very good at business. OK, I've a catch-up meeting at midday with our team which you should join, and we can plan how to take this forward. There are a lot of loose ends. I'm not sure what has happened to the government involvement. My friend Johnny says he thinks they have been told to back off for the time being."

"They have. Markov has a contact high up in the security services." He made a speech-quote sign with his fingers on the word contact.

"What's James Barton's next move going to be? I'm not sure why he hasn't tried to discredit us yet."

"He may be holding off until he sees if you've been frightened off. A lot of people would be. Once he's pushed that particular button your credibility might be shot but, on the other hand, you'll no longer have anything to lose and there would be people who would believe you and your colleagues, especially Dr Stirling. That could be a problem for Barton, because even if the ScotGene biobank has been trashed, there's living proof of your claims in the blood of subjects of his experiments. He's not going to be able to get rid of all of them. But tell me Kerry, where have you got to?"

There seemed little point in holding anything back, so Kerry filled him in on the early results they had on the changes in the X and Y sex chromosomes and what that might mean and lastly the evidence they had for how the mutation could be transmitted case-to -case.

Singh frowned when she mentioned the possible impact of the changes to the sex chromosomes and was wide-eyed when she mentioned the evidence they had for transmission case-to-case.

"My God! How quickly could it be spreading in the population? This is far worse than I thought! I expected there to be other changes, but a viral vector carrying a genetic mutation affecting fertility jumping from person to person! God, are we talking about the end of humanity?"

"Well, we don't know that the sex chromosome changes will do that, but it fits with the fall in pregnancies at St Julian's and certainly fits in with Barton's desires to reduce the population size. We don't know the mechanism of how it works or if its effects can be reversed. They may be. Anyway, we don't know any of this for certain. We may be jumping the gun, the fall in the pregnancy rate may be down to better education or a more organised lifestyle.

"The whole thing seems so far-fetched. If you'd asked me two weeks ago, I'd have said that no-one has the technology to do this sort of thing!"

"Your guy in Edinburgh, Emilio Sanchez. He was working on viral vectors. Alan and Donald were a bit suspicious of him. He seemed overly interested in what they were doing."

"He got a big grant a few years ago to pursue that line of work while he was working with NeoPharmatics. It was an odd set up which NeoPharmatics didn't like as he wanted to keep control of the grant and any intellectual property. That's one of the reasons they ditched him. When he came to us, he had softened his demands and was prepared to allow us to take a share in any IP for access to labs and equipment. The grant was big enough to fund his salary and two assistants and came with an extremely generous lab budget at a time when the company had a bit of a cash flow problem, so we accepted, and we have kind of given him free rein since. He said he was on the cusp of a big discovery."

"Do you know who the funder is?

"A company called Helical."

"Who are they?"

"Some Californian startup." Singh frowned, shaking his head. "Kerry, you're starting to make me feel a little bit nervous. Maybe we were a bit lackadaisical on the due diligence front when we accepted Sanchez' offer."

"I'll get Johnny on to it. If there's dirt to dig, he'll find it."

"I'll start getting in touch with some of our scientists to join our team to help. I'll keep it vague for now, but we can't keep it a secret for long… certainly not if it's spreading uncontrollably. "

CHAPTER 21

Alan and Donald were about to enter the Chi-Gen lab when a text notification cheeped on Donald's phone.

"Something from Kerry!" Donald whispered showing Alan the phone.

'Sanchez's grant is from Helical. Johnny says Helical is a subsidiary of a chain of other firms registered in the Cayman Islands and Isle of Man. One has James Barton as a director.'

"Well surprise surprise! How do we handle this, Donald?"

"Maybe it's time to have it out with him. Enough pussy footing."

Emilio Sanchez arrived around 10.00 AM and once more chose to set up near to them.

"Perhaps he's just being friendly" murmured Alan with a sceptical look.

Sanchez was glancing over at them, trying and failing to hide his interest in what was going on. Donald looked straight at him.

"Emilio, what do you know about Odyssey?"

Sanchez put on a quizzical expression.

"Odyssey? Not sure what you mean."

"I mean the Odyssey that is part of the same company that is funding your research. A company that has been carrying out research on children and young people without ethical approval. Research which has resulted in permanent changes to their genome and using a technology that looks suspiciously like the one you have been developing."

Sanchez paled.

"I… I… don't know anything about that."

"Emilio, you need to start telling us what you have been doing. I can tell you that the shit is truly only centimetres from the fan. At the moment the founder of this company is nowhere to be seen, and you're the man who is about to get a face full of shit. "

"What do you mean, changed the genome."

"What I said, the children's genome has been altered using a viral vector, probably respiratory. These changes are partly beneficial, improved concentration and cognitive ability, but the sting in the tail is, we believe, reduced fertility. We think you helped design the viral vector, we know you didn't do it all by yourself. You're not that good, nonetheless you helped, which is enough to get you jail time unless of course you help us stop it."

Emilio struggled to regain his cool.

"This is ridiculous. How do you know this? It sounds very far-fetched."

"Emilio, we know you were tipped off that we might be coming and were asked to keep an eye on what we were doing. We also know you were digging through our files after we left."

(Donald didn't know either of these things but thought it was likely.)

Sanchez's attempt at sangfroid failed. His face crumpled and there were tears in his eyes.

"I had no idea they were using it on people until you two appeared. I thought they were going to try it out on animals first."

"Did you use human cell lines to develop it?"

"I experimented with some human cell lines in the lab. The results were fantastic. It's some sort of modified lentivirus. The virus entered the cell and generated the CRISPR and test DNA using a reverse transcriptase and integrated it with the cell DNA with very quickly. The virus replicated but there was little in the way of cell destruction. Replication was limited. It seemed like a perfect vector I had never seen anything quite like it. Believe me, I had no idea what they planned to put in it!"

"So, you didn't actually develop it, you were asked to test it? Weren't you a little suspicious that you'd just been handed an amazing technology to test alongside what is really an astonishing grant for that type of work? What did they say to you. "

"They said it had been developed in a lab in Guangzhou, and that great claims had been made for it, but as the scientists there were relatively unknown, they wanted me to test different versions of it, as I was the leader in the field and that they could trust my evaluation."

"But it wasn't just the grant was it, Emilio. You were talking about papers in Nature. They were offering you joint authorship, weren't they? What about intellectual property?"

"They did offer authorship, but they have been holding back on that for months always finding reasons not to publish. They hinted at shares as a bonus payment if the tests turned out well."

"And what animals did they say they were testing it in and where were those tests done?"

"They said that the lab in Guangzhou would be carrying out the large animal testing, once I had demonstrated the virus worked in the cell lines."

"Do you still have samples?"

"No that was part of the deal. I wasn't allowed

to hold on to any samples." His voice breaking now

"Emilio, from what I've heard you aren't the kind of guy who lets rules get in his way. Are you sure you don't have any samples? People's lives may depend on it …. and certainly, your career"

Emilio was silent for a few seconds, eyes darting from Donald to Alan.

"No, I don't. They were quite definite about that."

"How did you communicate with these people?"

"Some video links, but mainly by email."

"Were they people you recognised?"

"No. One seemed like an older guy, an American, but the video link was always troublesome and heavily pixelated".

"What email address was the video link sent from?"

"I need time to think about this. I think I've said more than I should. Confidentiality was a cornerstone of the agreement. They said that at every meeting."

"Well Emilio, thank you for your honesty so far, but if you want to get out of the way of the ten-ton truck that is currently careering straight for you then you need to start co-operating with us. We're working with the UK security services. I think you can expect a call from them soon. Don't be tempted to start deleting files and emails. It looks to me that the people behind this didn't need you at all. Your role in this is to be the fall-guy if it goes wrong."

"We have to head out Emilio. We'll see you in a couple of hours."

Alan saved their work, they grabbed their jackets, picked up their phones from reception and headed through the Edinburgh drizzle across the campus.

"Well, he caved quickly! I hope he brought a spare pair of underpants because he looked like he was shitting himself when we left. Are you going to phone the secret service guys?" asked Alan.

"I think we have to let them know about this. I don't believe a word he said about having no idea about what viral vector was carrying or that he hasn't kept any samples. He couldn't help himself. Wouldn't be surprised if he wasn't planning a march on his collaborators to get a publication out. Do you believe the Guangzhou connection?"

"It's possible, Wuhan is the centre that's most advanced in this area in China, but people move all the time. We still don't know how they came up with this. It's so far ahead of the current state of the art. It's interesting what he said about the virus not being capable of repeated replication. It clearly is now as your own conversion attests to. I wonder if that was a new mutation or if Barton planned it?"

"Why a lentivirus, aren't they usually spread by insects?" asked Donald.

"I was involved in a study in Porton Down looking at lentiviruses as a possible bioweapon. They can definitely be spread by aerosol too and who knows how Barton's crew have altered it. Lentiviruses have the advantage that they can infect a wide range of tissues including brain and germ cells."

"Unbelievable! What if he'd got it wrong? He could have made a deadly super-bug so easily. He just doesn't give a damn."

Donald switched on his phone to call Speirs and noticed a message, unknown number. He opened it.

"Great if we could meet up! Call me!"

He turned to Alan with a concerned look.

"I think it's Brigitte Huber the school psychologist"

He tapped the phone to dial.

"Hello, great to hear from you again." He said in a measured tone.

"Thank goodness" sighed Brigitte. "I was

beginning to worry that I had the wrong number, I thought you'd have got back more quickly!"

"Sorry we've been in a building where phones aren't allowed."

"Is it safe to speak?"

"I believe so, what have you got for us?"

"I think I have a sample of the vaccine they use. I don't know for certain, but it was set aside for a new child at the school."

"Do they know you have it?"

"The authorities don't but, I'm sorry, one of the school kids saw me take it. He's a very smart kid, a friend of Kerry's apparently. He promised to keep it quiet for the time being."

"What does he know?"

"Pretty much what I know."

"Where is the vaccine now?"

"In my refrigerator in my flat here in Morningside"

"That's great work Brigitte, although you shouldn't have put yourself in danger like that. Text me the address we'll come and get it."

"Who do you mean by we? Do you mean Kerry? Is she OK?"

"She's fine, we spoke to her this morning, and we're going to speak with her again at mid-day.

I was going to come with my friend Alan who is working on the project with us. Would you prefer I came alone?"

"No, that's fine. Are you coming right away?"

"Yes, about fifteen minutes."

Donald opened the Uber app and ordered a cab. He then told Alan about Brigitte and what she had said.

"Bloody fantastic! Good for her. This should help us enormously! Wow! Who'd have thought it would be so easy to get."

"We don't know if what she has is the genuine article. We also don't know if someone will notice it's missing. I'm worried that one of the kid's knows she has it. Hard to be sure what his attitude will be. We need to get it as soon as we can."

As he was speaking a white Skoda drifted slowly up the road, the driver scanning left and right. Donald checked his app.

"Here's our ride."

Brigitte lived in the top half of a divided villa in a quiet tree-lined cul-de-sac in the south of the city. Donald texted her to say they had arrived. He asked the Uber driver to wait and promised a large tip. Alan opened his wallet and gave him £10. He said he'd wait ten minutes no more.

Brigitte had come downstairs. She waved at

Donald. She looked worried.

"Donald? *Great* to finally meet you"

"*Great* to meet you too. Do you have it?"

"Yes, here it is."

She handed him a bubble wrapped lined envelope.

"Brilliant, we'll get this to the lab right away."

"But wait! Before you go, I've just had the headmaster on the phone. Apparently, I tripped an alert in the nurse's room. There must have been a motion sensor camera there. The nurse has been off sick, but she must have noticed the alert on her phone. She just phoned five minutes ago asking what I was doing 'rummaging' through the fridge."

"I didn't know what to say so I said that one of the new kids was worried about the injections he was going to get and what were they and that I had come to see her, but as she was off sick, so I just looked in the fridge myself. I doubt she'll buy it for a moment."

"OK you need to get out of here too let's go now. Leave your own phone in the flat."

"It's there already."

"OK come right now. Leave your door. We can come back later to lock it."

They piled into the car and told the driver to move as fast as he could initially in the direction of the university lab. As they cleared the corner Donald caught sight of a black 4x4 turning the corner into the street.

Donald leaned forward. "Please! There's another ten pounds if you go a bit faster."

"Sir, I'm not going to lose my licence for you," he replied calmly in a strong Nigerian accent.

"Twenty!" said Alan pulling the notes from his wallet.

They were thrown back into their seats as the car accelerated.

"Where to Alan, Chi-Gen or the University?"

"My lab. We can hide it safely there I think, then we can ask Singh if he can get rid of Emilio if only for a little while. The equipment in Chi-Gen is much better."

"Switch off your phones Donald," said Alan fiddling with his own. "I know it's unlikely they have your burner number, but they could easily have mine. Remember we're dealing with someone who almost certainly has access to all sorts of tech."

"Can either of you tell me what's going on please. I feel like I'm being abducted here!"

"Sorry Brigitte. As soon as we get to the university. We'll tell you everything we know," said Donald flicking his eyes and head towards the driver.

The car came to a halt outside Donald's building, and after emptying Alan's wallet for tips they made their way up to the lab.

As they walked into his office, they found Speirs seated behind Donald's desk feet up on a precarious pile of books and papers at the side, talking on his phone.

"Make yourself at home why don't you!" exclaimed Donald with a twisted smile.

Speirs raised one hand towards them while he completed his call.

"Look they're here now. I'll call you later." Turning to Donald and with a curled upper lip he said

"I thought you were going to keep me updated Dr Stirling."

Donald gave a forced smile.

"The phone works both ways Mr Speirs, we understood that your department had … how shall I put it… suspended its interest in the case."

Speirs scowled.

"The department might have but I haven't."

"As it turns out we were on the point of phoning you, but it's a fast-developing situation. What is the government line on this? We thought you'd be all over it by now. Take this Alan," he said tossing the package containing the vaccine. Alan caught it and put it in one of the laboratory fridges.

"OK, I'll be straight with you if you're straight with me. Phil and I got told yesterday morning by our boss that there was strong suspicion that this whole thing was a hoax; a series of unrelated incidents cooked up into a crazy conspiracy theory involving mystery tech billionaires, rogue AI and vaccination or as he put it 'all the usual suspects from the lunatic fringe.' He said that the whole thing was being orchestrated by a bunch of hackers and mentioned Johnny McCabe by name."

Speirs stopped to gauge Donald's reaction before continuing.

"Apparently, the minister suggested to my boss that we hold back and let it fizzle out, so we didn't end up looking foolish. So, my boss told us to stop working on it. When I suggested there may be more to this than the minister realised, I was treated to a roll of the eyes and a suggestion that, if I didn't have enough to occupy my time, he'd find something for me that would. I was prepared to do that until I heard about the raid on ScotGene this morning. You know they'll probably blame McCabe for that don't you?"

"It wasn't Johnny McCabe and this isn't a hoax. It's huge, much bigger than any of us imagined. We have a video-call at 12. You should join it too. By the way, I don't think you have met Alan McPherson from Chi-Gen who is working with us." Alan smiled and gave an open-handed wave. "And this is Brigitte Huber, a psychologist working for Odyssey in St Julian's. She has very bravely, and possibly at the risk of her job, managed to get us a sample of what we think is the virus that they used as a vehicle to alter the children's DNA. On the call, I'll summarise what we know so we're all up to speed."

Donald texted Johnny to set up a video call with Kerry, warning him that her phone was possibly compromised. He linked his own phone to the VC suite in the lab. A few moments later Johnny replied on a different number providing a secure link. Alan, Donald, Brigitte and Speirs waited for the link to become active. After a few moments first Johnny then Kerry alongside Singh appeared on the screen.

Although she was black-eyed and appeared quite subdued, Donald felt a wave of relief at seeing Kerry. Singh was as immaculately turned out as before, looking more like a banker than a scientist. Donald introduced everyone, describing their role, Singh breezily insisting they all call him Raj. Johnny patently failed to control his facial expression when he introduced Speirs.

"OK. Here's the state of play as I understand it. We know that an odd genetic sequence started appearing in the last few years in blood samples held in ScotGene. One of those genetic sequences appeared to be close to an area of the genome associated with ADHD and cognitive ability, this led to a suspicion that extraordinary educational achievement in what was considered to be a failing school might be related, and indeed it turned out that the school had strong links with ScotGene. The transformation in the school had however been attributed to novel education and psychological processes led by Odyssey a subsidiary of CreativeCom.

We have since discovered that the mutation may affect more than concentration and cognitive ability. We *suspect* from behavioural changes in test sites here and in the US that it may have an impact on reducing addictive and violent behaviour."

"However, several additional mutations are on the sex chromosomes so the sting is that this may be at the cost of fertility. I emphasise that we don't *know* any of this for certain, nor do we know how it will manifest itself in different people or what the long-term effects may be. Altering DNA on such a vast scale could have unintended consequences.

The programme is much bigger than just St

Julian's and involves schools and at least one penitentiary on all five continents. We don't know if the same agent has been used in all these places or if they are trying out different approaches.

We have not proven for certain that the children's DNA has been altered, and if so, don't yet know how it was done. We *suspect* it was by use of a virus introduced during vaccination. A local scientist here in Edinburgh, Emilio Sanchez, has admitted to testing a viral agent which could do this. He claims to be unaware of the impact of its genetic payload or that it was to be used on children, but who knows? However, more worryingly, we have evidence that the virus can spread from person to person altering the infected person's DNA in a similar fashion, although we don't know how frequently or how rapidly this is happening."

"So, is it CreativeCom behind it?" asked Speirs

"Kerry has met with Abe Markov head of CreativeCom. He claims that Odyssey is a legacy programme created by, and which has continued to be directed by, an ex-partner, James Barton. CreativeCom kept it in place following his departure as it appeared to be a purely charitable educative programme which provided a good public face for the company. Barton was allowed to continue to direct it. However, he appears to have separately funded a large proportion of its programme including Sanchez and probably other research groups around the world. Markov says he knew nothing about these additional activities."

"And you believe him?" sneered Johnny.

"He seems as appalled at the possible outcomes as we are, and he says he wants to stop what's happening. However, I suspect his main concern is for the reputation of CreativeCom and his own skin. To help deal with this he's spent a fortune to buy up Chi-Gen, which, despite the fact that Sanchez was ostensibly one of their staff, also denies any knowledge of the programme."

"I can assure you that Chi-Gen knew nothing of this." Singh interjected. "Sanchez was effectively working independently. We're naturally worried about the optics of this. We'll be working with you to find out as much about this as we can and to help ameliorate its effects preferably before going public."

Donald continued. "James Barton always seems to be one step ahead of us. He appears to have carefully planned things so that in the event of disclosure, CreativeCom and Chi-Gen would be first in the firing line. He was almost certainly responsible for destroying the ScotGene database but has left a trail which seems to point the finger at Johnny, just as he previously tried to paint Kerry as an eco-terrorist. We're pretty sure he now knows we have the vaccine and expect he'll try very hard to get that back. We don't know to what extent government officials and ministers are involved in all this. I suspect there are a few in his pocket. I think that's about it unless anyone else has anything to add."

Donald looked around the room and at the screen. Speirs was shaking his head. Brigitte just looked stricken.

Johnny lifted a hand.

"Do you believe Markov, Kerry?"

"I think I do. He said this morning that he thought CreativeCom would probably not survive this, but that either way he wanted to stop it. He's more worried about winding up in jail."

Johnny gave a look that suggested that wouldn't be all that undesirable.

The screen suddenly added another picture. Markov in noise cancelling headphones, a background of plush beige upholstery with what looked like walnut trim. The people in the room glanced at one another. Of course, he had had access to Kerry's phone and they knew it might not be secure. If anyone could hijack the call it would be the owner of one of the world's biggest IT companies, joining from his private jet, somewhere over the Atlantic.

"Hi, I'm sorry to piggy-back on this without permission, but it helps me to know where everyone honestly stands. I thought it was better to come clean myself and I thought we couldn't afford to wait until this evening. Look, we could all of us end up in jail depending on how Barton lets this play out, but what do we do next?"

Donald was so angry at the intrusion he could barely speak. Singh broke the silence.

"First off, I'd say we have to clearly demonstrate that the children are affected by this."

"We need to map the DNA changes more precisely to the systems they are likely to affect to prove our suspicions," added Alan.

"There will have to be some long-term observation of the people affected," said Brigitte

"We need to establish to what extent this has spread beyond those vaccinated and if it is still spreading," added Donald.

Speirs interjected, his tone authoritative and sombre. "OK enough tiptoeing around! You need government help. This is just too big for you alone. The longer you keep it under wraps the more it looks like you're part of it. Markov, you might have meant well by buying Chi-Gen, but it looks pretty fishy to anyone who doesn't know the whole story. Barton is probably already making moves to incriminate everyone. His discourse won't hold forever of course, but probably long enough for him to get out of the way and to delay the people who know most about this from ameliorating it."

"And what happens to the kids? said Brigitte her brow lined shaking her head. "Just for once in their shite lives, they felt special, that through their own work they had achieved something. You must realise how this undermines those achievements. Who knows, when this breaks some people will think they're dangerous mutants and want them all quarantined. What a bloody mess!".

Brigitte continued.

"One of them *begged* me, the one who saw me take the vaccine. He *begged* me not to take this wonderful thing away from them, but we're going to, aren't we?"

"We need to establish they definitely have this mutation, Brigitte. Could you persuade a few of them to come and get tested?" said Alan.

"We should test their families to see if there has been evidence of spread," added Kerry.

"We also need to work out how these genetic changes manifest themselves in people. I can get our teams here to start working on that. We'll need to examine some of the affected people." said Singh.

"What do we do about Barton?" said Johnny. "How do we stop him?"

"I thought about asking to speak to him" said Kerry to general outcry from the group.

"Hang on, let me speak. Have you looked at his profile? Apart from the stuff about eugenics, certainly in the past he used to spend a lot of time posting about all he'd achieved. I think with the right sort of flattery we might be able to get him to talk."

"He wouldn't be that stupid Kerry," said Johnny.

"No harm asking, I could offer a meeting on his terms?"

Markov looked lost in thought slightly nodding his head.

"That might not be a bad idea, Kerry. You'll have to be careful. As you already know he is very slippery. He'll use anything you say to incriminate you if he can."

"Are you staying in London or coming home Kerry?" asked Donald.

"I've a flight booked home at 2.30PM, should arrive just after 4.00."

"Would you meet some of the kids with me Kerry and explain all this? asked Brigitte, looking down as she added, "They deserve to know what's going on and perhaps more importantly what may happen to them."

"Of course."

"I'll try and set up a meeting and text you with the details."

"If you could get them to come here so we could get some tissue samples that'd be great" said Alan, catching a dismayed look from Brigitte and quickly realising that this might be exactly the sort of treatment that she was worried about. "Or we could go with you?"

"Maybe see what they say first. They won't all necessarily feel the same way," replied Brigitte.

On the screen, Johnny's phone pinged, and he picked it up. Speirs phone pinged a few seconds later. At the same time the door to the VC suite burst open and Peter Munro barged in holding out his tablet.

"Have you seen this Donald!?"

He caught the surprised look on Donald's face and slowly turned to see Kerry and Singh on the screen and was that Abe Markov? He then noticed Speirs in the room.

Munro's tablet was open at a Daily Mail headline. 'World beating bio resource destroyed. Ecoterrorists suspected'

"What's going on?... Donald…. Kerry? Are you behind this?"

"An awful lot is going on Peter. We owe you an explanation. We could also use your help," replied Donald.

"The answer to your question is no we aren't behind this, but we want to get the people who are. If you have time, I'll tell you all about it as soon as we finish here."

Munro looked around him once more nodded and offered to see him in his office.

After his departure, the group agreed a list of objectives and time frames. Markov persuaded Speirs to hold out until the morning before involving his boss to give them time to collect some evidence. They agreed to meet again late that evening. Donald went to speak to Peter Munro, after which they planned to return to Chi-Gen, having arranged with Singh to get Sanchez out of the lab.

CHAPTER 22

As they ended the meeting, Kerry could see that their response to the threat was already beginning to fragment. Speirs was almost certainly right. They really did need to involve the government, although by the sounds of things he'd need hard evidence to do so. So far, no names had been mentioned with respect to the Scot-Gene destruction, but no doubt that would come with or without Barton's input and Johnny would be in the frame for certain and possibly she would too.

Alan and Singh were right; they needed the children to provide samples. She would have to persuade Brigitte to allow them to ask the children for help. She realised, however, that they might not want to. What would a positive result mean for them? That all their achievements of which they were rightly proud and which they had put down to their own hard work would suddenly be diminished, like an athlete caught using performance enhancing drugs. They'd suddenly become the focus of a huge research project. And how long before the social media trolls started to demonise them, seeing them as an insidious threat to the world. Super-smart freaks conspiring to rule over the rest of us. She could almost write the posts now.

Her reverie was interrupted by Eleanor knocking on the office door to ask if she was ready to head back to the airport. Kerry nodded and waved to Singh who was talking on his phone to Sanchez, explaining why he needed to come to London to talk about his exciting novel work with the new board.

"Are you hungry Kerry?" asked Eleanor. We have time for a bite if you like or you could pick something up at the airport. I've arranged for a car to pick you up at Edinburgh. The driver will take you anywhere you want."

"I still haven't recovered from that massive breakfast. The Eggs Benedict were, as you said, to die for," she replied patting her tummy.

"Well then, I'll say goodbye. Good luck Kerry."

Kerry smiled, but just as she was about to get into the car, she turned to Eleanor and gave her a long hard hug. Then looking at her square in the face said,

"You have been really good to me Eleanor. Markov is so lucky to have you working for him. When you're next in Edinburgh I want to take you for a really good night out."

Eleanor smiled and blushed. There were tears in her eyes.

"Oh Kerry! That's so nice of you! I hope whatever you're doing is a huge success and yes! Yes! I'd love to see you in Edinburgh."

She gave her another hug and a brief kiss on the cheek and said good-bye.

The driver turned around.

"Heathrow Ma'am?"

"Yes please," she said casually checking her phone then suddenly realising, as the car silently accelerated, just how quickly she had become accustomed to the high life. As if Kerry Pearson in a chauffeur driven Mercedes were an everyday event.

When she landed in Edinburgh, she decided she should get a new phone, uneasy that Markov was possibly privy to everything she used her old one for. Deciding to pay cash she went to an ATM where she discovered her account had £20,000 in it that hadn't been there yesterday. She wasn't sure how she felt about that. She wondered if she was now bought and paid for. Whether or not, that was how it was going to look. Still, she smiled, *On the plus side, nice to be rich!*

A smartly dressed chauffeur stood holding up

an iPad with her name in large letters. After he took her backpack, they walked to the short-stay carpark and drove to the University. As she thanked him, he handed her a card and said that his limo company was at her service, 24 hours a day, on the CreativeCom account.

CHAPTER 23
....

Brigitte needed to see Michael but, without her own phone didn't have his number. She phoned the school and, putting on her broadest Edinburgh accent, said she was his mother and needed to speak to him urgently. Mrs Ahmed frowned, this was the first time she had heard from Michael's Mum or Dad in years. She didn't quite sound as she remembered her, a little suspicious, she asked if she could get him to call her back, but Brigitte said she was in a call box. After a few minutes Michael said hello.

"Hi Michael, it's not your Mum it's Brigitte Huber. Sorry about the subterfuge but I need to see you urgently so I can get you up to speed with everything that has happened as I promised. I can't come to the school. I was caught on camera in the nurse's room. I'm pretty sure you won't have been as you just stood in the doorway, but I can't be sure. Could you come to the university after school? "

"OK Mum. It's alright I can come. Don't worry

about it. Where exactly are you?"

Brigitte gave him directions.

He turned to Mrs. Ahmed.

"My Mum is in a spot of bother, and she needs help. OK if I just head off now. I've a free period anyway."

"Yes of course Michael!" said Mrs Ahmed with a characteristic look of concern. "I hope it all turns out OK."

Michael heaved a sigh and quickly returned to the sixth form common room. There he saw Hana and Josh, who looked up at him expectantly.

"It's starting," he said. "I have to meet Huber. I think you should both come too."

Hana and Josh looked at each other then towards Michael, nodded and started to pack up.

They squeezed into a crowded tram and then ran just in time to catch a quieter bus. Initially each lost in their own thoughts, Michael broke the silence. He turned to Hana and Josh in the seat behind him.

"We always knew there was more to this than what we were told, even before Huber told me of Kerry's suspicions."

"Yeah, but whatever occurs today, we don't agree to anything straight off," said Hana. "Let whoever it is say their piece and then *we* decide what to do next. We have to try to keep it on our terms."

"Well, I for one don't want to go back to being a stoner loser; so, whatever happens, we're not giving it up," said Josh.

"Agreed. I've said goodbye to Mad Mick forever, regardless of what it costs."

Brigitte was waiting by the window for them to arrive and although a little taken aback when she saw Josh and Hana accompanying Michael she thought. "I'd have done the same. Too big a secret to keep at that age."

She borrowed Donald's ID and ran down to let them in. As they were about to enter a sleek Mercedes silently cruised into a parking spot beside the door. Brigitte wondered if Spitz was back, but the person backing out of the car, short, bleached hair, trainers and tattered jeans seemed somewhat inconsistent with the mode of transport. She turned around and shouted "Hi!", then, noticing the look of confusion on Brigitte's and the children's faces, smiled and said, "Not how it looks! All is about to be revealed!"

The young people were as solemn as if they were attending the funeral of a grandparent. They crowded together nervously as they entered the laboratory. Brigitte noticed Josh was gripping Hana's hand but wasn't sure which of them needed the reassurance more. They straightened as Donald came out of his office in his lab coat, and he and Kerry introduced themselves, waving towards Alan who was working on a laptop on the other side of the lab and who waved in return.

Kerry told them to grab seats around the bench.

"I guess you want to know what we know about what's going on. It's a lot to take in. I'm going to start from when I first began to think something was a bit odd, right up to everything that we know for certain now and what we don't know yet. At the end we'll answer all your questions if we can and we can discuss our plans for moving forward."

Kerry summarised what they knew. She decided not to mention their specific concerns about the potential effects on fertility at this point as it was far from certain. The kids listened in silence. As Kerry finished, she noticed a single tear ran down Josh's face.

Hana was pale, her fists tightly bunched and white knuckled. "So, that's how it goes. From feted to freaks in five minutes."

"You aren't freaks" said Donald or if you are I'm one. I have the new genetic code too. We don't know for certain what the long-term consequences will be, but the ones we do know about, the short-term ones, seem to be advantages. We have to make use of these to control our own futures."

"Nonetheless, up until now we were clever hard-working children who had overcome terrible disadvantages. Now we'll be portrayed as some sort of mutant. Do you really think those posh kids and their parents who we beat in all the exams won't feed fat on this?" replied Josh.

"Or that we won't be seen as a threat, some sort of Midwich Cuckoos," said Hana

Clocking the look of confusion on Kerry's face Donald added. "A science fiction story where a town's children are replaced by aliens".

Brigitte stood up. "Freak, or super-hero. We decide what we want to be. What's been done to us is completely unethical. The question is do we take it lying down and let others decide how this going to turn out or do we do something about it."

Michael looked at his friends then the scientists, inhaled smiled and said,

"Time to saddle up. Lock and load."

Donald smiled. "Platoon. I loved that movie."

"Nah, Star Trek, Mr. Data!" chorused the youngsters.

"The first thing we need to do is check if you

have the genetic changes. We're pretty sure you do. Then we need to see if members of your family who weren't deliberately infected by the virus have got it as I did by direct person-to-person spread," said Donald.

"How do we do that without telling the school and the other kids? If we don't then we're almost as bad as the people who did this to us."

From the doorway Speirs said. "You're right. As soon as it's been confirmed that you three have this then we have to let the school know, but how this is handled will be really important. We don't want widespread panic. I've been in touch with my boss again. Markov's involvement has changed everything for him. He's going to get in touch with the minister, but he says if we're serious about our concerns we need to contact the chief medical officer to make plans about what we do next, before this gets out of hand."

Donald was open mouthed, exasperated that Speirs had jumped the gun.

Alan shouted from the far end of the laboratory. "I thought we had agreed we weren't going to do that until we knew more about it. What do we say when the children's parents ask us about the consequences and all we can say is that we don't know. I vote we wait a few days to see what Singh comes up with and in the meantime, we run some tests on those who already know."

"I know the Chief Scientific Officer in London," replied Peter Munro, who had been listening at the door. All heads turned towards him. "He was in my year in medical school. He's a sensible guy, I can't believe he would be mixed up in this. I could contact him."

Michael jumped up, concern written across his face.

"Hang on a minute. This has to happen in a controlled way. The other kids and our parents have to be told before the whole world knows. What seems to be driving the speed of this is the concern that it is continuing to spread. From what you said Dr Stirling; you caught it from one of the teachers at St Julian's. The guy who was running that open day had recently joined the school and it is likely that he had just been given the vaccine…. At least I'm assuming the teachers got the same one as us. It may be that there's only a brief window during which the person is infectious. We can check how many members of our families who haven't been given the vaccine have the genetic modification. We could probably do that without arousing too much suspicion. I'm pretty sure my dad must have it as he's a totally different person these days, possibly my big brother, but I don't see any change in my Mum."

Kerry marvelled at how changed this young

man was and just how bright!

"I've not noticed any changes in my family, although my little sister seems to think up ever more ingenious ways of annoying me." said Hana,

"Nor mine," added Josh. Hana gave a look that seemed to say she disagreed.

"Well perhaps the R number is low, and person-to-person spread is a rare event." interjected Donald, "Although the results we got from ScotGene don't seem to suggest that. To be fair, those results could be seriously skewed by St Julian's enthusiastic participation in the biobank. We also don't know if people are infectious only once or if it is the sort of virus which can recur like cold sores or shingles although I think that is unlikely. However, you're right Michael. It would make sense to start with you and your families. If they were completely clear, then that'd be reassuring."

Alan joined the others. "Let's get started then" he said handing out specimen bottles. "All you have to do is spit into this, assuming that you haven't exchanged saliva with anyone else today!" he added with a grin.

"Guys, you don't have to do this if you feel uneasy about it. Do you want to discuss it with your parents first?" asked Kerry.

"I think we all understand what's at stake here

Kerry and the possible consequences. You'll only be confirming what we already suspect," replied Michael.

"Please also pick up kits for your families, label them and bring them tomorrow. By then I'll have your results," added Alan.

"So, are we agreed we hold off revealing any of this until we get the results from our families?" asked Hana

"I'd be for that. I'm not sure we can be entirely sure what Markov or Mr Speirs' bosses will do. What do you think?" he said looking at Speirs.

"I guess it makes sense to wait 'til tomorrow afternoon. How long will the analysis take?"

"Now that we know what we're looking for, hardly any time at all. I'll take these over to the Chi-Gen lab, right away. "

"Are you going to try to contact James Barton Kerry?" asked Josh.

"Yes, he seems to have disappeared from social media these last few days. Goodness knows where he is."

"He's in Rashwastan, I think," replied Josh

"What makes you think that?"

"Well, I've a sort of interest in aviation," he said quietly.

"He's a total plane nerd!" scoffed Hana.

Josh gave Hana a tired look.

"Anyway, I ran a search on locations where James Barton has been known to visit and private jets in those areas at the same time. There is one jet which turns up with him almost every time and that jet is currently in Rashwastan."

Michael looked up from the tablet on which he was typing.

"He's a big pal of the president. Donated a lot to 'Good Causes' there. I suspect many of these good causes fund the president's lifestyle. He'll feel pretty safe there I'd guess."

"Might make him careless then." said Speirs. "It's worth a try Kerry. Right now, we only have Markov's word that this is all down to Barton."

Kerry opened X on her phone. "He's thousands of followers. I doubt if he would notice a tweet from me. Nothing to lose I suppose."

She typed "@jamesxbarton, impressive project you have going in Scotland. Want to speak?"

"Ok message sent. We just have to wait and see if he notices…" She was interrupted by a ping.

"Wow! It says 'lovely to hear from you Kerry. Impressed by you too. Will be in touch.'"

"Bloody hell!" said Donald his expression as incredulous as that of everyone in the room.

"OK Kerry," said Speirs. "When he gets in touch let us know immediately. We need to record any exchange. Remember this could be the only thing keeping you and Johnny out of jail."

"Well thanks for that Mr Speirs, very reassuring."

Speirs shrugged. "Just telling you how it is Kerry. You have a tiger by the tail. Not my fault you thought it was a pussycat when you first grabbed it."

"We know Johnny had nothing to do with the Scot-Gene attack. It'll never hold water," interjected Donald.

"We know he tried to hack it. We know his electronic fingerprints will be all over it. Do you really think that the man whose firm designed the fastest quantum computer in the world, who almost *invented* AI won't be able to make it look like Johnny trashed it? Believe me, you guys are far from out of the woods!"

"OK," said Alan, "I'm off to Chi-Gen. I expect we'll have these results in a few hours. Guys when do you think you'll be able to get your families' samples to me?"

"Tomorrow morning. Hana, Josh, if you give me your families samples outside school tomorrow, I'll take them here to Donald and Alan," replied Michael.

"It would be better if it was me that did it, Michael," said Josh. "They may suspect you. We don't know for certain they didn't see you when Dr Huber was in the nurse's room."

"OK, tomorrow at 0800 we meet in Dobson's café, and do we take the samples to you Dr McPherson?"

"I'm happy to meet you there so you can get to school."

Brigitte raised her hand. "That black car that turned into my street as we left. Do you really think it may have been after the sample of the virus I took?"

"Maybe we were being a bit paranoid," said Donald.

Speirs threw back his head and guffawed.

"Are you serious? This guy has just trashed one of the most important scientific databases in the country, and tried to have you, Kerry, branded an ecoterrorist. Of course he's going to try to get his sample back. In fact, Dr McPherson I think it would be sensible for me to accompany you over to Chi-Gen. Where is it, have you got it in a safe place? Will you take the sample there?"

There was something in Speirs' tone that made him feel a little uneasy.

"Perhaps it would be safer there and I can start preliminary work on it. I'll go and get it."

He caught Donalds eye as he headed out of the room making it clear that he thought something was off. Alan went to the fridge in the adjoining lab where the sample had been stashed. He quickly drained it into another syringe filling the original with water and returned with it.

"OK, let's go," he said to Speirs.

"You guys should be getting home before your folks start to wonder where you are. Are you OK is there anything else you need to know."

"When do we meet again? How about tomorrow after school? You should have all the results by then."

A few moments later, Peter Munro ran into the room.

"There's something happening out there. We need to get the kids out of here right now. Have you secured the vaccine?"

Donald and Kerry ran to the window. Three large black cars had pulled up and 6 men were surrounding Alan and Speirs, their hands in the air. Four others were running towards the door.

"Josh, Hana, Michael, Brigitte. Go with Peter. We'll get in touch with you as soon as we know anything."

"What about the vaccine? Alan had it," whispered Kerry urgently.

"I don't think he did. I'm pretty sure it's still

here. Kerry, get out of here too. I'll deal with these guys."

Kerry hesitated as if to argue but then sprinted out of the door and along the corridor. She passed a seminar room. Peter appeared to be giving a talk to a group of people in white coats. Two were postgrads she recognised, the other four were Brigitte and the kids, who looked surprisingly mature in the lab coats. Clever plan!

Donald was deleting the computer history when four men in black, wearing masks, helmets and carrying automatic weapons burst into the lab.

" 'ands in the air where we can see 'em!" yelled the tallest in a strong cockney accent.

Donald slowly raised his hands.

"What's this about?"

"Where's Kerry Pearson?"

"Who are you? What has she done?"

"You know damn fine what she's done."

"Believe me, I don't. She's not here. She left a while ago. Gone to meet a friend. I don't know where."

Donald wondered if these men were connected with Speirs or in the pay of Barton. They seemed to have treated Speirs as an enemy outside, but that could be a front.

"Where's the vaccine Dr Stirling?"

"What vaccine?"

The speaker nodded to one of the other men who moved forward and hit Donald's face with the butt of his rifle. Donald fell to the ground, moaning. He then kicked him hard in the ribs.

"Ow! Alan McPherson has the vaccine," he grunted.

"Where is 'e?"

"On his way to the Chi-Gen lab to analyse it."

The tall one nodded to the man who had hit him. He stood on Donald's hand starting to press harder.

"And Kerry Pearson"

"Agghhh. She left about 30 minutes ago to meet her friend Johnny!" He was confident they already knew about Johnny. "I don't know where he is. She never told me." he shouted between gritted teeth.

"See, that wasn't so 'ard Dr Stirling. Perhaps next time we ask you questions you can just answer 'em and avoid this unpleasantness."

The man standing on his hand gave him another kick but was in turn punched hard in the shoulder by the man who appeared to be in charge.

"We're not animals," he snarled. He turned back to Donald.

"If we find out you've been lyin' to us, this is nothing to what's going to happen to you."

He touched a button on his helmet.

" 'e says his mate McPherson 'as the vaccine" then after a couple of seconds he turned to the others. "OK we 'ave what we came for. Nice meeting you Dr Stirling."

They turned and left. Donald lay coughing and grunting on the floor for a few minutes. *So much for playing for time. I must have delayed them all of 30 seconds. Still, I don't think I told them anything they didn't know.*

He slowly sat up holding his ribs. His face was stinging and starting to swell. He shuffled over to the window. The cars were heading out of the car park. Alan was nursing what looked like an injured arm and Speirs was on the ground.

"Shit!" He started to run, holding his side and grunting.

As he approached them Speirs was starting to get up. He had a large wheal on his forehead and a cut on his on his right temple was bleeding.

"Not your guys then?" said Donald.

"Well, if they are, someone's going to pay, but no, they seemed like a private outfit, ex-military. Certainly knew what they were doing."

"They've taken the vaccine and the samples," said Alan.

"Well, we can easily get more samples. A pity about the vaccine though. Are you two alright, you're holding your arm Alan and that's a nasty cut on your head Mr Speirs."

"Call me John. I think we're past formalities now. I'll survive. I've had worse. Pride's hurt more than my head. You don't look in that great shape yourself."

"I'm OK, but I think the bastard may have cracked a rib. Let's go inside. What about you Alan"

"I'll live."

When they returned, Peter Munro, Brigitte and the kids were in the lab. Peter paled when he saw them, and Hana gave an involuntary gasp.

"We're all OK. I think if we had any doubts about the type of people we're dealing with, we can forget them. We need to move fast. Kids they took the samples. Could you give us some more? Alan, are you OK still to do the analysis?"

They all nodded. Alan asked Donald to help him find new sample bottles and when out of earshot whispered.

"We still have the vaccine, what they took was largely saline but there may have been enough residue there to fool them that it was genuine if they run a DNA analysis on it."

"We need expert help with an analysis. We have to get in touch with Singh. Ironically, Sanchez has the skills we need but there's absolutely no way I'd trust that bastard."

"If he's any sense he'll have skipped the country. He must realise he's in deep trouble."

They returned to the group.

"Kids, I'm really sorry about what happened here. It must have been very frightening. We'll call a cab and get you home. I hate to ask you as I don't want to endanger you anymore, but are you still happy to keep working with us? If you say no, we'll completely understand."

Michael gave a twisted grin and raised his eyebrows. "Dr Stirling, we grew up in St Julian's remember? Until about 2 years ago this was normal playground stuff for us. I can't speak for the others, but I'm more convinced than ever that we need to do something. Where's Kerry? Is she OK?"

Peter Munro replied.

"I saw her slip past the seminar room. She may still be in the building."

Donald turned to him.

"Peter, you're still squeaky clean here. No-one knows that you have any idea about what's going on. If you want to pull out, you can. I'm sorry you've been dragged into it."

Peter blew though pursed lips and smiled, slowly shaking his head from side to side.

"There's no way on this earth that I'm stepping back from this now that I know what it's about. I have kids just a few years younger than them for God's sake."

"It's probably useful they don't know you're involved. They'll have eyes on all of us."

Josh's tablet pinged.

"Barton is on the move, or at least his jet is."

"I wonder where he's going?"

Josh typed a few more keys.

"The flight plan says Bergen."

"About as close as he can get to Scotland without entering the UK. He must be very sure of himself. Surely, he must realise this could all blow up on him. What has he got up his sleeve?"

"Probably a few cabinet members, senior police officers, and a legion of lawyers," replied Speirs holding a handkerchief to his head. "You might want to consider going public before he does. If I were him, I'd be dropping everyone in it before they got me. It puts them on the defensive and trying to make out that it is the whistle blower who is the guilty one always looks weak."

"We need evidence. No newspaper will take on Barton without concrete proof."

"Perhaps, but they may treat his intervention with a bit more caution if you have primed them with your story."

"We need to contact Markov." Turning to the three young people, "I know that this blowing up out of control is exactly what you didn't want, but do you see why we may have to do it this way? Perhaps there's still time to call a meeting at the school."

"I certainly think it's time the headmaster found out what's going on," said Hana.

Kerry appeared in the doorway.

"They've gone? Shit, did they do that to you?" she said clocking Donald then, "Shit!" again, when she saw Alan and Speirs.

"I've a missed call and a voice message from Mr Bhopal."

She lifted it to her ear, but he could be clearly heard by everyone. His voice was high-pitched and he spoke rapidly.

"Kerry, what the hell has happened. We've just heard Odyssey is shutting down their operation. Was this your doing? Please phone me!"

The kids looked from one to another in dismay. Michael shook his head.

"No surprises there. CreativeCom covering its ass."

Kerry looked stricken. "I'll phone Markov, get him to reverse this at least temporarily. First, I'll phone Mr Bhopal."

Brigitte frowned. "Oh dear! Everything you feared was going to happen Michael has happened. It's all going to shit."

"Once we heard the history of the whole sorry saga, it was clear what was going to happen. Kerry just inadvertently speeded things up a bit," said Michael.

"It was Barton that speeded it up. If he hadn't come in all heavy handed it could have been years before we put two and two together," replied Donald.

"Well, we're only going to lose some of the resources, but you Dr Huber and your colleagues, will you lose your jobs? That's much worse," said Michael frowning.

"I'll have no trouble getting another job Michael. No-one will. Don't worry about us. On another tack," she said, turning to the others. "Do you think Markov is about to go public?"

She was interrupted by Kerry on the phone to Mr Bhopal.

"Yes… I know… I'm sorry. I think we opened a can of worms. One which would have broken open anyway…. I feel terrible that I may have precipitated this, but when you hear… Listen Mr. Bhopal, we need to meet. When you hear what's behind this, losing the grant will be the least of your worries… I could come this evening. "

Kerry hung up and immediately dialled another number.

"Natasha? Hi It's Kerry Pearson. Yes, that's right. Natasha, I know you must get requests like this all the time, but I really need to speak to Mr Markov. Is there any way you can get a message to him to phone me? Really, that'd be great. Thank you so much."

Turning to Brigitte. "Brigitte, we have to go and see Mr Bhopal. He's in a hell of a state. Michael, Josh and Hana. Would any of you able to come too. We can explain to your parents."

"I can go. Believe me they won't miss me at home." said Michael with a wry smile.

Turning to Speirs, Donald said. "Mr…John that gash on your head is a mess. It needs cleaned."

"I'll do it," said Kerry. "The first aid Kit is in Lab 2. Come with me."

As soon as he left the room Donald whispered.

"Peter, they don't have the vaccine. We swapped it. Would you be willing to take it to Prof Singh in Oxford? You'd have to do it tonight, before they discover they don't actually have it."

"I could drive there. I'll head off in the direction

of my house initially then go straight there. If I'm back before tomorrow they won't know."

"We can't be certain that Singh and his colleagues can be trusted. If they subsequently discover it was you, you'd be in their crosshairs. Are you sure you want to do this?"

"I've never met Singh. I'm sure he won't recognise me. All I need to do is hand it over. Right?"

"We'll hold on to half of it here in case Singh isn't playing square with us. It's terrible we can trust no-one!"

A few minutes later, Peter was packing up his rucksack with a syringe containing half of the vaccine in a cold storage container.

"Peter. One more time. Are you sure you want to do this?"

"Yes. Just tell me where in Oxford I have to take it."

"I'll send you the address while you're on your way after I've phoned Singh to confirm the delivery location. Alan, are you OK to do the analyses on the kids?" Turning to them. "Guys would you give us some more saliva samples, before you head off? I'll set up a video call first thing tomorrow morning. There are just so many moving parts here!"

Before leaving Peter said

"Three people have been seriously assaulted. Should we not be calling the police?"

Speirs, with a bandage on his wound, returned with Kerry just in time to hear him.

"It's a good point but are you ready to blow this wide open? Because that's what'll happen. There's no way PC Plod will keep this under wraps. However, I'm escalating this with my Boss. He has to take it seriously now, if for no other reason than he'll have egg all over his face if he doesn't."

"I'll arrange a video call tomorrow at 7.30 AM," shouted Donald as they departed.

"Mr Speirs. That gash needs stitches, you need to go to the emergency room," said Kerry.

"That's OK, Kerry, we have our own resources for that. Donald, I'll call you later," he shouted as he closed the door. "

"Let me know how it goes with the headmaster Kerry," said Donald. "We can't keep a lid on this much longer. Let Johnny know what's happened too."

Donald winced as he hurried to catch up with Alan who was walking briskly across the campus to Chi-Gen.

"Hang on, wounded man coming."

Alan walked back to his friend

"Want a piggyback then?"

"Haha, a bit of respect would do."

"I got hit too you know!"

When they arrived at Chi-Gen the laboratory was quiet. Alan enquired after Emilio from one of the scientists and was told he had gone to Oxford at short notice to discuss future research plans.

"Just as long as he doesn't bump into Peter Munro," mumbled Alan.

"I'll call Singh when we leave here and ask him to make sure the handover is secure."

An hour later, the results were coming through on the kids' and Dr Huber's samples. They were all positive.

"We just have to check the family members now. I wonder how Kerry is getting on with the headmaster," said Donald.

CHAPTER 24

The meeting with Mr Bhopal was going badly. Kerry had tried to summarise the extent of the knowledge they had so far. He didn't seem to grasp the enormity of what Barton had done. He was pacing back and forward, speaking rapidly his head shaking from side to side.

"But all I can see is good! Now we'll be back to square one!"

"We won't be Mr Bhopal. We think the changes in people that have been infected will be long-lasting, so the improved concentration, better behaviour, these should all continue. It's the long-term side effects we don't know about," replied Kerry

"What about you Dr Huber and the other staff. You have all been fired."

"With six months' pay though," replied Brigitte who had received an email informing her of her immediate cessation of employment. "Not exactly a hardship."

"What about you Michael, how do you feel about this?" asked Mr Bhopal

"I guess, mixed is the answer. I think we all see the benefits of this, but we don't know if there may be other effects of which we are unaware or what the long term will hold. There's just so much we don't know. That's why we have to work with Kerry and her team."

"I've been trying to get a hold of Markov, but he's not replied so far. I was hoping he could be persuaded to change his mind about this. I think he's made the wrong tactical decision. Continuing to support the people who have been affected by this would play better."

"We need to find out how many people may have been affected. That includes you too Mr Bhopal. Would you give us a sample?"

The door between Mr Bhopal's and Mrs Ahmed's office had been ajar. She burst in.

"What about me? Could I have this? I had the flu immunization along with all the teachers. My Ayesha, she's trying to get pregnant. Could I have given it to her?"

"I think it's unlikely Mrs Ahmed, but we can test you and, if you're positive, Ayesha too. However, we're really concerned about managing how this is revealed. We think calling a meeting of the parents and older children in the school is needed, but only after we have some idea of how fast this has spread if at all. Until we know this it's better to say nothing and not cause unnecessary panic. Twenty-four more hours that's all."

"I don't know Kerry. If this is as serious as you suggest. We have to let people know," she replied frowning.

"OK how about calling a meeting for the day after tomorrow. By then we'll know how far it has spread. Although we won't know about other possible effects of the genetic changes at that point."

"OK. Will you address them?"

"Yes, but I'll bring some people with me who are experts. Can we take samples from you both? The children are going to get them from their families. Michael, I'll see you as planned in the café tomorrow."

Brigitte and Kerry stood in the foyer of the school clutching the samples. Kerry had phoned the limo company. They could hear Mr Bhopal consoling a tearful Mrs Ahmed catastrophising about her potentially affected daughter.

"I'm glad we decided not to mention the potential fertility problem. What are the chances of her keeping it a secret if that came out. I don't know about you, but I really need a big fucking drink," said Brigitte.

BRIAN MCKINSTRY

"Yup, I'm sure we could squeeze one in."

CHAPTER 25

The Californian Secure Youth Treatment Facility was a bleak functional building designed to hold what were considered to be the worst juvenile offenders. Three years ago, violence among inmates and against staff was common. Drug use was commonplace and there had been a couple of high-profile suicides.

Following a chance encounter at a Youth Facility Director's meeting, Caleb Farrel, who had recently been appointed Director had been approached by the Odyssey Initiative which offered an experimental package including enhanced healthcare, addiction counselling, psychology, education and a big investment in IT and IT training. All the organisation wanted in return was to observe the impact on the inmates of their intervention. It all seemed too good to be true. However, faced with a reducing budget and an increasingly vocal prisoner rights group, he swallowed his reservations believing that, if nothing else, it would look as though he was at least trying to do something.

The results had been outstanding. He had never seen anything like it in his long career. Rates of violence had fallen dramatically, and drug tests were increasingly returned negative. Literacy rates had soared, several inmates were doing college degrees long distance, some using their new-found skills to challenge their convictions and sentences. It had even rubbed off on the staff. He had never known morale to be so high.

Today, however, out of the blue he had received a message saying the project was being closed down. No reason was given. The two psychologists, the educationalist and the nurse who had been supplied by the project were equally in the dark. They had been exceptionally proud of their achievements, and rightly so he thought. They had however been informed that they would be given generous severance payments but were reminded that this would depend on adherence to the strict non-disclosure agreements they had signed. The director had had to sign one himself. He tried to phone the Odyssey headquarters, but there was just a recorded message saying that the company was no longer operating and an email address for outstanding accounts. Apparently, the facility could keep all the equipment they had been given.

His phone rang. Bernice, his secretary who had been in post since the facility opened thirty years ago and had worked her way through six different directors, was on the line. She could be a formidable ally but also a fearsome foe as some of his predecessors had discovered. She was a church-going Christian, who took her Lord's teachings seriously. She believed in the power of redemption, supported and sympathised with the families of the inmates, but was no push-over. Caleb had heard from one of the guards who went to the same church that she 'approved' of him; quite an honour he was told.

"What's this about Odyssey pulling out? It's the best thing to hit this place in years."

"I just heard this morning. The company seems to have ceased trading or something. I can't raise anyone there. It's a real disappointment."

"Those poor boys were just beginning to pull themselves up by their bootstraps. They had hope there for a while. How we gonna tell 'em?"

"I thought we could meet with a few of them and tell them, perhaps plan how to go forward. Who would you recommend we meet? We need to let the staff know. Would you call a meeting of the senior staff and the Odyssey staff?"

"You're free at 11.00 and Mr Novak and Mr.

Rossi are on duty. The Odyssey staff were told they were relieved of their duties immediately and could leave, but they are all in tidying up. I'll ask them if they'll attend. They're professional people and quite upset by this turn of events. I'd say the most sensible of boys are Darnell Williams and Tyrone Parker. Do you want everyone together or separate?"

"What do you think Bernice?"

"Well, normally, they'd all be seen separately, but on this occasion, I think everyone will be thinking the same way. How do we keep what we got goin'?"

Two hours later, two senior prison officers, two psychologists and an educationalist along with two inmates sat in a semi-circle in a small meeting room. Bernice sat to one side notebook in hand. The room was lit by two small windows high on the wall. Thanks to Odyssey money, the room had been brightly painted and fitted out with the latest computer and audiovisual equipment. All was quiet apart from the odd shout from the exercise yard below where a game of catch was in progress. They stood when the director entered. He waved them back to their seats. He outlined the news that he and the Odyssey staff had been given that morning and his futile efforts to find an explanation.

The prison officers made their disappointment

clear. Quite a bit of their workload had been taken up by the Odyssey team and there was no doubting the improved atmosphere in the facility which it had engendered. Like Bernice they queried why so sudden a cessation had occurred.

The Odyssey funded staff were bitterly disappointed. Graham Fairweather, a grey-haired man in his early fifties, one of the psychologists, said it had been the most worthwhile job he had ever had. He loved coming into work. He was now unemployed and had to find new work, although Odyssey had been generous with severance.

"They gave us six months' pay! Surely there's something suspicious about all of this. If this were down to a funding problem, how could they be so generous?"

"They've told us we can keep all the equipment. It must be worth hundreds of thousands of dollars," added the director.

"And what about the food and catering. That was subsidised too. I guess it'll be back to grits again," said the somewhat portly Mr Novak.

"Well," said the director. "Actually no. Odyssey suggested the dietary changes, and I'm sure you remember the resistance to that when it started! But I think you'll agree we have all been eating better. The thing is, since we cut back on the expensive stuff like meat and, as we're now growing a lot of our own summer vegetables, it's not costing any more than it did before. So that's at least something we can continue."

Darnell raised his hand.

"Yes Darnell," said the director.

"Some of us have been doin' a little checkin' since you told us this morning Suh. We got to thinkin'. There are a few things about this whole project which seem unusual."

He hesitated, the director nodded and gave him an open-handed gesture to continue.

"Dr Fairweather, have you ever in any of the places you worked seen results even approachin' what has happened in this facility?"

Fairweather shook his head.

"To be fair, Darnell we have never been resourced the way we have here."

"But so much has changed. I get that more time is being taken educating the boys here, I get that the lessons in logic prob'ly have improved the way people reason, I get that all this equipment has made us all, staff and inmates, feel a bit more valued. However, how does that explain the change in violence. Miss Bernice, you should close your ears for this part."

"Darnell, I've bin here thirty years. There ain't

nothin' that shocks me."

"The violence has almost stopped and the abuse. For example, when Tyrone came here three years ago. A handsome kid like him was picked on somethin' terrible. I recall night after night him cryin' himself to sleep. But that's all stopped. Now I'm not sayin' there no sex goin on now, but it's all pretty much consensual. For a while I wondered if you were puttin' somthin' in the food. I didn't care as long as it saved my ass… literally."

Tyrone flushed, and nodded. Several of the others looked down and nodded agreement. Bernice sighed, reached over and patted his shoulder.

"We weren't putting anything in the food, Darnell, I promise you. At least not that I know of," replied the director.

Turning to the educationalist Darnell continued.

"Mr. Johnson. I know you have been workin' really hard with the boys. Some didn't even know their letters when they arrived. Now they can all read, even the dumbest. I know the Odyssey method of recruiting students to teach other students, the courses they provided and all the equipment have helped. However, readin' about it, these methods ain't revolutionary and nothin' I've read has suggested the sort of success rate you have here."

"I agree. It's unprecedented, but not impossible if everything comes together at the same time."

"All seems a bit too good to be true. I figure there's more here we don' know about."

Tyrone raised his hand.

"Yes Tyrone."

"W-w- we ain't the only place that Odyssey is workin' in. Th-there's a school in some city called something like Eedinburge in a place called Scotland… th-that's the Braveheart place ain't it?"

"Yes, it's pronounced Edinburgh. I went to a conference there once. Lovely city," said the psychologist.

"W-Well, th-there's a newspaper article here about how the w-worst school in Scotland has suddenly got the highest exam results. Odyssey gets the c-credit."

"Well now, that *is* interesting. I wonder if they have had their funding cut too," said the director.

"One of the students is mentioned in the article. I called my sister and asked her to check. She's on Instagram. Least it looks like the same gal. I asked her to get her to follow her. Not heard anything yet," added Darnell

"Maybe I should just call the headmaster and ask?"

"Yes Suh. It's called St Julian's, but remember it's in a different time zone. Unlikely you'd get a reply right now."

"We need to put together a plan for continuing what we can without the Odyssey manpower. Guys I know you don't have to stay a minute longer, but would you help us plan some sort of transition?"

The former Odyssey staff nodded.

"Let's get going with that now and we can see what we can find out tomorrow."

CHAPTER 26

....

Hana was surprised to see a follow request from someone called Destiny in California. Normally she'd bin these, but the request mentioned Odyssey. Intrigued she connected. Within minutes she received a direct message.

- *Hi, my brother asked me to contact you. He is part of the Odyssey program in his secure youth treatment centre. It was cut today. He said you were part of that program too in Scotland. Is that true and were you cut too?*

Hana wasn't sure how to respond. She direct-messaged Michael copying in Destiny's message.

- *This could be the facility Kerry spoke about. It would be really useful to know more, but do we really know for certain this is genuine?*
- *I'll phone Kerry, but it looks genuine. Tell her she's right, the Odyssey program here is a matter of public record. Ask her for the details of the Institute and if there's a way to contact her brother, that we'd like to talk to him.*

Hana replied as Michael suggested and received.

- *Darnell ain't allowed to use social media. He's allowed contact with family by email and phone only. Everything he writes can be read by the Institute people. I'll let him know, He's phoning me later. What time is it in Scotland?*
- *9.00PM. I'll stay up to hear from you.*

Hana shared a bedroom with her younger sister Asha who took delight in telling her parents about any of Hana's transgressions and she had already been warned about hanging around with boys after school. Nonetheless, her spectacular exam performance was a source of pride for the family and, as any extra-curricular activities were always badged as 'educational', she got away with more than she might otherwise have. Asha, however, was suspicious, wondering when her big sister, who had planned a law career, had developed an interest in science and asked her with a sly grin in sotto voce if it was "Anything to do with the lovely Josh?" Hana smiled and mumbled. "One word and your life will be hell." Asha raised an eyebrow and decided to store this one up for another day.

Hana continued to read after their usual 'lights out' time. Her sister complained to their father, but Hana explained that there was a class test tomorrow and she felt unprepared for it.

"Alright but sitting test exhausted may not be good idea either," he replied in a strong Bengali accent.

Fortunately, Asha had fallen asleep when around midnight the phone vibrated. She turned off the light and went under the duvet.

- *Darnell says the institute director's going to phone your headmaster tomorrow. What do you think is going on?*
- *It's all a LOT more complicated than you might think. The headmaster may not be the best person to speak to. He doesn't know a lot of what's going on. I'd suggest one of the doctors that have been involved might be more helpful. We're sure that more than just money and educational techniques have been used.*
- *Some sort of drug?*
- *No worse than that, we think that our brains may have been altered.*
- *!!!!! You know that for certain?*
- *Not absolutely, but pretty sure.*
- *I knew it had to be something, I thought Darnell had found Jesus or something. He used to be a ball of fury when I visited, half the time making no sense, then in a matter of weeks, this new person was on the other side of the glass, asking about the family, telling me he was reading books! The only thing I ever saw him read before were the girlie mags he kept under his mattress. Whatever this is, it*

can't be all bad.

- *That's sort of what happened here too. We don't want to lose it. Destiny, tell Darnell what I told you and that the best person he and the director could speak to is probably Dr Stirling or Kerry Pearson. They discovered this. I'll get you their contact details."*
- *OK will get back to you*

Hana copied the text and sent it to Michael, hoping that she hadn't given away more than she should. But she was sure they had the right to know.

Michael responded within seconds.

- *Incredible. How many more sites are there? I'll phone Kerry and let her know.*

"Kerry? It's Michael here. Sorry to phone so late, but there's been a development."

"No problem, Michael. Brigitte, Donald, Alan and I are all together here, we're out for a... a meal."

Brigitte smiled as she shook her gin and tonic. The four were seated around a marble table near the horse-shoe shaped bar of the Café Royale, one of Edinburgh's classier bars. The bar was relatively quiet with just a murmur and the occasional clink of silverware coming from the few diners in the attached restaurant.

I'll put you on speaker. What do you have for

us?"

Michael outlined the exchange between Destiny and Hana.

"So, Hana told her that your brains may have been altered?" asked Donald looking concerned.

"Yes, but that's true isn't it, should she not have said it?"

The others around the table were frowning. Alan mouthed "Shit!"

"Well, we don't know for certain that's the case. Although we think it's likely. It is very interesting that the same thing that happened in Scotland has happened there…. It's just we were trying to keep it under wraps until we knew a bit more about it. It'll be a bit more difficult if people in the USA now know. Hard to believe the prison director won't feel the need to report this up the line. Still, I can understand why Hana felt she needed to tell Destiny. She's right that it's better that the director speak to one of us rather than Mr Bhopal. Send Destiny my number. I'm texting it now. I'm also sending my university details, so he knows that he is speaking to someone with some expertise. Tell Hana to hold back on revealing anything else just now. But tell her Well done. This is important information she's given us. See you tomorrow with the family samples as planned."

Donald turned to the others.

"We're going to have to move fast. Kerry, you need to get a message to Markov. Tell him it may be about to break in the States."

Kerry's phone started to ring again. Unknown number.

"Hello"

"Kerry, it's Johnny."

"Hi Johnny, remind me where we first met."

"Youth club, Corstorphine"

"Great, where are you?"

Kerry muted the phone.

"It's Johnny, wrong answer, something's up." She put the phone on speaker and unmuted

"In your apartment?"

"What are you doing there, you know that can't be safe"

"I saw some guys sniffing around our safe house and went there thinking they had probably already checked it."

"When are you coming home?"

"I was waiting for Barton to contact me so me and the others could talk with him."

"He's here Kerry."

There was yelp, then a rustling noise as the

phone was taken from him.

"Ms Pearson, delighted to finally speak to you." An oily Texan accent.

"Mr. Barton, I presume. We saw your plane was on the way here. No need to play the hard guy with Johnny. I was the one who wanted to meet *you*. I had hoped we could be civilised."

"Civilisation and its defence are dear to my heart Ms Pearson. Let's arrange to meet, but in the meantime, I think I'll hold on to your dear Johnny; and how hard we play with him will be entirely up to you."

"Where and when?"

There was a muffled shout in the background of "Stay away" followed quickly by a grunt.

"I do hope you have a bit more self-control than your friend. I'll send you the details of where and when. If I see anyone other than you it'll not go well for young Johnny. You have at most a few hours to save everything dear to you. By the way, your Mom and Pa, they send their love."

The phone went dead.

"Shit!" said Alan.

"We have to phone Speirs," said Donald.

"No! We can't risk that! He's threatened my Mum and Dad and Johnny."

"What do you think you can do that will make

them safe, Kerry? He's tying up loose ends here. He destroys the evidence and threatens to discredit us. I don't think any of us are safe least of all you."

Kerry's eyes were filling with tears her head shaking quickly from side to side. Speaking rapidly now her pitch rising,

"What if asks us just to drop it. Just to pretend I never found it. Most of the people who've been affected, well they'd probably have volunteered for it."

The others looked down, sympathy and resignation on their faces.

Donald blew a sigh through pursed lips.

"And what if it's leaping from person to person, possibly leaving them with God knows what sort of long-term consequences?"

"I have to go and see him."

"You need back-up, professional back-up, if you're going to do that."

"No. I caused this mess. I wrecked your lives and possibly my Mum and Dad's." Her voice broke, tears flowing freely.

"You wrecked nothing. Barton is the wrecking ball. You got in his way. You may yet save the world."

"It's my decision. I want to know what he has to say for himself. I want you to leave Speirs out it."

"OK, but don't go home yourself tonight. You can stay with…"

Her phone cheeped before he could finish. She showed it to Donald.

The message said an Uber would pick her up from Princes Street. It ended COME ALONE and switch off your phone!

"How did he know where we were? said Kerry.

"He's been one step ahead all along. Do you still have that tracker."

"Yes, but only Johnny can track it as far as I know."

"He may let Johnny go if he has you."

Kerry got up to leave.

"Kerry, before you go, message Markov first, tell him what Destiny said and that you're meeting Barton, then delete it. Tell him to phone me. I still think what you're doing is foolish. As soon as you can, let us know what is happening."

Kerry got up and without a backward glance left the bar. Brigitte looked stricken.

Kerry phoned her parents. *Please may they be there!*

"Kerry, what are you phoning at this time of night for? Is everything alright? "

"Yes mum, I had a missed call and thought it

might have been you. How are you both?"

"We're fine. We had a visit from such a nice American man this evening. He was hoping to speak to you. He said he hoped you'd be working together soon. He brought me flowers and left your father a bottle of Macallan malt! I hope you get the job; he'd be a great person to work with."

"Oh well, I'd better let you get to bed. I'll speak to you soon. Love you, Mum. Tell Dad I love him too."

"Of course. What's brought this on? Are you sure everything is alright?"

"Yes fine". Kerry switched off her phone, wiped tears from her eyes and headed to the building where she had been told to meet.

Back at the bar Brigitte was speaking.

"I can't believe we just let her go."

Alan was about to reply when he and Donald received simultaneous message.

"What tomorrow will look like if you cause trouble."

It had a link which led to a mock-up of the BBC news website. There were photographs of Johnny, Kerry, Donald and Alan. The headline read "Rogue boffins trash years of research" and went on to describe how a multimillion-pound project was destroyed by disaffected scientists angry at missing out on grants. The plausible lies were set alongside statements from the University and pharma company decrying their actions and announcing their suspension pending enquiries. It was very convincing.

"Well Alan, everything you said on that first night I told you about this thing may come to pass. I really have fucked things up for you. What do we do? I just wonder if he knows about Singh and has leaned on him too. We really need some serious firepower here to fight back. Where the hell is Markov?"

Donald's phone rang. Unknown number.

"Dr Stirling?" said a pleasant cockney voice. "I have Mr Markov for you"

"Eh, thank you. Eh put him on."

"Has he bugged our phones?" he mouthed to Alan.

"Dr Stirling. I just had a message from Kerry. Has she gone yet? If not stop her. Barton is dangerous and at the moment he feels cornered. We've been doing some work which clearly proves his involvement in all this, and he knows it."

"Kerry's worried because he has Johnny, and he's threatened her parents."

"Damn. Has she gone? Go after her now! Stop her!"

"OK! On my way."

Turning to Alan and Brigitte.

"We have to stop Kerry. Let's go."

The three raced out of the Café Royal, Donald still wincing from his injuries. Brigitte ran ahead. The pick-up point was just around the corner in Princes St. opposite Waverley train station. As she sprinted round the bend, she just caught sight of the door closing on a silver Uber. Despite a last-minute burst of speed, she couldn't reach it as it drove off towards the west of the city.

"Where's a damn traffic jam when you need one?!" she gasped as Alan and Donald caught her up."

Donald pressed redial on the phone. Natasha answered.

"Putting you through to Mr Markov"

"We missed her. She's gone."

"Well, I'm sorry to hear that. You need to tell Mr Speirs. Barton is dangerous."

"We might be able to find her if Johnny gets free."

"Please let me know if there's any news."

"Did she tell you about the news from the States? Not sure how long we can keep a lid on that. We're not sure if the removal of funding is helping."

"As you can imagine I was keen that we should not be seen to continue to support what is really an illegal operation. We did provide money for the transition. Depending on how this pans out we may be paying quite a bit more. Any word on the analyses yet?"

"As expected, all the children and the one member of staff we tested are positive. We get the families' samples tomorrow."

Donald remembered that Markov wouldn't have known about the raid on the laboratory.

"Barton's men paid us a visit at the lab and took away some samples as well as what we hope they'll think might be the vaccine used to deliver the genes. They didn't get it, and we're hoping that we'll be able to find out more about what's in it in the coming days.

There are a lot of people itching to come clean about all of this. We wanted to hold off until we know more about it, but we're really struggling to keep a lid on it."

"We would prefer to manage the revelation. I've a first-rate PR team working on different possible scenarios and how they'd be best presented. Please do nothing without speaking to me first."

"OK, but I think we're talking about a couple of days max before this explodes."

"Please contact me as soon as you have the

results of the families' samples. Everything hinges on those."

"We should have results by midday tomorrow, 4.00AM California. How early do you want to be woken?"

"When you have them. Use this number. Signing off now."

Donald turned to the others, shaking his head and scowling.

"He doesn't give a damn about Kerry, Johnny or anyone. The only thing he gives a shit about is himself and his company. He'll drop us like a stone when he no longer needs us. We can't trust him. I'm not sure how much we should've trusted Singh either. He talks a good talk but do we know he wasn't as involved in this as Sanchez?"

"Let's focus on the here and now," said Alan. "What are we going to do about Kerry. Maybe he's right we need to tell Speirs".

Donald nodded and phoned Speirs, he outlined all that had happened. Speirs listened without interruption to the end."

"OK, so we have no idea where she is. She has a tracker but without Johnny no means of finding her. We don't know where Johnny is or if he is still being held by Barton's men; which is likely. Did you get the number of the car that picked her up?"

Donald turned to Brigitte.

"It was an Uber. It was a silver Skoda Octavia KS 63 HYR"

"OK, well done Brigitte! At least we can find out where he took her. I suspect there will have been a car switch along the way, but it's a start," replied Speirs. "I'll phone you when we have anything."

CHAPTER 27

....

The Uber driver, a young Asian man, turned and said, "Royal Bank Head Office?"

That sounded odd to Kerry. She knew it was a large complex on the West of the city.

"Is that where you were told to go?" replied Kerry.

"Yes Miss, I always check though," he replied a little defensively.

"Of course, quite right. Were you told exactly where?"

"Yes Miss, outside reception."

The driver felt something was amiss. She looked anxious. He wondered why she didn't know where she was going.

"Is everything alright Miss?"

"Not really, but don't worry it's not your problem."

He thought of his wife's advice. "You're always worrying about other people. Worry about me and the children for a change!"

The traffic was light and after about 30 minutes he pulled into the drop-off beside the main entrance. There were a few lights on, but the area was deserted apart from a black Mercedes people carrier with blacked out windows ahead.

"Sorry," said Kerry. I've no change for a tip.

"That's OK. Don't worry. Are you *sure* you're OK Miss?"

"Fine," she smiled. "Thank you for asking though."

Two tall muscular men got out of the people carrier, impassive, focused. Salim had seen their type before in Afghanistan. It was because of men like them he had fled the country. His unease doubled, but what could he do? He checked his dash cam. It was on. He pretended to look at his phone as Kerry got into the back of the van. When it set off, despite his wife's entreaties echoing in his head, he followed. He passed quickly through the exit barrier, keeping them at a distance but in sight.

The van drove towards the airport but took a detour around the rear. This part was less well lit, the car moving from pool of light to pool of light from the overhead LEDs. At the far end of the airport, it passed through a security barrier. This was as far as he could go, but he watched as the vehicle headed towards a jet parked off to one side of the runway.

Salim now knew something was very wrong. This girl hadn't even known where she was going and now was being taken to a private jet. Was she being trafficked? He had picked up many sex workers in his job. Nice girls most of them, down on their luck, but she didn't look like them in her jeans and hoody. Should he phone the police? Would they care or think he was wasting their time. All he could say was that he had dropped a worried looking girl off at the airport and had jumped to the conclusion that she was being abducted. His previous run-ins with the police hadn't been that positive. Before he worked cashless for Uber, people had run off without paying and one had robbed him at knifepoint. Then, the police he spoke to looked at him as if he was making it up and spent more time checking his immigration status and his right to work in this country. He shook his head and told himself to forget it. His wife was right. It wasn't his problem. He was about to drive off when his phone rang.

"Good evening. Mr Kharzai? Sorry to bother you. This is Lothian and Borders police. We're making enquiries about a young woman about whom we're concerned. We believe you may have just picked her up," said Speirs.

"I knew there was something wrong! I know where she is."

Salim went on to describe what had happened and his concerns. He had dash cam footage if they needed it.

"Well done Mr Kharzai. You have been very helpful."

Speirs phoned flight control at Edinburgh airport. A private jet had posted a flight plan to Rashwastan scheduled take-off in sixty minutes. He made it clear that it was not to be cleared for flight until he said so. The controllers were to make any sort of plausible excuse.

He phoned Donald.

"I want a straight answer Donald. On a scale of one to a hundred how certain are you that this thing is spreading person to person."

"100%, but we don't know at what rate. It could be slow like tuberculosis or fast like influenza. I suspect it is somewhere in between."

"Is it containable?"

"We don't know. At the moment, it looks that way, but we need to know more. When we get the test results from the children's families, we'll have more of an idea. I think we have to try and do something though."

"OK. We need to find out what Kerry has

gleaned."

"Where is she?"

"At the airport on Barton's private jet."

"But he could take her anywhere!"

"I've arranged for the flight to be grounded. Security at the airport is keeping an eye on it and my men and I are on the way."

Speirs could hear an incoming call and put Donald on hold. About two minutes later he picked up again.

"Barton's captain has just posted a new flight plan to Rashwastan now for immediate departure. He's been asked to put that on hold because of "an emergency landing". We're going in."

CHAPTER 28

Kerry sat in the rear of the people carrier. The men who had picked her up looked ex-military to her. Unlike the visitors to the lab, they were unmasked and wore dark well-cut suits. Both had close shaved heads one of which bore several scars. She revised her opinion from ex-soldier to just thugs, or maybe a bit of both. They were polite but assertive. They had checked her phone was off and removed the battery, but they returned it to her in two parts. She felt slightly easier, believing that they wouldn't have done that if they hadn't intended to let her go.

I'm pathetic, but I'd have been very upset to lose that fancy new phone.

They said nothing as they drove the short distance to the far end of the airport where a large private jet stood, gangway down, dim light bleeding from the doorway.

Kerry's stomach was turning. She started to sweat.

Oh God, they are going to abduct me!

Her mind raced through different scenarios. It wasn't too late to make a run for it, but then she remembered Johnny and the veiled threat to her parents. She had to stay. No-one would know where she was, although Josh might tell them in the morning that the jet had been in Edinburgh, by then she could be God knows where. The door opened.

"This way Miss," from the unscarred shaved head. *Was that a South African accent?*

Kerry climbed down from the Mercedes and up the aircraft steps. Before admitting her, a female dressed as a flight attendant carefully searched her and declared her clean. The inside of the jet was dimly lit, richly furnished in white leather and walnut and had a pleasant smell which Kerry couldn't place. Quiet classical music was playing. A middle-aged man at the back of the plane watched her enter, gave a half smile and indicated the seat opposite. This must be Barton, she thought. She had had no idea what he looked like. Odd, Markov's face was everywhere, but Barton, for all his wealth and fame had managed to dodge the limelight in recent years.

As she moved closer, she took in a slim, pale-faced-clean shaven man, brown eyes, thinning on top, an earpiece in his right ear. To her surprise he was in what looked like a well-worn

Adidas track suit. This was one of the richest men in the world, wearing something even her poor brother would have thought was a little chavvy.

"Good evening, Kerry. Thank you for joining me," he murmured in a mellifluous Southern accent.

"Did I really have a choice?"

"We always have choices Kerry. We just have to decide what we're prepared to sacrifice for them," he said with a wry smile.

"What do you want Mr Barton?"

"Why, straight to the point. I like that," his smile broader but not quite making it to his eyes. "I want you and your colleagues to stop. Just stop. All I've tried to do is give some very disadvantaged young people a leg up, albeit not in a very conventional way. Is that such a crime?"

Kerry resisted the impulse to shout back at him. *He doesn't know the extent of what we know yet*. She took a breath and replied in as even a tone as she could muster.

"The intention may have been noble, but do the ends really justify the means? You could have researched and developed this properly and, hell, if it had worked people would have paid for it. Why did you not go down that route, properly testing it in trials, observing long-term outcomes?

"I suppose I could say it's not my style. I have always been the sort of guy who just likes to get things done. It's always worked before for me. Can you just imagine the push back we would have got from all the woke liberals accusing us of mind control or undermining so called civil liberties? Hell, some of the world's biggest scientific advances have never been subjected to your randomised controlled trials from parachutes to penicillin for heaven's sake!"

Kerry knew she needed to maintain her calm. This was an opportunity to find out more about the project. She told herself to get off her high horse.

"It is a stunning advance," she admitted looking down and nodding her head slightly. "We could hardly believe what we were seeing. How on earth have you achieved this in such a short time? No-one in the world is even close to doing what you have done. You must be at least ten years ahead of everyone else."

Barton hesitated and looked a little past her.

Is he listening to something?

He turned his attention to her again.

"Why thank you. Much appreciated. "

"You're a tech guy. I had no idea you were interested in biology. I looked you up. It's all quantum computing, generative AI, large language models. Shit, that's it, isn't it? That's the connection."

Barton smiled. Kerry could see her flattery working, but again he seemed slightly distracted.

"Sorry Mr Barton. Are you listening to someone. Is someone else watching us?"

"I'm sorry Kerry. I have an AI digital assistant Janus who nags me with what she thinks is good advice. Just now warning me not to say too much," he replied with a smile.

"However, I'm going to take a chance. You're right. Put together the worlds most advanced quantum computer with state-of-the-art artificial intelligence programs alongside the collected genomic, medical and social data of every biobank in the world and the genetic changes required to improve the race just pop out. Use those same tools to model changes in CRISPR technology and viral vectors and there you have it. It's a revolution. What we have done so far is just a test bed.

Think of it. A world without crime, addiction, stupidity. Who wouldn't want that?"

Who indeed thought Kerry. She decided to go for more.

"We got the impression, although we can't be certain, that the changes may also affect fertility. Are we wrong?"

The smile disappeared. He was listening again.

"Impressive. May I ask how you worked that out?"

"An AI algorithm, probably based on one of your designs."

"Touché! Now there's an irony. My views on overpopulation are well known. Let's talk about that though. What is it that most people in the world want Kerry?"

"Health, a safe place to live, enough money to eat well."

"Yes, bang on, the basic Maslow's needs, but what do you think the *rich* world wants?"

Kerry hesitated and then with a resigned sigh,

"More."

"Yes, more of everything," continued Markov on the same even tone. "Yet the whole world can't have what you and I have now. We are destroying the world so that the few miserable years we do have are spent in relative luxury. We spend our resources as if there is no tomorrow… and for many there is no tomorrow. They think they'll be long dead before the climate collapses so won't pay for the consequences of their profligacy. Unscrupulous politicians in hock to purveyors of dirty energy assure the ignorant of their right to consume, mocking or demonising those who try to warn them.

In the poor world people are pumping out children in the hope that they'll be supported by them one day. They have nothing, so nothing to lose. They are caught in a vicious cycle of poor education and ravaged intellect, often borne of malnutrition."

"But there are signs that the population growth is slowing."

"Too little too late, the African population is estimated to quadruple to 4.2 billion in the next 100 years. Carbon dioxide levels in the atmosphere are reaching a tipping point. Our AIs give a 90% chance of irreversible runaway greenhouse effect in the next fifty years. I'll be dead, but this is your world, Kerry. One that my generation has destroyed. The politicians are too craven to do anything about it. Someone needed to take action."

"Then why not give people the choice? There are plenty of people who would sacrifice fertility for what you're offering."

He raised his eyebrows, smiling once more, now speaking enthusiastically.

"That was the original plan, once we had proof of concept, but then Janus… the AI, modelled the likely reactions to the technology. Most people in this world have very little choice about what happens in their lives Kerry. Most, only just get by. Most, addled by poor diet or disease, aren't smart enough or educated enough to see the bigger picture. Those most likely to opt for this offering would be people already of above average intelligence who wanted their children to be a bit smarter, possibly keeping one child to breed. The major religions and not a few despotic or manipulative politicians would limit it, possibly to social and political groups or races they'd like to see the back of. As always those most influenced against the innovation would be the very people we most wanted to stop breeding. The impact would be slower than it needed to be to save the world."

"So, you did intend to fix it to spread faster."

The smile disappeared.

"My, my, Kerry, let's not get paranoid. And just what makes you think that?"

Kerry blew through pursed lips, looked down then up and with a grimace which made Barton flinch a little shouted,

"Paranoid! Paranoid! You know if you hadn't played hardball with me and had just left me to it, it would probably have been years before I'd have made the connection between St Julian's and this. It was a quirky finding in a PhD project for God's sake! Instead of just keeping an eye on things and seeing what developed, you made me out to be a criminal. Then you trashed ScotGene! That biobank was ten years in the making and has facilitated countless research projects. Talk about a sledgehammer to crack a nut! I can't believe your supersmart AI came up with that."

"You'd posted your query online, for God's sake. We had to get rid of it and to make sure you didn't do it again. We also needed to get rid of the evidence. For what it's worth I regret my hasty actions now. Things got a little out of hand. However, we have the opportunity to contain these problems. I want to make you an offer."

Here we go. Another offer I can't refuse.

"For your silence, we agree to stop the program where it is right now and observe the long-term outcomes."

"How can you stop it when it's spreading from person to person without a vaccine."

Again, he was listening.

"We had heard that you'd made that false allegation."

"We have proof of it. We know that the changes the virus has made go well beyond improved cognition, we have evidence of non-vaccine spread. I can't believe you let a *machine* make a decision that could destroy humankind."

"The *machine*, as you put it was programmed specifically to create an intervention which would curb and *improve* but *not* destroy humankind. No matter, I'm getting the impression you don't want to take my generous offer. That will have consequences."

Kerry hesitated. This man was dangerous.

"I haven't said that" she said quickly. I just don't think our group being silent will keep your secret for long."

"I only need a few years. One way or another this is happening; the wheels are already in motion. All we're debating now is how fast they'll spin."

The jet captain came out of the cockpit and nodded to Barton.

"Excuse me Kerry, I won't be a minute."

He was speaking quietly to the captain and at times was listening to his assistant.

Kerry's anxiety was rising. "Are they going to abduct me. Are they mad?! What would that achieve?"

"Sorry about that Kerry. A minor hitch. I think you were telling me that you hadn't completely made up your mind to oppose me."

Barton tipped his head to one side displaying what Kerry assumed was meant to be a concerned and reasonable look.

"As I see it you have two options. Forget this all happened! Disappear to travel the world with Johnny for a while, with a very generous payoff!" The smile disappeared. "The alternative is to see you and your friends' careers ended and your boyfriend almost certainly in jail. Your mother and father have had so much to cope with over the last couple of years do you want to add to that? Particularly if in the long run it is all for nothing."

Kerry opened her mouth to answer when the captain came into the cabin again.

"Sir, you should see this."

Barton looked out of the porthole. Two police cars had pulled up in front of and beside the jet.

"I warned you Kerry. Now you can reap what you have sown."

"I know nothing about this! Nobody knows I'm here. I didn't know where I was going for God's sake!"

There was a knock at the door. Barton nodded to the flight attendant. Speirs came in accompanied by a uniformed police officer.

"Sir, I'm a roving ambassador for the state of Rashwastan and have full diplomatic immunity. You're currently trespassing on what is Rashwastani sovereign property."

"Actually Sir, I think you'll find your attendant here invited us in. We haven't come for you sir but have reason to believe you're harbouring a suspected felon."

"I'm harbouring no-one. Ms Pearson is here of her own accord. Are you not Ms Pearson? I was unaware of any criminality on her part."

"Kerry Pearson, I'm arresting you under the Computer Misuse Act 1990. You do not have to say anything. But it may harm your defence if you do not mention when questioned something which you later rely on in court. Anything you do say may be given in evidence. Come with us please."

Kerry, open eyed and open mouthed, cast a sideways glance of incomprehension at Barton as she was led out of the cabin.

"I'm sorry to have intruded Sir. Thank you for your co-operation. May I ask you why Ms Pearson was visiting you."

"No sir you may not. Unless you plan to arrest me, I would ask that you leave my airplane," spat Barton, furious that the hold he thought he had had over Kerry had just been neutralised. He turned to the captain. "Get us out of here."

At the bottom of the aircraft stair, Speirs opened the back door of the waiting police car and indicated to Kerry to enter. The steps of the jet rose up behind them.

Closing the door, he instructed the uniformed police officer to drive. As they were leaving the private part of the airport Barton's jet was starting to taxi.

"Don't worry Kerry, you're not under arrest. We believe he was about to take off and were concerned he was going to take you with him. If he had got you to Rashwastan, we couldn't have helped you and he'd have had an irresistible hold over Donald and Johnny. They'd never risk anything happening to you."

"I was so relieved to see you come through that door, although when you started reading my rights, I thought what a creep! I shouldn't have doubted you. But how did you know where I was. Did Josh track the plane?"

"No, you can thank your Uber driver Mr Kharzai. He very presciently thought there was something fishy going on and that you were in trouble, so he followed the car."

"And I didn't even give him a tip!"

Kerry looked out of the car window as Barton's jet rose in the night sky strobe light flashing.

"That bastard admitted everything. He is sure this thing is going unfurl across the world. All he was concerned about was how quickly it was going to happen. I think he wanted to be alive to see the result of his work."

"It's all got to come out now Kerry. You're going to be the centre of a maelstrom in a few days as will those poor kids at St Julian's."

"Is there no way we can keep them out of this?"

"Maybe for a while, but the press will dig and dig until they get there in the end."

"Those kids don't know about the fertility problem. We didn't tell them because we weren't sure, but Barton has admitted it. We need to find out how it works, if it is 100% effective or will just result in reduced fertility and if it can be reversed. We also need to know how fast it is spreading."

"We're running out of time Kerry. Someone is going to break this soon."

"We need to let Markov know what happened this evening. He has the resources to manage this. Yes, I know his focus will be purely on what's good for his company, but at the moment it looks like his interests, ours and the world's are aligned. The most vital information will be the test results from the family members. We'll have those tomorrow. Speaking of which I better let the rest of the team know I'm OK. May I use your phone? Bastards pulled mine to pieces."

CHAPTER 29

....

Donald, Alana and Brigitte stood outside the Café Royal.

"I can't believe we just let her go like that," said Brigitte frowning.

"I don't see how we could have stopped her," replied Donald. "Once Kerry makes up her mind…"

"What do you think he's going to do? Why did he need to see her face to face? He could have exacted promises from her with the threats to Johnny and her mum and dad. Did Speirs give you the impression she was in danger?" said Brigitte.

"He was pretty definite she shouldn't go. Maybe Barton just needed to see her to impress on her how powerful he is or possibly try to reassure her that the virus is not dangerous. I'm beginning to wonder what the limits of what Barton might do are. Hell, I don't know! I just hope to God Speirs gets to her in time."

"OK where do we go now?"

"I think we should stick together until we find out what has happened to Kerry and then plan our next move. We can go to my flat," replied Donald.

"Not safe. After Kerry you'd definitely be next in his crosshairs. Why not stretch that giant bank balance Markov gave us. Let's stay at a hotel" said Alan nodding at the five-star Balmoral across the road.

"Too posh for me. There's an Ibis around the corner"

"You used to be fun, "said Alan with a grimace.

As they approached the door of the hotel Donald's phone rang, Speirs' number.

"What's happening? Is Kerry safe?"

"I am," replied Kerry. "Barton is on his way back to Rashwastan we think. Where are you? …OK we'll join you."

While they drove back into the city centre, Kerry re-installed the battery on her phone and asked Natasha to contact Markov. She then phoned Johnny. There was no reply on the first number she tried. She asked Speirs to swing past the safe house.

Markov phoned as they were driving there.

"Hi Kerry, I'm glad you're OK. The more we find out about James Barton the more unhinged he seems to have become. I was worried he'd try to kidnap you or worse."

"Well, as it turns out that came very close to happening and I have Mr. Speirs to thank for avoiding it. Barton more or less admitted that everything we suspected about the nature of the genetic manipulation and the transmissibility of the viral vector is true. There may be other things we haven't uncovered yet."

"We think we need to start letting authorities know about this. We don't know how far he got in the other centres; they were a few months behind Scotland, but I suspect they are all active. The one thing that is certain is it's going to be a mess. My advisors here suggest we start with the US and UK governments before involving the other countries, at least until we have a more definite idea of how big an impact the genetic changes will have on fertility and how fast it is spreading. On the other hand, we have to be very careful not to be seen to be hiding what could become a catastrophic pandemic if unchecked. It's hard to believe some governments won't make political capital out of this, and who could blame them."

"We won't know for certain about the likely degree of spread until after we get the results from the families tomorrow. What do you think Barton's next move will be? He thinks I've been arrested for the ScotGene hack. In a way that has eased the hold he thought he had over us."

"He may now be desperate and, as we know, he has form in shooting from the hip. That's why we must grab the narrative early. We have already set the wheels in motion. Contact me as soon as you have the family results." He ended the call.

They were approaching Johnny's safe house; a light bled through orange curtains in an upstairs room.

"I'll go first" said Speirs, pulling out a gun.

"Careful! Johnny doesn't know who's on whose side. Let me shout first."

They pushed the door open, and Kerry called his name. There was a muffled noise from above and the sound of furniture moving.

"Johnny, it's me your old Leith buddy. I'm OK and Barton is gone. I've got Speirs with me. We're coming up."

They had difficult pushing open the door and were met with grunts and a muffled cry when they did.

Johnny was on his side on the floor tied to a chair and gagged, wedged against the door. There was a large bruise on his right temple and his nose was swollen.

"Johnny! Those bastards!" She squeezed through the door and started to untie his gags and binds. When she had managed to move him, Speirs followed her in.

"I'm OK" whispered Johnny. "Just a bit sore and feeling a bit stupid that I let those guys get the drop on me. I was terrified of what they'd do to you." Kerry succumbed to an overwhelming impulse to hug him hard. Stopping when he winced, realising she was probably squeezing broken ribs.

"We should get you to hospital."

"No need, I've had worse. There's no serious harm done."

"Let's go then," said Speirs. "We're meeting the others."

In the car, Kerry recounted her meeting with Barton.

"Sounds like Markov was telling the truth after all. Who'd have thought it?" said Johnny in a resigned tone.

It was just after midnight when the group got together at the hotel.

Taking in the multiple bruises and abrasions of those present, Johnny coughed, winced then smiled.

"We look like we have all been on quite a night out! What's the game plan?"

Donald gave a wry grin and was about to speak when Kerry replied,

"I don't know what Markov has planned, he mentioned approaching authorities in the US and here, but we're still waiting for test results. We also have to hope that Peter has managed to get the sample of vaccine to Singh and that he can/will analyse it reasonably quickly."

"You're all welcome to stay here if you like, the budget will rise to it."

"I have another place said Johnny. Brigitte, come with Kerry and me, we have spare rooms."

CHAPTER 30

At 3.00AM Donald received a call from Speirs.

"It's out there. My boss has just phoned me. Said that they have been informed by Markov of an unethical trial conducted by the rogue ex-director of CreativeCom. My boss had the nerve to ask me what the hell I had been messing about with and why had I not told him what was going on! I told him I couldn't have made my concerns plainer to him if I had projected them on Edinburgh castle! Anyway, it's going to the highest level. There's a meeting planned tomorrow at 10 AM. Any chance you'll have your analyses ready by then?"

"Possibly, but what are the chances Barton knows about this? You said you suspected there were some highly placed people on his payroll."

"I think you should assume he already knows and wait for the counter strike"

The counter strike wasn't long in coming. A message from Johnny at 5.30 AM with a link to multiple news sites.

"*Boffins hail spectacular break-through in genetic research which can make us all geniuses.*"

"*An end in sight for addiction and anti-social behaviour claim scientists.*"

The press release, which purported to come from Emilio Sanchez, claimed that trials in several countries with 'pioneering volunteers' had shown stunning results. The articles went on to list the outcomes but did not identify the centres involved. Chi-Gen and CreativeCom were named as the sponsors of the research. The treatment was described as an easy to apply nasal spray. No mention was made of any potential side effect except for mild head-cold symptoms. Comments from a variety of politicians and medical 'experts' were appended, occasionally cautious but largely positive. The manufacturers hoped to make it available to buy soon.

"This is outrageous! Surely, they can't get away with that," exclaimed Alan

"Governments may be able to act fast on public health grounds, but even 'fast' takes time, particularly if new legislation is required. God! He is always one step ahead! Does he really have the facilities to prepare large batches of the virus?"

"Emilio mentioned a lab in Guangzhou. He also

has apparent carte blanche to do what he likes in Rashwastan, but I wouldn't have thought that country had the necessary scientific expertise or infrastructure."

"That can be bought though. What about India? It's the world's biggest vaccine producer? Could it be being manufactured there or perhaps the know-how could have come from there."

"The Russians too, could do this I suppose, and certainly the Americans."

"We need to get warnings out there as fast as possible about the potential effects of this 'miracle breakthrough'. Let's get up. We're not going to sleep now anyway"

"We still don't know a lot for certain though," Alan said with a sigh.

"We don't have *proof* yet, but we know what he told Kerry. Let's get ready for when the results confirm what we already know."

Donald replied to Johnny asking him to set up a conference call to the others.

Thirty minutes later. Everyone was online. Kerry took the lead, summarising what she had gleaned from Barton and the subsequent news posts. Speirs outlined the intended British response so far to Markov's warning and asked Markov what response he had had from the US government.

"Nothing yet. I'm not sure what the response is going to be. It's an election year. The current president is a sensible sort of guy, but the main opposition candidate, the current governor of California, is taking a very strong stance on law and order. I could see him hailing this as a solution rather than a threat."

"He might not be so keen if he sees it spreading to the non-criminal population," said Alan.

"We'll have to convincingly prove that." replied Kerry

Markov raised his hand.

"Our coms team have a statement ready to go, denying prime responsibility for this, that it was research conducted without our knowledge, and which questions the safety of the product. At this point we won't specifically say what the safety concerns are. I think we need to launch that now. In the meantime, they'll be watching the social media feeds and responding where need be. We have also prepared a statement for Chi-Gen. It's probably best if it comes from you Professor Singh."

"Please. Call me Raj. I've a meeting of the board later this morning, after our scheduled meeting."

"I'd bring that forward. How much do they know?"

"Nothing yet. I was waiting for definitive

evidence."

"They're in for a surprise then. I'd tell them not to get too comfortable with the share price which has risen on the rumours of all this. When the truth comes out it'll be a sadder story."

Alan interrupted.

"Professor Singh… Raj. Have you received the vaccine yet? Any progress on analysing the DNA sequence changes?"

"No, your colleague hasn't arrived yet. He was supposed to be delivering it here to my home. He phoned around 7.30 PM while he was in his car and gave me the impression he'd be arriving around midnight. I sent a message around 3.00AM, but although it has been received, he hasn't answered. Has he been in touch with you?"

Kerry and Donald exchanged a worried look.

"That's really not like him. I'll phone him now." said Kerry.

Singh continued.

"With regard to analysing the DNA sequence changes in the dataset you gave us Kerry; yes we have made some progress. Compared with the unaffected population there are specific micro-deletions on both the X and Y chromosomes. We're still working on these. Apparently, the changes in both are often found in people with reduced fertility. Perhaps the most concerning are the deletions we found on the Y chromosome. If the germ cells are affected, then any male children born will inherit these microdeletions. We suspect, but don't know, that these changes will reduce fertility, however, they may not render the individual completely sterile. I've a telephone meeting with some of my colleagues who are interested in fertility genetics later this morning. I'll know better then. It may be that sophisticated techniques may be required to restore fertility unless these gene changes can be reversed."

He continued. "We have a different group looking at some of the other specific changes. We specifically looked for DNA sequences thought to be associated with addictive behaviour and some of these were definitely less frequent in the affected individuals. The genetic basis for violent behaviour is much less well documented so we can't be sure if that has anything to do with the genetic alterations."

"Dynamite!" said Johnny smacking his fist against his palm.

Alan looked at Brigitte on the screen. She had tears in her eyes.

"Are you OK Brigitte. Hopefully Raj's right and something can be done about it. "

"It's OK," she replied shaking her head. I always thought I didn't want kids until now, but I suddenly realise I'd at least like to have had the option."

"You probably still do have," replied Alan.

"Shit sorry Brigitte. That was so crass of me" mumbled Johnny, turning towards her.

"Peter's not answering. It's not like him. Something's wrong!" interjected Kerry.

"Shit, why did we involve him? Johnny, I know this is extremely unlikely but is there any way you can find out where his phone is."

"Shouldn't be a problem if his phone is still on. Send me his number".

"His phone is in a service station just north of Birmingham," Johnny shouted.

"I'll get someone on to it," said Speirs. "Can you send me the exact location".

"It's coming up for time to meet the kids to get their families' samples. What do we tell them?"

"What we promised them… the truth," replied Brigitte.

"We also need to let Mr Bhopal know. We said we would meet the parents. That's going to be a hell of a meeting. The St Julian's parents aren't famed for their quiet restraint," said Kerry. "Remember that California prison director is going to phone you too Donald."

"Would you like me to handle that?" asked Markov.

"Perhaps you should contact him later. We saw the way Mr Bhopal reacted to losing his funding, I'm not sure the director will necessarily be in the right frame of mind to talk to you."

"Well, please tell him that what has happened was done without knowledge of, or permission from, the current company leadership and, that in the light of what we have now discovered, we'll continue to support the Institute as well as investing in research to ameliorate any possible adverse effects. I suggest that we say we're looking at potential drawbacks and that there are some worrying gene alterations the impact of which we don't yet know. Is that fair?"

"Might be better to be honest. If they find out about our specific concerns from other people … and, let's face it, I don't believe the US Government is any less leakproof than the UK one, they'll be very pissed off. I'll emphasise that at the moment these are just concerns; nothing we have proven yet."

"Can we say that to Mr Bhopal too… that you'll continue to support St Julian's?" asked Brigitte.

"Yes of course."

The meeting ended with an agreement to

call again after the results of the family specimens were known and the meeting with the UK government. The sky was beginning to brighten in Edinburgh as Kerry and Brigitte set out to meet the kids.

CHAPTER 31

Michael and Josh had decided not to give a full explanation to their families and instead described it as a school science genetics experiment.

"It's not a complete lie," said Michael

However, obtaining the specimens wasn't going as smoothly as they expected.

Hana's father, a political refugee, was wary of providing a sample.

"You never know what they can do with these things. I heard the Home Office is using these to say that people are imposters and sending them back."

"Dad, this is for a school project. The Home Office won't get anywhere near this," replied Hana, with a frustrated sigh. "And anyway, you aren't an imposter, so you don't need to worry." However, a sideways glance to his wife and the almost imperceptible shake of her head suggested that maybe he did.

"Let your daddy alone! Take my sample and your sister's. That should be enough for you. You spend enough time at that school anyway. It's about time you started doing a bit more around the house."

Hana knew when she was beaten. Her younger sister smirked and when she was having her cheek sample taken, made a fuss.

"Hana's hurting me, Mum! She almost tore my mouth!"

Fortunately, her mother wasn't having any of it.

"Be quiet, it's nothing."

Hana hoped the others were having fewer problems.

Michael had to wake his older brother Mark.

"What the fuck time is it?! Fuck off with that swab!"

"I'll pay you a pound."

"Five"

"OK."

The mouth opened, followed quickly by an open hand. The fee deposited, he added,

"Any time, *any* bodily secretion, I'm your man" said his brother with a wink and a grin, pushing his hand deep down under the covers."

Michael gave a disgusted look and went to

his parents' bedroom where his request was met with sleepy, resigned acquiescence. His young sister, up and dressed and preparing her breakfast, happily provided it.

Josh, whose parents praised and thanked the Lord every single day for the transformation in their son over the last two years, gladly submitted to the tests and bullied his two older brothers to do the same.

They met Kerry and Brigitte around 8.00AM at the café near their school.

"There are two samples here from the two younger sisters which we would expect to be positive, but none of the others have had the vaccination," said Michael. "Have you any news for us?"

"There have been quite few developments and there are one or two meetings to take place this morning. Would it be OK to leave off telling you about them until early this afternoon when we have these samples analysed. I promise you we'll let you know absolutely everything we know then," replied Kerry in a serious tone.

"Sounds ominous," said Hana. "Should we be worried?"

"I'm not going to lie to you. There are some troubling findings. We'll have a better idea of what's happened and what may be happening soon."

"Is this to do with this?" asked Josh holding up his phone with the 'Boffin's breakthrough' headline.

"Yes, and quite a bit more besides. You'll see St Julian's isn't named there, but, honestly, I don't know how long it's going to take for the newshounds to put two and two together. If you hear about press activity at the school, call me immediately. How will we meet this afternoon?"

"It's a half day. I could come to the lab," replied Michael.

"Josh and I are supposed to be in a chess tournament, but it's online," said Hana. We can say our video's broken and do it in the bus. The team we're up against are pretty hopeless so it should be a doddle."

Kerry smiled. *Changed days, St. Julian's winning chess tournaments! There was a time when there was hardly anyone who could play checkers.*

When Brigitte and Kerry arrived back at the lab, Johnny and Speirs were there. The mood was sombre.

"They found Peter. He was bundled in the back of his car unconscious. He's now in hospital and recovering. He seemed unmarked so it's not clear what the cause is. We suspect some sort of drug. Bastards poured alcohol on him to make it look like he was just drunk. At least we found him before the local police. The vaccine is gone."

"Well, if we were ever in doubt, we know what we're up against now. This guy will do anything. How long before he kills someone?" spat Kerry.

"Still don't have a whole lot of evidence that proves it's him behind it. He could find fairly straightforward explanations for just about everything we know so far, and he could say the money trail was fabricated by Markov. Otherwise, it would be just your word, Kerry, against his… and of course his armada of lawyers. Markov must be a worried man. While the heat is on, I doubt Barton will leave Rashwastan," said Speirs. "I'm going to report back to my boss. Remember the meeting at 10.00."

"Let's go across to Chi-Gen and run these analyses. I'll phone a virologist colleague to look at the vaccine we kept back to see if it contains a lentivirus. I wonder where Sanchez's got to? He's got to be concerned that Barton appears to have put him squarely in the crosshairs."

"I wonder if we could offer him a deal, he must know more."

CHAPTER 32

Back at St Julian's Mr Bhopal called Michael and Hana from their English class into his office. Michael had never seen him in such a state even in the bad old days when he had been a regular attender there. He was pacing back and forward and literally wringing his hands… something Michael had until then thought was just something you read about in books. He was very black-eyed and clearly had slept little since their last encounter.

"Any more news?" he asked in a very high-pitched version of his usual impeccable Oxbridge accent.

"Tell me, could Kerry possibly have got this wrong? Could it be she's just upset the people at CreativeCom and that they'll come round if she gives them an apology?"

He looked so desperate. Michael wondered about tossing him some sort of crumb of comfort, but Hana answered first.

"We think everything Kerry has said is true.

She also says there's more to come out, possibly worse if I'm guessing correctly. Don't worry about the financial support, CreativeCom are now working with us, and something tells me that if anything we'll be getting more."

Hana was attempting to smile, although at the back of her mind she wondered if CreativeCom would survive this, in which case the gravy train would definitely hit the buffers.

"At least that won't be so bad," he replied with a sigh and plonked his ample form down on his seat, with a loud creak.

"We'll have more information this afternoon," said Michael. "I promise you we'll let you know then. Now can we go back to our English class?"

Mr Bhopal sighed again and nodded. Hana thought he looked defeated. She had always thought of him as just a man who was very well paid for doing a job, but in that moment, she realised that he really cared about the school and the kids.

"Sir, thank you for everything you have done for us. No matter how this turns out we know that every day you have done your best for us."

Mr Bhopal sat up straight, astonished but with a slight smile and eyes filling.

"Why thank you Hana. You don't know how much that means to me," his voice breaking.

They left the office nodding to a worried

looking Mrs Ahmed as they went past.

"The last thing I feel like is Mrs Rossetti banging on about her 'beloved bard'," said Hana in a hammed-up accent. "Let's get a coffee in the form room. She thinks we're with the headmaster, she won't miss us."

Josh had a free period and was in the form room.

"Have you seen the latest?"

"What?"

Josh showed them his tablet. The narrative on twitter had changed from generally hailing an advance to conspiracy theorists suggesting that there was an Anglo-American plot to keep the breakthrough to themselves. They suggested that these countries had been stockpiling the treatment to boost the performance of their own people to give them an advantage, holding it back from the rest of the world, particularly the developing world, counselling caution because of 'alleged' side effects even though there wasn't a shred of real evidence for any. "*Once more the rich world hogs it all. It's the COVID vaccine story all over again. Well not this time!*" screeched one of the twitterati. "*Release this to the whole world!*"

"You can see their point," said Josh.

"In my, albeit short, life experience though, every so-called 'silver bullet' appears to have a lead lining," replied Michael. "I think Kerry and Donald are right to be cautious. Anyway, where have this crowd got all this info from. No-one here has said anything yet about side-effects. This has all got to be coming from Barton."

"Well, let's hope Kerry is true to her word and tells us everything they know this afternoon."

"Careful what you wish for Josh! Let's get some coffee, I really need it," added Michael.

CHAPTER 33

Policemen were milling about the entrance of the Chi-Gen laboratory when they entered. The receptionist called them over.

"Sorry Sir, we've had a break-in and the labs are closed."

"What? This place is like Fort Knox, how could that happen," exclaimed Alan

"It seems to have happened in the early hours of this morning. Whoever did it had full access to the building, we don't know how."

"But what about the iris identification?"

"Yes, we have the identity which was used, but we think it extremely unlikely that this person could have used it and that and it must have been copied or the system bypassed in some way. Must be a hell of a computer whiz to breakthrough this security."

Alan phoned Singh and told him. Almost immediately the receptionist's phone rang and what appeared to be a fairly intense debate followed. On hanging up, the now somewhat red-faced and resentful looking receptionist informed him that 'Apparently, against the advice of the police' he was to let them through.

Fortunately, the police, who were going floor to floor, hadn't reached their lab yet. One of the refrigerators had been jemmied open, but to their relief the Forrest 3000 sequencer had been left intact.

"Let's get to work, before the cops realise we're here and shut us down," said Alan.

The equipment worked like a dream. They only had to check for the presence of one particular genetic sequence and within forty-five minutes they had their results.

"Shit! All but one positive. Could we possibly have a contaminant? We should run it again.

The same result was returned. The genetic change was detected in every family member apart from Michael's mother.

"This is worrying. We clearly need to do much wider testing, but we have enough now to know that there's a serious risk of spread from person to person. We need to speak to Michael to see if he can think of any reason why his mum might have been spared"

"There are several possible reasons. Maybe she wasn't around when he or his sister were active with the virus, maybe she has a natural resistance to the viral vector. I wonder what effects if any it's had on these relatives? It's possible that the changes may only be noticeable in younger brains."

"Why thank you! I'm clearly still young."

"Just keep telling yourself that," said Alan grinning.

"It's time for the government meeting. Let's get across to my lab we can join it there."

They heard the police coming out of the lift in conversation with the receptionist as they slipped into the stairwell.

"I know sergeant, that's what I told my boss, but he insisted. They are through here," remarked the receptionist in a tired resigned tone which suggested that his job was full of many such trials.

"Well, that was close!" smiled Alan as they entered the main foyer. Luck stayed with them as one of the security officers was showing a policeman the security panel and they were able to sneak past and out through the barrier.

"Clearly Barton cracked their computer systems. We're lucky he didn't put the whole place off-line."

They had left their phones in Donald's lab, but on their return they found a message about the latest online chat from Josh.

"He's not wasting time, is he? Cleverly twisting the narrative. Only a matter of time before governments start asking questions and then it really hots up. What a mess!"

"It's 10.00, time to start the meeting." Donald called Kerry and Speirs to the conference room. Brigitte, who hadn't been formally invited, sat to one side out of view of the camera.

They were admitted into the meeting at 10.15. There were around ten people present and there had clearly been some discussion beforehand. The chairman, Lord Lazenby welcomed them, particularly Mr Markov who had joined them at 'an unearthly hour' from California. He suggested a round of introductions. The group included the home office secretary Philip Lawrence, the Scottish deputy first minister Shona MacFadyen, Director of the Security Service Sir Jeremy Cohen along with Speirs' boss Commander Malcolm Smith, the Chief Scientific officer Sir Andrew Ross, deputy Chief Medical Officers from Scotland and England, Professor Singh, a press officer and several senior civil servants.

Lord Lazenby briefly summarized why they were there. His tone seemed to question the need for such a high-level meeting normally reserved for national emergencies and hinted that there may have been an over-reaction. Speirs' boss was squirming uneasily in his seat. Lazenby asked Donald to describe the events leading up to the present day and his concerns around them. He turned to Kerry as if to offer her the opportunity to speak, but she nervously shook her head. Looking at the screen he saw several people scrolling phones and wondered how seriously they were taking this.

Donald started, a little hesitantly, but gradually gaining confidence. He outlined how the problem had come to light and their initial findings, the attempt to discredit Kerry, their meeting with Markov, the subsequent raid on the laboratory, the attempted abduction of Kerry, the destruction of the ScotGene biobank, the attack on Peter Munro and the content of Kerry's conversation with Barton. He went on to describe the break-in at the Chi-Gen laboratory and lastly the evidence they had found that morning for person-to-person spread of the virus.

Lazenby thanked him and asked Markov if there was anything to add. Markov apologised for any part his company had played in what had happened but wanted to assure the committee that if there was any sin, it was one of omission, poor oversight, but not completely unforgivable given the sophistication of the operation Barton had set in place and quite frankly the almost unbelievable scale and ambition of it.

Singh's contribution came next. He corroborated the information that Donald had given and emphasised the concerns he had about the potential unwanted effects of the genetic changes. However, 'as a scientist' he to say that, as yet, they had no evidence of any actual impact on fertility, the most serious concern.

Donald's phone cheeped while Singh was speaking. He was annoyed with himself for not having put it on silent, but noticed it was a message from Johnny marked urgent. He quickly checked it.

Philip Lawrence's wife is on the Odyssey board! Also, Jenkins, one of the civil servants formerly worked for the education secretary and was a paid advisor to the Rashwastan government. He met Barton last year. Checking the others.

A little surprised that Johnny had somehow hacked into the meeting unseen, Donald forwarded it to Speirs, whose eyes widened. He in turn forwarded it. On the screen Malcolm Smith looked to his phone just as Singh finished and pushed it toward Sir Jeremy Cohen. Sir Jeremy frowned.

Lazenby turned to Smith and asked him for his assessment. Smith looked towards Sir Jeremy. After some hesitation he said, "Before Mr Smith starts, we need to make it clear that Barton appears to have strong connections within the UK government and wider parliament as well as several scientific institutions.".

"Well, I don't expect any of us have such connections, although I suppose I should have asked for declarations of interest at the start. Would anyone care to declare an interest? No. I think you can continue Commander."

"With respect Sir. I don't believe that is correct," replied Commander Smith.

Lazenby raised the corner of his upper lip into a scowl and added in a resigned tone

"Perhaps you need to be more specific Commander."

"Mr Lawrence, your wife is on the board of Odyssey. I would regard that as an interest."

Lawrence gave a surprised and sceptical look then smiled.

"Really? She's on so many things. I wasn't aware of that. I can't see how that'd compromise me."

Lazenby sighed again.

"Come on Philip! Of course it does! You know better than that. I think you *will* have to recuse yourself."

Lawrence looked like he was going to explode. He cast a foul glance at Smith as he got up to leave.

"Anyone else?"

Smith stared at Jenkins, who looked down and said nothing. Smith shook his head and outlined Jenkins potential conflict of interest.

Lazenby looked like he was going to burst a blood vessel and in an exasperated tone said

"Oh, for God's sake! What on earth were you thinking Mr Jenkins! Please leave. I have to apologise to the meeting for not making this clear before. Can I just say now if anyone else has met Barton, worked with him in any sort of capacity please say so now!"

A young female civil servant from the foreign office tentatively raised her hand.

"Barton was on an interview panel when I applied for and won an internship at CreativeCom eight years ago, but I haven't met him since. The work I did there had nothing to do with this."

"He does get about this James Barton, but you may stay Ms Patel," replied Lazenby

Message from Johnny. *I think she's lying. Her departmental record shows she was in Naples in June last year for one day, supposedly on an educational trip. Barton's jet was there just for that day.*

This was forwarded to Smith. He looked at

it but decided that it was perhaps a little to circumstantial and it might be better to let her think she had got away with it. He wouldn't be surprised if Barton had hacked the whole meeting anyway.

"Your opinion Commander, please."

"My lord, I believe this may be a serious threat not only to the people of the UK but globally and, at the very least, one to our international reputation. As we have just seen this morning, James Barton has managed to inveigle himself at every level of our government and no doubt into many relevant scientific, educational and medical organisations throughout our country as well as others. He's demonstrated his desperation to stop us uncovering and stopping his plans."

"OK, well that couldn't be clearer. Any questions for our visitors?"

The English deputy Chief Scientist raised his hand.

"At the moment, we know that close family members have been infected. Have we any idea of spread to the wider population?"

Donald looked to Kerry again but answered.

"Ms Pearsons original work seemed to show a growing number of people affected. This research was limited to the ScotGene cohort, one which we know was enthusiastically supported by St Julian's so it may give a false impression of the infection rate. However, it would be surprising if it had not spread further. I myself was infected after a relatively casual association with the school."

The Scottish deputy medical officer raised her hand.

"Just to be clear, we seem confident that this genetic trait is passed by a virus and that at the moment all the evidence points to relatively positive effects. We suspect but don't know it may have a negative effect on fertility. How do you propose we see if there has been? I'd be reluctant to go public about this unless we had some evidence. It could cause real panic."

"But in the meantime, Barton is hinting that he'll make this stuff available online. He is also very cleverly manipulating social media to increase demand. I'd suggest very strongly we ban this in the UK and involve the WHO. To our knowledge there are sites all over the world where this has been distributed and it must be spreading rapidly."

"We don't know that yet though," replied the English deputy medical officer.

"Jesus this is COVID all over again! The house is on fire! We need to call the fire brigade, not check the thermostats!"

"OK, Dr Stirling," replied Lazenby assuming his

most emollient tone. "Let's try to keep calm here. We're very grateful for the information that you and your colleagues have provided, but **we** have to manage this now. Mr Markov, do you think we need to be as worried as Dr Stirling suggests?"

"I'm not an epidemiologist; the only viruses I know about are computer viruses. But it seems to me that this is like a trojan horse virus hidden in a program. A program that everyone thinks is brilliant and wants to use. The trojan sits in your system for a while before breaking out and causing havoc. You have to believe that James Barton is a man who is completely driven. He's been fixed on the idea of saving the Earth from humanity for years, his views becoming increasingly extreme year by year. It was one of main the reasons he was finally asked to leave CreativeCom. He is a genius and a perfectionist. He's clearly been planning this for years and were it not for Ms Pearson he would almost certainly have achieved his aim, which, despite the reservations expressed here today, is clearly to reduce the size of the human population, perhaps to zero. I'd be very worried indeed."

"As Professor Singh said, we don't know that yet, "said the English Deputy CMO leaning forward pronouncing the last five words slowly and clearly."

"He admitted it to Ms Pearson. That's good enough for me."

"Perhaps, but try to get that to hold up against a billionaire legal team."

"Use another billionaire legal team. CreativeCom will provide support."

There was a silence for a few seconds.

Lazenby looked from side to side.

"Well thank you all for your very helpful information. Please keep us appraised of any future developments. Here *in London* we're going to start planning our response. Please sign out. We'll be in touch soon about next steps."

Donald opened his mouth to speak but Speirs tightly gripped his arm and leaned forward to disconnect the call. He turned and spoke clearly and quietly

"Donald, I know this seems frustrating, but this is how government works. Believe me arguing at this point will just annoy them. It may take a little while for the penny to drop, but they'll soon realise how important this is. In the meantime, we need to be building up evidence of harm. Are there tests we could be doing on the affected people for example?"

Donald's phone was ringing. Markov. He put him on speaker.

"We can't wait for them to make up their minds we should start work on proving this is dangerous. Twin-tracking that with seeing if it can be reversed. Where do we start and who do we need"

Kerry, whose dismay up to that point had been evident, spoke.

"We don't know how the effect on fertility will be manifested, but I guess we could check out sex hormone levels and sperm counts, but we need to find a few more people who have been infected. Obviously, St Julian's is a start."

Donald inwardly laughed at the lack of difficulty in persuading teenage boys to produce semen samples but decided to keep the thought to himself.

"We need to bring in some infertility experts. This is way outside our skill set", said Alan.

"Professor Singh's group are still exploring other potential effects, there may be other stuff we don't know," added Markov.

"We have to get a hold of Sanchez if he is still in the country. He almost certainly knows more than he makes out."

"What about the social media side? Who will handle that?" asked Speirs.

"My team are on that. You should start to see the results of that quite soon," replied Markov.

Another message arrived from Johnny. *"See the latest"* with a link to BBC Scotland.

Police are rumoured to have made an arrest in the ScotGene hacking case. The world-renowned research BioBank was wantonly destroyed by hackers a week ago. Kerry Pearson, described as a 'failing student' at Edinburgh University has been identified as the person arrested. Police are on the look-out for her accomplices which include some well-known for their anarchist views. There was a picture of Kerry from the University website.

Almost immediately, Donald's desk phone rang.

"Hello? Oh, Good morning, Sir Basil. No, Peter Munro is in hospital following an attack. …. No Sir Basil, of course it wasn't Kerry Pearson. Peter has been working with Kerry Pearson… Yes I *have* seen the report on the BBC… No, she wasn't responsible for the ScotGene hack, and she's not been arrested by the police… I have a British Intelligence officer standing here alongside Kerry working with us. No! No! She shouldn't be suspended. She's done nothing wrong, in fact she is a hero, her work has uncovered an appalling conspiracy the nature of which will become clear only too soon. We'll get that libellous report taken down immediately."

He ended the call and turned to the others, with eyes, mouth and hands open wide in disbelief.

"That was Basil O'Leary the head of the medical school. Mr Markov is there anything that can be done about this post on the BBC. It needs to come down. We'll send the link."

Kerry attempted to copy the link

"Wow! It's already gone."

"There are clearly some advantages to working with tech billionaires!" murmured Alan, with a grin.

"We have people surveying all the major news sites and social media platforms, backed by legal teams and reacting as necessary," said Markov. "We are also starting to place warning messages. I'll warn you; you may be somewhat disturbed at the people we have enlisted, but they have millions of followers particularly among the more easily led sections of the population," added Markov.

Kerry could guess the sort of shock jock, vaccine denying conspiracists to whom he referred. Johnny was obsessed with them. All they were interested in was getting online hits. The more controversial the topic the more money they made.

"They could turn on us, just as easily."

"They certainly will if we don't get in first."

Alan phoned Singh to ask his advice on whom

they might approach who had an interest in the genetics of infertility. They came up with a shortlist of three but decided to let Johnny check them out before they called them, given that if they thought they were the best then Barton may have already got them. Two had grants from a foundation linked to Barton.

"Good God, has he nobbled everybody?!"

"I wonder how much idea they have about what is really going on. I suspect not a lot. I would be amazed if they wouldn't be horrified by what's unfolding."

"Sure, but they'll be just a little more resistant to begin with as they'll be worried about their funding stream."

"Unless of course we suggested that it is possible that their research had been used to help design the virus. In which case if they had any sense they'd be scrambling to help," added Singh, fully aware that he and his company fell squarely into that category.

"Let's stick with the 'uncontaminated' people first. Professor Joan Al Shahi works at Imperial. We call her first and see how we get on."

"I know her," said Alan. "It's been a while, but we worked together on a WHO project in Brazil, after the Porton Down trouble. She's a solid researcher and more importantly one with a social conscience. I'll contact her."

"Johnny, can you try to find Sanchez? My guess is he's holed up somewhere. He can't be happy that he's been hung out to dry by Barton. He may co-operate."

"We have the kids coming this afternoon and you have the American juvenile prison director calling then too. After we speak to them, we have to let Mr Bhopal know. Their parents too. It's only a matter of time before they start to suspect something is wrong and we need to get ahead of it."

"My boss has been trying to raise Barton, but he's been told that he is ill and cannot be disturbed. The UK ambassador to Rashwastan has requested an urgent meeting with their foreign secretary although she isn't hopeful of any sort of useful response. Barton apparently invested millions into several companies owned by high-ranking government members," said Speirs.

"What else can be done to stop him?"

"Well, if we can get governments behind us, freezing his assets would be a start, but that won't happen for a while."

"So basically nothing."

CHAPTER 34

Josh, Hana and Michael arrived at the lab at 1400. Josh and Hana had just seen off the competition from a prestigious private school on an online blitz chess tournament while travelling on the number 36 bus. At the end of the tournament, the teacher in charge of the opposition hinted rather strongly that Josh and Hana may have used a computer to cheat. Hana responded that they were more than happy to thrash them in person and to name the day. She was still fizzing about it when they arrived.

"OK Hana, let's leave it behind us!" said Josh. "We know they think we're scum and that they should've hammered us, but they're the ones nursing their egos not us. I'll phone Miss Cooper and tell her what was said. She'll enjoy getting stuck into that pompous prick!"

Kerry smiled as she listened to the interchange, thinking how good she'd be feeling if she were in their shoes at that moment. She remembered only too well the way other schools had talked about St Julian's and how nice it was for them to be the smug ones for a change.

Her outrage at the casual way these kids had been treated by Barton was partly tempered by seeing this play out, but now it was time to tell them what they knew and suspected. They couldn't hold off any longer. They needed their co-operation for further investigations.

"Hit us with it, Kerry!" said Michael. "Don't hold back, I don't think what you're about to tell us can be worse than anything we haven't already thought of ourselves."

"What have you been thinking of?"

"That as time goes by, we go back to being stupid or even stupider," replied Josh. "I read a story like that once."

"That it gives us brain tumours," said Hana. "Or we go mad."

"That it means we can't have kids," mumbled Michael. "That's what that guy wanted isn't it. To stop the lower orders breeding."

Kerry couldn't hide her surprise and looked at Brigitte.

"Oh God, I've that right, don't I?" said Michael catching the interchange

Kerry sighed and started at the beginning working through everything they had discovered, what was certain and what was suspected but unproven, what they thought should be their next steps. She also described her meeting with Barton and the discussion with the government that morning.

The kids sat quietly throughout sometimes looking at the floor. What seemed to upset them most was when they heard that it had spread to their families.

"My mum will be so upset if she doesn't get grandchildren," said Hana. "Her sisters back in Bangladesh are always bragging about them."

"Mine too. I just don't understand how my brothers have this, and it doesn't seem to have any impact on them," said Josh.

"Josh, your brothers have just created a video-game startup. You've seen it. You know how good it is. I know they were probably bright boys to begin with, but…" replied Hana

"Patrick has a girlfriend. He's serious about her. What if he can't have kids? Would she want to marry him?" he interrupted.

"Hang on. Let's not get ahead of ourselves. We don't know for certain what the impact is on fertility. It may work differently in different people. It may reduce your chances of having kids rather than stop it altogether, it may be reversible with treatment. We know there have still been some pregnancies at St Julian's. We need to find out more," Kerry interjected.

Michael considered his older brother Mark who had been a typical St Julian's graduate, no qualifications and no job. He recalled a recent conversation between Mark and his dad about something they had seen on the news and noted at the time that he sounded a lot more coherent than usual. He also realised that the daily mild but irritating abuse he had suffered from him ranging from sarcasm to rubbing knuckles on his head had stopped lately. He had put it down to maturation. Maybe it was something else. He turned to Kerry.

"My mum and dad split up for a while. She was away when we first got immunised," said Michael.

"Well, that explains your mum's result and it does suggest there's a relatively short window of infection. However, when that window is open, it seems to be very infectious and of course your families in turn could have infected other people, friends, workmates," replied Kerry.

"What do you need us to do next Kerry?" asked Josh.

"Well, first, Mr. Bhopal wants us to tell the parents and other children about this. We need to see if there really is an impact on fertility. This will involve some blood tests and ideally the males producing semen samples."

"Wow, there'll be a riot at St Julian's when you break this news," said Josh.

"Better we tell them than they hear it second hand. Don't you think," said Hana. "Is it OK to tell our own families?"

"I guess you can. Would it not be better they heard about it with the others? Then we can answer any questions they have," replied Kerry

"I'll go and see Mr Bhopal. We'll get a meeting set up."

Brigitte asked Kerry what the government people would think about this as they clearly wanted to be in control of the narrative and wouldn't approve of this early revelation.

"Bugger them! They're a bunch of corrupt, inept, pompous asses."

CHAPTER 35

Facility director Caleb Farrel calmly listened to what Donald told him about what they knew about Odyssey, the suspected viral vector, the genetic changes it caused, and their concerns about how it may yet manifest itself. Donald wasn't sure why, perhaps too many Hollywood apocalypse movies, but he had expected more of a gun-toting, shoot from the hip kind of response. Instead, Caleb revealed that they had already sussed that something odd was going on. His relaxed demeanour may have had something to do with a phone call his secretary had received an hour before restoring Odyssey support for the Institute. That had caused some celebration, but this had put the cork in it.

Caleb thanked Donald, asked him to keep him abreast of what was happening in the United Kingdom, but that he'd have to contact colleagues in the United States to take this further. He hung up and leaned back in his chair. From what he had heard, the Federal Government were already aware of this. He was annoyed and a little embarrassed that as an American citizen that he had had to hear about it from a British scientist.

His next call would be to the state Governor. Caleb despised Parsons. A billionaire, Democrat in name, but a social conservative. Caleb had seen him working at close quarters in meetings of other prison governors and facility directors. As a man of colour himself he winced at the memory of Parsons' casual dismissal of any ideas his black colleagues came forward with and his constant references to the race problem in prison. "What is it about you boys that you keep winding up there?" he had said, as if the follow up "I'm jokin', can't you take a joke?' somehow made that OK.

The call went as expected. Parsons listened without interruption although Caleb could hear the clacking of a keyboard, suggesting that he did not have his full attention. However, when Caleb finished he said.

"I had heard a whisper about this. Someone suggested I sell my shares in CreativeCom. You know anything about a connection there?"

Caleb shook his head reflecting that this was how people like Parsons became billionaires. Casually receiving nudges and winks about his old frat pals' insider trades, the privilege passing on to his own kids via Harvard, Yale or whatever Ivy League college he pledged them to. Caleb said he believed Odyssey and CreativeCom were connected.

"Well, that is interestin' must get on to my broker! Anyhow, so what you're saying is that this virus calms these guys down, gets them off dope and boosts their brains. Not only that but has the added advantage of stopping them producing another generation of criminals? Hell Caleb, what's not to like? We could offer this to people who are given long sentences with a guarantee to shorten it if they agree. At $100k a year to bang these boys up, we could save the state millions!"

Caleb, bristled at his use of 'boys' but stayed focused and mentioned the concerns that the virus was spreading beyond the immediate prison setting and that it is possible some of the guards, the prisoners' relatives, even some court officials may have been infected.

Parsons dismissed this, clearly excited at what he thought were the positive aspects.

"That could be a problem but what if we give it to them then put them in isolation? Heck, we managed with COVID!"

Caleb remembered only too well what the Governor had suggested they did with COVID in the prison. He had seen it as a solution rather than a problem and made a play of having 'personal concerns' about vaccination. At least so he said, although rumour had it, he had been first in the queue when it came on the market. Caleb shuddered to think this man was thinking of running for president.

Parsons continued. "Let me make a few calls. I'd keep this under wraps for the time being. The last thing we need is a bunch of woke liberals crawling out of the woodwork and battening this down before we make a plan."

Hanging up, Caleb thought about his own family. What if he had infected them? He and Martha had no plans for more kids, but like everyone else he wanted grandchildren. Could his kids have been infected? He thought about his son Luther's transformation in the last couple of years, from tearaway to model student. He sighed and shook his head. Almost certainly. Dr Stirling had said the fertility problem wasn't definite and that it may be able to be overcome. Caleb certainly hoped so. No point in saying anything to Martha yet until he knew more. He pressed his intercom and asked Bernice to recall the people in yesterday's meeting. To hell with the Governor, he wasn't keeping this under wraps when he, his staff and the prisoners were affected.

An hour later and the group sat grim-faced in the conference room.

"Well Darnell. You weren't wrong."

"I spoke to my sister, she told me some of this. I kinda knew there'd have to be a sting in the tail. What do we do?"

"Sue their asses is what we do!" said Novak.

"Dead right!" agreed Rossi.

Donald Johnson, the psychologist, looked thoughtful.

"It was quite a liberty they took. Anyone looked at the agreement we signed when we took the money? I've a vague recollection of signing some sort of consent form for research, but I'm not sure how well I read it."

"We all signed it s-sir," stammered Tyrone. "They gave us phone cards if we s-signed up."

"They didn't tell you they were cutting your balls off though, did they?!" shouted Novak.

"Let's not jump to conclusions too soon… we don't know for certain yet if it affects fertility. The scientist in the UK says as soon as they have more information on that they'll contact us."

"Suh", asked Darnell. "Do you think it would be possible for us to speak to some of the students in Scotland. See if we can find out more about what's goin' on. They may be more willin' to talk to us than some of the scientists."

"That's not a bad idea Darnell. Bernice, would

you change the computer privileges to allow Darnell and Tyrone to do this?" turning to the boys, "now don't you be abusing this now yuh hear!"

"What's next?" asked Graham Fairweather. I see we have our jobs back. I suspect we have our Scottish friends to thank for that."

"Still, I'm glad we still have the severance pay in our banks. Can you see Odyssey surviving this?" replied Johnson.

"I've been in touch with the governor," mumbled Caleb to universal sneers from the group.

"Sure, that went well," answered Fairweather sarcastically.

"He's looking into it," replied Caleb making a quotes sign. "He could hardly contain his enthusiasm for it. He sees it as a way to cut costs and no doubt claim credit to help him on his way to the White House. Dr Stirling the UK scientist said we should all get tested but that'd have to be arranged by our own people here in the USA. I suggest we wait until we hear from our own government and any further news our UK friends have. Until then I suggest we keep this to ourselves and not worry other people until we have a better idea of how big the problem is and how it can be addressed. It's better to go forward with a plan. The UK scientist said he'd contact me again tomorrow. I'll let you know as soon as I know anything."

CHAPTER 36

Early that day Mr. Bhopal's eyes had filled with tears as Kerry explained the background.

"I was only trying to do my best for them Kerry. I promise you. When they first approached me, they hinted at financial rewards if I could get the school on board, but I said I'd prefer any money to go to the school. I'd never, never have agreed if I had known this was going to happen. Oh God! What will the parents think! They are bound to be furious. Will you help break the news, Kerry?"

"Of course. I'll get Dr Stirling to come too, to answer any questions."

"I'm going to speak to them myself Kerry, but what did the children think of this? Do they blame me?"

"Not for a moment. No-one could have predicted this. The strange thing is, that if they could reverse it and go back to where they were before Odyssey, I don't think they would.

They like what they have become. Barton knew what he was doing. Of course, when they get older and settle down, they may start to think differently if they can't have children.

There may be things we can do to reverse the genetic changes or ameliorate their effects. When you think about what happened with COVID; a solution found in just under a year when the world's greatest minds focussed on it. Hopefully we can do the same again."

They called an urgent meeting for staff and parents the following evening. They discussed having a separate meeting for teachers in advance but decided as increasingly wild and inaccurate accounts were rapidly unfolding across social media that an early combined meeting would be better. The only thing the attendees had been told about this meeting was that the headmaster had some troubling news to impart to them and that it was essential that all staff and at least one parent came.

*

The school assembly hall had had the Odyssey treatment. The venue was brightly lit with rows of bright blue padded seating arranged on a spotless pale engineered wood floor. A large video screen at the front and several smaller screens down each side displayed the school badge and motto alternating with images of recent successes: the examination results; the soccer triumph in the local league; the chess trophy; the trip to Downing Street, Hana's victory in the Burns poetry contest. Even knowing what she did, Kerry couldn't help but be impressed. This was like prize giving at an elite school.

In the past St Julian's had abandoned such large meetings. In part because so few parents came, but worse because those that did sometimes took the opportunity to settle old scores, usually resulting in the police breaking it up.

As the room filled, much of the chatter was about the reason for the meeting. A portly woman with dyed-blonde hair in short skirt and sleeveless top sporting a tattoo of three children's names on her arm shouted at her old school pal a few rows ahead.

"Hey Lorna. Wi' ye look at this place! I kent it was tae good to last, it'll be money he's after."

"Aye, I expect he'll be getting the begging bowl oot afore the end of the evening."

"You could buy oor flat for the cost of that big screen. No way am ah coughing up."

"Still, they have done pretty well. Do you remember whit this place was like when we were here?"

"Man, it wis wild!"

"It wis very handy fae gettin dope tho," she

smiled.

"And a quick knee trembler behind the bicycle sheds!"

Both laughed.

"Ah, the good old days. The kids these days are sae serious. Oor Jamie disnae ken how to ha'e fun."

"Aye, but it is good see them gettin on ah s'pose. Oor Neil wants to go to university to study medicine. Can ye believe it?"

"I sometimes think they think they're a cut above us noo. Ashamed to be seen wi' us."

"I ken. I think that too sometimes. Sort of feel, well, left behind ken?" The smiles now gone both looking down.

"Still, we didnae have them for our benefit."

"As a recall neither of us planned them!" They laughed again.

Meanwhile near the back of the room, two men faced off scowling. Both stocky, one with a close shaved head, red chopped liver face, the other greying mullet and unshaven, both in denim bomber jackets.

"Charlie McGonigal! Whit rock did ye crawl oot from under. Did they finally let ye oot?"

"Dinnae think I dinnae know why I ended up there, Wilson. Ye fuckin' grass."

Wilson made a dive across the hall, but was

intercepted by Colin McLaren the gym teaching assistant, a former pupil and a Scotland under 21 boxing championship contender.

"Right stop the pair o' youse! You can take this ootside after. We're no wantin' trouble here this evening. This is important."

"What's it aboot Colin?" said the shaved head.

"Ah'm as much in the dark as you are. All the teachers had a three-line whip tae come, with nae details. But we're aw pretty sure it'll be nothin' good."

The hall was now almost full, school staff lining the sides eyeing the parents as if they were still kids.

"This is the biggest turn-out we've ever had!" said Mr Bhopal. "Typical it should be about this," he added sotto voce shaking his head. "Well let's get it over with."

As he stepped up to the podium which stood to the left of the front of the hall, his image appeared on the screens and the general hubbub started to subside.

"Ladies and gentlemen. Thank you all for coming this evening. I'm sure that you'll be wondering why I called you in and at such short notice.

Over the last three years you'll have seen extraordinary changes in the school. Not just in the buildings and equipment, but also in the development of the children. Their achievements have also been extraordinary. St Julian's has moved from having among the worst examination results in the country to among the best. This was achieved through the hard work of the staff and students but also as a result of a large investment from Odyssey. The reason I have called you this evening is because it has become increasingly clear that this investment had a darker side."

A murmur rippled through the audience. One voice louder than the others.

"Ah god dinnae tell us they're kiddie fiddlers"

There was concerned murmuring throughout the audience.

Mr Bhopal rapped the podium. "No nothing like that. I've asked Kerry Pearson a former pupil here to explain what we believe has been going on. Her colleague Dr Donald Stirling from Edinburgh University will also be able to answer any questions you have."

He nodded to Kerry.

Kerry rose and took his place at the podium. Every face, some well-known to her, turned towards her. The room uncharacteristically silent.

Slowly, and in as simple terms as she could manage, Kerry outlined the events as they had unfolded. She mentioned that many changes had been made to the genetic make-up of the children the consequences of which were as yet unknown. Finally, she delivered the bombshell that it was suspected that this likely had affected many family members too.

Multiple conversations broke out across the room. Many people looked thoughtful taking it in, some alarmed, some angry. Finally Michael Flannigan senior, stood up.

"So, what you're sayin' is that some big corporation has infected us with a virus which has probably made us more intelligent, but maybe more docile too. There was me thinkin' ah was brilliant for kicking the fags after thirty years and ten previous attempts. Was that aw down to that an aw"

"It may have been. Drug use fell dramatically in one group in America that has been given this treatment."

A woman in the front row turned to her husband, Jack Kelly, an alcoholic of many years who had been abstinent for 18 months. She nodded at him, and he stood up.

"Youse a' ken me. The toon drunk. Well, some o'youse will ken that ah'm dry now and huv been for a while. These guys shouldnae hae done this, but so far, I can see only good."

Flannigan stood up again. "Folks. There's gonnae be money in this. We can sue these fuckers. Pardon ma French. Class action here we come." He punched the air grinning.

This was greeted with more murmuring some head shaking as well as the odd smile and nod of agreement.

Malcolm Stewart the biology teacher, raised his hand. This was acknowledged by Kerry.

"What are we worried about Kerry? As Mr Kelly says, so far, it seems it's all good. Turning to Flannigan. "To sue someone, you have to show they have harmed you." Turning back to Kerry. "What have they done that has you worried?"

Kerry swallowed. This was the bit she was dreading. She looked out at the sea of worried expectant faces.

"We have a lot of people poring over the changes in the genes trying to work out what they may mean. Several areas of the genome that have been altered are associated with fertility. We don't know what effect it has, but that is certainly the area in which we're most concerned. That's why we would like as many of you as possible to help us with some tests to find out what if anything these changes have caused."

"Hang on! Are you saying they've neutered our kids…. and us!" yelled a red-headed man in the front row.

"We don't know that. That's what we need to

find out."

There was an explosion of chatter and concerned looks in the audience.

"As ah said. Someone will huvtae pay for this," shouted Flannigan with a gap-toothed grin.

Kerry noted Michael had flushed with embarrassment.

"Wid ye sit doon, shut up and let the lassie speak!" replied Mrs Flannigan.

"Whit dae ye need us tae do next," she continued.

"First, we need to find out how many people have been infected. All we need for that is a mouth swab. Many of you have already provided one in the past for ScotGene, but that information has been destroyed."

A voice from the back. "We heard that it was you that did that."

Kerry looked distraught and turned to Donald who stepped towards the microphone.

"The people who are behind this are extremely powerful. They are very angry that Kerry uncovered this plot before it had become unstoppable. They have tried to discredit her. She's the hero here not the villain."

"And what's in it fae you."

Donald hesitated, immediately wishing they hadn't taken Markov's money and worried they might be seen to be part of the problem.

Before he could reply, Charlie McGonigal slowly raised his bulk from the seat and turned to the speaker.

"Shut. The fuck. Up! This lassie is clearly here tae help us. Fuck sake ye know her Ma and Da she's ane o' us."

Brigitte raised her hand and Kerry made way for her at the podium.

"Hi, I'm Brigitte Huber the school psychologist. I want to make a point about what the kids may be facing. There's already a lot circulating on the internet about this. Some of you may have seen it but not realised that it was referring to St Julian's. The kids here have worked really hard and for the first time in years have been able to hold their heads high. We can't let this in any way diminish what they have done. Genes and equipment are only part of it, but they had to put the work in. However, you know what social media is like. You have to be ready for some negative trolling. There are a lot of people out there whose noses have been put out of joint by their success. They'll only be too happy to stick the knife in. Your kids'll need a lot of support over the coming days."

Mr Bhopal took to the podium again.

"We intend to address all the children tomorrow and tell them what has happened we felt we need to tell you and the teaching staff first. Kerry and Dr Stirling are here to answer any specific questions you many have"

Kerry spoke briefly to reiterate the need to determine how much this had spread and that kits for mouth swabs were at the back of the hall and that some of the senior students were on hand to show people who needed help how to take them. She promised that the results would be returned to them as soon as they knew them, with a follow up meeting on the implications. Until they knew what they were facing, scientists couldn't start to fight it.

It was over! The attendees formed orderly queues to provide samples. Kerry couldn't believe it. She had expected a riot. A few worried individuals, mainly teachers, came to speak to Kerry and Donald to ask specifically about whether it was likely they were affected and their plans to have children. One had already embarked on infertility treatment and was now pregnant. She mentioned the cost of the treatment and wondered if Odyssey was likely to pay for it. Kerry said she had no idea about what sort of compensation was likely to be available if any and indeed if the company was likely to survive this long enough to pay it out. Kerry however, felt her hopes rising that this successful assisted conception might indicate that if this person had the genetic transformation there was a way to overcome the fertility problems.

As Donald left the meeting there was a message from the Scottish deputy first minister asking him to join a Teams meeting that evening. He checked his watch and decided he had time to return to the lab with the specimens they had collected before then. Alan, Kerry and he had planned to spend the evening running the tests. There was also a message to call Johnny.

He pulled Kerry into an empty classroom and put him on speaker phone.

"I found Sanchez. He changed phones but switched on the new one in the same location… rookie error. He's in Edinburgh. A new block of flats in the West End. I can't pinpoint which one, but if you like I can do a reccy."

"Great let me know when you find him. Alan and I'll pay a visit."

"Also, I've been doing a bit of digging around that Westminster committee. The Scottish deputy first minister, Shona MacFadyen, has a connection with Barton, well indirect. Remember the Spitz lady?"

"Yes," said Kerry her lip curling contemptuously.

"She has had several meetings with Spitz. She also went to the Monza Grand Prix and spent a few days on a 'fact finding tour of educational facilities' in Milan, courtesy of guess who."

"I think Spitz's assertion that she knew nothing about what has been going on is beginning to look a little thin. However, it probably suits Markov not to recognise this as she is a direct link with his company."

"I've a contact there now, a girl-Friday/ factotum whom I got friendly with. She says that Spitz appears to have been sidelined," said Kerry.

"Anyway, it looks like Barton has a substantial number of people in his pocket."

"Let's see what Shona MacFadyen has to say this evening."

CHAPTER 37

On the teams meeting Shona MacFadyen was flanked by the Scottish Chief Medical Officer David O'Farrell and an administrative assistant whom she didn't deem worthy of an introduction. She scowled and went immediately on the attack. She was unhappy to hear first about this problem from her English counterpart and said that any concerns Donald had had should have been raised with the CMO. However, the important thing now was to avoid widespread panic. So far nothing so terribly bad had happened. Yes, the methods were unorthodox, but they had produced a good outcome, and we should be honoured in a way that Scotland had been chosen as a test bed. Any scaremongering about infertility should stop right away. In the meantime, he and his colleagues were to stop all work on the project and that the CMO would be appointing a new team to look at it in due course. He was reminded that tests on individuals for research purposes required proper ethical approval.

Donald listened in silence, grateful for the information that Johnny had shared with him. He was tired, he had been attacked by Barton's men, his body had been violated by his virus. He returned her scowl.

"Sorry Deputy First Minister, but I believe you'll have to recuse yourself from making these decisions."

"What?! How dare you..."

Donald interrupted, leaning forward to the camera and clearly pronouncing every word.

"You have had multiple meetings with high-ranking members of the organisation that is responsible for this disaster and have accepted lavish hospitality from them. You chose not to reveal this at the COBRA meeting, despite specifically being asked to reveal any such connections. I'll leave it to others to decide your motives for that, but when it comes to ethics, I don't think you're in a position to lecture anyone. Professor O'Farrell, I don't know how much Odyssey has involved you in their plans, but I have to tell you that you're under investigation too. Anything you want to come clean about now?"

O'Farrell looked furious but said nothing.

"Well, I don't hear any denials, So I'll tell you what's going to happen. We *are* going to carry on with our work, publishing it at every step. We'll also be revealing everything we know about the sordid connections you have with a company that has almost certainly sterilised a whole school of working-class children, a company whose head is on record as singing the praises of eugenics. I don't know what this guy has offered you both, but it must have been **huge** for you to agree to be part of this."

He hung up.

Later that evening Donald sent a wave of emails to colleagues around the world outlining his concerns about new genetic changes which had appeared in the ScotGene database, the attacks on the lab and his team, and the Scottish government attempts to stop further work. He provided links to multiple copies of the data they held, adding that more data would be available in the coming hours.

The result was instantaneous. The world's leading geneticists whose interest had already been piqued by the rapidly growing twitter traffic about the 'wonder treatment' on offer started contacting Donald.

Kerry sighed. "Oh well, it was only a matter of time anyway I suppose. It was always going to come out. Just annoying that a lot of other people will steal a march on us now. Good-bye paper in *Nature*. Good-bye Nobel prize," said Kerry.

"But let's face it Kerry it's better that the whole world starts looking for a solution and not just us."

"Just have to wait for Barton's backlash."

"Never mind Barton, I think you'll have pissed off the government. Possibly we should have run this past Markov and the others too".

"Oh, there's a missed voice message".

It was Basil O'Leary the head of the medical school. Donald shook his head.

"I don't have time for him."

"Aren't you going to listen to it?"

"No. Those assholes will have got to him. Let's help Alan."

CHAPTER 38

Around 1 AM, they finished the last of the samples. Alan had refined the process to look for a specific sequence typical of the infection. It meant that the samples could be processed in minutes and in parallel. Of the two hundred or so people at that meeting one hundred and forty were positive. The teachers had been given the virus in a vaccine, but the rest had contracted it from their children.

"This is massive," said Alan. "We're looking at something which is as infectious as the flu or measles."

"What about the girl who had the infertility problems, the pregnant one?" asked Donald.

"She's a member of staff and probably been given the virus in the flu vaccine. She tested positive for the gene changes. She'd have been infected a while ago. However, at least that's something positive." replied Kerry.

Alan screwed up his face and raised an eyebrow. "How's that positive"

"Well, I guess that means there's a way of getting pregnant even with these genetic changes, thank goodness"

"Only if you live in an advanced country that can provide assisted conception, and you can afford it," he replied.

"Well. Let's not get ahead of ourselves. We don't know for certain that it is the virus that caused her to be infertile. Lots of people have problems getting pregnant," added Donald.

"Barton admitted it to Kerry, Donald. It spread like wildfire in St Julians families. It may still be spreading. If we don't act soon to stop him spreading it further, it will be too late."

"I'll upload our latest findings to the web. Can you set up the machine to work overnight to provide a more complete genotype. Our colleagues will want that."

"What's to stop Barton from staging another break-in and trashing all this?" asked Alan.

"Let's phone Singh. He'll want to know what we found anyway. Maybe he can lock the place down and make it more secure. Anyway, Barton can trash it as much as he likes, he can't trash all those people out there who have this in their cells."

They picked up their phones from security as they left the facility. Donald noted fifty new emails. He scanned them. Some asked if his communication was a scam of some sort. Many were interested and wanted to know more. Quite a few were very critical, particularly so of his methods and the lack of peer review before going public. These latter had been copied to multiple colleagues. Donald, raised an eyebrow, making a mental note to get Johnny on to some of these names. He'd be very surprised if a few weren't bought and paid for by Barton.

There was text message from Johnny. *Target sighted* followed by an address.

"Very cloak and dagger. He's loving this," said Donald smiling as he showed Alan the text. He sighed and decided to leave Sanchez to the morning. It had been a very long day.

"What about Basil O'Leary? Are you going to listen to that."

"God, I had forgotten about him. Let's get it over with."

"Basil O'Leary here. Dr Stirling. I've just had the Scottish Chief Scientist on to me. He has some very worrying things to say about you and Ms Pearson. Please phone me. Until this is clarified, in view of the risk of reputational damage to the University, I've been advised that you should remain away from work. I look forward to hearing from you."

"Let's go home. I'll phone him in the morning."

The phone started ringing. Markov. Donald

thought about ignoring it, but they really needed him on side. He expected him to be furious about going public. He put him on speaker. All three stood anxiously around the phone the chill night starting to seep through their clothes. However, Markov's voice sounded resigned not angry.

"Hi, I see you decided to release the information to the world. A heads-up would have been nice. You have pissed off a lot of politicos here in the States, but honestly, they were stalling so to hell with them. Barton seems to have a hold on so many of them. It *has* to be more than money. The movers and shakers in this government have more money than they can spend. "

"It's the same here. We thought they'd all be jumping up and down and moving fast but it's all 'This doesn't seem so bad' and 'let's set up a team to look into it.' He replied in a reedy voice.

"Anyway, the story is beginning to hit the major press outlets, they haven't made the link yet to CreativeCom, but that should only be a couple of hours then we can watch the share price plunge." He sighed. "Our media people are primed ready for the push-back. Expect some very rough treatment at your end. Barton almost certainly has some of the press on board. He's been planning this for a long time, and he is always meticulous."

"We just completed the analysis of 200 odd people in the school. Most are infected. This is a highly contagious virus," interjected Kerry.

"Isn't it amazing they didn't get a lot of symptoms and that this wasn't spotted sooner?" asked Markov

"They maybe did, but they probably put it down to COVID. There was still a lot of it around then. That's what I thought I had when I contracted it. We all know the COVID antigen tests aren't 100%. Barton didn't plan the COVID pandemic, but he must have been very happy with the convenient cover it provided," replied Donald

"Have you told Singh yet?"

"Yes, he knows. Not a happy guy at the moment," answered Alan.

"Who is? One way or another it's looking like we have all been shafted. Quite frankly the ruination of our careers, your company, Chigen.... all of it is nothing compared to what is about to happen to the world." Donald breathed out heavily and yawned. "Sorry Mr Markov. Can we meet up again later? Its 2.00AM here, we have had a hell of a day, and I'm desperate for some sleep."

"Sure, let's meet at 2.00PM your time. Try to get some sleep."

"Switch the phone off Donald," said Alan. "You

can switch it on again tomorrow morning. There's nothing more we can usefully do tonight. Let's go home. Kerry, are you coming with us? I'd be happier if you did."

CHAPTER 39

The alarm woke them at 0800. Alan opened his iPad at the Sky News website expecting a front-page splash, but a cruise missile attack on the American embassy by Islamist rebels in Rashwastan dominated the pages. Miraculously no-one had been killed as the staff had been at a state dinner hosted by the president.

"Islamist rebels my arse! This is 100% Barton," he said showing it to Donald.

Kerry knocked on the door and burst in. "Have you seen this?!" She held out her phone, showing the same headline. "Our revelations hardly get a mention. All of the news websites are carrying this. Tucked into a corner of the home page is a headline. 'Concern about mystery virus prompts government investigation. The Chief Scientific Officer In London has warned against empty speculation about the origins of a recently discovered virus which appears largely harmless. Hysterical reports in social media about impacts on fertility should be treated with extreme caution. Further information will be available in due course, but at the moment there's no cause for alarm.' I don't bloody believe it!" Kerry's tears were falling as she spoke.

"Shit. Looks like they got to him too. Peter said he was a good guy. We have to hope that some of our other colleagues will start to look seriously at the information we have sent them. We should go over to the lab and send the complete genome information this morning. We have to keep pressing this. I wonder what Markov will make of this…. It takes the pressure off his company for a bit longer."

"Gives him time to sell his shares!" snarled Kerry.

"Let's not be too harsh. So far, he has played fair. Let's get up. Alan, will you go to the lab and send the information to the community and Singh? Ask Singh if he and Joan Al Shahi have come up with anything further on their analysis of the fertility genes. Joan is well respected. Surely they'll listen if she speaks out.

Kerry, you and I and Johnny are going to pay our friend Sanchez a visit."

CHAPTER 40

Johnny met with Donald and Kerry at the foot of the private road where he had found Sanchez. It was in one of the most expensive areas of Edinburgh, a carefully restored nineteenth century school, set in acres of rolling grass and trees which had been converted to luxury apartments only minutes from the centre of the city. The carpark was a hymn to high-end marques.

"And to think I thought Alan had been doing well for himself! You could buy two of my apartments with what that Maserati costs!"

The entry system used video communication and keyless access.

"What if he won't answer?" asked Kerry.

Johnny gave her a wry look, fiddled with his phone and held it to the entry pad. The door buzzed open.

"Give me a Yale lock any time," laughed Donald.

The long corridors had automatic lighting

which slowly illuminated in sections as they advanced.

"God, this is spooky," said Kerry. "I keep expecting him to jump out at me."

The apartment had a normal bell and a spy hole. Johnny and Donald stood to one side as Kerry buzzed.

After a delay of a few seconds a muffled voice from behind the door.

"Who are you? What do you want."

"I have a package here for Dr. Emilio Sanchez."

"I'm not expecting a package."

"It says it's fragile and must be delivered by 12.00MD. If you don't want it, I need a signature to say that delivery was refused."

The door opened. Johnny and Donald pushed in. Sanchez looked terrified, his eyes darting form Johnny to Donald. He was unshaven, he smelled of body odour and alcohol.

"For God's sake Sanchez, you're a mess. What the hell has happened to you?" exclaimed Donald, screwing up his nose.

"You can't come in here. I'll call the police."

"Somehow, I think that's a bit of an empty threat Emilio. I suspect the police are the last people you want to see. A foreign national responsible for forcibly sterilising Scottish children. I don't think they'd be particularly well disposed towards you."

"I didn't! I didn't know about that! I swear! I thought it was all going to be animal testing. I thought they'd get permission. But they've put all the blame on me. I had to switch my phone off. The press people have been hounding me for interviews. "

"We believe you," said Kerry quietly. Sanchez looked toward her. Donald was amazed; Kerry was really turning on the sympathy look. Good call, time to change tack.

"We all do." He said kicking Johnny, to banish his look of incredulity which Sanchez hadn't spotted.

"We know how devious Barton is. He all but kidnapped me. He's played everyone for fools or bought them. The best thing you can do now Emilio is to join us to fight him."

"You don't understand. He knows things about me. Things that could finish me." Sanchez had started sobbing. "Stupid, stupid stuff I did when I was younger."

"Whatever he knows can't do more harm to you than the trouble he's put you in just now. He's threatened all of us. If you help us, it could go a long way to reducing whatever consequences may come from any revelations he may make. The question is, do you want to be the hero or the villain?" continued Kerry in a gentle consolatory voice.

Sanchez head fell forward.

"You really think we can fight him?" looking up, a desperate hope in his eyes which darted between Donald and Kerry.

"He's strong, and has some very powerful people on his side, but we too have a billionaire in our corner Emilio and the whole scientific community is looking at this right now. He can't keep it hidden for much longer," replied Donald.

Sanchez shook his head gently, tears dropping freely from his chin onto the wooden flooring.

"You don't know all of it. "

Kerry pulled a handkerchief from her pocket and gave it to him. "Why don't we sit down, get us a cup of coffee and you can tell us what we don't know. Then we'll see what we can do to remove the hold this bastard has on you."

They moved to the living room. Floor to ceiling windows gave views of the Pentland Hills. Dark clouds were moving swiftly across the sky, one narrow patch of blue rapidly being obliterated. Donald looked at his smartwatch which was flashing a storm warning. Johnny was manning the Nespresso machine and handing out coffees.

"What is it we don't know?"

"There's more than one vaccine. The one you know of was only used in schools, but they did some work in retirement homes too."

"A treatment for dementia? That'd be astonishing."

"That wasn't the intention, this one impacts on telomere length and several other areas of the genome associated with ageing. I don't know what the results were in the retirement homes, but they seemed very cheery about it at one of the meetings."

"What was your involvement?"

"Same as before, to provide the viral 'wrapper' and check it could infect mammalian cells without destroying them."

"Which mammals?"

"To start with mice."

"And afterwards?"

Emilio looked down. "Human cell lines...... but I swear I didn't know they were just going to deploy it like they did."

"So, the actual code came from where?"

"Same as before, I don't know. I assumed some lab; I presumed in China."

"Do you still have samples of it?"

"They told me to destroy them."

"Emilio, you know that's not what I asked you.

If you kept some of it, we need to see it."

"There's some at the Chi-Gen Lab. I relabelled it and stored it under another project."

"What are you all talking about? What does this mean? What could it do" asked Johnny.

"It sounds like Barton has got himself a way of extending human lifespan," replied Donald. "Strange for someone who wants to reduce the size of the human population."

"That explains why the politicos are dragging their heels. That is quite the bribe," said Johnny.

Donald rolled his eyes and shook his head. Then he asked, "But surely once they have had the gene treatment, they could do what they like."

"That's the clever part. From what I could see it's not like the other vaccine, it doesn't last. The treatment needs boosted every so often and the carrier virus has to change as the body becomes immune to it. If they want the extra years they have to stay in hock to him."

"No Present Like Time," replied Kerry quietly. Seeing their quizzical looks she explained. "It's the name of a fantasy novel where loyalty is bought by an all-powerful emperor in exchange for longevity, which can be withdrawn at any time."

"How good is it? How much life extension does it offer?"

"I don't know. All I know is that they seemed very pleased with the results from the retirement home."

"Have you tried this?"

"You must be joking. We have no idea what the long-term consequences would be. I'm still young. Something to try when I'm fifty perhaps."

Kerry remembered how young-looking Markov was. She had wondered if it was all down to healthy living or plastic surgery. Now she wondered if he was playing with a straight bat. Did he know more about this than he let on. However, Barton himself looked his age or older. Why would he not take it himself?

"There's got to be a catch. Barton knows what he's doing. He wouldn't want to take the risk that everyone could eventually get this treatment. Sure, he'd restrict it as a reward for a blind eye to those in power, but they couldn't keep it that way for long. The demand would be incredible."

"Where have you stored it? Alan is over there now."

"What about me? Are you going to help me? If they know I told you this, I'm finished."

"You're one of us now Emilio," replied Kerry. "Of course we will."

"It's in cold storage 4, labelled Frog semen

2ZE. Some of the guys from the vet school are working on a way to make amphibians resistant to the chytrid fungus."

Donald tried to phone Alan.

"We'll go there now. Alan's phone is switched off. He must still be in the lab."

Kerry was checking her phone.

"It looks like he's posted the latest data online."

Donald, checked the site, still smarting from some of the comments he had received yesterday.

"Let's see what our smart-Alec colleagues make of that," he mumbled curling his lip.

"What do I do now?" asked Sanchez.

Johnny pushed forward towards him. Sanchez jumped back eyes wide. Johnny shook his head and smiled.

"Do you think I'm going to hit you or something? You move location and don't switch on your own damn phone even for a second. It took me four hours to find you. If I can, they can." He pulled a burner phone from his pocket. "Only use this one to get calls. Don't phone anyone who knows you on it. If you must phone us, use a public phone, there are still a few around."

"Time to go. OK Emilio, we'll call you again this evening, but don't turn that phone on until you're well clear of here," said Kerry.

"Let's head over to Chi-Gen and see what Alan has for us," replied Donald. "It'll be interesting to hear his take on this latest development. As I recall he did his PhD on the genetic basis of longevity in mice. This is an area he knows a bit about."

CHAPTER 41

As their Uber pulled into the Chi-Gen car park, there were several police cars and an ambulance outside. Their lightbars were flashing. The ambulance doors were open.

"What the hell is going on?" exclaimed Kerry. "Have they ransacked the place again?"

They jumped from the car and made for the door to be stopped by a policeman.

"Sorry folks, you can't go in there."

"What's happened. My friend is in there. Has someone been hurt?" yelled Donald.

"Who's your friend sir?"

"Alan McPherson, he's one of the scientists."

"And your name is?"

"Donald Stirling. I've been working with him."

"Come with me Sir."

Donald signalled to Kerry and Johnny to wait, mouthing that he'd sort it out, but as he passed the open ambulance, he could see the paramedics conducting cardiopulmonary resuscitation. He paled, stretched over to see what was happening wide-eyed.

"Please no!" he thought "Please, please no!"

"Is that Alan in there?" he said indicating the ambulance

"We believe so Sir. Which floor was he working on?"

"The tenth."

"That's where we found him."

"What happened to him? He was perfectly fine this morning."

They were joined by a tall man in a blue suit with an open neck shirt and fashionable stubble who introduced himself as Detective Sergeant Sinclair. His look and manner seemed designed to meet the gritty media stereotype. He took over from the uniformed officer with a nod of dismissal.

"He was attacked by a group of armed men. The security staff called us about 30 minutes ago. They came through the front door. They appeared to have the codes to enter the building and move at will through it. By the time we arrived they had gone again. We found him on the floor badly hurt but alive. He had sustained several blows to the head. Do you know who would want to attack him?"

"Yes, I do. Is he going to be alright?"

"I'll be honest with you Sir. It's not looking good. We need a statement from you."

"Yes of course. I need to phone someone.... One of your colleagues who's involved, well he's in the security services. Is it OK if I do?"

"OK Sir. Is this a terrorist situation?"

"No, but probably worse than that. Look I'll tell you everything, but I need to phone this man first."

He pulled out his phone and called Speirs.

"John, they've attacked Alan, it's bad. We're at Chi-Gen."

He disconnected and turned back to the sergeant. "He's on his way. Let me start from the beginning."

The policeman listened in silence. At the end he said.

"How well did you actually know your friend?"

"Very well, we've been friends for years."

"What about the company he keeps. The people who attacked him... we recognised one from the CCTV, he's part of a known local drug cartel. We contacted our colleagues in the serious crime squad in London, and they say they had recently been given information linking Dr McPherson to production of class A drugs. Seems he has quite a lifestyle in Oxford."

"That is complete nonsense. He's a geneticist not a chemist. He wouldn't have a clue how to start making crystal meth!"

"How did you know it was crystal meth?"

"I didn't. Like everyone else, I've watched 'Breaking Bad'."

"Well Sir. Common things occur commonly. Just now, there seems a pretty good reason for your friend's assault without, dare I say it, the need for the science fiction theory. However, we'll of course keep an open mind."

Donald knew he was going to get nowhere and that the DS's mind was about as open as Fort Knox. He decided to wait for Speirs.

"Can I see him?"

"I think the paramedics are still working on him."

At that moment one of the paramedics came in. He shook his head.

"Oh God" whispered Donald. "Is he dead? He's not dead is he?!"

The paramedic looked sombre. He looked at Donald with genuine concern and said he was sorry that they had done everything they could, but they couldn't save him.

"This is all my fault," he murmured, remembering their row in Oxford and how angry Alan had been at Donald involving him.

His eyes filled with tears.

"I have to tell the others. He has a partner, a girlfriend in Oxford."

"Do you have a number?"

"No, but I've an address."

Donald could see the concern etched on Kerry and Johnny's faces as he came out of the building. Kerry realised immediately what had happened.

"No! No! No! No! No!" She leaned back on the wall sobbing. Donald hugged her, openly crying too.

Johnny, grim faced, said quietly. "That bastard Barton will pay for this. Well, we know what we're dealing with now. Gloves are off."

Speirs' car screeched to a halt. His side-kick Phil was driving. He quickly took in the scene, nodded to the trio and headed into the building displaying his ID to the constable intercepting him.

It was clear from the look on the DS's face that he had little time for spooks.

"I suppose you're going to tell me to back off here," growled the DS.

"No. It's a murder pure and simple. The guy is innocent. The drugs are a red herring. Everything you were told by Dr Stirling holds water as far as we know. These thugs were hired, presumably to stop them revealing any more. I don't suppose they meant to kill him, but they did. He was one of the good guys in this. Round the bastards up."

He took out his mobile and called his boss, with one eye on the distraught trio. He nodded several times. Hanging up he called them over.

"You three must be super careful from here on in. None of you should be alone and you should not stay anywhere unless you're certain Barton won't know about it. I'll phone Singh and tell him. He needs to take care too. What about your colleague? Is he home from hospital yet?"

"He's back home. Donald and I were going to visit him today. Is that still OK?" replied Kerry.

"Well, his wife was certainly furious and looking for someone to blame when I saw her, although she may have calmed down a bit."

"Well, that would be me," said Donald. "All of this is down to me dragging people into stuff."

"Excuse my French but please don't talk such shite! There is one person responsible for all of this, and we all know who it is. Alan and Peter knew exactly what they were dealing with. They both could have pulled out at any point, but they knew what was at stake and took the chance because it was worth it. Alan was a very brave guy, despite being duffed up by those thugs earlier, he carried on. Just as you three have carried on. Now we just have to convince the assholes in government that this is urgent and to get moving."

"Well, we have a bit of information which might explain the heel dragging."

Donald explained what they had learned from Sanchez.

"For God's sake! It just gets worse and worse. Who'd have thought a bunch of politicos would put their own interests before those of the people they represent," he said sarcastically. "It does change the perspective though. Are you going to reveal this?"

"We haven't got the definitive evidence yet. We think there may be some in there," replied Donald.

"Well let's get you in there."

Speirs started what seemed like a heated argument with the DS. In the meantime, Donald asked Johnny to start looking at the profiles of the type of people in power likely to be making decisions, particularly with respect to meetings with Barton or his cronies.

"Do you have somewhere safe to go to do that?"

"Yes, I've another place. A friend. I don't see how they'd know about it. I've a few friends, hackers…. They all hate CreativeCom. I'll leave out the bit about Markov being a 'Good guy' for the time being. These guys can hack anything.

Those conniving bastards will have no secrets by the morning."

Speirs came back.

"You're in. You can't use the equipment though, but you can pick up the sample."

"The university has shut us out on the advice of the chief scientist… not sure what we can do with it."

"It's Saturday. Anyone working there that'll see you?"

"It's getting in might be the problem if our privileges have been revoked."

"Well, that's another reason for visiting Peter Munro I suppose. Good luck with the wife though!"

CHAPTER 42

Josh, Hana and Michael sat in stunned silence with Brigitte in her office. Just a few hours ago, Alan had been taking samples from them and now he was dead.

Normal schoolwork that day had come to a halt as all the talk had been about the previous evening's revelations. The emotions ran from anger to denial to feeling a little bit special to be the centre of such a scandal. Some were feeling guilty at infecting their parents and siblings. Michael was amazed there hadn't been more of a blowback, possibly an effect of the gene manipulation. *We really have been neutered.*

He looked around the room and realised they had to pull it together.

"Barton's made a mistake. They won't be able to cover this up."

"I don't know. All those guys in power have a lot to lose if it all comes out. They won't give in easily," replied Hana, wiping away tears.

"The story is really starting to blow up now. The American embassy bomb is already yesterday's news, and the journos are looking for a new hook to grab the viewers. Toss in the allegation that the embassy attack was a deliberate distraction and some of the more serious news outlets will take notice, not just the internet conspiracists. We can help with that. We need to get all the students here working on it," said Josh.

"That's a great idea. Let's get the students together and plan a campaign. Twitter and Insta won't know what's hit them. Harder for Barton to block it all. Do we need to co-ordinate with Markov?" asked Michael

"No, I'm sick of taking orders let's get going."

Brigitte looked concerned.

"You saw what happened to Alan. Do you want to risk that?"

"He died helping us," replied Michael.

Josh looked up. "They can't kill us all! I'll head off to the sixth form room and start co-ordinating it."

Hana's phone cheeped. "It's the guys from the juvenile prison in America. They want to speak. They've sent a link."

The three headed off to the meeting room and called up the link. After a few seconds of holding music and a message that the host would join them shortly, the screen opened to two young black men in orange overalls.

"Hello, Tyrone and Darnell?" asked Hana. "Hi, I'm Hana and this is Josh and Michael."

"Oh! They's b-black!" said Tyrone

The trio laughed.

"Michael's an honorary black. What were you expecting? People who looked like they had fallen out of Downton Abbey?"

The pair looked confused.

"I think it's your accent Hana, I don't think they get Scottish," laughed Josh.

"Sorry g-guys, we wasn't expecting a black gal speakin' like Groundskeeper W-Willie!" said Tyrone

"Fortunately, a rich diet of the Wire, Eddy Murphy and Fresh Prince, means we understand you," said Michael.

"We ain't got much time on this. We have a few questions."

"Darnell, we got some awful news today that we have to tell you first. This has got really ugly. One of the scientists who was helping let the world know about this was murdered today."

"Dr Stirling?!"

"No, his friend Alan. He was a really nice guy. The police are out looking for the thugs that did it. You need to be careful and tell the facility director about this. He needs to be careful too. These guys are trying really hard to keep a lid on this for as long as possible to give it time to spread."

"Ain't nothin' happenin' here. I think the bosses here don't see any harm in it."

"Yeah, well there's more to it than that. They've been offered a bribe. A pretty big bribe. Barton has developed another genetic modification. One which will extend their lives. We think he's been offering it to politicos and plutocrats. All they have to do is do nothing."

"Well, that'd explain a lot. Doin' nuttin'pretty well sums it up here. Las' thin' we want is those bastards living longer, sorry Hana for the language. What are you doin' in Scotland?"

"Dr Stirling and Kerry have spread the word to the genetics people around the world. We think they are beginning to take notice, but there's a big push to discredit them and their work. Let's face it, it's a hard one to swallow."

"Like somethin' you'd read in the National Enquirer. You know that magazine?"

"Yes, we've heard about it… 'spacemen ate my baby' and the like. We're going to get going with twitter, TikTok and Insta here in the school. We're getting as many of the kids here as we can to take part. We'll send Destiny the links. Maybe she could help with her contacts but tell her to be careful. Barton will sue anyone who drags his name into it."

"Huh! And what's he going to sue. We ain't got jack shit."

"Same here! One of the drawbacks of using a sink school for your experiments!" said Michael with a wry grin.

Tyrone leaned forward. "Y-You tell Dr Stirling sorry for his loss and that we're prayin' for him."

Hana swallowed a lump in her throat and her tears started again, moved by how those two boys who had had everything taken from them still had compassion to give.

"Thank you I will. Take care of yourselves and keep in touch. Tell Destiny she'll be hearing from me."

The boys waved and the screen went blank.

"Nice guys," said Josh. "Makes you wonder how they ended up there."

"You and I might be there if we lived in the States," replied Michael. "OK, let's get going with the social media campaign."

CHAPTER 43

....

Kerry and Donald pushed open the gate to Peter's house, a stone-built detached villa in the south of the city. The garden path was scattered with yellow leaves from an old sycamore. Donald rang the doorbell, and a dog started barking from deep inside getting alarmingly louder as it approached the door. They could hear someone moving through the house shushing the dog, its nails skittered across the floor and there was a thud as it jumped at the door. Donald jumped back with a start. He was a cat man and nervous around dogs. However, despite his precautions, when the door opened the large golden retriever jumped up and licked him on the face.

"Get down Monty! I'm so sorry he gets excited," said a small, portly, flustered looking woman with dyed black hair and bright blue piercing eyes. She looked up and a flicker of recognition passed over her face.

"Hi, Mrs Munro, I'm...."

"It's Dr Munro and I know who you are. We met at a departmental soiree." Turning to Kerry with a scowl. "And you I take it are the cause of all this trouble young lady."

"Kerry Pearson, Dr Munro."

A voice from inside the house.

"Moira for goodness' sake let them in! As I keep telling you, none of this is their fault! Don't shoot the messengers!"

"Hmm!" She pulled the dog backwards and made space for them to enter. Peter smiled and steered them into a chilly, high-ceilinged front room decorated in what Donald thought of as a neo-baronial style.

"Apologies for Moira, she's looking for someone to blame"

"I suppose you'll all be wanting coffee!" answered Moira adopting a resigned exasperated tone.

"Please don't go to any trouble. We won't be staying long. We just have some news for Peter."

"Is it about the incident at the Chi-Gen lab?" said Moira.

"What incident?" replied Peter.

"Sorry dear I didn't want to trouble you with it. After all that's happened, I thought it was the last thing you needed. Apparently, there was a fight of some sort and someone was hurt, it was on the local news."

Peter looked quizzically at Donald.

"Alan was beaten to death this morning by Barton's thugs."

"Moira for God's sake woman! What on earth made you think for one moment I wouldn't need to know about that. Make the coffee!

Goodness Donald I'm so sorry. What are the police saying?"

"They were fed some cock and bull story that Alan was involved in fabricating class A drugs. Speirs arrived though and put them straight. They seem to have been local goons. We suspect they didn't mean to kill him, just scare him again, but whacked him too hard."

"What else has been happening. I feel really bad that I haven't been in touch but it took a day or two to recover and obersturmfuhrer Moira has been watching me like a hawk."

Donald outlined the events and revelations of the last few days ending with the need to examine the new virus which Sanchez had told them about and the problem of not being able to access either the Chi-Gen or university labs.

Moira had been setting out the coffee cups alongside some very tasty looking home-made biscuits. She was looking more serious as the explanations went on.

"Oh! This is just awful! I'm so sorry. I didn't pick up from the news that he had died, just that there had been an attack on the premises," exclaimed Moira then, turning to her husband and frowning, "Peter, I don't want you to have anything more to do with this. Promise me you won't."

Peter looked at Donald then Moira.

"Moira, don't you see? This is a war now. Our children's future is at stake. How can we just sit back and let others do it?" Turning to Donald. "I'll come with you. We'll work on this together."

Moira dashed her cup to the floor and stormed out.

"God, I'm so sorry Peter," said Kerry. Everyone and everything I touch seems to be being hurt."

"Don't worry about Moira. She'll come around. She just got a shock with what happened to me. We'd had a few words the day before I left to go down south and when the police came to the door… well I think she thought they had come to tell her I was dead. She's been ultra-protective since."

"I don't blame her. Look you don't need to come in Peter; you really have done enough. Kerry and I can do this."

"No, I'm more determined than ever to stop that bastard."

They set out in Peter's ancient Volvo estate to the university. Kerry's phone cheeped. Unknown number. She wondered if it could be Johnny, but the message just contained a link. She showed it to Donald.

"I don't think this is Johnny. I'm not too sure about opening the link."

"Agreed, wait until we get to the lab. We can open it on an old tablet there. My guess is Barton, probably to do with what they did to Alan."

"We should let Sanchez know. He may be a prick but he's almost certainly a threat to Barton and must be at risk. I hope he's taken Johnny's advice and got out."

She switched off her phone and asked Donald for one of his burner phones. She dialled Sanchez on the phone Johnny had given him. It was answered after one ring.

"Emilio it's Kerry."

"Oh! Thank God! Have you seen the news? They were at the lab, they say a scientist was killed. Was it Alan? God, they were probably looking for me." His speech high pitched, rapid and heavily accented.

"We know Emilio. Are you somewhere safe? Don't say where, just if you're safe."

"I think it's safe…. I don't know… is anywhere safe? Why shouldn't I say where I am? Do you think they can trace this call?"

"No, calm yourself, your phone is new, and this one is too. I think we can be very sure it is secure."

"But Johnny found my new phone."

"That was because you started using it in exactly the same location as you stopped using your own phone. We're in a moving vehicle and my own phone is switched off. They can't trace this."

"I want to go back to Spain. I don't feel safe here."

"I understand that, but you're dealing with someone who is a tech genius who can hack anything. Can you be sure he won't be looking out for someone at airports using facial recognition or using the automatic passport scanners. We'll arrange to meet you. Stay where you are for the time being. When you do leave, cover your face as much as possible and wear dark glasses, even change the pace of the way you walk normally. We'll text you an address. Do nothing until then."

"Please don't forget about me! I know I've been stupid, but I would never have had anything to do with what happened to Alan."

"We know Emilio, we'll be in touch."

Kerry hung up and sighed

"Not sure that helped him much."

"Can't say I've a lot of sympathy though. We probably need to bring him in," replied Donald.

"The sooner we analyse this sample and tell the world about it the better. Once the secret's out we'll all be a bit safer."

As they drove towards the university in the distance Kerry spotted a black people carrier with blacked out windows. Her heart started pounding. She reminded herself that there were hundreds of these on the road but indicated it to Donald and Peter.

"We know they know your car registration Peter. Probably stupid of us to have used it. If it's Barton's men, then they know where we're headed. Turn left here and see what it does."

The car followed. Donald phoned Speirs and filled him in.

"Where are you?"

"Salisbury Road."

"OK you aren't far from St Leonard's police station. Tell Peter to keep driving but to turn towards town again then turn right towards St Leonards."

"Yes, I know where it is."

"If he follows you there, then he's paid them a hell of a lot, because they must know how hot they are just now. I'll alert the force there."

The black car continued to follow them at a distance but suddenly hit a burst of speed. Peter put the foot down and shot forward executing an amazing hand brake turn to turn down St Leonard's Street The car was just about in touching distance when whoever was driving realised where they were and went racing past the police station. The sound of a police siren was heard a few seconds later and a patrol vehicle shot out of the station.

"Bloody hell Ayrton Senna where did you learn to do that?!"

"Formula one fan. My dad and I used to spend weekends at the racetrack."

Donald shook his head. "You think you know someone!"

"Safe to go to the university now?" asked Peter

"I guess so. I suspect our friends will be occupied for a bit. I'll see if Speirs can get us some security."

They nervously entered the laboratory. Barton would almost certainly know to where they were heading and would throw more at them. They had to work fast.

"I'm not sure what we should be looking for," said Donald. "Alan had some expertise in this but it's not my field at all. What about you Peter?"

Peter shrugged. "I know that ageing is

associated with the length of telomeres at the end of genes and that's about it."

"Kerry, would you do a search on the latest known genetic associations with longevity. I guess we should be looking for something which codes for telomerase, but what else? Let's stick this vaccine in the fridge and get the machines started up."

Donald stored the sample in the fridge and started switching on equipment.

"There are several genes associated with longevity," said Kerry looking up from the search results on her tablet. "There's no magic bullet of course or else someone would have been on to it and made their fortune already."

"And yet there is," said a voice from the back of the lab.

All three sharply turned towards the grey-haired be-suited man, partially silhouetted by the autumn light streaming through the window.

Kerry jumped, her immediate reaction was that it was Barton, but the dress and more conclusively the voice wasn't right.

"Sir Andrew," replied Peter to the English Chief Scientific Officer.

Kerry and Donald looked at each other anxiously then glanced at the fridge. Whatever happened, they had to keep a hold of the sample.

"You too then," continued Peter moving slowly to one side to get a closer look. "You know you're consorting with murderers now, don't you?"

"So, I've heard." His tone was flat. He sighed. "It is amazing how easily one gets sucked into this sort of thing. A phone call from one of the world's richest men, dripping with flattering words about my research followed by an offer to fund it. Then, later, sympathy about the plight of my wife who has early onset dementia and the revelation of a possible revolutionary cure, the result of a hitherto unpublished AI research programme into longevity." He smiled ironically. "Well, I think we all knew these tech billionaires were chasing immortality, so it seemed a possibility and when it was described it seemed a dream come true, with a chance to have my soulmate protected."

He hesitated, looking down before continuing. "There was a price of course, but he was persuasive. The world was heading towards self-destruction; drastic action was required and the solution… one which benefitted the living over those still to be born, seemed benign, even beneficent. So, I was persuaded. I wasn't alone as I'm sure you already know."

Kerry opened her mouth to speak but a brief shake of the head from Donald caused her to pause.

Sir Andrew sighed. "I knew young Alan's father. We were very good friends. Did you know he was biochemist too? He was exceptional but died in his early forties with a subarachnoid haemorrhage when Alan was sitting A-Level exams. I continued to follow Alan's career at a distance. The ups and downs… some of those downs due to the company he kept." His eyes flicked to Donald who shifted uneasily. "I saw the chance to get him a decent job and put a word in at Chi-Gen. I thought he was settled."

"He never said…"

"He didn't know, his mother and I never really got on."

"Believe me Sir, there hasn't been a minute I do not regret involving Alan in this," replied Donald, his voice breaking.

"I know. And I know he was very fond of you Dr Stirling. I'm not a prude, I know what goes on between people. If you and he had been in the opposite situations he'd have done the same as you. Anyway, the reason I'm here isn't to stop you… although Barton thinks it is. You know you could be months trying to work out what's in that vaccine. So, take this. When I was considering it for my wife I researched it thoroughly. All the information you need is in there." He held out a data stick.

"What are you going to do Sir?" asked Peter.

"I've resigned my position as Chief Scientist and my chair at Oxford with immediate effect citing family illness. I'm going to take my beloved wife to our cottage in the Isle of Arran where I hope Barton will leave us alone. I wish you good luck. There are large numbers of people in the government and opposition as well the scientific establishment who are in tow with Barton. It's not just here but in countries in every continent. You'll need that good luck."

With that he stood bowed to the three scientists and left the room.

"Wow! This could really help us. Let's look at it. What time is it? We said we'd link up with Markov and Singh at 2.00. Hang on… that message you got Kerry… did you ever look at it."

"No, I completely forgot about it. "

She switched her phone on. The message was just an internet link. The sort of thing she wouldn't touch normally.

"Let's open it on one of the burners. I don't want to ruin my new phone."

It opened on a video file. An image of her parents' house. Her father was working in the garden. It seemed to be in real time. She tried to work out from where the image was being recorded. Underneath the text read 'JUST STOP NOW'

"What's wrong?" asked Peter noting her concern

"Barton has someone outside my mum's house. I have to go."

"Let's phone Speirs. After Alan, the police have to take it seriously, you going there won't help."

"He thinks that if he can pull me away from you that it'll slow up our analysis. Peter, be sure you didn't get the same sort of message. You can't risk your kids."

Peter opened his phone and saw a similar weblink. It led to an image of his house, this time from above.

"He has a drone above the house."

"Shit. You need to warn them. It is almost certainly just to intimidate you, but he's killed once already. Hopefully, he doesn't know that thanks to Sir Andrew we may already have all we need. I'll upload it now. I'll get Johnny to spread it everywhere. He won't be able to stop it," said Donald.

"You only have Sir Andrew's word that it's bona fide. He could be setting us up with duff data to discredit us. We need to check it," replied Kerry.

"We can start here, and I'll send a copy to Singh

and Markov.... God, can we trust them? Singh has a family too and he must be spooked by what happened to Alan."

Peter started speaking to his wife.

"You and the children need to leave the house now. You're in danger... Moira for once please don't question and please don't argue! Get them out and go to your mother's you can shout at me later... Now Moira! You're in grave danger. There's a bloody drone above the house! Take the car to the multistorey car park at Leith Walk, leave it there and spend some time in the shops or buy the kids lunch then get a cab." He gave an exasperated sigh. Forget the parking charge I'll pick the car up later. Go! Go! Go!!!"

He hung up.

"Well, that went as well as expected."

"I don't know how to get my Mum and Dad out."

Donald was speaking to Speirs

"Peter's wife is getting out and will try to lose them. Can you help with Kerry's parents? Great thanks." Turning to Kerry. There's a squad car on the way. It looks like the camera on your Mum's house is on the ground in a car or handheld. The squad car should be able to get them or chase them."

Peter continued to view his house from the phone. He saw Moira and the children, dog in tow, being ushered into Moira's Volkswagen Touran. As they set off the drone began to follow. Peter's eldest boy had his head out the window looking up.

"They are following her!"

"Your plan is a good one Peter. I'll message Speirs and tell him what she's doing."

Turning to the lab equipment he continued.

"We have to get on. Look we won't be able to check all of this, but let's cross-check a random selection of genetic sequences highlighted in Sir Andrew's information to see if they check out. If we do, then we upload the lot to the web with appropriate caveats."

"Kerry, will you contact Johnny?"

Kerry was fixed on her mobile watching images of a squad car screeching to a halt outside her parent's house. The camera didn't shift either suggesting it was fixed somewhere or Barton's men had bigger balls than she expected. She could see the door opening and her mother speaking to the police. Angry tears ran down her face. They didn't deserve this. Memories of the day the police turned up to tell them her brother had been found dead came back to her. One policeman was approaching the camera his face getting larger as approached. The image went blank.

Donald cursed himself for being so crass.

"Sorry Kerry. You have enough on your plate. I'll call him."

"No, it's OK. The police are there now. I'll do it. You start the analyses."

CHAPTER 44

At St Julian's Josh and Hana were working with most of the sixth form on their social media strategy.

Lewis, the school's resident computer genius, raised a hand.

"My X account has just been blocked."

"Mine too," said another.

"And mine."

"OK let's switch to Instagram, TicToc, Threads and even Facebook if we have to," said Lewis. "Those of you who haven't been blocked yet, we need to vary the message. They are probably searching for specific terms and blocking it as it appears. Almost certainly some sort of AI program. Also, if you have access to VPNs, use those or get friends to forward from their home computers. They have identified our server as a source and are blocking it too. Hana, warn Destiny what may happen and strategies to avoid it."

"Kerry's friend Johnny might be able to help. He has troupe of hackers working for him, they must have hundreds of usernames and passwords we could use," replied Josh. "Clearly we're causing a nuisance or they wouldn't have gone to this bother."

At that moment, Mr Bhopal came into the sixth form room.

"Hana, there's a gentleman here from the Scotsman. He's picked up on the social media posts and wants an interview."

Hana shrugged. "Well, it's not the Times or the Guardian but it's a start and sometimes the big boys pick up on the local press"

"I thought he was here to interview me about the International Day of the Child this week. I had been in touch with them a few weeks ago to complain about the lack of events here in Scotland when all over the world it is a really big affair."

"I think we have more to worry about here Sir," said Hana with a benign smile.

"Yes of course I know. Forgive me. How's the campaign going?"

Josh was looking quizzically at the headmaster.

"Hang on! Sir? What sort of events are happening around the world?"

"Oh, it's really exciting," replied the

headmaster enthusiastically. "There will be literally thousands of conclaves of school students in I think at least 100 countries to celebrate and promote high quality education. The biggest celebration there has ever been"

"Who is supporting it Sir. UNESCO?"

"Yes, it's usually them but this year they have managed to get a huge amount of support from…" his voice trailed off, his smile fading. "Industry."

The headmaster looked at Hana and Josh. Michael said. "I'm on it!"

After a few minutes. "Well, the generous funding source turns out to be… drum roll… Odyssey of course. Marion Spitz is the lead for the company.

"The lying cow!" spat Hana.

"Hana! Language!" scolded Mr Bhopal.

"Sorry Sir. We need to tell Kerry."

Michael blew through pursed lips.

"If this isn't going to be a super-spreader event, I don't know what is."

"Sir, do you have a list of the participating institutions around the world?" asked Josh.

"I might have, but for some reason we weren't invited this year."

"'Cos we were already infected," replied Hana with a scowl.

"I'll start trying to track down the institutions attending and try to find some contacts. We need to agree a text to send them. This is where we wish we had a stronger languages department," said Josh.

"Steady on. We did really well in languages this year," remonstrated Mr Bhopal.

"In French and Spanish, but not Mandarin, Farsi, Arabic, Russian, Japanese."

"For everything else there's always Google Translate," said Michael. "Look, I'll call Kerry and ask her to get Johnny to phone you Josh. Hana don't forget the Scotsman reporter."

CHAPTER 45

Caleb Farrel was reeling from what he had heard from Darnell. He and Tyrone had asked to see him straight after their video-call. One of the scientists murdered! The prospect that narcissists like Jeb Parsons were being bought by the promise of eternal youth would certainly explain why nothing appeared to be happening Stateside. He felt helpless. What chance did they have. Darnell said that his sister Destiny and her friends were trying to tell the world by social media, but how much clout would a bunch of kids have against the might of Barton's organisation? The whole thing seemed unbelievable. He kept hoping himself that it was a bad dream or just a crazy conspiracy theory, but the evidence just kept stacking up.

The prison guards had asked for a meeting again. Maybe if they started kicking up a stink with the local press people would start to take notice.

Now… If they were to threaten industrial action that might attract a bit of attention! As a facility director of course, I couldn't suggest it but…

"Bernice, could you come in here a second?"

Caleb told Bernice everything he knew about what was going on. She sat and shook her head.

"It never stops, does it? Did Darnell tell you that the school in Scotland is full of poor kids of colour?"

"I hadn't looked at it in a race sort of way…. Just a poverty sort of thing…. Barton choosing people with the least ability to fight back. Could be a race thing I s'pose though. What about the white guards and their families? Are they just collateral damage? No. I'd hold off playing the race card… at least until we know more about other institutions that have been affected. We have to get people to take notice, and we need everyone on board. Whites have to feel as threatened by this as blacks. I want you to help organise a strike."

"What! Say that again!"

"Everyone listens to you Bernice. You're the font of reason in this prison. I can't be seen to be fomenting industrial action, but a few words from you about the unfairness of it all and what you'd heard about reasons for inaction…. Well, I think that just might get things goin'. A threatened strike here will have the reporters here like flies on manure."

Bernice scrutinised him for a few moments.

"You're right," she smiled. "The prospect that law and order might break down and felons would be released on the street should get their attention! Leave it to me. By the way. Darnell has found a flaw in his trial process. The sentence was crazy for what he was alleged to have done anyway. However, looks like there was poor handling of the evidence and the policemen that arrested him have just been accused of fabrication in another case. Hopefully he won't be here much longer."

"Half these kids shouldn't be here Bernice. I know that's not exactly a comment typical of a California prison director, but it's true. Let me know what happens with the guards."

He lifted the phone and dialled the state governor's office. The receptionist apologised assuring him that the governor was in an important meeting but would be sure to call him once he was free. There was little point in arguing. Jeb Parsons wouldn't phone back. He'd be playing the odds and working out what was best for Jeb Parsons Inc.

Let's see what he does when the shit hits the fan, and it's clear he's done nothing but rather liked the idea of enforced sterilisation for 'degenerates'.

CHAPTER 46

Moira Munro and Peter's family had safely entered the multi-storey car park. After a few minutes the drone had given up and flown off. The feed went black. Speirs phoned Kerry and put her mother on to speak to her. Her apologies were shooed away as unnecessary.

"Mr Speirs has told me how important your work is. I can't believe that that Barton man had me so fooled. He seemed so nice! Now of course your father is saying he hadn't trusted him from the start. Not what he was saying then however! Anyway, you look after yourself and don't worry about us. We're fine. Mr Speirs is going to take us to your Auntie Jessie's house in Dunfermline. I don't see how Barton would know about her."

"Don't be too sure about it, Mum. He is a very powerful man. Please be suspicious of everything and phone the police if you're worried."

Kerry realised that Speirs couldn't have told her parents about Alan's murder or her own near kidnapping or her Mum might not have been so sanguine. She turned to Peter.

"Peter if you phone Moira, use a burner. Barton will have your number. You don't want to reveal her location."

"I was putting that call off I have to admit, but you're right I probably should call her. The sooner we get this information out to the world the better. Once it's there for all to see, hopefully, Barton will have no reason to pressure us. Unless he's a vindictive sort of guy."

"I'd say cold and calculating. I doubt he wastes much energy on revenge. Speaking of cold and calculating, it's time for our call with Markov and Singh," replied Kerry.

As Kerry started to set up the call her phone rang. Michael. He told her about the International Day of the Child meetings and the Odyssey involvement.

"Listen Michael I'm going to put you on speaker. The others have to hear this.

"God, every hour there seems to be another twist of the screw it just gets worse! He is just one step ahead all the time. What are the chances of being able to cancel all these meetings?" asked Donald.

"Not a hope I'd have thought, these things are years in the planning, but we could start warning people," replied Kerry.

"How might he use a meeting like that to disseminate the virus? Something that could produce an aerosol maybe?" asked Josh.

"I guess he could use air-conditioning systems. These UNESCO meetings are largely in hot low- and medium-income countries; some will have air conditioning but not all." replied Kerry.

"But think of the organisation that would be required. He'd need hundreds of people all over the world to organise a mass infection. Surely, he could not have done that without someone gabbing," said Donald. "Could be he is just going to use the day to advertise the advantages of the genetic change without mentioning the drawbacks."

They could hear Josh's voice in the background. He came on the call.

"Mr Bhopal has just given us a list of the schools taking part. There are thousands around the world. A couple in Scotland and several in England are meeting in London. Just about every country has school representatives going to big meetings on every continent. All travel expenses have been covered. There are huge numbers in South-East Asia and especially Africa. Our school has an ongoing relationship with a couple of schools in Malawi, and it appears that there are about thirty schools are taking part in a session in Lilongwe alone. We're going to get in touch and see what they have been told about the day. Mr. Bhopal says he'll contact the headmasters of the Scottish schools to let them know about our concerns. However, the programme he was sent seems to consist of a series of telecast inspirational speeches from speakers around the world, then what looks like a side session for educators on the "Odyssey Method" as well as some local showcasing."

"What are the chances that the leadership in UNESCO will listen to us?" asked Michael

"We don't really have much to go on. We haven't proven a link with infertility. We haven't yet got concrete proof of a conspiracy to bribe major stakeholders and leaders with longer lives. Also, Barton's social media campaign has been going full pelt insinuating that western countries have made up a scare story as a means of hoarding this major advance to themselves. I suppose it's just possible that they might just listen to Sir Andrew. He has the international clout, but I got the impression he just wants to go away and forget about it all."

"It looks like Markov is a big donor?" said Josh his keyboard clacking in the background.

"Really? In addition to the money that's coming through Odyssey? We have a meeting with him now so we can always ask, although I get the impression that Markov is in two minds about all of this. I'm sure if he could get out from under this with CreativeCom still intact he would." replied Kerry. "If you have contacts with the Malawi kids though, try and find out if anything unusual is planned or if they have heard anything about the 'miracle IQ fix'".

CHAPTER 47

Markov and Singh were on-line and on screen. Both looked like they had slept little over the last twenty-four hours, Johnny was attending but had blocked his video. Markov started by offering his condolences to Donald. He said he knew that they had been close and asked how his partner had taken it. Donald squirmed, with all that had been happening he hadn't phoned Emma yet. He assumed the police would have called her. He didn't have a number but knew that wouldn't be a problem for Johnny. He wondered if his postponement of that task had more to do with avoiding what was going to be a distressing encounter. He resolved to call her after the meeting.

Singh said his family had been threatened. He too had been sent drone footage of his house. The police in Oxford had been sympathetic, but in the absence of an actual threat did not feel they could do anything about it. He had moved his family and thought they were probably safe now but, like Peter, he had come under extreme pressure from his wife and her family to stop his work against Barton.

"They found out that Professor Al Shahi was helping us. I got a phone call from her in the early hours of this morning. She was hysterical. Her brother and his family are in Iraq. He was arrested under trumped up charges and has been imprisoned in a notorious torture jail. She was told that if she did not stop working on the project, they'd come for his wife next. After what happened to Alan, we know he is capable of anything," said Singh his voice breaking. "I can't take the risk with my family Donald. I'm going to stop."

"But once we get this information out to the world there will be no reason for him to threaten you," replied Donald. "Let me tell you what we have discovered in the last few hours."

Donald recounted the meetings with Sanchez and then with Sir Andrew and the need to test the sample of the longevity virus they had against the information he had provided to ensure it was bona fide before publishing it.

"I had heard rumours that something like this was on offer," said Markov. "However, so much of this kind of talk is just that… talk. I hadn't taken it seriously. It's quite an offer though. I know a lot of people who would trade a lot for it including any ethical reservations they may have."

"Would you really take something like this that hadn't been properly tested?" asked Singh.

"No doubt James Barton has some 'impressive research' to back it up. Whether that research is true or not… who knows? You have to realise that the sort of people he is trying to influence tend to be risk takers. Hell, a lot of the tech guys I know are taking all sorts of unproven shit to improve their creativity or prolong their life. Most of the politicos I come across aren't very different. Dress it up with a scientific paper, liberally laced with a few impressive so called "real-life" testimonials and they'd be queuing up."

"We need to test the vaccine to see if Sir Andrew's information is accurate. Raj…. I know it's a big ask, but could you not put a few of your folks on to it while keeping at a distance yourself?" asked Donald

"Do you honestly think he won't know? He seems to know everything we're doing… almost before we start. It's too risky. I'm sorry. I promised my wife that I'd do nothing to put the family in danger. She'd be appalled to know that I'm on this call."

"The Chi-Gen lab in Edinburgh is a crime scene so we don't have access to rapid analysis. We can do it here at the university, but our equipment is very much slower."

"What do you need?" asked Markov.

"A Forrest 3000, but they aren't due to be released until later this year. Sanchez had a test unit."

"Anyone else testing it?"

"John Gillies at Glasgow University had one," replied Peter.

"How far away is that?" asked Markov.

"About two hours."

"Make him an offer. Whatever you think will persuade him."

"There's something else," added Kerry.

Kerry outlined the plans for the International Day of the Child in two days' time and Odyssey and Spitz's involvement.

"Hmm. I think it's time to deal with Ms Spitz," murmured Markov.

Kerry stopped herself from a sarcastic correction of the honorific.

"The kids at St Julian's are trying to find out more about plans for the conference. We're concerned it could be a super-spreader event, but not entirely sure how Barton could pull it off. Can we stop it" asked Kerry.

"The only thing that could possibly stop it is a viable terrorist threat. Although mass infection would certainly meet that criterion, it seems we have little actual evidence to support it. Although Barton's plans are starting to unravel, the murder of a respected scientist will pull in the attention of the media, it may not be sufficient to cancel something that has been years in the planning," replied Markov.

"What about the online campaign? At least, even if it all goes ahead, we can say we warned them," asked Donald. "The kids at St Julian's attempted an X and Instagram campaign but they were blocked comprehensively. Johnny, have you been able to help?"

"Check your X now. It's all over it. Barton of course has gone into full swing dismissing it as conspiracy theories from the usual suspects, but our message is beginning to gain traction especially with Alan's death," replied Johnny.

"My people have been amplifying it," added Markov, "but I'm not sure it'll be enough. I'll contact the Director General of UNESCO. I know her. I'll say that we have strong reasons to suspect there may be a terrorist bio-attack on the meeting. Whether it'll be enough or not I don't know."

"My phone has been filling up with more requests for information from the genetics community. Several have confirmed our findings based on the information we sent. They want source material though to show we haven't staged the whole thing," said Donald

"I'm sure the St Julian's kids and families will supply that if they want it. I'll get Brigitte to ask," said Kerry. "We'll never organise that in time to stop this will we?"

"I'd imagine there will be a more than a few people in positions of power who having supped with the devil have a bit of indigestion right now. Most of them won't have read the small print when they signed up to support Barton. Some will just be annoyed that their next shot of what they think is the elixir of life might be in danger," added Markov.

"I've been reading the information that Sir Andrew gave us. He really arranged a thorough analysis. He concludes that some of the genetic changes associated with slowing cell death may increase the risk of cancer. For people like his wife who was facing an imminent slow death from dementia he probably considered that that was a risk still worth taking, but for people in their forties and fifties it's quite a gamble," said Peter.

"That explains why he doesn't seem to have taken it himself and why someone whose avowed aim is to reduce the world's population was prepared to offer it," replied Kerry.

"Well, that'd really spook them. We need to get that published. Do we absolutely have to wait for confirmation first?" asked Donald.

"I think you have to set aside the tenets of good science. Forget the measured statements laced with caveats and do what Barton does.... full blast scare tactics. Think tabloid headlines. OK you're putting your reputations on the line, but what's the worst that will happen? If it's all wrong, and it isn't, you'll look stupid for a while, but it'll soon all be forgotten," answered Markov.

"My guys have been compiling a list of people with suspected contacts with Barton and Odyssey. It's a long list with some very famous and powerful people on it. We can start uploading it in batches," added Johnny.

"Perfect, prepare yourself for some pretty heavy libel threats though."

"Two things. First for something to be libellous they have to prove that what we say is wrong, and it's not, and second, who they gonna sue. Do you think I'll be putting my name to it? And if they find out it's me, I've got nothing worth suing."

"I'll take the sample through to Glasgow and start work on it. In the meantime, you start blasting the press," said Peter.

"No Peter. No way am I having you risk your life again. I'll go. You and Kerry start preparing the press releases."

"Phone Speirs, Donald. He'll know what to do. Barton is desperate right now. He almost certainly has people or a drone watching this building," replied Kerry.

"I'm on the call," interjected Speirs. "Sorry I was late. The police have picked up one of the guys that attacked Donald. They are sticking with the drug war trope. I've made it clear that that it is bollocks, but the chief constable keeps talking about Ockham's razor whatever the hell that is."

"That the simplest explanation is usually the most likely," answered Kerry.

"More like the one that gives them the least work is the most convenient to go with," said Johnny sarcastically.

"Anyway, when we're off-line, I'll tell you what we'll do to get you safely to Glasgow," said Speirs

"OK. Let's go. Can we all meet again in six hours?"

CHAPTER 48

Donald couldn't believe how smoothly it had all gone. Peter had phoned his friend John Gillies in Glasgow at home. He had been on Donald's email distribution list so already knew the concerns that had been raised. He was among those who provided initial confirmation of the data they had been sent but had asked for confirmatory evidence. He agreed to meet Donald at his lab and help run tests on the second vaccine.

To get there, Speirs had arranged a car to take him initially towards the city's Western General Hospital, but in a tunnel in Abbeyhill they changed cars, the original now containing someone who looked like Donald along that route while Donald after a few moments' delay headed towards Glasgow.

As they approached Glasgow they heard on the radio breaking news of an exchange of gunfire in the north of Edinburgh. The reporter said that early indications suggested a police sting operation, involving armed police in several unmarked cars. One of the criminals was seriously injured the other three arrested.

"Good for Speirs!", exclaimed Donald to his driver. "Did you know he had planned this?"

"Glad it worked Sir. We deserve a bit of luck. Hopefully the bastard who got shot is the one that did for your friend."

Professor Gillies was waiting at the laboratory when Donald arrived.

"John, thank you for this. I really appreciate it."

"I knew Alan McPherson. We collaborated a couple of times. He was a solid reliable guy, easy to work with compared with some of the obstreperous assholes we have to cope with. Did you know him well Donald."

Donald's eyes filled with tears answering the question.

"Sorry Donald let's get on with this. If even half of what you say is true, then these bastards must be called to account."

Gillies took the precious sample and started the analysis.

"We need to just confirm the highlights of what is in Sir Andrew's report to be sure that it isn't just a clever ploy to wrong foot us. I really don't believe it is though. Are you prepared to go on the record for any results we get here today? I promise you we'll publish regardless of how it turns out."

"Of course, but I want to be an author on the paper when it comes out. This is going to be a cracker!" he smiled.

Three hours later, the first results were available. Everything stacked up.

"What a bunch of bastards!" exclaimed Gillies. "To think they'd sell the futures of all these children for a few extra years. I can't believe Sir Andrew would let himself be dragged into something like that."

"He was desperate to help his wife. I felt quite sorry for him. He's lost everything now and, without his help, we could be weeks trying to find out exactly what this vaccine did. I'd hope he comes out of this with a bit of dignity," replied Donald. "What do you think of the cancer risk of this vaccine John?"

"I'd say it's very high. These changes effectively prevent cell death and, as Sir Andrew's report indicates, some of the genetic sequence changes are more frequently found in tumour tissue than normal tissue. Put it like this. There is absolutely no way I'd take this."

"Well then, it's time to let Barton's 'special friends' know."

Donald uploaded page images of Sir Andrew's report to his geneticist colleagues in a post which also informed them of Alan's murder and Peter's abduction. He decided to cast Sir Andrew as a whistle-blower rather than an offender. John Gillies subsequently uploaded the result of his independent verification of the main findings of the report.

There were immediately multiple messages of shock and sorrow from the genetics community. Alan had been well known and liked. There was no doubt that Barton's strongarm tactics had massively backfired. There were none of the knee jerk rejections he had from the first postings, such was the gravitas that Sir Andrew and John Gillies brought to the revelations.

Donald phoned Kerry to confirm the findings. Kerry and Peter had been working on a variety of statements for the press and social media with Johnny gleefully providing suggestions to turn their carefully crafted words into the sort of attention-grabbing headlines beloved by social media scrollers.

"Let's not dwell too much on the upside of the genetic manipulations, let's leave that to Barton," said Kerry

"It looks like from the list that Mr Bhopal gave us that Odyssey is concentrated on Africa," said Johnny.

"Well, I guess it's where most of the population

growth is happening," replied Kerry

"Just thinking that if we were to imply a possible racist element it would garner a lot more clicks."

"Do you really think Barton is a racist?" asked Peter.

"If he was it didn't show in the people he surrounded himself with. I suspect he's focussed on Africa because of the projected population increase. The schools and institutes he chose may have just happened to have more ethnic minorities. He says he selected them because they were poor, easy to influence and less able to push back but let's not worry about the nuances here. He certainly hasn't been," replied Kerry

"Need to be careful though, we want the *whole* world to be outraged not just ethnic minorities," said Johnny.

"Ok let's drop 'White supremacist's plot to neuter a generation'" and use 'Mad boffin's plot to decimate humanity' instead" replied Kerry

"Personally, I prefer 'It's like they cut my balls off!'" replied Johnny

"We're certainly not losing that one!" laughed Kerry.

"We need to emphasise the science," said Peter. How about 'Scientists line up to verify Edinburgh discovery of widespread genetic tampering of Scottish school kids.'

Or maybe 'We're all at risk! Says Edinburgh top scientist as he confirms the sterility bug is contagious.'

The later posts focused on the bribe promising extended life and the sting in its tail. They published this alongside lists of influential people known to have associations with Barton and Odyssey. They realised many of these would have been innocent and so were careful not to make definite allegations.

"Take Mr Bhopal's name off that list Johnny. You know he's not involved. There must be loads like him," said Kerry uneasy about the lives they may be trashing.

"We haven't time to check them all out Kerry."

The headlines started to spill out.

"Grasping politicians sell their children's birthright for elixir of life."

"They swapped the dream of eternal youth only to risk a slow death from cancer!"

"Sting in the tail of elixir of life"

"Leaders linked to deranged tech billionaire scramble to distance themselves from bribe allegations."

The St Julian's computer club, working with Johnny and his associates spent the following 24 hours plastering their messages across social media. There was a continuous battle with Barton's people who fought back by cancelling and removing their accounts, but using Johnny's software, new ones were created as quickly. The kids laughingly compared the texts of the threats of lawsuits and cease and desist messages they received with one another and the increasingly vicious attempts to discredit them. They were portrayed as scaremongering conspiracists.

"The lack of corroborating evidence is a problem though," remarked Peter to Donald who had returned from Glasgow." We really needed Prof Al Shahi's confirmation of the fertility impact".

Donald was scrolling through responses in his email.

"Hang on! Wait till you see this!" he said handing his phone to Peter.

There was an email from Professor Bernard in Colombia University, an international expert in the genetics of infertility. He said he had reviewed the data he had been sent and thought it extremely likely that if these multiple changes were made to the genome they'd very likely result in subfertility.

"Wasn't he someone who was on the links with Barton list?" asked Johnny.

"Yes. That's why we didn't ask him for help

initially. Well, I'll be damned. Still, he's a prime example of why we shouldn't assume that just because people have had apparent contact with Barton that they are necessarily part of the plot," replied Kerry. "Anyway, let's get his analysis up on the web and add it to the online debate. This is brilliant!"

Gradually the St Julian's team started to dominate the discourse, with Barton's team's denials sounding increasingly desperate as they sought to discredit well respected scientists who had joined in confirming the analyses. Many people who had been listed on Barton's contact lists were posting that they knew nothing of any genetic manipulation, but two mentioned that they had been approached about a potential life extending treatment which they had turned down as probable nonsense.

There was a message from the California Secure Youth Treatment Facility director with a link to an article in the San Francisco Chronicle about a threatened strike at the facility, the reasons behind it and the 'wall of silence' from government.

"Fantastic! That is a really big newspaper, some of the bigger American outlets will surely follow," said Donald.

"I wonder how Markov got on with the UNESCO director general?" asked Kerry.

"We have a meeting in two hours. We need to see if Hana had any luck with their contacts in Malawi. Maybe they can give us a clue as to how he might spread the virus there, if indeed that's what he wants to do."

CHAPTER 49

In California the governor was screaming down the line to Bernice.

"What do you mean he's busy?! Tell him the damn governor wants him."

Caleb and Bernice smiled as they sat together beside the speaker phone. Caleb gave the absent governor the finger to a look of disapproval from Bernice. Bernice, however, had played it perfectly. Over early morning coffee, she, Novak and Rossi had let the other prison guards know that as far as she could see the state governor considered the genetic tampering that had occurred with the prisoners 'all good' and any impact on the prison staff and their families as 'acceptable collateral damage'. Like Novak and Rossi many guards were veterans of the Afghanistan war and bristled at the term. They had seen so-called 'collateral damage' close up. She went on to 'subtly' drop the bombshell about the longevity bribe being offered to the rich and powerful.

Their fury boiled over, curses alternating with embarrassed apologies for the language to Miss Bernice. Within hours the guards had threatened an immediate walk-out if an immediate investigation did not take place. The San Francisco Chronicle had been contacted who in turn phoned Caleb. Caleb of course 'felt duty bound' to confirm the expressed concerns of the prison staff but that he was 'sure that Governor Parsons had it under control', but that 'no, he wasn't aware of any action that had been taken yet'.

Caleb waited twenty minutes before calling Parsons. *Let him sweat.*

"Where the hell have you been?!"

"Just finishing up a workshop on facing up to life outside the penitentiary for some of the young men who are about to be released. It went well."

"I don't give a damn how it went, but I do give a damn that you thought that it was more important than speaking to the Governor!"

"But Governor, you've always maintained that recidivism was our biggest problem, so I gave it priority. But what can I do for you?" replied Caleb in his most unctuous tone.

"You know damn well why I'm phoning. What the hell do you mean by telling the press about the Odyssey situation? I told you to keep it under wraps."

"The wraps, as you put it governor, had already well and truly come off. The whole institution has been talking about it. We have some very talented young inmates who have sussed the whole thing out. They are in communication with other institutions in the UK. Now I'm sure that you personally had nothing to do with the bribes everyone is talking about, but you can see how inaction might make people who are a little less disposed towards you infer the opposite." Caleb and Bernice looked at each other and smiled.

"This whole thing is nothing but a conspiracy theory. That's the message I'm putting out and that I want you to put out too."

"Have you seen Twitter or X this morning Governor? It may be a conspiracy theory, but it is certainly gaining a lot of traction from some very influential people. You might be interested to know that you get a mention yourself for your connections with Mr Barton's Odyssey programme. Not a particularly positive mention either. You should consider suing Sir."

Bernice was quietly clapping her hands with glee.

"Now listen here boy and listen well. Start

denying this or your job will be on the line. Do you hear me?"

"Sir, I'm not 'your boy', and something tells me it's not going to be my job that's on the line. Good-day Sir."

Parsons started to reply but was cut off by Caleb hanging up.

"Man, but that felt good! Bernice, should Governor Parsons phone again, please tell him I'm not available to take calls for the rest of the day…. or better still… ever.

"I'd like to be a fly on the wall of his office at the moment," laughed Bernice.

"Can we organise another meeting of our group to discuss ongoing strategy now that everything is on the table so to speak. I can't believe what those kids in Scotland and Destiny's kid sister and her friends have managed to pull off."

"They are super-smart remember."

"Yes, they are," he sighed. "At least they have that." Looking down, thinking of his own son, and how his family line could end with him, he continued. "I just hope they can find a way to reverse the bad things he's done, but I can understand that with what these kids have been given, they wouldn't want to lose it no matter what it cost."

He sighed and continued, "I was lying in bed

last night and I got to thinking about how this will all play out. All those evangelists you see on the television praying for the so called 'End of Days', predicting a nuclear war beginning in the Holy Land that'd bring their 'rapture' closer. But it won't be that way… will it? The ending of a poem we learned in school kept going around and around in my head.

'This is the way the world ends, not with a bang but a whimper.'"

Caleb shook his head.

"Sorry for being so maudlin Bernice."

"If these kids are as brilliant as we think, then they goanna find a way out of this director. They have to."

CHAPTER 50

"Anyone hungry? I'm starving," said Donald.

"Oh my God is that the time? I need to phone Moira!" exclaimed Peter. "May I borrow a phone?"

Peter walked to the back of the lab. It was clear he wasn't getting an easy time, his voice starting hushed but getting louder

"I know, I'm sorry I should've called earlier, but we haven't stopped……You know that's not true. You and the boys *are* my top priority… I'm not sure how long you'll have to stay there, but I don't think much longer. All this stuff has come out now and there is little point in him threatening us anymore…… Yes, I know it must have been terrifying, but you were brilliant giving them the slip… I hadn't realised I was married to a female James Bond… I'm not trying to soft soap you. It's true. You were brilliant. I'll phone you later tonight and I'll check with the special branch guy if it'll be safe to go home after that… I will of course… I promise I won't take any more risks."

Peter returned to the others shaking his head.

Kerry frowned. "Peter, so sorry for dragging you into this. I realise we won't be in Moira's good books for a while."

"You know, I've a sneaking feeling she actually enjoyed this a bit. What are we having for dinner. Pizza anyone?"

They were finishing the remains of their pizza when Kerry's phone rang. Unknown number. The three looked at each other. She put it on speaker and set to record.

"Hello Kerry" came the distinctive Texan drawl. "I felt I had to call you after what happened to Dr McPherson. I wanted to tell you that that was not planned. Whatever you may think I'm not a monster, and I hate using violence. I wish to apologise. I realise that my apology is unlikely to help much but there it is all the same."

Donald flared with anger. He opened his mouth to speak, but Kerry held her hand up. She replied

"He was the kindest sweetest man I knew. He hadn't an enemy in the world… apart from you. If you have phoned for forgiveness, we have none to give. If you really feel any sort of sorrow for what you did, then stop all of this now."

"Too late Kerry. The die is cast, the horse has bolted, the genie is out of the bottle, Pandora's box is open. Choose your metaphor. There really is no going back now. The only thing open to debate is how quickly it'll happen. I dare say your bright boys and girls have put a dent in our timeline… and don't forget how they got bright by the way… but the locomotive tearing down that track isn't yet derailed. And now you've got me mixing my metaphors. Time to say goodbye. You're a bright girl Kerry. I like you. Another time another place we could have worked well together. Pass my apology on to Dr Stirling. I know they were close. Good night." The phone went dead.

"The fucking bastard!" screamed Donald. Bitter tears now flowing freely. So much had happened that day, they had had no time to grieve. Hearing Kerry's words about Alan had breached the dam. She reached out and hugged him.

Peter stood up sensing they needed time alone. "I should try to see Moira and the kids and pick up the car from the car park. Can you manage without me for a while?"

"Sorry Peter, yes of course, but take care. Maybe phone Speirs first and get advice on how to get there."

"Don't worry, there are lots of ways out of this building. He can't be covering them all. I'll leave the car. I'll contact you later. Do you think he's right though? That we can't stop this thing?"

"Possibly. Probably. So many people have something to gain from it. Ambitious parents, students desperate for good marks, grasping politicians, heavens maybe even a few folks from the green lobby would see the good side. Still, that doesn't mean we should make it easy for him. Anyway, we have his confession recorded, that's something," replied Donald shaking his head. "Rookie mistake for one of the world's greatest geniuses."

"We'll need to convince the police that it's him of course although hopefully it'll be enough to scotch the crazy 'Alan was a drug lord' theory," replied Peter.

"It's all going to come out eventually. I suppose history will decide if he's a hero or a villain and if we're the reactionaries. One way or another, he has to pay for Alan. I want to see him suffer for that."

"Time to phone Markov," said Kerry.

CHAPTER 51

Johnny kicked off the discussion. He reported that they were beginning to win the online debate. A California republican senator who had been defeated for the governorship by Parsons had called for a full enquiry into the serious allegations of illegal genetic research among prisoners and the government corruption that facilitated it. Two left wing members of parliament in Westminster had asked for the Secretary of State for Health to make a statement. Most surprising of all, the president of Rashwastan announced that his government was looking into worrying media assertions linking persons residing there to illegal experiments on children and young people.

"I suspect he's less worried about experiments on young people and more rattled by the revelations of a potential sting in the tail of his life-extension treatment," mused Johnny.

"How did you get on with the Secretary

General, Mr Markov?" asked Kerry.

"Not well. She says she'd need stronger evidence of a clear and present threat to cancel something which had been three years in the planning. While she accepted there were some worrying findings which required more investigation in America and the UK, she had seen no evidence of this in the countries primarily targeted by the Day of the Child events.

The problem is that our concerns about the impact of the genetic changes are just theoretical. I suspect we need physical proof of the treatment's impact on fertility. How will we get this? Just wait until the birth rate drops?"

There were a few seconds of silence

Singh, who until then had been quiet, said

"We talked about looking at sperm counts in males. We could do this now that we know a lot more people have been affected. The alterations affecting female fertility appear to be multiple but subtle. Professor Barnard suggests that one of the alterations is seen in women with impaired fallopian tube function, another in maturation of the ova, another with premature menopause. Do you think we could get co-operation from the St Julian's kids and their parents?"

Josh remembering his big brother's attitude

said to general amusement

"Asking a bunch of adolescents to jerk off for the benefit of mankind…. I think they could be persuaded."

Hana blushed, smiled and replied, "I think I might have more of a problem asking my Dad!"

"The kids would be enough I think," replied Singh. "We would need a local lab willing to do the analysis and the samples would have to be produced freshly. Let's talk about this later."

"Hana, what about you? Did you have any luck with the kids in Malawi?" asked Kerry.

"Unfortunately, no. They were all excited and looking forward to the conference. Their transport and accommodation costs had been paid. They had all been given new sweatshirts to wear. They seemed reluctant to accept that there was much risk involved. They thought we looked pretty good despite what we 'claimed' had been done to us. More worryingly, they didn't seem concerned about what might happen to them ten years down the line. One even said that there were too many kids in Malawi anyway!"

She continued. "I told them to keep an eye open for anything that could be used to spread a virus, which they agreed to, but I really got the impression that they thought we were over-reacting, and one hinted that we were just a bunch of first world rich people selfishly trying to hold on to an advantage. Us rich! Well, that's new."

Michael added, "Mr Bhopal got nowhere with his colleagues. They more or less accused him of being a cheat for claiming that he and his staff had been responsible for the St Julian's results and for wanting to keep hold of an unfair advantage. They rejected the fertility concerns as just scare stories."

"We have emailed as many of the other schools as we had contact details for and sent them attached copies of all the information you put on-line. We couldn't send links because we have to keep changing the site as Barton's people keep closing them down. However, Mr Bhopal has already had several complaints about the information we sent out asking us to desist from alarming their students and staff. Interestingly the email complaints all look pretty much the same, suggesting some sort of co-ordinated response" added Josh.

"Do you really think this will be a super-spreader event? How could he do it? Maybe we *are* over-reacting," said Kerry with a sigh.

"I don't think so," said Markov. "This looks meticulously planned to me."

"So, what do we do?" asked Michael.

"We're not going to be able stop this event.

That's clear. We just have to wait and see what happens. Hana and Josh, keep in touch with your colleagues in Africa, ask about how the conference is progressing, try to see if anything unusual takes place and importantly if they report coming down with any viral illnesses in the next few days," replied Donald.

"Barton thinks he's going to win," sighed Kerry.

"What makes you say that?" asked Markov.

"Oh sorry, I should've said this right at the start. My head is scrambled. He phoned again briefly. The bastard had the nerve to say it was to apologize for Alan's death, but he used the opportunity to make it clear that the spread of the virus was inevitable and that at best we were delaying it. However, one good thing is that we have a recording of him effectively making a confession of his involvement in the murder. Wouldn't have thought he'd be so stupid."

"Well not really given the other important news I have," said Markov. He hesitated before speaking again. "Barton is dying. I got my people to explore the US contacts Johnny had unearthed. We noticed some of them were cancer specialists whom Barton had seen on several occasions. Long story short, we got access to his medical records. He has stage four lung cancer. He's had just about every experimental treatment going, some of which worked for a while, but the tumours have started to grow again. This probably explains his need to accelerate his programme. He has secondary tumours in his brain, for which he is taking large doses of steroids. That could explain some of the untypical mistakes he's made, such as his recent heavy-handed tactics."

"Heavy-handed! He's a fucking murderer!" exclaimed Donald.

"Sorry, of course, that was a crass way of putting it, I apologise," replied Markov.

"No, no, sorry, I should apologise. Sorry kids you shouldn't have had to hear that."

"For goodness' sake Donald you're talking to St Julian's kids here. The F-word is our favourite adjective, and Barton absolutely is a fucking murderer!" said Michael.

"If word gets out that he has cancer himself then there will be wide-spread panic among the political and scientific elite he's bought off with the promise of eternal youth."

"How long do his doctors think he has?" asked Kerry.

"Not long…. Certainly not long enough to bring him to justice."

"His Rashwastani pal may not be too bothered about due process, and he seems a bit pissed off," said Josh.

"Let's hope so," replied Donald. "That'd be the sort of justice he deserves."

"Can we meet again tomorrow afternoon. We'll get some indication perhaps on how the Day of the Child has gone," asked Kerry.

"With regard to testing the boys. I've a pathologist friend in the Royal Infirmary, he works for the infertility clinic there. I'll call him and ask him to about the best way to check semen samples. I know that they need to be fresh so we'll have to get them to the hospital within two hours. Do we have to check this is OK with the boys' parents? Will the headmaster be OK with this?"

"We just did a social science project on this. In Scotland the age of consent is 12+, but if you want to avoid controversy, we could restrict it to the kids over 16 years. How many samples would we need?" replied Hana.

"If what we think is true then not many. Let's aim for forty. Do you think you could get that many?"

"Only one way to find out. We'll call a meeting tomorrow morning and tell them about it and ask for volunteers. If we have to, we could ask our dads and older brothers too. I know my dad is furious about the whole thing. He's putting together a legal action," replied Michael. "Poor Mr Bhopal thinks the school will go bankrupt, but I think it is you he has in his sights Mr Markov."

Markov gave a 'Que sera, sera' look.

"Pretty sure you're one step ahead of all that eh?" snarled Johnny.

"We have been considering steps to make sure everyone is treated fairly, while preserving the company," responded Markov in a measured tone. "James Barton has extensive assets. We believe he should be first call for any reparations."

"We should ask Brigitte to help with this," said Kerry. "We don't know how the boys are going to feel when they get the results. Before they have it done, they need to be warned about what it might mean for them and some may need support afterwards. Especially since we don't know if anything can be done to reverse or ameliorate it. Donald, your friend in the fertility clinic might be able to give us some idea of prognosis, do you think?"

"Of course. Given that that pair of teachers we spoke to had managed to get pregnant, albeit with help, I am optimistic."

"OK tomorrow afternoon everyone."

Donald's phone cheeped, a message from Speirs. Would he speak to Alan's girlfriend with a telephone number.

He phoned Speirs.

"Have they got the guys they thought did this to him? "

"They have three in custody and looking for two others. All deny dealing the killer blow of course. Not that it matters as they'll all be treated as guilty through joint enterprise. They are still spouting the drug baron crap, but even the chief constable knows that's wearing thin now."

"I'll call her. I've never met her. I'm not sure what to say?"

"Just tell her what you know."

"That it's all my fault he's dead."

"Rubbish! Alan could have sat back in Oxford and done nothing. Yes, he maybe helped at the start because he was your friend and felt a bit guilty about the way he had treated you, but he was 100% committed once he realised what Barton had done. That could just have easily been you in that lab. It's Barton's fault that he's dead. His and the murdering assholes' he sent to scare him."

Donald ended the call and told Kerry.

"Do you want me to join you on the call to her?"

Donald sighed.

"No. I have to do this myself I think."

With another sigh he clicked on the number Speirs had given him.

"Hello, is that Emma? This is Donald."

Donald started sobbing expressing regret at having involved Alan. He told her how Alan had been his best friend and that they had been through a lot together in the past. He started to tell her why he had asked him for help but Emma gently interrupted. She told Donald that Alan had told her about his visit and his bitter regret and guilt about not being more supportive. She had encouraged him to make contact and to travel to Edinburgh to help. So, if anything it was her fault too.

"Oh Emma, it is not your fault. He loved you so much and was looking forward to having a family with you… now all that is lost."

"Well not entirely lost…I'm pregnant. I found out only today for certain, I was going to let him know this evening."

"But that's wonderful. Oh God he'd have been so pleased…. Oh sorry Emma, I'm jumping the gun as usual. I can't imagine how hard it might be to raise a child alone, maybe it's too much to expect… I promise you, if you think that if I can help at all, I will. I owe you and Alan so much."

"What would please him most and me too is that you beat that bastard, Barton. Please keep me informed."

"I promise you Emma. Barton and his cronies will be made to pay."

Emma ended the call. Kerry who had been anxiously watching and listening pulled Donald toward her and hugged him. The pent-up emotion of the day finally finding some release.

They decided to call it a day and were slowly walking home when Donald's phone rang. Speirs.

"John here again. I just had a call from Malcolm Smith my boss…well actually my boss's boss. Apparently, Lord Lazenby is up in arms over the list of Barton's contacts that young Johnny put up on the web. Seemingly the satirical magazine Private Eye phoned him about it asking him if he realised that half of his group looking into the Odyssey allegations had been compromised by connections with Barton. The Chief Scientist's revelations and resignation and Alan's murder put the tin hat on it so to speak. Anyway, they published a comprehensive account of his failure to act in a timely way and his execrable attempts to cast blame by dint of being poorly informed, alongside a very unflattering somewhat jowly picture of him with the headline 'Flabbergasted'. He's furious wants to call the group together again."

"Serves the supercilious old git right. When's the meeting?"

"It's scheduled for the day after tomorrow at

noon. Can you make that?"

"Wouldn't miss it for anything. I do hope they'll be serving up humble pie. We may have the results of the semen analyses by then. That should make his day."

CHAPTER 52

....

Josh's phone cheeped later that evening, Chisomo, one of the Malawian schoolkids messaged, did he have time to speak.

Josh clicked the WhatsApp telephone symbol. After a few rings Chisomo answered.

"Hi Chisomo, what's up?"

"Hi, Josh. It's just that I've been searching the internet since you spoke to us today. At first, we all thought it was just another conspiracy theory, but I wasn't so sure and now I see that there are some very important people beginning to confirm what you were saying, and I'm a bit worried about this Day of the Child meeting tomorrow. Do you really think they'll try something?"

"We don't know, but Abe Markov knows Barton really well and he thinks he will. We don't know how he'll do it."

"Some of my friends… they say that the worst that can happen is that they'll end up smart like you. They say you're making up the stuff about fertility."

"We don't know for certain about the fertility, but a lot of respected international experts believe that the changes that come with this virus could cause infertility. We're running some tests, and we think we'll know more in the next few days, but I realise that's too late for you to make a decision about tomorrow."

"I'd like to be smart, but I want to have children too. If my mother thought I was risking that, she'd be furious."

"I don't know what to tell you Chisomo. It's great to be smart. I was pretty much a deadbeat stoner and now my life has been transformed. So, it's definitely not all bad. If you were asking me, would I go back to what I was, then the answer would absolutely be no. However, perhaps another thing to factor in is that the people who were smart and focussed to begin with probably gained less than people like me. You and your friends may fit that category."

Josh sighed and continued.

"We just think people should know what they are getting into and that they should have a choice. Barton put the infertility changes into the genes as some sort of trade-off. That was his agenda… to save the world. Well at least that's how he sees it. He had given up on humans being persuaded 'to do the right thing'. And you know, if I'm being truly honest, there may be something in that. I'm not helping, am I?"

"You *are* being honest Josh. I appreciate that."

"The other important thing to consider is that this virus spreads. Even if you and your friends go into this with your eyes open you may spread the virus to people who don't feel the same way as you. That could get you into trouble if people discover subsequently that you knowingly got infected."

"I hadn't thought of that. Oh goodness, I don't know what to do."

"I'd speak to your friends again or your Mum and Dad if you thought that'd help. If you go tomorrow, keep your eyes open for ways the virus might spread. We think it could be in the air conditioning unit."

"That building doesn't have air conditioning. It's a modern construction that encourages natural ventilation."

"Well then, we're not sure how he'll be able to spread it. Perhaps we are over-reacting Chisomo. Maybe it will all be OK. Perhaps it'll all be about Odyssey teaching methods and nothing more. If you decide to go, please keep your eyes open and contact me if you think anything is suspicious."

"Thank you, Josh. I'll let you know what's happening."

After hanging up, Josh called Hana and Michael and told them about Chisomo's misgivings.

"What do you think he'll do?" asked Hana

"My guess is that he'll go. I think I probably would myself if I were in his shoes. He said he'd let me know what he decides."

"We've done everything we can," said Michael. "Nothing to do now but wait. There are thousands of different Day of the Child events sponsored by Odyssey all around the world. If we can't persuade the Malawi guys who know us, there's little hope that the rest will listen to our advice."

CHAPTER 53

Hana decided to leave the requesting of volunteers for semen analysis to Michael and Josh.

"I can imagine the sort of requests that might be made of any woman present!" she pronounced somewhat haughtily.

However, as it turned out, Mr Bhopal insisted on being involved. Josh and Michael were waiting for an excruciatingly painful presentation of the request, but to their astonishment, the headmaster addressed the fifth and sixth year boys in a very matter of fact way explaining why the test was important, how they did not have to take part if they didn't want to and how when the results became available they'd be fed back personally and that perhaps it would be wise to discuss it with their parents, but only if they wanted to before taking part.

To their amazement there were no embarrassing questions about how to produce the sample, no jokes no jibes. Almost everyone agreed.

Josh called Donald who had spoken to his colleague. Mr Bhopal arranged for transport for them to go to the Royal Infirmary. It all went amazingly smoothly. Apart from the somewhat prissy school bus driver Alfred making the mistake of chastising one of the students who had called another a wanker to much jeering.

"He is Sir, we all are. Only Ah dinnae think that Jackie here could have had much left to give he works his sae hard."

"It was hard as steel… still is if ye want to check."

"Aye, ye'd like that."

Josh felt his phone vibrate and reached into his pocket. This generated more raucous laughter and a chorus of jibes. It was a WhatsApp call from Chisomo.

"Josh?"

"Hi Chisomo"

"Haha. Did he say jism homo?!" shouted one of the boys.

"What's that in the background," asked Chisomo

"Ignore them they are just a bunch of tossers."

"You can talk" yelled someone from a few seats

down. Josh covered one ear and walked to the front of the bus.

"Are you at the meeting Chisomo. How's it going."

"It all seems fine. They have been incredibly generous. We were greeted with breakfast, fresh fruit coffee and pastries after our long drive here. All very posh, like a five-star hotel, even ice-cold face and hand wipes to cool down after the journey."

Josh hesitated.

"Did everyone get the face towels. Tell me Chisomo, were they individually wrapped?"

"Yes... Oh, my goodness you think that's how they are delivering the virus?"

"I don't know but it's possible. Chisomo would you try to get one of those towels preferably unopened. I'll phone you back with what to do about it. "

Josh phoned Kerry.

"That must be it. We need someone to look at the towels and see if there is any evidence of infection. I'll speak to Peter. He seems to know everybody everywhere."

Peter did. The university had an ongoing relationship with Malawi and the previous year Professor Moyo, who worked in Lilongwe University of Agriculture, had given a lecture on millet virus genetics to the university department and Peter had hosted. He called the professor and told him about their concerns.

"And why is this meeting still going on?" asked the alarmed professor. "I had seen the emails but really didn't think it had anything to do with crop genetics or Malawi so hadn't paid much attention."

"We have tried very hard to get it cancelled both centrally with UNESCO and with the schools but without success. It is happening all around the world we suspect. No-one with the power to stop it believed us and we may of course be wrong."

"What do you want me to do?"

"We have a sample which we think may contain the virus responsible. If we get it to you, could you arrange for it to be examined with electron microscopy and arrange to preserve it in viral transport media and freeze it?"

"I certainly can. When can I expect to receive it?"

"We have a student who has the sample, he should be with you within two hours."

*

In Edinburgh by the end of the day, they had forty-two samples all of which had been tested for sperm density and motility. Samples were also frozen for further analysis.

The results showed that the boys (and Donald who had also contributed) were not sterile, as they had feared, but they did have very low sperm counts with low motility. According to Donald's friend this meant that natural conception might prove difficult, but not impossible and that in vitro fertilisation should be possible.

He phoned Peter and Kerry and told them the news.

"It's better than I expected. However, it's likely that the males in their families if they were infected will have been similarly affected and we have to let them know in a sensitive way. We still don't know how this has affected the girls. Testing them may be a lot more difficult. We could track their cycles to see if they are ovulating, but one of the genetic changes was also found in women who have problems with fallopian tube motility. That will be a lot harder to measure."

"The kids will have to get their results individually in confidence."

"What about their parents, should we ask them if they want them to be told or if they'd like them to be there?"

"Some of the parents might be a little irritated that we did this without asking them even though the kids were considered competent to make that decision themselves and advised to tell them."

"I think they'll be much more annoyed about the result than us testing their kids. It'll certainly give some impetus to continue their lawsuit against Odyssey or CreativeCom."

"I'm still waiting to hear from Professor Moyo. Chisomo managed to get the towel delivered. I really hope that this is a wild goose chase, but it seems like too big a coincidence that a perfect delivery system for the virus would be made available on this very day.... hang on that may be him now, I'll put you on hold.

Professor Moyo. Any result? I have some colleagues on the line. May I add them to the call?"

"Yes of course. The results are if anything a little worse than we expected. There are two viruses in the wet towels. The first is the COVID virus SARS-CoV-2 the second is a lentivirus which I've not been able to identify as yet."

"The virus in Barton's vaccine is a lentivirus. It's almost certainly the same," replied Donald.

"But why the COVID virus?"

"He's smart. Infection with the lentivirus causes headache and high fever. Anyone testing the kids and the people they come in contact with would also be COVID positive and doctors would assume that was the cause of the illness. A COVID outbreak facilitated by a large meeting is classic. What we don't know is how these two viruses will interact and if there will be more serious reactions," replied Peter.

"In general, COVID wasn't a big problem for Malawi. We have a very young population and many of the older people have been vaccinated."

"Barton's lentivirus sometimes results in unpleasant symptoms but to our knowledge no-one has died of it. However, we now know, as of this afternoon, that it has a considerable impact on male fertility and we expect will also do so on females too. It may be that assisted conception will be necessary for many couples trying to have children," said Donald.

"What can we do!?"

"We're about to post our results online once more. We'll also inform UNESCO. Will you preserve the towel? We'll also ask the other centres to see if they can hold on to any that they may have left and warn them to watch out for a lot of ill children," replied Donald.

Kerry added, "It's possible that timely antiviral treatment might help, but we don't know that and in any case I doubt if that could be arranged on the sort of scale you'd need. Looking at recent meetings that Barton has had; I'm afraid that some members of your government appear on his list of engagements. We believe he may have offered them a substantial bribe either in the shape of life extending treatments or perhaps just good old-fashioned money. We have been wrong about some people though".

"No-one here would be surprised by government corruption."

"Are you happy for us to name you as an independent verifier? When we come to write this up you'll be a joint author."

"To be honest. I'm not sure. It sounds like some very powerful people are behind this. I'm heavily reliant on government grants for my work."

"If we arrange transport, could we have the sample sent to us here in the UK?"

"Yes of course. Chisomo is a bright boy. He managed to bring me four un-opened towels. I have only opened one. We can freeze the others and send them to you."

"It might be better if we had it sent to an independent verifier. There are more and more geneticists getting interested in this. We'll be in touch about arranging the transport Professor Moyo. And once more, thank you for helping us with this."

"Thank *you* for exposing this," he replied

sombrely. "I'm still reeling from it all. I have children and hope to have grandchildren. Assisted conception isn't common in this country and beyond the reach of most people. It'll be a disaster if it unfolds as you suspect it will."

"It may be possible to reverse some aspects of this, Barton clearly has the knowhow to do this, though I doubt he'll be willing to share it. However, I should warn you that the benefits of this virus are quite impressive and given the choice to roll it back completely I think many of the young people we encountered would be reluctant to do so."

"What?! They'd remain eunuchs by choice!"

"It appears so. Certainly, in our country having children is dropping down the priority lists of many young people. They worry about climate change and resulting war and famine. Some just worry about the cost of childcare and how it'll impact their preferred lifestyle."

"There has always been war and famine. I think we have grown too rich, too used to a soft life and now we have let this happen. I feared it would be AI which would undo humanity not this."

"Well AI certainly had a hand in it," answered Donald.

Kerry looked anxiously at the other two and

sighed. "Professor, we have to let the people of Malawi know what we have found. It'll be difficult to do this without revealing your contribution to it"

"I realise this. Do it. How soon before the children start to show signs of infection?"

"About three days."

"Once that starts happening it'll be difficult for them to deny it."

"They may try to put the blame on others for spreading it though. Certainly, the members of the government who took bribes will be striking out to preserve themselves. You won't be alone. This virus was probably released all over the world."

"Then name me."

"Initially there may be pressure on you to go back on your findings or attempts to discredit you. That's what they tried with us. However, as news of this unravels around the world, they may instead try to paint you as part of the conspiracy. Even this won't hold up for long as different members of your government are implicated. To be fair many of them will genuinely be ignorant of the enormity of what they turned a blind eye to and will be appalled at what has happened. They will, with considerable justification, portray it as an international conspiracy. I suspect there may be considerable civil unrest."

"I'll warn my wife and children there may be consequences. How much time do I have?"

"A few hours at most. Thank you again professor for all you have done and will do. You're one of the heroes in this. We'll keep you fully informed of developments."

Peter ended the call.

"He's probably more to lose than we do. He's a brave man."

"Let's call the others and plan how we reveal this to the world."

CHAPTER 54

In California Governor Parsons knew he was in trouble. He couldn't believe he had been blindsided by Caleb Farrel. It must have been him. There was no way those inmates and prison staff had orchestrated the sort of media storm surrounding him. They were barely literate for God's sake! They had to be getting help, if not from Farrel from some sort of pinko lawyer collective.

Just that morning he had had a submission, supposedly from one of the inmates. In it he outlined defects in his criminal case particularly with respect to the reliance on statements given by two police officers. Those officers had subsequently been clearly shown to have perjured themselves in previous cases and to have been in the pay of an organised crime syndicate. It was certainly convincing, but where did he get help to write it? Was Farrel right? That this boy was super bright because of the virus? Parsons had been delighted to hear about the virus's effects on aggression, addiction and fertility effects. He had spoken to the vice president about it and how it should be offered to all the delinquents. However, he could now see that a whole bunch of suddenly clever criminals could be problematical.

That guy whom Barton sent to talk to him couldn't be raised now. It had all been too good to be true. All he had had to do was nothing for a few months and there would be $200,000 dollars in his special account; and then there was the promise of a new anti-ageing treatment. Could that be true? He was beginning to feel his years… especially the last few days! There was no doubting Barton's crew were smart, and if they could do the sort of things they had done to those felons maybe they could turn back the clock too.

Well, it was now clear he couldn't do 'nothing' so goodbye $200K! He had called in the Public Health Director to investigate, suggesting the whole thing was something and nothing. Initially the guy agreed, believing it all to be ridiculously farfetched, but after doing a bit of online research suddenly decided to take it a lot more seriously. He had been in touch with the scientists in Scotland who he said had made a convincing argument and would be providing more information soon. He was arranging for blood tests and semen analysis on the inmates. Half of those junkies he'd be lucky to find a vein, although no doubt they'd have jerking off down to a fine art!

Well, damn the lot of them! There was no evidence suggesting he had been bribed. Yes, that'd be his line; he had been approached but had turned them down. Of course, the media were already crying about racial bias and unfair sentencing and that this virus was just another way of putting down the black man. Well, he could seem moderate if he had to. He'd start by pardoning that 'uppity' felon Darnell Williams. After all, pardoning didn't admit that any court wrongdoing had happened. Hopefully that'd satisfy the newshounds baying at his door.

CHAPTER 55

Professor Moyo phoned his wife and three sons. He explained what had happened and that there may be an attempt to denounce him by government officials caught up in Barton's web of corruption. He told them that they should leave the capital and head for their family home in the Shire Highlands and stay there until he told them it was safe to return.

"Edward, you should come with us."

"I need to be here. When the word gets out there has to be someone who can answer questions. Things are coming to a head very rapidly. If I'm at risk, I think it'll only be for a short while. My colleagues in Scotland will be releasing this information very soon. Go now."

"May the Lord guide you and keep you, Edward. You're a good man. You're doing his work."

"And may He keep you and the boys safe too. Leave now."

His phone had started to ring. It was the

Malawi chief medical officer. She had been alerted by a colleague in the WHO who in turn had been contacted by the Scottish scientists.

"How bad is this?"

"If my colleagues in Scotland are correct, very bad. Almost every child at that conference will have contracted the virus along with a dose of COVID which will probably help the spread both to their family members and anyone else with whom they come in contact."

"Then we need to isolate them."

"That should slow it down, but from what they have seen in Scotland, it is highly infectious. They did say anti-viral meds might be effective, but they haven't been tested."

"There were two thousand students at the conferences in Lilongwe and Blantyre from more than two hundred schools across the country. I don't know how we could begin to start isolating them. We need to send a message out to their families and to local medical centres. We don't have enough anti-viral meds in the country and should we really start experimenting with our kids? Tell me is it true that it causes sterilisation."

"It would appear that it isn't complete sterilisation. Procreation will be much more difficult, and conception may need to be assisted in many cases. They don't know how many yet. They only know for certain about the impact on boys. They haven't determined yet what effects if any it'll have on girls, but they are confident it has some."

"And there's an upside? I heard it can help with mental focus, aggression and addiction."

"Yes, those features have been observed. The benefits are so great they say that given the choice young people would choose not to reverse them even if it meant they lost their fertility."

"Maybe in those Godless Western countries! I do not believe that will happen here."

"Let's hope not."

"I'll start the alerts. You'd better be around to help field the inevitable onslaught from the press and worried parents. Just as Africa starts to be stronger and more assertive this happens. It can't be a coincidence. The Western nations want to weaken and dominate us once again."

"I can understand that it may appear that way. However, all over the world in rich and poor countries this Day of the Child is being celebrated sponsored by Odyssey. This is one man's obsession, fuelled by billions of dollars. The outcry once it is clear what is going on will be massive, but, if anything, from the so-called developed nations it'll be even bigger. They are already struggling with low birth rates."

"They at least have the resources to tackle this. Where will we find means to provide assisted conception to millions of people?"

"My colleagues in Scotland say it may possibly be reversed but, for now, only Barton and his team may have the technology to do that."

"I have spoken to the Minister of Justice. There will be warrants for the arrest of Barton and the people who are responsible for disseminating these infected hand towels."

"I suspect the people who dispensed them had no clue about what they were handing out. I'd be more concerned about finding out if any of the towels had 'gone missing'. The Odyssey logo looks quite sophisticated and attractive. I'd not be surprised if a few batches had found their way into the hands of friends who own restaurants or even their own family and friends."

"Of course, and that will have happened all along the supply chain!"

"Not that Barton will care…. The more the merrier."

"We'll have to get a message out that these towels are contaminated and must not be opened but returned to the nearest health centre for destruction."

"Be careful Madam Director. From what I've heard, Barton has great influence in the government. Some ministers are bought and paid for. If you corner them, they may strike out."

CHAPTER 56
....

The revelations came too late for most countries to take action to halt the Day of the Child conferences and the dissemination of the hand towels. Only in Hawaii where the conferences were opening a full twelve hours after Malawi were they able to react in time. Over the following days, the contamination of the towels was confirmed in multiple locations.

Around the world from Aukland to Anchorage children started to exhibit signs of the viral infection. Doctors found that in most cases this was mild, but some with underlying chronic disorders required hospitalisation. The symptoms in their family members and other contacts started a few days later. It was a mild strain of COVID that had been included with the lentivirus and only a few of the most debilitated and unvaccinated died.

There was world-wide fury. The press screamed for justice and for action to protect other children.

After much debate the WHO declared a pandemic and encouraged countries to invoke their national plans. In the best organised countries participating schools were temporarily closed and potentially infected children isolated in their homes. In others little or no action was taken. Parents took to the streets to demand anti-viral treatments despite any evidence that they would be effective. There was a huge demand online for these and stocks quickly ran out. As it happened, a subsequent trial in Denmark of two likely antiviral candidates showed no impact on ameliorating the infection.

In a world worn down by COVID people had little appetite for new lock downs. Most schools remained open, mask wearing was patchy and in the absence of widespread deaths a general belief that the scientists would get on top of it as they did with COVID prevailed. The virus spread widely.

The political fallout started when it became clear that a potential problem had been suspected for some time. First the director of UNESCO resigned after admitting to having been warned about a possible threat. The press quickly uncovered links between her and Barton. Lord Lazenby who had failed to take seriously and act urgently on the warnings of the Edinburgh group went shortly afterwards. Around the world journalists started to investigate Johnny's online list of officials who had been in contact with Barton. Several resigned, many were suspended pending investigation. To Speirs disgust it became clear that Sir Jeremy Cohen, the security service director had been feeding information all along to Barton.

Emilio Sanchez was arrested on his way to Spain… as predicted, a convenient fall-guy. His stated inability to identify the scientists that created the virus was not believed. His employer Chi-Gen was caught up in the general melee. Raj Singh, despite effusive and at times hysterical denials of involvement, was held accountable by his board for failing in due diligence and fired, bitter that Markov, minimising his own involvement, had abandoned him.

The factory owner in China that had manufactured and packaged the face towels was dragged, screaming his innocence, through the streets by a mob. He had, he said, only followed the instructions of the purchaser. He thought what he had been asked to include was an exclusive but fragile skin rejuvenating treatment. He swore he had given the towels to his own wife and daughters. The source of the 'rejuvenating' liquid he had applied to the towels was eventually narrowed down to a newly opened state-of-the-art biotech factory in Guangzhou, abandoned by the time the authorities found it. CCTV in the surrounding area was found to have been altered, a sophisticated AI programme providing a near-real illusion of everyday life. The scientists and technicians who worked there had disappeared.

Social media conspiracists were in a frenzy although this time even the most sober of commentators had difficulty dismissing their wildest theories and accusations given that what was thought to be the truth was about as wild as it could get.

Barton had gone to ground. His onetime ally, the president of Rashwastan, made a great show on television of displaying the warrant for his arrest. Barton had however, by then, and almost certainly with government help, skipped the country leaving behind his private jet and many millions in the nation's banks, which the president declared forfeit, 'for the people of Rashwastan'. Across the world his assets were frozen, but most forensic accountants believed that much remained hidden. An intense worldwide search failed to find him. His medical records were leaked and many assumed that he had died or possibly committed suicide. Johnny and his associates along with many in the Twittersphere were convinced the medical issues were a ploy and that he was still alive somewhere pulling strings.

Marion Spitz too had disappeared.

CreativeCom's share price plummeted and the company filed for Chapter 11 bankruptcy which enabled the business to continue. Markov performed well in interviews, laying the blame squarely on Barton and emphasising his own role in funding research by the Edinburgh and Oxford groups to identify the problem and his early warnings to the US Government and UNESCO which had been dismissed. Multiple class actions were initiated across the world. He promised that CreativeCom would continue to fund research into reversing or ameliorating the effects of the virus. He argued that the best way for people to gain compensation was for CreativeCom to continue to operate and to pay this from profits alongside the use of Barton's companies' own considerable assets.

Kerry, Donald and Peter were almost continuously interviewed and became the heroes of the hour. Alan's sacrifice was mentioned in every interview. Moira Munro enjoyed vicarious celebrity regaling anyone who would listen about her family's 'death-defying dash' through the backstreets of

Edinburgh, 'willingly risking their lives' to support Peter and his colleagues.

Hana, Josh and Michael took on the mantle of spokespersons for those who had been affected by the virus. St Julian's and the California Secure Youth Treatment Centre came under intense media interest. Darnell, newly released, supported by Caleb Farrel, fronted the questions at the Facility and pushed strongly for reconsideration of sentences for all the inmates, not just because of what had been taken from them, but because psychologists believed that the mutation had greatly reduced, addictive and violent tendencies and therefore the chance of recidivism. Governor Parsons, desperately trying to gloss over his 'alleged' initial support for controlled release of the virus to prisoners and rejecting 'vile' accusations of racism, supported the idea. He declared "I have prayed, consulted my spiritual advisors and concluded that some good should come of this evil."

Determined to prevent another worse man-made disaster, world governments quickly enacted legislation to ensure similar research was carried out only in licensed regularly inspected premises with serious repercussions for any rogue laboratories. The USA, UK, Japan, EU and Chinese governments offered lavish funding for research into reversing the effects of the virus. It was thought that if they offered amnesty and generous rewards that the scientists involved in its creation would come forward, but none did. Some online conspiracists theorised that Barton had ordered them all murdered, others that there were no mastermind scientists and that a rogue AI running on a super-fast quantum computer carrying out the wishes of Barton had been responsible for design and production of the virus.

CHAPTER 57

Five years on the effects of the virus were dramatic. Across the world the number of pregnancies fell precipitously with a birth rate around one fiftieth of that previously. The changes were felt mostly in those countries with younger populations with little easy access to assisted conception, the only intervention shown to overcome the effects of the virus on fertility. Their pleas for reparations from the rich countries, perceived as the instigators of the crisis, were largely ignored

However, funding from CreativeCom and Barton's companies was used to set up some no-frills 'assembly line' fertility clinics in poorer countries. Access to these was restricted in some states. In Rashwastan, applicants had to pass a 'Good Citizenship' test to be offered the service; ensuring it was only available to people who toed the governing party line. In conservative countries only married mixed sex couples could apply. In others bribery was commonplace. Cowboy clinics and internet 'cures' mushroomed around the world as desperate people sought solutions. The poor and those lacking influence were restricted to one child (The rich of course, as always, did what they pleased). This was a profound change for countries where four, five or six children were the norm, whereas in the West, once resources were diverted from family planning and obstetric clinics to fertility clinics, it was less impactful.

The beneficial aspects of the virus kicked in quickly. Crime rates especially violent crime rates started tumbling. Alcohol sales steadily reduced and so called 'narco' states began to recover from the grip of drug gangs as demand for their products faltered. One of the legacies of Odyssey was that a range of online courses, similar to those that had been taught in St Julian's was made available free of charge across the world to all students. Examination results soared everywhere.

There were many who raged against this 'mind control', who thought that humanity had 'lost its spark' suggesting that man's innate drive to violence was linked to creativity, ambition and success. An influential mullah declared with disgust that it had 'made us all think like women'. A view that at least half the world's population applauded. Bright kids, Odyssey online-schooled in logic and critical thinking, were immune to these baseless arguments and also to those of the climate change deniers. With a stake in the future and new-found skills they began to have a profound influence on governments' environmental policies.

Newly qualified Josh now worked alongside Donald and Kerry who jointly headed one of the world's leading cytogenetics institutes, spearheading an international research drive to find a permanent way to ameliorate the fertility limiting impact of the virus. However, emulating Barton's work proved challenging with many failures. In Malawi Professor Moyo, initially attacked for spreading false rumours but then later hailed for his role in discovering the virus in the hand towels was appointed head of the task force to ameliorate the effects of "the infertility plague" as it came to be known. He continued to collaborate with the Edinburgh group and became a mentor to Chisomo who later won a scholarship to do a PhD in Edinburgh with Kerry and Donald supervising.

Michael worked in the legal department of the institute. He joked that he was the first of the Flannigan family to be on the right side of the law. Hana was part of an international think tank which sought solutions to manage the impending global demographic change, as going forward there would be far fewer young people to look after and pay pensions for older people.

The so-called Generation-X and Millennials were furious that their retirement age was going to be pushed higher and there were large, loud protests in many countries with demands for higher taxes on the 'Boomers' who were seen to have retired early with gold-plated pensions and who, although considered the architects of the disaster, continued their profligate use of the earth's resources into their old age. Once a powerful force at the polls the elderly feared the increasingly strident rhetoric of the young and acceded to many of their demands.

Donald became godfather to baby Alan.

Darnell had his criminal record expunged and went on to win a seat in the California Assembly with plans on a senate seat when he came of age. Alongside Caleb Farrel, he fought hard for a review of sentencing. A pilot programme of early release of 'genetically improved' prisoners who had exhibited behavioural change, demonstrated that the policy was safe and very cost-effective. In that policy, Darnell and Caleb had the unlikely backing of Jeb Parsons, who, to no-one's surprise, admitted to nothing, denied everything and not only held on to his governorship but, making a virtue of his 'inclusive forward-thinking attitude', went on to be elected president. Darnell's sister Destiny set up her own agency managing the online presence of politicians and celebrities.

EPILOGUE

Ten years since the release of the virus and after many failed attempts, Kerry, Donald and their international collaboration had managed to develop a virus which looked like it could overcome the fertility impact of Barton's virus without removing the advantages which most now accepted had been beneficial. No adverse consequences had appeared.

Kerry, with infant Ellie on one arm and five-year-old Donald playing with trains on the floor beside her, had just started to empty the dishwasher when her laptop started to peep, an incoming videocall. She shouted to Johnny to take Ellie while she answered.

She clicked on the receive button and gasped. James Barton smiling at her. Very much alive, and not looking much older than when she last saw him that fateful night in Edinburgh

"Hello Kerry."

Kerry immediately wondered if this could be some sort of trick, an AI generated simulacrum. She turned to Johnny... it was just the sort of prank he'd pull... but he looked as shocked as she.

"Mr Barton?"

"Surprise!" he made a clown-like grin. "Just thought I'd give you a call. Did you know this is exactly the tenth anniversary of you posting your findings on the GenCom website?"

"We thought you were dead," she replied, her tone making it clear that that'd have been the preferred outcome.

"Still upset Kerry? Seems to me things have turned out darn well for you and Johnny. You run your own institute, you have beautiful kids, a great home..."

Kerry calmed herself and replied slowly in a measured tone.

"You are responsible for the deaths of literally thousands of people around the world and the enforced sterilisation of billions, not to mention the murder of one of my friends. Yes still, as you put it, 'upset'."

"And how many deaths have I prevented? The murders, the wars, the deaths from addiction and reckless behaviour. What about the numbers of children, especially girls, now completing education in the previously most benighted countries. It's not been all bad, has it Kerry? All I ever wanted was to halt the earth's crazy population growth and prevent humanity from destroying itself along with all the other species on this planet. I think I have succeeded. The world overall is a better place for it."

Kerry's heart was beating hard; she took a deep breath. She hated this man, but she knew there was some truth in what he was saying.

"You have ensured that the only way humanity can now survive is through the application of very sophisticated technology. If anything were to happen to roll back civilisation. If there were some sort of disaster which led to us losing such technology that'd be the end of us."

"Let's face it Kerry, the way the world is organised, so specialised, so interdependent, a disaster such as you are describing would end human civilisation anyway."

"Why have you called. Why now?"

"I've been following yours and Professor Stirling's research for a cure; one that will remove the fertility block without taking away the benefits of my virus. I know that has proven difficult for you. Given the success of facilitated conception, I suspect there will be few takers for one that takes away all the advantages too. Except perhaps in the sort of countries whose administrations are abhorrent to you. For example, religious maniacs who value women rather less than your own society does. The reason I called is that I want to make a deal."

"Why on earth should we trust you?"

"You don't have to trust me. What I have to offer is easy enough to check out."

"Go on."

"I have a curative virus which will do exactly what you want; in large part reverse the infertility but maintain the other advantages. However, according to my AI models the earth needs another ten years of low birth rates to be safe. I'm pretty confident that the social changes that have come in the wake of the first virus; the increase in education in girls and improved infant survival will lead to a voluntary reduction in fertility; something which had already happened in many richer countries. It just needs a little longer to gel."

"So why are you telling me now?"

"Two reasons. The first is that the virus-cure you have been working on and are about to trial at scale won't work as intended. Every analysis conducted by our AIs shows that it'll have a catastrophic effect particularly in people with a certain genetic pattern, one mainly found in people of African heritage but to a degree in all races. Despite your efforts to make it self-limiting and non-transmissible it does have limited ability to reproduce in this group."

Kerry frowned. "How do we know this isn't a ploy. We have spent months checking it out."

"I know. However, your research cohort was mainly Caucasian and if you carefully check out the few people of African heritage you included, you'll find that, one year on, they are beginning to develop some minor neurological problems. Without preventative treatment these will accelerate to something that looks very like multiple sclerosis. I can send you the evidence and also information on how you can manage this side-effect. It's compelling. You must not deploy your cure."

"You said there were two reasons."

Johnny had put Ellie down and was furiously typing away from the camera trying to trace the origin of the video call. Young Donald was clawing at his leg for attention.

"The second reason is that this time I really am dying. The immune boost from the 'longevity' vaccine, which, as you know, I offered several people, has run its course. It's no longer effective and my tumour is now advancing rapidly. I know you think I'm a monster, but it was always my plan to reverse this. I developed the cure at the same time as I developed the original virus.

My 'fertility-restore' virus has been engineered

and tested. You may have read about some people in Oregon who had had some success with an unlikely collection of herbs. A success which wasn't replicated. Well, suffice it to say it wasn't herbs. We have been following them for five years and they show no ill effects. Unlike your virus it isn't transmissible so people will be able to choose if they want to stay relatively infertile or not. Kerry, I want to leave the solution in your hands."

"And you'd just give this to me?"

"Yes, but not right away. Ten years from now you'll be informed of the location of the freezers in stable safe areas around the world containing the agent. I've set up several methods of contacting you and other experts in the field in case of war, meteorite strike, plague or any of the other disasters which seem to worry you so much."

"What? And we're supposed to stop working on this in the hope that you'll provide this?"

"Kerry you can do what you want, but I can assure you, you were about to unleash a disaster. If you call in these people who had 'the herbal cure' but who actually got the fertility restore virus which I engineered, you can check them out. I 'll provide their names. You'll see that many of the beneficial changes have been retained but the fertility blocks have been largely removed.

Now, I see that Johnny there has been trying to trace me, so I think I'll sign off now. Good luck Kerry. The screen went blank and her email pinged. Several documents were attached.

Kerry opened the first of these which fleshed out the detail on the potential side-effects of the cure she and her team had been working on. It seemed convincing. She phoned Donald and outlined the conversation.

"You're sure it was him?"

"Well, if it wasn't, it was a pretty marvellous deep fake which interacted very convincingly with me. But who knows? It may have been an AI simulating him."

"How could he still be alive?"

"Possibly the cancer scare was a ploy or maybe the life extension treatment wasn't the scam we thought it was."

"We should look into that again, find out what happened to the people who took it. I was pretty sure that no-one would have continued with it when we showed it had such a high chance of causing cancer. I wonder if he continued to supply them with it? Sanchez said it had to be boosted."

"Maybe they found a way around the cancer risk... You know, I always wondered if Markov was in on that too?"

"The life extension? Really? I know he had

a youthful complexion, but I thought he was going grey the last time I saw him. I thought the stress had got to him."

"Yes, but that's easily faked. I'm not sure he was ever completely on our side. It was he, remember, who told us about Barton's cancer. I know he helped us a lot, but could he have helped his old partner get away? Despite what he subsequently said, at least at one point his viewpoint and Barton's were aligned."

"The last I saw of him was a month ago in an article in the Guardian. He was about to go to the Cayman Islands, to celebrate his retirement after he converted Chi-Gen to a non-profit, declaring all proceeds were going to go to genetic research for 'the benefit of mankind'," replied Donald with a slight sneer. "Here's the link to the article"

"Well, whether Barton's alive or dead is the least of our concerns," she said. "What about our test subjects to whom, if Barton is correct, we may have given terrible side effects."

"The third paper here suggests that it can be managed. We can re-infect them with the original virus or it can be ameliorated with a cocktail of high dose vitamins B12 and D. Note that he cautions that he's not tried this on anyone who has had our experimental treatment, but he believes it'll be effective."

"How does he always know what we're doing?" asked Kerry, her exasperation plain.

"He clearly always has. Either someone in our team is supplying the information or he's hacked all our computer systems."

"Anyway, we need to bring in our test volunteers right away and check them over. If he's right, and he probably is, then we give them the choice of maintenance with vitamins or re-infection with the original virus. Not a conversation I'm looking forward to," added Kerry with a resigned sigh.

"What about this ten-year offer from Barton?"

"Well, if he can be believed… We can certainly check out the people he said he's treated to see if the treatment he gave them is bona-fide. If it turns out it is a safe solution and, given what has happened with the one we devised, I could see a lot of people holding out for it no doubt with a massive baby-boom among older women once it is deployed with all the consequences that has."

Donald sighed and shook his head. "We need to call a meeting of our colleagues, cancel the launch of our virus trial and call in all the people in the pilot study. This will set us back a hell of a way. The decision to delay for his solution will be one government has to make. It may seem self-serving, but I think we still have to keep working on a solution in case it turns out that he's lying."

He hesitated and continued tentatively "I suppose we could still offer our cure to people of non-African heritage"

"Seriously?! Would you take it Donald?! I wouldn't. Never mind the appalling optics of a cure for white and Asian people only. No, that treatment is a dead duck like all the others. We're going to have to offer reversal with the original virus to everyone in the trial. We don't know what other problems there may be. No-one is going to trust anything we do after this," she sighed.

"Let's speak again tomorrow. We need to let Josh know. He's going to be pissed off. He did warn us that we had restricted our ethnic diversity too much in the trial."

"Maybe he's right but, if we hadn't, we'd have even more people to have a difficult conversation with!" Shaking her head she continued. "How did Barton get it right first time, but we have failure after failure?!"

"We don't know that, Kerry. He was careful to try this out on marginalised people. There may have been many failures we don't know about in individuals and communities whom few people cared about if they became ill. Anyway, let's talk tomorrow."

She hung up and clicked on the link to the article Donald had sent. She scrolled down and stopped at a photograph of the ceremonial handover of Chi-Gen on the steps of the United Nations Building in New York before Markov's departure to Grand Cayman. President Parsons was shaking his hand. Kerry was just about to scroll down further when she noticed a woman near them with a Mulberry handbag.

Surely not! She zoomed in. Next to Markov, a new hair colour, wearing glasses, but seemingly not a day older, almost defiantly looking at the camera, was that Marion Spitz?!

"Look at this Johnny! Who's that?

"Fuck me! She has some nerve!"

Kerry looked silently at the photo of Markov, Spitz and Parsons, slowly shaking her head. "Some radical greens are already calling that murdering bastard Barton a hero. He and his fellow travellers, whoever they are, they've won, haven't they?"

Johnny sighed nodding. "For now, maybe, but we're not giving up. One way or another they'll pay."

Acknowledgements

Many people helped me get this off the ground. My old pal, now lost to us, Patrick Kelly provided the inspiration and encouragement for me to write. I got great feedback from friends and family who looked at many drafts. Thank you, Ruth McKinstry, Mairi McKinstry, Alistair Liddle, Justyn Comer, Julia Lowden, Heather Hewitt, Alison Worth, Lucy McCloughan, Donald Cameron, Jim Cowan, Donald Macaulay, Mary Paterson, Sandy Gallander, Lynn Gee and Beth Hacche.

Printed in Dunstable, United Kingdom